EXPIATION

THE WHISPER OF DEATH

A novel by

Elisa S. Amore

Translated by

Leah Janeczko

Sign up for the TOUCHED saga newsletter at:
http://eepurl.com/bR8EuT

Join the conversation about the Touched saga using the official hashtag:
#TouchedSaga.

Visit the official site to discover games, quizzes, book trailers, and much more: www.touchedsaga.com

Follow Touched on:
Facebook.com/TheTouchedSaga
Twitter.com/TheTouchedSaga
Instagram.com/eli.amore

Join the Official Group on FB to meet other fans addicted to the series:
facebook.com/groups/251788695179500

If you have any questions or comments, please write us at
touchedsaga@gmail.com
For Foreign and Film/TV rights queries, please send an email to
elisa.amore@touchedsaga.com

Artwork by Nathalia Suellen

PRAISE FOR THE *TOUCHED* SAGA

"As seductive as *Meet Joe Black*. As mysterious as *City of Angels*. As powerful as *Twilight*."

"Elisa S. Amore is one of the few phenomena in Italian self-publishing." **Vanity Fair**

"Girls who dream of love, a new novel just for you has come out in bookshops." **Marie Claire**

"*The Caress of Fate* is the literary success of the year." **Tu Style**

"A winning novel that's fresh and interesting, one that belongs on your bookshelf." **Io Donna**

"Italy, too, is seeing the rise of the fantasy genre served with a side of romance. Its undisputed queen is thirty-one-year-old Elisa S. Amore." **F Magazine**

"A sensationally successful debut." **La Sicilia**

"Elisa S. Amore is an unquestioned star of the supernatural fantasy genre." **Metro**

"For those who think emotions shouldn't die out as you grow up, this novel has a lot to offer you." **Vero**

"With *The Caress of Fate,* Elisa S. Amore makes her bookstore debut, but if you look up her name on the web you'll discover a whole world. Elisa S. Amore's narrative skills are clear; it's like reading a classic American-made saga." **Pop Up Literature**

"A truly incredible fantasy novel in which love is masterfully combined with the supernatural. A new saga whose readers are already anxiously awaiting the second—and no doubt spectacular—installment." **Il Recensore**

*"The universe will never be extinguished
because just when the darkness
seems to have smothered all,
to be truly transcendent,
the new seeds of light
are reborn in the very depths."*
Philip K. Dick

PROLOGUE

"Simon, behind you!" I shouted from atop one of the boulders, but my voice was drowned out by the explosion of the fireball hurled at my brother. I held my breath in alarm, but moments later Simon emerged from the cloud of dust, a thousand shards of rock still raining down.

"Where'd he go?!" he shouted, agitated, shielding his eyes with his arm to avoid the shower of shattered stone.

I hadn't seen where the Subterranean had gone, but a fleeting movement caught my eye. "Over there! By the wall!"

Simon narrowed his eyes and disappeared into a crevice in the rocks.

"You take care of him, little brother," I murmured. "I'll keep climbing."

I had no idea what that hellish place was. It looked like a world in ruins from one of Drake's video games. The wreck of an old galleon stood among the rocks like a sentry and small pools of water dotted the sandy earth. Around me, the rocks rose in a circle all the way up to the ceiling of the cavern, where light streamed in through a hole. It was as though a giant hand had descended from above and punched through the rocks, opening a passageway to Hell while groping with its fingers to dig channels all around it. The result was a bizarre labyrinth of tunnels that made their way up toward the surface.

A movement to my left. I gripped my dagger and stood motionless, all my senses alert. The Subterranean materialized behind me but I spun around in time, blocked his fist, and slammed him against the wall. He shot to his feet and rushed me at warp speed. My blows were brutal and direct, but the young redheaded Subterranean put up a good defense. He broke off a jagged piece of rock and wounded my bare chest with it. I gritted my teeth, absorbing the pain.

I jumped up, grabbed hold of a vine dangling among the rocks, and pinned the Subterranean's head between my legs. I whipped him around, releasing my grip and dropping him several levels. Keeping my eyes trained on him, I opened my hand and summoned the poison-tipped dagger that had slipped to the ground.

The Subterranean shot me a glare brimming with contempt and raced off through one of the infinite number of clefts in the rock. I slid my weapon into my belt and set off after him, swinging from vine to vine. Barehanded, I climbed up one of the vertical passageways that looked like a tunnel burrowed through the ground by worms. The place hadn't actually been designed for escaping; it was a prison, and sooner or later the Subterranean I was chasing would realize it. I'd seen the flicker of fear in his eyes when he discovered he couldn't dematerialize any more, that he couldn't escape me. The perimeter had been sealed off. It wasn't time to run—it was time to fight. And we were going to exterminate every last one of them.

I followed the sound of his footsteps racing through the unpredictable twists and turns. A mortal wouldn't have been able to handle the dizzying pace of the obstacle course, but with me chasing him, that Subterranean was doomed.

"You can't keep her away from us forever," he shouted.

I pounced in front of him and shoved him against the wall. "But I'll never stop trying." As I drew my dagger its blade hissed and I pressed it against his throat.

"Others will come," he warned, his eyes full of fear.

"I have a plan for that too," I shot back, my expression threatening.

We'd spent a whole week, day and night, formulating a plan, studying every detail. Now that Gemma had sworn loyalty to the Witches she'd never been more in danger. The Màsala wanted to take her before she transformed, but I wasn't about to let anybody touch her.

The Subterranean cringed, bracing for the blow. Instead I grabbed his hands and pinned them to the rock. An arrow whistled past my ear. I spun around and her eyes pierced me, as golden as those of the hissing Dakor coiled around her wrist.

A Witch.

The Subterranean let out a wail of terror but she continued to stare at me, a mix of excitement and bitterness in her eyes. She had a proud face, dark skin, and a long ponytail as black as ebony.

Bathsheeva.

She set another poisoned arrow against her bow and took aim at me, but a second before she released it her arm tipped up and she hit her real target. The Subterranean who'd just materialized in midair crumpled to the ground, the arrow protruding from his leg.

Like a bolt of lightning, another arrow flew straight toward us and lodged inches from the head of the Subterranean I'd immobilized.

With a fierce snap, a black leather cord whipped around his wrists, binding him to the wall. The Angel of Death howled with pain from the poison the cord had been soaked in and passed out, scarlet trickles of blood streaking the mark of the Children of Eve on his arm.

The Witch narrowed her threatening eyes at me once again, then took a mighty leap and set off to track down her next prey. The Subterranean she'd hit in the leg was writhing on the ground just steps from me, his flesh sizzling from the arrow's poison. Framed by long black hair, his face was covered with welts, painful testimony to his personal battle with the Witch.

I clenched my fists. He was about to die, but in his gray eyes there wasn't a shadow of fear or remorse—only the proud awareness that with his death others would come to complete the mission. I raised my foot and kicked him hard in the face to erase that satisfied smirk.

The sounds of the battle echoed off the walls. There was no time for long farewells because we weren't done fighting yet. I ran in the direction of the shouts and leapt off the rocks into the void. Aiming for one of the two Subterraneans Simon was battling, I landed on him with all my weight, like a hungry lion pouncing on its prey. I was well aware of my peers' blind dedication during battle, but my strength had another source, another energy, another name. My need to protect Gemma was unstoppable. I could feel the fire grow stronger inside me every time I struck. And struck. Again and again. I would slaughter them all, each and every one of them. No one was going to take her away from me again.

I dragged the Subterranean back and slammed him against the ground. My hair fell over my face, my breathing ragged and my muscles quivering as I held him in place.

He stared at me in terror as the earth cracked beneath him. What scared him most, I could tell, were my eyes. They were the same ice-color as his, but mine held a fire he'd never seen before.

Someone clapped, deliberately, and I slowly raised my eyes.

"What an exciting show. I'd almost forgotten how ardently you used to battle in the Opalion." Devina emerged from the shadows, moving with feline grace as four black panthers stalked from different crevasses in the rock and positioned themselves in a circle.

Terrified, the Subterranean beneath me tried to break free, but I tightened my grip. "Too bad the show didn't feature you," I shot back at the Witch, my sarcastic voice overflowing with hatred.

She leaned over and stroked my cheek with her black-painted fingernail. Her fiery eyes told me she still desired me. She slid her finger down my neck and across the long, deep scar on my shoulder. A dark shadow veiled her gaze at the memory of when she'd left her marks on me, almost as though she'd branded me as her property. Her Dakor slowly slithered out of her thick red hair and hissed close to my face.

I grabbed the hand she was touching me with and glared at her with contempt.

"Such bitterness," she lamented, her voice honeyed. "After all the time we spent having fun together . . ." One of the panthers roared and she sneered.

In a silent challenge, I held her ardent gaze as her serpent circled down her arm. The blond Subterranean struggled beneath me, terrified, as the Dakor slithered closer and closer to him and the air filled with tension.

Another panther roared, and this time the sound filled the entire cave.

"Oh, all right! You're all so tiresome!" Devina stood up and cracked her whip, winding it around the Angel's throat. She jerked it back and smashed him against the galleon's fragile wooden hull, shattering it and revealing what was hidden inside: a cluster of Subterraneans bound to tall posts.

I went to stand beside Simon, my muscles tensed. He too had captured a Subterranean. The two panthers facing them transformed into Witches, seized his prisoner, and bound him to a post beside the others as more Sisters leapt down from the rocks with their prey.

Devina smiled at me, in her eyes a glimmer of nostalgia and a hint of promise. I turned to follow Simon, but something stopped me. The burning pain registered before the crack of the whip; Devina's poisoned lash had coiled around my wrist. "Leaving so soon? The fun is barely starting."

Simon and I exchanged glances. He seemed worried about my intentions, but I grabbed the whip, ignoring the pain, and jerked it out of Devina's grip. Before she realized what I was doing, I threw myself on her, forcing her backwards with my body and pressing the whip tightly against her throat. "We're not in your world now, *Witch*. Just because we've formed an alliance doesn't mean I'm willing to put up with you. Try that again and I'll incinerate you."

Three panthers crept toward us threateningly. "Evan," Simon called.

I looked at the Witch again. Would I ever manage to wipe that smug smirk off her face? I turned my back to her and followed Simon to the waterfall above. There, behind the curtain of water, was the way out. I opened the door and behind me Simon pressed the black carbonado button. Our surroundings changed: the ruins slowly turned into the familiar walls of the workout room. The rock beneath our feet flattened out to form the floor, like a lake gradually freezing over, sealing the Subterraneans in our dungeon below, guarded by a group of ferocious panthers who were prepared to devour them.

"Luring them here was a great idea, bro. Well done!" I told Simon, throwing myself down onto the sofa in the living room. He straddled a chair and started munching popcorn. After various days of nonstop battling the Subterraneans sent in to kill Gemma, we'd come up with a strategy. Originally, we'd only had to deal with one Executioner at a time, but this time they'd sent in nine of them at once. The Witches had helped us secure the training room area, and one by one the Executioners had fallen into our trap. Once they'd been lured in, they had no way out. Now they were under round-the-clock surveillance by a group of Drusas—guardian Witches—who were keeping them in a weakened state with their powerful venomous blood. Even if they broke free, the perimeter of the workout room was sealed off so they couldn't dematerialize. We had them in the palm of our hands.

"At least we're playing on our home field now," Simon replied. "The enchanted workout room is a perfect battlefield."

"Yeah. There's no better way to train, and the simulation scenarios made everything more fun. Let's hope the plan works and more don't turn up."

"I'm sure this'll keep them at bay for a while. Besides, we had no choice. There were too many of them this time. I counted seven prisoners."

I too had counted the posts to which we'd bound the Subterraneans. Two were missing. "One died right before my eyes. He was about to attack me when a Witch ran him through."

"Eight Executioners in one night? Not bad. What sons of bitches. The Màsala have decided not to cut us any slack."

"Nine, actually," Devina called out nonchalantly, suddenly appearing out of nowhere.

"You mean you killed another one?!" I shot to my feet and confronted the Witch. I'd assumed one of them had escaped, but instead Devina had killed him, risking ruining our plan.

"Calm down, Spartan," she said in a lilting voice. "I understand the rules: only prisoners."

"Couldn't you have understood it before?" Simon reproached her.

"Don't you realize what this might mean for us?!" I growled, inches from her face. "We have a plan. Follow it."

"Evan is right, Dev," Anya spoke up, walking through the door with two other Sisters. She was the one who, in panther form, had growled at Devina when she provoked me. I'd recognized her by her emerald eyes. "We can't kill them any more. For every Subterranean we get rid of, another one will show up. Or maybe more. Who knows?"

"Imprisoning Desdemona worked," Simon reassured her. "It'll work again this time."

"I think so too, but we need to be careful and not let our instincts get the better of us." Anya cast a reproachful glance at her Sister who hadn't been able to hold back in battle.

"What a bore! You're taking all the fun out of it!" Devina complained. Anya rolled her eyes. "I killed a Subterranean, but I wasn't the only one. Why are you taking it out on me?!" She looked accusingly at Bathsheeva.

"Hey, it's not my fault!" Bathsheeva protested. "I saw you, you killed him on purpose. I *had* to do it. There were three of them and that bastard was making things rough for me. He was armed to the teeth and he wounded my Dakor. He had these strange razor-sharp brass knuckles—I'd never seen anything like them. They got smeared with my Dakor's poison. While I was capturing the other two he got away. He was about to attack Evan with that weird weapon of his and would have killed him if I hadn't shown up in time." The Witch sent me a fleeting glance and I nodded to her in acknowledgement.

"So what? Sophìa's orders are to protect Gemma, not her boy toy," Devina said with a sneer.

I glowered at her. I couldn't stand how she jeered at me like she owned me. I knew what she was thinking: if the Subterranean had hit me with his poisoned weapon, I would have ended up back in Hell where she could do with me as she pleased.

"Forgive her," Anya said. "She's a real Witch when—No, she's like that practically all the time."

"It's nice to know you speak so affectionately about me behind my back, little Sister."

"I wasn't speaking behind your back. You know for yourself you act like a bitch. It's what you do best."

"Touché." Devina gave a shrug of satisfaction.

"Do I really have to stay here?" Simon asked.

The grimace that twisted Devina's face got a smile out of me. Maybe once in a while it had to get to even her to know her company wasn't enjoyed.

"Is Gemma with Gwen?" Anya asked, suddenly worried again. I nodded to reassure her and looked outside. Beyond the hexagonal picture window, darkness shrouded everything.

"Nerea, Safria, join Gwen upstairs. We should reinforce our surveillance."

The two Witches nodded and left us, morphing into panthers before climbing the stairs. I nodded to Anya, grateful for her consideration. Though Gemma hadn't transformed yet, most of her Sisters were already treating her as one of their own. In recent days I'd been surprised by how loyally the Witches had helped us protect her.

"We have to keep up our guard," Anya said. "Bathsheeva killed an Executioner to protect Evan, and Devina slew one because . . ." She looked at her Sister reproachfully. "Well, because otherwise she wouldn't be Devina."

"Blah blah blah," Devina said, responding to the accusation in a singsong voice.

"We've imprisoned seven, but we know for certain two more will soon be after Gemma. Over the last few nights we've had time to study each of them, but we have no idea who they'll send in now. We don't know when they'll attack next. Still, there's no doubt that—" A sudden hiss sliced through the air, cutting Anya short.

We spun around in alarm and Devina smiled at us, pleased. "Problem solved." The Witch filed her nails with the shaft of her whip as we all stared at her, wordless. On the ground, an Executioner who'd appeared from nowhere writhed beneath the iron grip of her heel, while another hung from the wall, unconscious, behind the Witch. "You might consider thanking me at this point."

Simon's relieved laugh filled the room and I shook my head, my tension draining away. He loathed Devina, maybe even more than I did—she was the one who had betrayed Ginevra and made the Sisterhood drive her out of her world, putting both their lives in jeopardy. However, crossing the latest two Subterraneans off our list would make life easier, and for once it was thanks to her.

"Great job, Dev," Anya said sincerely. "Now let's take them down to join the others."

"I'm not guarding the Children of Eve if I can't even kill them," the redheaded Witch complained, heading toward the workout room.

"Yes you are, if you want at least to have a little fun with them. I bet you can't wait." Anya winked at me. They dragged the two unconscious Subterraneans through the door leading downstairs and closed it behind them. I was infinitely grateful for her gesture: it finally left me free to go to Gemma.

"The best way to start the day, don't you think?" Simon slapped me on the shoulder and I grimaced from the pain of the cuts and bruises on my chest. "Nice work with that Carpathian," he said, grinning.

"Carpathian?"

"That's what Drake would have called him. You see how big that guy was?"

"Yeah, I'm sure Drake would have had a blast this time." I missed my brother Drake terribly—we all did—and the awareness that I would never see him again was devastating. Still, I couldn't blame him for deciding to stay in Hell with the woman he loved. If I were in his shoes I would have done the same thing. "Things aren't so bad for him down there. He has his Stella. I wish you could've met her. She's a tough one."

"Just what Drake needed to get his act together!"

We both burst out laughing.

"Anyway, you weren't bad yourself, though that gash in your side is pretty gruesome," I said, teasing him. We were both bare-chested, our skin dirty and scratched from the battle.

"Yeah, those fireballs sure are annoying when they hit you."

I laughed. Annoying? I well remembered how blindingly painful it was when a Subterranean struck you with his angel fire. The battle with Drake's impersonator had really put me to the test. "Want me to give you a hand with that?"

"Stay away," he warned me with a little smile. "We both know you can't wait to run up those stairs. Besides," he said, waggling his eyebrows, "battle wounds are the world's most powerful aphrodisiac, didn't you know? Now get out of here. And while you're at it send the blond down to me. Go on, leave me alone before this gash heals." He added in a whisper, "Ginevra goes crazy for little games like this."

"You two are completely insane."

"What can I do?" Simon shrugged.

I shook my head, leaving him in the living room. I'd battled Subterraneans all night long, so I should have been exhausted. Instead, the thought of going to Gemma filled me with pure energy. I took the stairs three at a time, electrified at the idea of being with her. I still hadn't forgotten the feeling of that terrible void deep in my heart when they'd torn her away from me. At times, when the memories of Hell filled my head, that same terrible sensation of loss returned and it felt like I was losing my mind. Now that we were together again, I wanted her beside me every second.

I stopped outside the door to my room where she was sleeping. Two Drusas—Nerea and Safria—were standing guard in their feline form. They had shiny black fur and sharp yellow and blue eyes that glinted in the half-light. Beneath Nerea's coat I glimpsed a faint spotted pattern, while Safria's was as clear as night. They both bowed their heads and moved aside for me. Inside the room, a large black panther with jade-green eyes rose majestically to its feet and a shiver ran through me. I still wasn't used to seeing Ginevra in her feline manifestation. In animal form, the Witches could better perceive their Subterranean enemies, which was why they often transformed when given the task of acting as Drusas. I studied her, fascinated. Within the walls of the house they looked larger, yet they moved so gracefully. If you stared at them for too long, you were in danger of being bewitched. Ginevra was beautiful and intimidating at the same time. Her threatening green eyes struck fear into the heart. On her forehead, a white droplet-shaped patch stood out against her black fur. She moved forward elegantly and assumed her human appearance.

Simon had insisted she be the one to watch over Gemma so she would stay out of the battle. I'd immediately backed him up, because with Ginevra guarding her I would feel more secure, more able to focus on the fight. It was surprising to see the bond that had formed between her and Gemma while I was away. Ginevra had been at her side and had protected her like a Sister even before she'd known Gemma was destined to become one. Even Simon had proven to be protective toward her, and for that I would be eternally grateful to them.

When I'd lost everything, including myself, they'd taken me in and given me a new life. I realized part of Ginevra's affection toward Gemma was due to the dark nature buried inside her—a nature they shared. Yet I'd known Ginevra for centuries, and seeing her so attached to the person I loved most in the world filled me with pride. It was unique, sensational.

Ginevra smiled at me, reading in my mind how anxious I was to be alone with Gemma. "Shouldn't you take a shower first?" she joked, gesturing at my bruised, soot-covered chest.

"Somebody told me war wounds are really sexy." I ran a hand up my neck, grinning. "Speaking of which, that somebody is waiting for you downstairs." I winked at her.

"Better not keep him waiting, then." Smiling, she stole out of the room.

"Hey, Gin," I said before she shut the door behind her. "Thanks."

"I'll have the Drusas stand guard downstairs. That way you can have a little time to yourselves. Just be sure you don't make too much noise—you and your *war wounds*," she teased with a sly grin. I chuckled and she closed the door softly to avoid waking Gemma.

A blue book lay on the floor. I picked it up. It was her diary. She must have dozed off while writing in it. I stroked the embossing on the cover and set it on the nightstand, then stared at her in the dim light. Her skin glowed like silver and her ebony-black hair was spread out on the pillow. I clenched my fists to contain the wave of emotion that flooded me.

Gemma was lying on her side, fast asleep. I moved closer to the bed. The sheet was pulled back, leaving her legs bare. I stroked her knee and thought of covering it so she wouldn't be cold, but instead my hand slowly rose up her thigh, moving the fabric away. I breathed deeply, forcing myself to get a grip, but just then Gemma parted her lips and desire threatened to overwhelm me.

I lay down behind her, our bodies nestling together like two perfect halves, and stared at the soft curve of her bosom as it rose and fell to the tranquil rhythm of her heart. Brushing the hair from her face, I touched my nose to her ear and breathed in her scent. I closed my eyes, overcome with love for her. My hand ran down her side and slowly slid to her belly, where a tiny creature was growing inside her—a creature I already loved with all my soul. I sought her hand beneath the covers and squeezed it, impatient to join her in her dream.

Do not destroy this tacit silence
but leave me, I beg you,
to these melancholy shadows.
Let me perish with the sun.
Giuseppe Strazzant

THE COLORS OF THE SOUL

"Hey." Gemma opened her eyes and squeezed my hand, turning to face me.

"Hey," I whispered back, stroking her palm with my thumb. I raised her hand to my mouth and kissed it, gazing at her the whole time.

She closed her eyes, turned all the way over and slid her knee between my legs. The gesture set my blood on fire. I drew her to me and was on top of her in a flash, my lips on her neck and my hips pressed against hers. "Jamie . . ." I sought her mouth and she arched her back, yearning for my body. I cupped her bottom with my hand and pulled her against me roughly, responding to her need as our breathing mingled, trembling with desire.

Gemma clutched my dog tag in her fingers and kept me pulled against her, burning with the same passion that consumed me. She kissed me sweetly on the mouth, quenching my instincts. I prolonged the kiss, moving slowly. Resting my forehead against hers, I tried to regain control of my breathing. "Good morning." I looked her in the eye and she smiled at me.

"This is a great way to wake up. Just be careful—I'm going to expect this every morning."

"Well, I don't know about that. I'm a pretty busy guy." I shot her a teasing grin and she punched me on the shoulder.

"Hey!"

I laughed, swept her up in my arms, and pulled her on top of me. "I'm yours. Every morning of every day to come." I fixed my eyes on hers to make sure she knew I meant every word.

Gemma pretended to think it over and then decided to smile at me. She ran her finger down my chest, looking me in the eye. "Now will you explain why you're half-naked in my bed? What are your intentions?"

"To unleash your most deeply buried instincts. Wasn't it clear?" I raised an eyebrow, still teasing her. Her jaw dropped in pretended shock. "I must say I'm surprised by how easily I managed to do it. Clearly some of your instincts aren't buried so deeply after all." I laughed, enjoying the range of reactions Gemma was trying to hide from me, even though I could sense her every emotion. "Besides, have you always slept in only your underwear?"

She let out a playful gasp, covering herself with the sheet.

"It's not my fault you got uncovered in your sleep."

"And you didn't even bother to cover me, I bet!"

"Uh . . . Yeah, sure. I mean, I was just about to."

"You . . . !" She pulled the pillow out from under my head and started to hit me with it.

Unable to block the blows, I grabbed her wrists and both of us laughed like little kids. When we finally ran out of laughter, she turned on her side, facing me.

"She was haunting his soul and he vowed to haunt her dreams," I murmured. I tucked a lock of hair behind her ear as she watched my every movement, mesmerized. How could love cause such restlessness deep in one's heart? Immense joy, tumultuous passion . . . the agonizing fear of losing her. Love was a generous thief. It had stolen my heart, taking me prisoner, but never had a prison been so sweet and so necessary. It didn't matter how long I'd fought it or how hard I'd tried to control it. In the end, it had conquered me, my instincts, my desires. All I had to do was look at Gemma to understand that my world had changed. She was both my Heaven and my Hell.

There could be no Evan without Gemma.

"You didn't answer my question. Did you think I wouldn't notice?" Gemma raised an eyebrow slyly. "Well? Why are you shirtless? And more importantly, why do you have blood and dirt all over you?"

My wounds had healed, but maybe I should have taken Ginevra's advice and washed off all traces of the battle. "Let's just say last night was a bit *lively*."

"What happened? Did they hurt you? Why didn't you wake me?" she asked, agitated.

"We carried out our plan," I said, point-blank.

"Last night?!"

"They tried to attack us all at once again. It was the perfect opportunity. One of them even came in here."

"What? How?!"

"Don't worry. He didn't even touch you. Ginevra took care of him. We had to act fast. The Witches relaxed their defense of the house, convincing the Executioners they'd found a way in. At that point we lured them into the workout room."

"Did the simulation scenarios work? And the defenses?"

I nodded. "It was a perfect battlefield. None of them managed to dematerialize and we got them all."

"All of them? You mean nine Subterraneans captured *in just one night*?!"

"Actually, there was a slight delay with two of them, but Devina handled the problem."

"Devina? You mean redheaded Devina the Witch slash Cruella de Vil?"

"That's the one."

Gemma closed her mouth and I smiled. She was so sweet when she got jealous. I pulled her by the wrist and rubbed my nose against hers to ease the agitation that the memory of Devina and me in Hell caused her. "Hey, weren't you the one who had the idea of imprisoning the Subterraneans instead of killing them?" She nodded, pride sparkling in her eyes.

"What was the name of the one who tried to off you when I was gone?"

"Desdemona. Have I told you I was the one who killed her?" she replied, secretly pleased.

I feigned surprise and shock. "And how did you do that, pray tell?"

"I shot her." She shrugged, as if she'd just told me she'd made scrambled eggs.

I laughed and pulled her closer. "Well, you did fight your way through Hell to save me—I always knew you were brave," I whispered, my mouth close to her ear.

"What choice did I have? I had to go get you and she was in my way!"

"A terrible decision, really." I shook my head, pretending disapproval.

"Moron!" She laughed too when she realized I was joking. She covered my face with her hand but I pinned her wrists against the pillow and stole a kiss from her.

"When are you going to stop teasing me?"

"When the moon meets the sun. Now get up—I have a plan."

Gemma rolled her eyes. "Every time you say that I have good reason to be scared."

In spite of her words, I could sense her enthusiasm growing from the beating of her heart. "Don't lie to me."

She climbed out of bed, instantly noticing the many cans of paint I'd stacked up in the back of the room. The floor was covered with a white drop cloth.

"What does all of this mean?" She looked at me, surprised.

I smiled and led her toward the paints. "It means we're going to paint your room."

The walls of Gemma's room were covered with photographs. In many of them she was with Peter. I would never have asked her to take them down because, all things considered, I was grateful to the guy for being there at her side as she grew up. Peter had been as important to Gemma as Ginevra was to me, though the feelings Peter had for Gemma had led her to loosen the bond between them. Every so often we would all meet up—our group and Gemma's friends—and at school sometimes the two of them would even spend time alone. Inevitably he would take the opportunity to make a move on her, and when that happened I would have to fight the urge to break his neck. Knowing that he wanted her made a fire burn inside me. If it hadn't been for Ginevra I probably would have slaughtered him long ago. But then I would look at the pictures of Gemma and me sharing our everyday lives together, and the fire would die down. She was mine and no one else's.

"Well? What color should we start with?"

I turned to look at Gemma and my breath caught in my throat. Her golden skin glowed in the light coming in through the window. She still wore the clothes she'd slept in: a soft blue satin camisole and shorts. She walked toward me, barefoot, and showed me her index finger tinged with red paint. While I'd been trying to control my homicidal instincts toward Peter, she'd already cleared all the walls, taking down the photos and removing the books from the shelves. She was so electrified by the thought of painting her old room! She'd wanted to do it for a long time, but the thought unsettled her. Gemma was very attached to the memories objects held for her. She was afraid that if she changed the color of the walls, hiding the scattered pencil marks or flaking paint, she would erase part of her life. There were even lines on the wall marking her height and Peter's as they'd grown up over the years.

"What do you say to this?" She slid her finger across the wall, leaving behind a wavy line of red paint.

"Actually, what do you say we use them all?" I suggested, heading toward her laptop. Typing in the password—*Gevan*—I started up her playlist. I adjusted the volume and the sound of Passenger's *Let Her Go* filled the room.

"All of them? What do you mean?"

"That you don't have to choose the color you want right away."

Gemma moved closer, suspicious. "Okay . . . So what do we use to paint?"

With a flick of my foot, I swept two long paintbrushes off the ground and caught them in mid-air. I twirled them in my fingers and offered them to Gemma. They were thin but as long as her arm.

She looked at them, puzzled, before taking them. "Where do we start?"

"Let's play a game." I took her hand, pulled her in front of the cans of paint and stood behind her. "Close your eyes," I whispered in her ear.

"Huh?" She turned to look at me, confused.

"Shh . . ." I squeezed her hands at her sides. "Close your eyes."

"How can I paint if my eyes are closed?"

"Trust me. It'll be fun."

Gemma took a deep breath and did as I said. I rested my palms on the backs of her hands and laced my fingers with hers, holding the brushes along with her. Guiding her hands, I had her dip the tips in two different colors—yellow and red—then raised the brushes, marking two spots on the wall.

"Ready?" I whispered again. Gemma nodded. "Now free your mind and follow your instinct. Let yourself go, move as though it was just you and the paints. There's only one rule: never take the brushes off the walls and don't open your eyes for anything in the world."

"Those are *two* rules."

"Just focus on yourself."

"Okay," she murmured trustingly. After a few seconds, she moved one of the two brushes over the wall and the other one followed close behind.

I also closed my eyes and breathed through her hair, surrendering to her movements. Gemma followed the rhythm of the music and the paintbrushes danced through the air as though she were an orchestra conductor.

She took a step and then another, and I followed, my fingers still intertwined with hers as though we were one being. Under my control, the yellow turned to orange, the red transformed into green, then blue and purple. The colors blended together from wall to wall, morphing into still other hues as Gemma advanced slowly, following her need to fill the entire room. My eyes still closed, I let myself be guided by her movements, melding with her, her heart beating against my chest almost as though it were my own. From time to time Gemma trembled, and her shiver spread to me.

Antar may as. Yata tvam may asi.

She was inside me, in my heart, in my soul.

Finally she stopped, satisfied. Slowly, I raised her hands over her head and ran mine down them. I stroked her neck, her shoulders, then moved down to clasp her hips. When I kissed her softly behind the ear, she turned slightly, rubbing her head against mine, then lowered her hands as the notes of Lana Del Rey faded. I opened my eyes and smiled, my lips on her ear. "Now you can look."

Gemma raised her eyelids and trembled. I could sense her amazement even before reading it in her eyes. She didn't say a word, just turned around, her mouth slightly open and her gaze captivated by the walls full of colors. The lines were as soft as the harmony she felt deep in her heart, marked here and there by sharper segments that expressed her uneasiness. Some areas stood out more than others. I'd perceived feelings of fear and distress arise in her when she painted them. The lines ran parallel, followed each other, parted, and then rose up together to touch the sky. To the rhythm of *Glory and Gore* by Lorde, Gemma had painted the boldest segments. With Adele's *Set Fire to the Rain*, she'd let herself go with long, interwoven lines. Lana Del Rey had reawakened grimmer thoughts, bringing out her fears. At those moments, even the sunbeams had grown dimmer and the darkness behind her closed eyelids had turned to gloom.

"Evan, it's . . . Did we do this?" Gemma continued to stare at the stunning weavings of colors on the walls, fascinated.

"I didn't do anything. It was you."

"Incredible," she murmured to herself.

Smiling with satisfaction, I took Gemma's hand and whirled her around. She locked her big dark eyes on mine and for a second I was left breathless. I pulled her to me gently and moved her away again, guiding her movements to the sound of Ed Sheeran's voice in an unplanned dance. Colorful droplets of paint rose from the cans into the air, drifted through the room and encircled us. Amazement and wonder filled her eyes as she watched them.

Taking me by surprise, Gemma did a spin, never letting go of my hand, and leaned back against my chest, swaying to the rhythm of *Thinking Out Loud.* I closed my eyes and rubbed my head against hers, overcome by the sensations.

The song ended, interrupting that brief moment, and the faster rhythm of Pink boomed against the walls. Gemma turned to go, but I pulled her back, spinning her around quickly and back into my arms, laughing. "You can tell the drops of paint to stop now too. One of them was about to land on my face."

I caught a drifting sphere of paint on my finger and smeared it on her nose. "What, like *this*?"

"Why you . . . !!" Gemma's eyes opened wide and her jaw dropped with surprise. She caught a droplet of her own and drew a line down my face with it. I let her do it and then raised an eyebrow: a clear warning that she should run, and fast. Gemma understood and let out a shriek before rushing over to the paint cans and dunking both brushes in them, challenging me.

"You sure that's a good move?" I said, letting a this-means-war grin escape me. I shot toward her. She let out another shriek and ran, dropping both paintbrushes. I chased her around the room and in a flash grabbed her from behind and spun her around as she squealed with laughter. I pinned her to the ground beneath me, her sweet laughter filling my soul. She tried to defend herself and counterattack but I showed no mercy, painting her arms, legs, neck. Each touch triggered something inside me. I caressed her inner thigh and moved my fingers upward, leaving a blue streak on her skin. Gemma's laughter grew softer when I rose to her belly. In a single movement I ripped her camisole in two, her beauty leaving me breathless. Her chest moved quickly, her breathing ragged from what had just happened—or maybe from what was about to happen. Like a tidal wave, her emotions crashed down on me: anticipation, impatience . . . desire.

I gently stroked her belly, then kissed it over and over. Gemma smiled at me. My immense love for the baby filled her with joy. But instantly my eyes found hers, like those of a wolf. My hand rose over her middle and found the clasp to her bra. I propped Gemma up and slipped it off her as she slid her hands down my chest, then sat on the floor and drew her to me, holding her tightly by the waist. Gemma watched the little drops of paint floating around us. She lifted her hand and moved her fingers through them.

A sweet melody filled the room. I brushed the hair from her face and sought her eyes, whispering the lyrics: *"'Cause all of me loves all of you. Love your curves and all your edges, all your perfect imperfections."*

Gemma closed her eyes and rested her forehead against my cheek, then lowered her hand, dipped her finger in the little pool of paint that had formed there, and drew symbols on the white drop cloth that covered the floor.

"Give your all to me. I'll give my all to you. You're my end and my beginning. Even when I lose I'm winning." I stroked her fingers, following her lines, weaving together our movements, seeking her hand. Our thumbs playfully touched and clasped together to complete the tattoo that united us. *Stay together, fight together:* the writing connected to the two rings in the infinity symbol. I rested my palm on her hand and led it to the drop cloth, our laced fingers dancing together, creating new colors. I felt like we were making love. It was the most sensual moment of my entire life. Every movement was so erotically charged that the paint almost felt hot against our skin. Or maybe it was me, boiling with desire for her. I raised our clasped hands, spread open her palms and gently took her wrists, pulling myself against her skin as our fingers continued to seek each other out, touch each other, slide at times tenderly, at times with need. I felt I was losing my mind: it was a sweet hell from which I wished no redemption. Overcome by those sensations, I squeezed her bottom and pulled her on top of me.

In my ethereal form my emotions were more intense—they flooded me with a force that was uncontrollable, devastating, vital. A multitude of tiny explosions that changed my universe. I sought her lips and our tongues touched, teasing each other playfully. She moaned and I let out a long breath, yearning to rip off the fabric still dividing us. As if sensing my need, Gemma undid the button on my pants and unzipped them, leaving me breathless. Anticipation was killing me like never before. My hand slid into her shorts, stroking her underwear. Gemma trembled with pleasure, gripping the mark of the Children of Eve on my forearm. She arched her back, yearning for contact, and rubbed her hips against mine, her hot panties pressing against my erection. I moaned, her reaction leaving me stunned, and kissed her intensely on the mouth as our bodies burned, melting together. I grasped her nape with one hand while with the other I pushed her underwear aside and penetrated her, groaning with pleasure.

Gemma panted, driving me wild. I gripped her nape tighter and she raised her chin, letting my lips slide down her neck in slow, sweet agony. With my other hand I pulled her against me more firmly, her hot breasts on my chest sending quivers through me as I moved inside her. I could feel Gemma's emotions growing with mine, so powerful they clouded my senses. I perceived the exact moment when her pleasure reached its peak and at that very moment I climaxed inside her, overwhelmed by the intensity of the emotions.

Cradling her neck, I rested my forehead against hers and a smile escaped us both. I swept her hair out of her face, tucked it behind her ear and kissed her—a long kiss, sweet and necessary—as shivers of pleasure shook my body once more. A star had just exploded inside of me. Its name was Gemma.

POTENTIAL

Gemma laughed. "You have my handprint on your back."

"Where? Oh, that's okay. It'll be my spoils of war."

"Hey!" She hit my shoulder. "What do you mean?"

"Well, you know, I did fight for you all night long." I raised an eyebrow to provoke her. "This way I can show Simon it was worth it." I laughed, teasing her.

Gemma's jaw dropped and her face turned bright red. "You're not showing Simon," she warned me. "Now go straight to the spa and take a shower!"

I moved my lips to her ear. "Only if you'll join me," I whispered, gently sucking her earlobe.

Gemma trembled and closed her eyes, at the mercy of her emotions. Then she pushed me away and laughed. "I bet Simon would get himself injured on purpose just to have Ginevra heal him."

"You would win that bet."

"So tell me, did the two of you plan all this last night? Otherwise why would you want to show him my handprint on you?"

I raised my hands. "I didn't tell him anything. I came here with honorable intentions, I swear." I tried to hide a grin but failed.

"Yeah, right. You expect me to believe you weren't planning on *this*?" she said, gesturing at our entwined bodies on the floor.

I leaned over her and nibbled her neck. "I *always* plan on this."

Gemma laughed and let out a shriek when I pinned her beneath me and tickled her. I stroked her belly, growing serious again. It was unbelievable that a tiny creature was growing right there inside her. Gemma toyed with my dog tag but I continued to stare at her belly, enchanted. I leaned down and rested my ear against it as I continued to stroke it.

"Hear anything?" she asked, curious.

I listened to Gemma's breathing, then heard a rapid flutter and smiled. "I can hear his heart beating. Tell me again about how you heard him. Are you really sure it's a boy?"

"Not a hundred percent, but my instinct says so. I heard something while I was talking to Simon and Ginevra. I thought it was because the baby had powers, but instead they were mine. *I* was the one reading his mind. But it hasn't happened again since then."

"It must be amazing." I kissed her belly, but as I caressed the silvery streaks on it I grew sad.

She instantly realized why I looked concerned. "Evan, do you think the baby will be human?"

"I ask myself that question every day." I raised my head to look her in the eye. "Whatever his nature is, he's ours and we'll protect him together." Gemma's eyes moved to the matching tattoos on our hands, her expression a mix of fear and concern.

Stay together. Fight together.

She'd made a pact with the Witches to save me, but I still couldn't accept it. Gemma was convinced the transformation wouldn't obliterate her, that she would manage to cling to our love to drive the evil out of her, but I was consumed by doubt. I couldn't allow her to transform. I couldn't run the risk. I had to come up with a way to prevent it.

"A penny for your thoughts," she said, stroking my head.

"I'm thinking about how happy we'll be together with him."

Gemma smiled. "Do you think the Màsala will ever give up and let me be?"

Only two things could make the Màsala stop hounding Gemma: her transformation or her death. In either case, I would end up defeated because I would lose her. I propped myself up on my elbows and moved closer to her, looking into her eyes. "No," I admitted, "but we're not about to give up either."

Gemma nodded in silence. I stroked her cheek. I would have turned Heaven and Hell upside down to be with her—no one was going to take her away from me. I pressed my lips to hers and our kiss burned with passion, kindled by our caresses. I slid my hand up her thigh, ready to start all over again. Gemma clung to my biceps, letting me kiss her neck and breasts. I sensed the desire growing in her, but suddenly it was replaced by something else: astonishment and wonder. She darted around me and rose onto her palms.

"Oh my God." Gemma's jaw dropped, her eyes widening as she peered up. On the ceiling had appeared the image of the two of us entwined in a starry sky. She got to her feet, still staring at the painting, entranced.

"Wow." I also looked up, stupefied.

"You mean it's real? It's not my imagination?"

"Well . . . Define *imagination*."

"Don't kid around, Evan. It's—"

"It's us," I whispered, holding her from behind, "and it's magnificent."

"But how? *When?*"

I laughed and moved my lips to her ear. "Want me to tell you a secret?" She nodded eagerly. "I didn't do anything."

Gemma turned to look at me, amazed. "What? You mean . . . ?" I nodded for a long moment as she reflected. "It was *me?*" she asked, still confused.

It was the truth. As we made love, the paints had danced across the ceiling, creating the incredible image of the two of us locked in an embrace in our universe. Gemma's soul was what had given life to that magical dance.

"Looks like you gave it a finishing touch." I smiled at Gemma.

She ran her hands through her hair. "But I don't get it. Usually I realize when my powers are awakening. Oh my God! How am I going to explain this to my mom?"

"I bet she won't even notice." I winked at her, still teasing her. I'd given Gemma clues, but it still hadn't dawned on her.

"What do you mean she won't notice? How could she not notice? It looks like a paint bomb exploded in here! Maybe I should've left my room the way it—Wait a second . . . I always sleep at your place. What are we doing in my old bedroom?" She turned to look at me and her eyes slowly went wide, the smile gradually spreading across her face as she figured it out. "I'm . . . dreaming," she murmured to herself. "This is a dream, isn't it? We're inside my head."

I nodded and smiled back at Gemma. She was electrified. Few times before had I made her aware she was dreaming because I didn't want to deprive her of the emotions she would have missed out on. In dreams, my soul was closer to hers. I could read her subconscious and perceive her slightest sensation as though it were my own. To me, it was a parallel universe in which everything was amplified. Gemma knew that on those occasions I could read inside her, so if she realized she was in a dream she held back, reluctant to stay so open to me. Instead, I wanted her to experience every emotion to the fullest.

"If you meant to tell me, you could've done it sooner!" she reproved me with a little smile.

"Well, looks like you played your part anyway," I teased, gesturing at the ceiling. In her dreams, Gemma had always had the ability to recreate incredible scenarios and this time her spirit had painted a picture of the two of us.

"So when I wake up everything will be like it was before? What a shame."

"Will you remember it?" I whispered in her ear, squeezing her from behind. She nodded. I could sense her heart brimming with joy. "We can always redo it, if you want . . . but for real."

Gemma turned around and folded her arms around my neck. "No, I don't want to risk spoiling this memory."

"You never could." I kissed her on the lips but she pulled away.

"Besides, from now on when I look at my old room, I'll see it with different eyes."

"Why's that?"

"Well . . ." She slowly moved away, holding my hand. "Because now I know its potential. I know what it could become."

Potential. The word had a double meaning: Gemma was trying to distract me, but I realized she was actually referring to *her own* potential. She had something in mind and I could already sense her attempts to keep me from picking up on it. She'd always been good at that.

"Hey, where are you going?" I asked suspiciously.

She smiled and opened her bedroom door. Sunlight burst in. Before us was a white beach gently lapped by waves. "It's my turn to play."

I smiled, shaking my head. Gemma shut the door behind her and disappeared. I gave her a few seconds' head start and then ran after her.

HIDE-AND-SEEK

Telling Gemma we were in a dream gave her enormous power and she knew it. She could do anything she wanted, go anywhere. She had full control over her desires and this time she'd decided to take advantage of them.

"Gemma . . . Come on! You can't hide from me," I called out. I heard her laughter in the distance. "You're going to regret that joke you played on me with your father!"

When I'd opened the door after Gemma closed it behind her, I'd found myself in the hallway of her house. Her father had just come out of his bedroom and went ballistic when he saw me barefoot, shirtless, and covered with paint. I'd bidden him a rather sheepish goodbye and opened various doors before ending up in the dream where Gemma had hidden. We were in her mind and she was having fun playing hide-and-seek with me.

The sand was so white it blinded me, the sea an endless expanse of blue and green.

"Gemma . . . Do you really mean to leave me here all alone?"

You're not alone, her voice whispered on the wind. *I'm right here.*

I spun around, but the beach was deserted. "Okay, keep on toying with me." Gemma laughed, amused. "You know what I'm going to do to you the second I catch you?" I concentrated on her soul like never before as I waited for her reply.

First you have to find me . . .

Guided by the sound of her voice, I lunged to one side and grabbed her. Gemma laughed, pinned beneath me. "Well? What were you saying?" I raised an eyebrow, satisfied.

"You found me." She smiled, her gaze provocative.

"I will always find you." I rubbed my nose against hers and she touched my lips. "You can't escape me," I warned.

She looked me in the eye and kissed me more passionately. Resting a hand on my chest, she deftly inverted our positions, rising up and straddling me. "Are you so sure?" she whispered against my mouth. I tried to kiss her but she pulled back, forcing me to lean up to follow her lips.

"You bet," I said, grinning.

Gemma bit my lip, leaving me in a momentary daze during which she pushed me down, leapt to her feet, and raced off. "Start running, then!" she challenged me, dashing away across the beach.

"You know I'm going to catch you!" I shot off after her.

It didn't take me long to catch up with her. She tried to escape me, laughing and shrieking at every attempt to grab her. She ran along the water's edge, hoping to gain ground, but there was no way she could elude me for long, and soon I grabbed her by the waist and picked her up, cradling her in my arms. I waded into the water until it was up to my hips, ignoring Gemma's protests as she clung to my neck, afraid to get wet.

"So, did I win the bet?" I asked.

"It's too soon to say!" she replied stubbornly.

"Oh yeah?!" I raised an eyebrow, a threatening look on my face.

"No, wait! No!" she cried, guessing my intentions.

Ignoring her, I bent down and stood up again with Gemma dripping wet in my arms. She shrieked from the contact with the water and then laughed, kicking her legs as she tried to get free, but I dunked her another time and then another.

"Hey! I'm not a teabag, you know!"

"And yet I would willingly drink you."

Gemma managed to pull me down and throw me off balance. We toppled into the water and a splash fight ensued, both of us laughing like crazy. All at once I grabbed her wrist, just because I felt like it, and pulled her against me. Even with only that small distance between us I already missed her. I missed touching her, missed the contact of our joined bodies. She responded by holding me tight.

"I knew I should never let you know when we're in a dream," I whispered into her hair.

She looked at me, resting her hands on my chest. "Because I can do whatever I want?"

"Because you always trick me."

Gemma smiled. "I always trick you when we're awake too."

"It's true, you're right." I touched my forehead to hers.

Gemma stroked my chest, washing away the paint. I did the same, pouring water over her shoulders and seizing the opportunity to touch her, because there was no denying it: I never tired of her.

"You wanted to take a shower together, right? Well, we're getting clean," she said provocatively.

I looked at her, a sparkle in my eye. "My idea of a shower was a little different, if I'm going to be honest."

"Because you never get enough."

I leaned closer and kissed her neck. "Because I never get enough of *you*," I whispered, brushing my lips against hers. I grabbed her thighs and lifted her up. Gemma wrapped her legs around my waist, our bodies wet and our tongues touching. All her emotions exploded inside me and she let me explore them: the infinite joy she felt, the hope she nurtured, her fear of losing me—the same fear that lurked inside me. Yet there, in the dream, it was just the two of us holding each other tight, hidden from the whole world. Just for that moment, I wouldn't let fear overpower us. We deserved to be happy. We'd been through a million trials and tribulations so we could be together and that moment was all our own.

With Gemma still clinging to me, I walked toward the shore, set her down at the water's edge, and lay down beside her as the waves caressed us only to draw back fearfully.

"Evan, are there hierarchies among Angels?" she asked out of the blue.

"Not exactly. There's us and there's them, the Màsala. The orders come to us like a whisper and the information appears directly in our heads."

"So no guardian Angels?"

"Those are legends dreamed up by humans to satisfy their need to feel at peace. True peace, if you earn it, isn't in this world, but humans feel comforted by the belief that someone's watching over them. Life on Earth wasn't made for peace—it was made for decisions. Every decision or reaction—even the smallest one—is a step toward good or evil. Only decisions made toward good will lead man to the peace he seeks by nature. Still, not everyone is strong enough to resist the power of darkness. So no, there are no guardian Angels. There's good and evil. Life and death. You, however, can consider me your own personal guardian Angel." I winked at Gemma and she smiled at me.

"You already were. How much longer do we have before the alarm goes off?" she asked. "It's so nice here."

"Not long, I'm afraid."

"If we could stay here I would sleep forever."

I smiled and took her hands on the sand, staring at the sky. "If you did, you'd miss the Winter Carnival," I teased her. Gemma had fought long and hard with the school faculty. Because of her pregnancy, they'd told her she couldn't participate in the school games, but the tomboy in her had rebelled. If it had been up to her, she would even have signed up for broomball and the alligator walk, but in the end they'd reached a compromise.

"They don't want me to take part this year anyway. I'll read about my classmates' heroic deeds in the *Blue Bomber Times*."

"They're only keeping you from competing in a few events," I reminded her.

"I'm not good at singing, and you're better than I am at ice sculpture."

"I can always make one for you. Besides, you're forgetting the pie-eating contest. If you sign up for that, my bet is your team will score tons of points!"

"Hey!" I laughed and barely dodged her blow. "Why does everyone keep saying that? Do I really eat so much?"

"Only slightly above average." I grinned. Staring at the sky, I squeezed her hand. Recently Gemma's appetite had grown to amazing proportions. It wasn't only because of the pregnancy but also because of the Witch nature buried inside her. Gemma's body was burning lots of energy and producing just as much. Luckily for her, the food burned off quickly and had no effect on her figure. Quite the opposite, in fact; she was five months pregnant but it was barely noticeable. Still, pregnancy had left her glowing. Gemma's curves had softened and she was sexier than ever. Looking at her made my heart race but scared me just as much, because it meant that with every passing day she was closer to her Sisters.

To protect Gemma we'd formed an alliance, but their presence stimulated her senses, like a summons her body couldn't resist. The Witch in her was waking up and I could do nothing to stop it. Gemma was certain the transformation wouldn't drag her away, that she wouldn't leave me to follow them to Hell. If I'd been as certain of it as she was I would have wanted her to transform so we could stay together forever, like Simon and Ginevra. That was what she was planning on: transforming and then renouncing evil. But I saw the doubt in Ginevra's eyes and that was enough to convince me: I wasn't going to let Gemma transform. No matter what it took, I would prevent it.

A little bird flew overhead, tweeting a relentless melody. It turned back and flapped around us. Gemma propped herself up on her elbows. "Do you hear that strange chirping? I've never seen that kind of bird before," she murmured.

I laughed. "I know that sound . . . and so do you. Open your eyes, sleepyhead. It's time to wake up."

I opened my eyes and Gemma grumbled in my arms. We were back in my room. "No, no . . . let's stay here. Go away, nasty old bird!"

I laughed into her hair and switched off the alarm that Gemma still believed was a strange bird. She relaxed, pleased because it had flown away and stopped bothering her. I hugged her from behind and she slowly opened her eyes.

"Good morning," I whispered.

"Mmm . . . Why are we here? Let's go back to sleep . . ."

"You can't go back to sleep. It's late. Ginevra's already waiting for you."

Gemma bolted upright and looked at me. "Aren't you coming too?"

I shook my head. "Maybe later." I only had a couple of missions but I wasn't sure I'd manage to get to school in time.

Gemma grumbled and got out of bed. As she dropped her shorts to the floor and took off her camisole I couldn't take my eyes off her. She was so sexy in her gray cotton underwear . . . I clenched my fists on the bed, fighting off the impulse to reach for her and keep her from going to school. She sensed my intentions and laughed. Her camisole hit me in the face, surprising me. "Peeping Tom."

"It's not my fault I can't resist you."

"Oh, really?" She raised an eyebrow and came closer, her gaze seductive. "Are you saying it's my fault?" She moved my knee aside and slipped in between my legs.

"I'm saying you should buy longer pajamas if you want to keep me away from you."

"I never said I wanted to keep you away from me."

My hands slowly slid up the backs of her thighs, unable to stay still. I rested my head on her belly, breathing in her scent. Gemma rested her knees on the bed and sat down, straddling me. Provoking me was becoming her favorite game. "He tried to resist her, but she wouldn't let him," she murmured, her arms around my neck.

I raised an eyebrow. She didn't realize what she was getting herself into. I grabbed her by the bottom and swept her onto the bed, my erection pressing against her. My hands slowly moved over her body. "*Correction*," I replied, playing along. "He would never try to resist her. He wanted her and didn't hide it. He knew he would never be able to control himself, as his fire was fueled by the very air she breathed." I stroked her lip with my thumb. "An undeniable need."

"So you're saying you can't resist me, *despite yourself?*"

"I'm saying I don't want to and never will, unless you decide to stop me."

"Then I'll have to follow your suggestion and buy longer pajamas," she teased. "You sure that will be enough to calm your instincts?"

"I'm afraid it won't help at all." I lowered my mouth to hers and surrendered to a kiss, my hands clasping her bottom tightly. "Jamie . . ." I kissed her neck and groaned, on the verge of losing my mind.

"Hey . . . you two!" Ginevra knocked insistently on the door and Gemma laughed.

"Not a good time. Go away," I grunted.

"It's morning and Gemma's going to be late for school."

"There's no school today," I called back, continuing to kiss Gemma.

"Get out here or I'll forced to come in!"

I ignored her and Gemma rolled on top of me. She started to kiss my chest tenderly, looking me in the eye as Ginevra continued to knock, undeterred. "Don't say I didn't warn you!" She opened the door and stood there, arms crossed. I plopped my head onto the pillow and Gemma smiled at her Sister.

"Good morning to you too."

"Man, what a pain in the ass!" I grumbled loud enough for her to hear it.

"Gwen, why the big rush to get to school?" Gemma asked.

Ginevra smiled and clapped her hands, bouncing. "The games start today. Put some clothes on or I'll take you to school as you are!" she goaded her, literally dragging her away from me.

"Trying to cause a mass extermination, are you?" I retorted. The thought of Gemma naked in public made my blood boil. No one could see her without clothes on and live. She was all mine. Gemma turned to look at me and shrugged, powerless.

The Winter Carnival games were a perfect occasion for Ginevra to prove to everyone that she was the best. "Try not to attract too much attention," I warned her. "These aren't the little games you play with your Sisters in the kingdom of darkness."

"It's broomball, Evan. Why are you so worked up?" she scoffed.

"There are mortal Souls there and somebody could get hurt." That day they would be taking Nausyka and Anya to school too, to protect Gemma. I just hoped Ginevra wouldn't get carried away by her enthusiasm. "Don't let Gemma out of your sight."

"Relax, Evan. The Subterraneans are under close surveillance. Gemma will be safe with us and we'll have loads of fun!"

Gemma, who meanwhile had gotten dressed, came over and planted a kiss on my mouth. "Don't worry, I'll be there to keep an eye on them," she whispered. "You go do your duty, Soldier." She winked at me and hurried out of the room. Ginevra stuck her tongue out at me and followed her.

I interlaced my fingers behind my head and lay back down on the bed, listening to the noises in the house. For days, the Executioners who'd come to kill Gemma hadn't let up for a second. They'd even attacked her at school once, but Simon had protected her, knocking the Subterranean out with a single blow. Gemma, who was the only person able to see him, had let out a scream during class, drawing everyone's attention. She'd flicked an imaginary spider off her desk and the teacher had resumed the lesson. They hadn't attacked at school since then but, as a precaution, at least one of us was with Gemma at all times.

I heard panthers growl in the hallway and, a second later, voices. Things would go better now that all the Subterraneans were under our control. Once the simulation scenario was deactivated, the galleon had gone back to being a normal cell and the prisoners found themselves chained to the walls with a group of black panthers guarding them. The Drusas had to be careful not to injure them because their teeth and claws secreted their serpents' venom. A single scratch was enough to kill a Subterranean, and if that happened, others would show up. In any case, they wouldn't escape, as dazed as they were by the Witches' blood. I'd learned the hard way the effect it could have on our minds.

The Witches had the power to modify it based on what they wanted from us. In some cases, it could even enhance our strength, like it did during the Games—or it could annihilate us. The prisoners would never be able to rebel.

Hearing the engine of the BMW starting up, I jumped out of bed and went to the window. From the looks of the girls' clothes, they'd had a snowball fight. Gemma was laughing with her Sisters and was so calm as she got into the car. I should have been happy, but instead I was jealous—jealous and worried they would take her away from me. Gemma's bond with them would make the transformation easier for her, but it would also make it harder for her to renounce evil.

Ginevra, on the other hand, didn't seem the least bit worried. Being reunited with her Sisters had given back to her something she thought she'd lost. She was beaming. On top of that, though at times she harbored doubts that she didn't dare voice, she had endless trust in Gemma. She was convinced that once Gemma transformed she wouldn't lose herself, that our love and her love for our baby would eradicate the evil inside her. Gemma wouldn't be human any more— she would be a Witch—but she would keep all her memories and human emotions. Still, not even Ginevra could be sure.

Gemma noticed me staring at her and waved to me from the front seat. I returned her smile and waited until they drove off. Then I balled my fists against the windowpane, frustrated. I couldn't risk it. No, I would never allow Gemma to transform.

FOUL PLAY

I got into the shower and washed away the dirt from the battle. Maybe it wasn't appropriate to feel this way, but I'd had an awesome time fighting the Subterraneans. Simon and I had worked as a team, defeating over half of them, though many of them were strong and battle hardened. Still, they hadn't been as determined as I was. Once we'd subdued them, the Witches had taken over. It wasn't that long ago I would never have believed it if somebody had told me I would form an alliance with the Witches—with *Devina*. I hadn't forgotten the 'special treatment' she'd given me in her world to try to dominate me, and I couldn't wait to repay her the favor.

I put my head under the jet of water and tilted it back, hoping to rinse away my anger at Devina. We were allies. I had to force myself to remember that. And although we'd imprisoned the nine Subterraneans who'd attacked us over the last week, I had to stay focused and never let my guard down.

The Màsala were willing to do anything to kill Gemma. What they might not realize was that *I* wasn't going to let a Subterranean take her away from me. If they managed to make her soul cross over, I would lose her forever, and with her, our child. The stakes were too high. An unexpected smile spread across my lips. A hundred Subterraneans wouldn't have been enough to stop me. I was willing to kill them all.

The blood and dirt washed away, tinting the water, and my chest trembled at the memory of the paints blending together in our hands, the warmth of our intertwined bodies, the intense emotions that flooded me when I was in my ethereal form. It had been an otherworldly experience. I smiled, remembering the picture of us that Gemma's soul had created. While the entire world tried to separate us, Gemma and I became more and more closely bonded. Our love was growing as intensely as the passion that burned whenever we were alone. I rested my palms on the stone wall and closed my eyes, the sensations sweeping me away. Gemma satiated me, yet I was always hungry for her. Her attempts to seduce me made me lose my mind . . . and all control. She'd realized that and had fun toying with me. Most times desire consumed me and I let it take me over, burning together with her.

I shook my head and ran my hands over my face. Making love in her dream had been all-consuming and I still felt a bit dazed. I should have been focusing on the orders I was about to carry out but I couldn't think of anything except her, the scent of her skin, her lips on me, my hands on her body. Gemma was my obsession. It had always been that way and I had no intention of resisting it. I was hers. Mind, soul, body . . . and my stilled heart, which beat only for her.

I turned off the water and got out of the shower, wrapping a towel around my waist. I looked at myself in the mirror as I dried my hair with a towel and noticed writing on the fogged-over glass:

I'll be waiting for you ∞

I smiled when I recognized Gemma's handwriting and walked out of the room barefoot. I was a Soldier of Death who was about to kill two people, but Gemma made me feel like a little kid who couldn't wait to finish his homework so he could see her. The towel still around my waist, I went into my room to get dressed, tossing my dirty boxers onto a chair.

The door closed behind me and I straightened up. I didn't need to turn around to know who had followed me. "If you're looking for cat kibble, the kitchen is downstairs," I snapped.

Devina walked up and touched my shoulder, stepping around me. "I'm hungry for something else right now." She slid her finger down the scar she herself had inflicted on me.

I stood stock still, my jaw clenched and my eyes burning into hers. "I'm afraid you'll have to make do," I said curtly. "I'm not on the menu."

She sat on the bed, hoping to seduce me, but I turned my back on her and went over to the dresser where I let the towel fall to the floor. She whistled. I pulled on boxers and jeans without blinking an eye.

"I'm confused, Evan. Undressing isn't the best way to get me out of here—you should know that."

I approached the bed and grabbed her by the throat, catching her off guard. "And you should know that I'd like nothing more than to tear you limb from limb. Now get out of here before I decide to follow my instinct. I haven't been very good at holding back lately." I jerked my hand away.

She rubbed her throat, vexed. "Mind your manners. I just stopped by to say hello."

"Stay away from me, Witch. I'm trying hard not to incinerate you, but you're not making it easy."

Instead of leaving, she spread her legs and snapped her whip between them, her eyes glittering like molten gold. "You've already lit a fire inside me, right here. Only you can put it out."

"You can burn for all I care."

"Why don't we let bygones be bygones? We're allies now, aren't we?" She stroked the bed with her hand suggestively, looking me in the eye. "We could seal our deal right here . . ." Her whip cracked again. "I like the thought of doing it in your bed."

I snorted. "Aren't you Witches bound by claiming rights?"

"We'll talk about that when she's a Witch and she's claimed you. Until then, she isn't your Amìsha." She raised her eyebrows and a subtle scent wafted in my direction.

"Keep your pheromones to yourself—they have no effect on me."

Devina stood up and came close. "Are you so sure? I heard your thoughts while you were in the shower and figured you might need someone to have a little fun with," she whispered in my ear, touching my bare chest. "We're alone. Gemma will never find out."

"Have fun with you? What, are you offering me your head on a platter?"

"I'm offering you much more than revenge, don't you see?" Her hand slid up the inside of my thigh until it reached my crotch. "I'm offering you *expiation*. I can give you much more than myself. I can give you my heart." Devina stroked my lip with her thumb and tried to kiss me. On her mouth sparkled the trickle of blood with which she hoped to subjugate me.

I grabbed her wrist and looked her in the eye. "The only place I could want your heart is in my fist," I growled. "You're insane if you think you have the slightest chance with me."

The amber in her eyes seemed to melt, extending over their whites, and her pupils lengthened like a serpent's. "Be careful how you speak to me, Child of Eve. Your princess is still sweet and vulnerable."

The second she mentioned Gemma, a burst of rage blinded me. "Threaten her again and I'll personally scatter your ashes in Hell," I hissed, snatching my shirt off the chair and heading for the door. "Oh, and have fun on your own. The bed's still warm. Use your imagination."

Devina cracked her whip and I smiled without turning around. I went down the stairs just as Simon appeared in the kitchen.

"Morning. Long night?" he said, grinning.

"Not long enough," I shot back, pulling on my shirt. "What happened to your battle wounds?"

"A sweet young maiden cured them for me last night."

"Just like you'd hoped."

Simon filled two shot glasses with bourbon and held one out to me. A panther nonchalantly glided through the room and I cast my brother a glance.

"I'm afraid we'll have to get used to that," he said.

"I'd rather die."

Simon laughed and raised his glass in a toast. "To the battle."

"And to those to come." I downed the liquor in a single gulp to celebrate our victory. Another panther jumped onto the railing at the top of the stairs and leapt down. Simon and I stared at her and she snarled. I didn't need to check for the red patch on her paw to know who it was: Devina. Her eyes challenged me, glittering like drops of amber.

"You're right. I'll never get used to this." Simon refilled our glasses. The panthers exchanged growls, crossed the living room, and headed toward the dungeon. The door closed behind them.

"You, on the other hand, should clean yourself up," I suggested. Simon didn't seem to have washed away the blood or dirt from the battle.

"I know. I just need to recharge my batteries first."

"Nine Subterraneans too much for you?" I joked.

"No, Ginevra on her own is enough to zap my energy. Being with her is like taking on a hundred Executioners all at once. Speaking of which, I checked on Gemma at school before coming back here. She's fine, having fun with the girls." I nodded to thank him, but my face clouded. It didn't escape Simon's notice. "You worried?"

"Wouldn't you be?"

"Take it easy, Evan. Ginevra's there with her. Besides, if Gemma is finally able to have fun it's only because you're back here with her."

I looked at Simon, thankful for his words. He lowered his voice, though there was no risk the Witches would hear him, since the workout room was soundproof. "Do you have any idea what she went through when she thought she'd lost you? She didn't want me to take the pain away because she didn't want to lose a single memory of you. Do you think she would accept the thought of losing you forever to join them? That's insane. Gemma would never give you up, Evan. She would never give up the *two of you*. She would accept the transformation but she would stay herself. I believe it, and you should too. Her plan is going to work."

"What if it doesn't? What happens to me?"

"It *has to* work—it's all we've got."

"Wrong. What if there was an alternative?"

My brother looked at me. I had his attention. I clenched my fists, preparing to lay it on him. "What if Gemma ate of the Tree?"

"Have you lost your mind?! You've always had insane ideas, but this one tops them all."

"Why? It might work! What if the Divine Fruit eradicated the evil inside her? What if it purified her soul? She would be one of us: immortal."

"Okay. You must have ingested too much poison in Hell," he said, raising both hands. I sighed. Why didn't Simon understand me? "Evan, did you hear how many *what ifs* there are in your plan? Here's a couple more for you: what if you were both punished for it? What if it had catastrophic consequences?"

"What punishment could ever be worse than the one I'm already suffering? Anything would be better than this. I'm not going to let the Witches obliterate her."

"Evan, no one who isn't a Subterranean has ever eaten of the Tree."

"Then she'll be the first," I shot back, determined.

"Evan . . ."

"I hoped at least you would understand me!"

"And I do." Simon rested his hands on the table and looked me in the eye. "But you have to think of the consequences this might have for her and everyone else."

"You think I haven't?" I stared at him steadily. "I think about that *every minute*. And for now it's all I have to cling to. I need this hope." I knew my brother was right, that I should assess everything down to the smallest detail, but no one could give me any certainties. "Simon, I've thought it over long and hard, honestly, and I'll keep thinking it over, but it's a possibility we need to consider."

"All right. We'll talk about it later. Give me some time to reflect."

I nodded, grateful that he was at least making an effort. "It's late. I've got orders to carry out."

"And I'd better take a shower," he said. We fist-bumped and I disappeared behind him.

The conversation with my brother left me with a bitter taste in my mouth. It was true, my plan still needed to be ironed out, but at least it was something. I refused to give in to the idea of losing Gemma. Only a few months were left before she would transform into a Witch and begin to hate me. The thought was devastating. I ran a hand over my face. I had to concentrate. I focused on the flickering lights illuminating the night and went to the scene of the accident. My assignment had taken me to Japan.

The headlight of the downed motorcycle cast a sinister shaft of light across the asphalt. The families of the two kids hit by the car had just arrived. The boy driving the bike was loaded onto one of the three ambulances while his mother wept at his side, calling his name. I walked past him. The life was gone from his legs, but no Subterranean was there for him. The girl was loaded onto another ambulance and I got in with her. The rear doors closed and the inside filled with the sobs of her mother, who was gripping the girl's hand. The sirens screamed their urgency as the vehicle began its desperate race against time. *Against me.* It was a race they wouldn't win.

"Mmm . . . mmmom," the girl moaned.

The mother wiped away her tears, forcing a smile. "I'm right here. I'm here, sweetheart."

"I'm . . ." The girl's chest rose and fell with effort.

"Don't strain yourself. We'll be at the hospital in no time and you'll get better."

A tear slid down the girl's cheek. "I love you."

The woman burst into tears. "I love you too. Now don't talk. You'll be better soon. You'll be better soon."

"I'm . . ."

I held my hand over her chest and paused, waiting for her last words.

"I'm sorry, Mom."

I lowered my hand and the life left her body. Her eyes stared blankly into space and her mother began to shriek, tears of despair running down her cheeks. The paramedics intervened to resuscitate her daughter as the mother huddled in the corner, but there was nothing they could do. The girl, Sachiko, was already staring at me from the far side of the ambulance, ignoring the chaos around us. She came over and tried to touch me. "Who are you?"

"I'm here for you. I'll take you to safety."

Sachiko thought over what I'd said and seemed to understand. She looked at her mother, who was clutching her daughter's jacket to her mouth to stifle her sobs. "Is she going to be okay?" she asked.

I stared at her, searching for an answer. I couldn't guarantee that in this life she would forget her pain, but if she made the right decisions on Earth then yes, she would be all right and the two of them would be together again. "One day," I reassured her.

Sachiko hung her head. "It's all my fault. We got into a fight. I ran out of the house with Takeshi, my boyfriend. Mom didn't trust him. She wanted me to dump him . . . Is he okay?"

"They only entrusted me with you."

She huffed. "He only had one helmet and said it would be too big on me."

I balled my hands into fists, wishing I could change ambulances. "Parents often understand things their children aren't willing to listen to."

"I get that now, but it's too late," she said softly.

I held out my hand and she took it, vanishing like a puff of smoke. After I'd guided her through the worlds, the sounds in the ambulance hit me again, like someone had turned up the volume with a remote control.

The paramedics had stopped trying to revive Sachiko and were now holding the mother still as one of them sedated her. I sat down beside her and held her hand, hoping to give her a bit of comfort. Would she feel better if she knew her daughter would be all right in the place I'd led her to? If she knew that one day they would be together again, in a world without corruption, without pain, without darkness . . . a world that was denied to me.

All I wanted—all I had ever wanted—was to know that even if Gemma died I wouldn't lose her. Instead I was condemned to an existence of solitude. Not a Soul in Eden could see me. To me, a descendant of the Children of Eve, it was a deserted place. Gemma and I could be together only on Earth. If she crossed over, I would never see her again.

My power flowed into the woman and she fell asleep. The thoughts that had been running through my head triggered within me the compelling urge to see Gemma. I would have to make it fast, since I still had another execution order, but I couldn't resist my need for her. I concentrated and the ambulance disappeared.

Gemma was sitting in front of me, so engrossed in the story she was reading she didn't notice me. The seats in the auditorium were dimly lit, so when I was sure no one would spot me I materialized. The only lights were pointed at the stage, where Jeneane was singing a number from the musical she would be performing in. The boy at the piano played the notes wrong, angering her and leading to a heated argument. Gemma didn't move, as though she couldn't even hear them. She seemed to be in another world—a world where there were no Executioners who wanted to kill her. It was nice that she had a means of escape and could hide away in a place where negative thoughts wouldn't hound her. For a second, sorry to pull her out of that world, I considered leaving, but then she smiled. I leaned toward her, wondering what she was reading.

"You going to stand there spying on me all day long?" Gemma turned. She'd smiled because she'd noticed I was there.

I smiled back at her and folded my arms behind my head. "I was just wondering whether I should leave you to your book boyfriend or demand your attention."

"What did you decide?" she asked, raising an eyebrow.

I shot forward and snatched the book out of her hands. "That I'm better." I planted a quick kiss on her mouth and darted away, the loot in my hand.

"Hey! Give that back!"

"Let's see, who do we have here?" I opened the book to scan a few words as she leaned over the back of her seat. "Damon and Kitty. Interesting names . . ."

"That's not all. If you must know, he's quite the hunk," she teased.

"Oh, is that so?"

"Yep," she said, her expression sly.

"Are you saying I should be jealous?" I dematerialized to change places and seconds later she was sitting on my lap. She looked around, confused. I'd moved so fast she couldn't even tell how she'd ended up there.

"Well, actually . . ." She touched my nose with hers. "Damon's a really hot alien. On the other hand, you're here in flesh and blood."

"Oh, is that the only reason?!"

She shook her head and moved her mouth to my ear. "It's also because . . ." She stroked my arm provocatively and nimbly whisked the book out of my hands. "Gotcha!"

I laughed. "So it's true? I'm competing with that guy? I'll have to work hard to capture your complete attention."

"C'mon, cut it out!" Gemma laughed and hit me on the chest. A tremor ran through my body the instant she touched me.

I went serious again and brushed my thumb against the paint on her cheeks. "These look good on you. They remind me of last night." With her so close, sitting on my lap, I was in danger of losing control.

Gemma touched the yellow streaks on her face. "Yeah. I look like a warrior."

"You *are* a warrior," I replied in a heartbeat, and she kissed me. I slid my hands under her loose yellow jersey and she stopped, laughing against my mouth.

"Hey . . . People can see us, you know!"

"So what? I don't care." I pulled her closer and continued to kiss her.

"Evan!" She looked around to draw my attention to the kids on stage who were stealing glances at us.

I relaxed in my seat and raised my hands. "Okay, you win this time, but only because I can't stay for long anyway." She nodded without asking questions. "Aren't you going to the game?" I asked, pulling at her jersey.

"My class is outside playing snow volleyball in the Olympic Oval and I'm not allowed, so I'd rather stay here."

"Why's your friend still up on stage?"

Gemma looked at Jeneane, who had started reciting her lines. "It's the guys' team on the field. They're holding auditions for the spring musical in a few days and she wants the lead role."

"Doesn't she always get the lead role?"

"Yeah, but this time she has competition. There's a freshman girl who's really good and might steal the part from under her nose."

"Jeneane's giving it all she's got, I see."

"Yeah. She won't stop rehearsing. By now I know all her lines by heart."

"How'd the pie-eating contest go?" I asked, hiding a smile.

"I didn't stand a chance. Ginevra, Nausyka, and Anya creamed everybody. To compensate, Jeneane outdid everyone at the opening ceremony and clinched our team's victory during the sing-thing."

"Which would be . . . ?"

"A competition among all the classes to see who sings the LPHS Alma Mater best. It's what kicks off the Winter Carnival, and the winners get a ton of points."

"What else is planned?"

"Let's see . . . they've already done the relay race, the tug-of-war, and the alligator walk."

"Sounds like a dangerous game," I joked, making Gemma laugh.

"I didn't take part in it, anyway. The broomball match starts in half an hour. Today it's the girls' team's turn and I'll just be cheering them on. What a drag."

I glanced at the stage. Her friend also wore the senior team's yellow uniform for the Winter Carnival games. I could read in Gemma's subconscious how much she wanted to play. She'd always been a tomboy and she liked a challenge. It must have been hard for her to accept the faculty's decision, but after all they had no way of knowing the baby could withstand far more than a game of broomball. Gemma's fear of having to leave her life behind was right there around the corner and she clung to the need to live every day to the fullest.

"I bet they'll win, with you cheering them on," I said, trying to boost her spirits.

She crinkled her nose. "There's no way they can lose, with Ginevra, Anya, and Nausyka on the team."

I looked over my shoulder. From the back row, Nausyka shot me a scornful greeting. She was pretending to read something as she watched over Gemma. "But they aren't even on the team," I said in disbelief.

"Ha, that's nothing! You should see what they did to their uniforms."

"I can imagine." I grinned. There was nothing surprising about that. With three Witches in the rink, I was sorry to miss the game. It would have been fun to watch. I pushed the hair from her face and smiled. I adored the feisty side of her. I'd probed the souls of thousands of mortals, but Gemma's was like no other. "I'd better go. I wouldn't want someone to miss their big date," I joked.

"Well, whoever it is, I bet they'd be more than happy to miss their date with death."

I laughed, assuming my angelic guise. It was quite rare for Gemma to manage to joke about my duties as a Subterranean. That aspect of me still upset her—which was understandable, given that she herself had been one of my targets.

"See you later," I murmured, just as Jeneane called from the stage: "Hey, you two!"

We turned to look at her. She shook her head and squinted, confused. "What happened to Evan? He was there a second ago."

Gemma cast me a fleeting glance, smiling. My eyes must have been shining like liquid silver in the half-light, but Jeneane couldn't see me. "Yeah, and angels have wings. Evan left a while ago. You were just too wrapped up in yourself to notice."

"Hey, is the pregnancy turning you into a bitch?"

"If that's what causes it, then you must be pregnant too," Gemma called back.

"Very funny!"

I wasn't sure whether I should laugh at how they were needling each other or worry that Gemma was becoming more like Ginevra.

"So tell me, did you even listen to me singing? That's why you came here, wasn't it?"

"For that and to have some peace and quiet so I could read."

"You mean you prefer make-believe stories to my beautiful voice?"

Gemma smiled. "A story is a big lie that everyone loves listening to."

"Not me. Close that book and experience the real world—that is, *me*."

"No, you get down here or we'll be late for the game."

"Is it so late already?" Jeneane jumped down from the stage and walked up the aisle to her. She was glowing. "Well? How was I?" she asked casually.

Was Gemma becoming more like Ginevra? Maybe I was just imagining things. I was getting more nervous with every passing day. Jeneane bounced up and down, clapping her hands. "C'mon, I'm psyched for the game! We're going to bring home lots of points, I know we are!"

"I bet you're right," Gemma said softly, glancing my way. She also knew they were bound to win, thanks to her Sisters. I took her hand in mine and she squeezed it to say goodbye before I vanished. It was time for me to focus on my other assignment. My work wasn't done.

I found myself in the corridor of a hospital, in front of the heavy door that separated me from my target. Something caught my eye. I turned and saw a man staring at me through the window of one of the ORs. He was an Executioner, like me. Hospitals were always full of us. Still, it had become hard for me to look at other Subterraneans without suspicion, without thinking they were my enemies. Once I used to ignore them. The only thing that had mattered to me—the only thing I knew—were orders. But Gemma had changed all that. She'd changed me. My dedication to my obligations as a Subterranean hadn't changed; ferrying Souls to prevent the Witches from claiming them was still an essential principle of my nature as a Soldier, but now my priority was to protect Gemma. That was why I could never let my guard down. In every Subterranean I encountered, an enemy might be hiding.

A gurney was rolled out of the OR and the Angel of Death followed it. I went back to focusing on my mission and entered my operating room. I walked slowly among the doctors, who moved cautiously. A twelve-year-old girl, Yoko, was lying face down as the doctors stitched up her skin after having operated on her kidneys.

I moved farther into the OR, to another bed where a young woman was lying in the same position. Her name was Corinne. She was twenty-two years old and American, the one who'd been driving the car that had crashed into Sachiko's motorcycle.

A single heartbeat ran across the monitors, letting out a steady *beep*. It was the little girl's. Corinne, on the other hand, had been dead on arrival. She must have been an organ donor because the doctors had just removed one of her kidneys to give it to the girl so at least she might live.

I waited for the doctors to finish with Yoko and then freed the Soul trapped in Corinne's body.

"Hands off, perv." I spun around. Corinne was behind me, glaring at me. "Well? You one of those types who's into corpses?"

A smile escaped me and I stood up straight. "You're pretty lively for somebody who just died."

"Oh, no!" She touched her face, pretending to be shocked. "I'm dead? Gasp! Why?!" A second later she was serious and condescending again. "I figured out I was dead when I was screaming my head off and nobody even noticed, Einstein. I mean, c'mon! They could at least have covered me up, don't you think?! I'm dead for ten minutes and the first thing they do is take my clothes off. Practically the story of my life," she grumbled, waving her arms in the air. "Speaking of which, shouldn't I be transparent?" She turned her hands over and back again, examining them.

"Would you stop pacing?" I asked with a smile. "It's making me dizzy."

She stopped and took a closer look at me. Her hair was black, cut short, and she had big blue eyes. "So who the hell are you, anyways?! Was it you who freed me? If it was, then thanks. I couldn't keep on screaming like that. I was out of breath."

"I can believe that," I muttered, given how much air she was using even now with her nonstop talking. "Just so you know, you don't need to breathe any more."

Her eyes bulged. "You don't say!" She closed her mouth and pretended to hold her breath, then exhaled hard and shook her head, rolling her eyes at me. "You think I hadn't noticed that?! It's the first thing you notice when you die. So where'd you get your Undead License anyway? I've never seen the handbook, but I'm pretty sure the first rule is: always answer questions. Well? You want to tell me what you're doing here? Are you a voyeur or what?"

"What," I replied, grinning.

"Right, so this is a guessing game? Okay, let's see . . . Are you my spirit guide? Are you here to teach me all the tricks of being an evil poltergeist?"

"In a way."

"I bet you're like that guy in the movie *Ghost*. What was his name? You know, that guy, the ghost in the subway."

"I don't know what you're talking about, but no, you're not an evil poltergeist. If you were, I wouldn't be here."

"Buddy, if you don't know the movie *Ghost* you definitely are weir— He didn't have a name! That's why I couldn't remember it! *No name*, can you be more pathetic than that? So what about the tricks?"

"I'm not here to teach you tricks." I tried to dam the raging river, but the woman was a hurricane of energy.

"Then what do you want from me?! Who are you?" she asked, finally serious.

"I'm your ride." I smiled.

Incredibly, Corinne finally closed her mouth. My revelation seemed to have stopped her in her tracks, but it only lasted a second. "Whoa! So I have to come with you in order to go . . ." She moved her hands up and down, simulating scales. I took one of them and raised it to show her we were going up and not down. She twisted her mouth and nodded, pleasantly surprised. "Can't say I expected it. Nice that they sent me a hottie!"

Her brazenness made me laugh. I held my hand out to her. She looked at it hesitantly. "So now what happens? I take your hand and we start flying around the room?"

"Something like that."

Corinne glanced one last time at little Yoko and her face fell. "She'll have to find another nanny. I won't be much good to her dead," she joked, but the sarcasm couldn't hide her sadness. She loved the little girl.

"She won't forget you," I promised. I took her hand and she smiled, but then, just as she was fading, something crossed her mind.

"Hang on! I've got more ques—"

I shook my head and ran a hand over my neck. Rarely did you encounter spirits like Corinne. I materialized in the corridor and glanced at the other rooms again. There was no trace of the Subterranean I'd seen before, but in a quiet, dimly lit room, a woman was kneeling at the foot of a bed, praying under her breath. I paused to study her, listening to her words. She wasn't praying for her elderly father to get better—she knew he was suffering and there was nothing more they could do to help him. She was praying for his soul, asking her God to give him peace and put an end to his pain. The woman had no way of knowing it, but a Subterranean was already there for him, waiting beside the window.

A group of doctors ran toward me and I dodged out of their way, then walked to the waiting room, where a doctor was talking to the little girl's mother. She'd left her husband to pursue her career, but it hadn't left her with much time to dedicate to her family. I didn't need to enter her dreams to know she was reflecting on her decisions—I'd learned to read the human soul. Later that night she would phone her husband. If the nanny's kidney wasn't compatible, their daughter might not survive either. But that wasn't what was written; her time hadn't come yet. The little girl had been very lucky because my work was done for the day. I smiled and turned away, anxious to return to Gemma.

It was pitch dark in the little room I materialized in but I could already sense Gemma's heartbeat as she neared. I opened the door a crack and saw her. She was walking with Nausyka and Jeneane, who was talking nonstop. The Witch seemed interested in her chatter and was giving her advice better left unfollowed. Gemma, on the other hand, was engrossed in her book. The hallway was deserted. The students were all at the game. When she was close enough, I grabbed her hand and pulled her inside.

Gemma let out a shriek but I covered her mouth, gesturing for her to be quiet. When she realized it was me she nodded, so I let her go. I pricked my ears toward the hallway, where Jeneane had just noticed she was gone. "Gemma? Where are you?! Where'd she go? Did you see her?" she asked Nausyka.

The Witch didn't reply but I knew she'd spotted me. In fact, she'd sensed my presence even before hearing my thoughts. It was almost impossible for a Subterranean to hide from a Witch. I could, though. Gemma laughed and I pulled her against me. "Shh . . . or they'll find us," I warned her in a whisper.

"Evan, what are you doing?!" she reproached me, still laughing.

"I thought that since you can't play games with the others, you could still have a little fun with me." I kissed her neck.

"Are you going crazy?"

I kissed her again. "I've always been crazy."

"Evan, they might see us!" she protested, laughing. She tried to break free but I held her tighter.

"Nobody's going to see us in here." I drew her close, my breath coming quickly against her neck.

"What do you think you're doing? We're at school!" She put her hands on my shoulders to push me away but then sank her nails into my skin, her breathing growing ragged from my kisses.

"I have every intention of making you forget that guy Damon."

Gemma's breath came fast when my lips closed on her earlobe. Her fingers gripped the tattoo on my arm. "I forgot him the moment you grabbed my hand to drag me in here."

I smiled and pulled back. "Good: mission accomplished."

"What are you doing? Why did you stop?" she protested. She stumbled and I pulled her against me to keep her from falling. She reached one hand over her head and with a click a dim light barely illuminated the cramped closet we were in.

"Didn't you tell me to stop?" I loved teasing her, especially when she looked at me with those mischievous eyes.

She rested a hand on my chest, but something happened when she touched me—an image burst into my mind: *the two of us, our skin sweaty and our breathing mingled as we made love in that broom closet. My lips moved over her, my hands touched her all over . . .* Gemma pulled away from me and the vision vanished. We stared at each other for a long moment, stunned, trying to understand what had just happened. My ravenous eyes were drawn to her lips and desire overwhelmed me. In a flash, my mouth found hers and I pushed Gemma against the wall almost brutally. She returned my kiss passionately and yanked my shirt up. I pulled it off, trying to maintain the contact between our bodies, and she did the same. My dog tag clinked against her necklace, both of them cold against our burning-hot skin. I grabbed her by the thighs and lifted her up, wanting to meld with her. Overcome by the same need, Gemma wrapped her legs around my waist and sank her fingers into my hair.

"Oh, Jamie . . ." I panted against her lips.

All at once, the door flew open and Gemma let out a shriek, crossing her arms over her bare chest.

"What the hell's going on here?!" the janitor bellowed, looking back and forth between us.

I clenched my fists and pushed Gemma behind me to hide her. Locking my fiery gaze on the man's, I saw the fear in his eyes, almost as if he realized who was hiding inside me. "Get. Out. Now," I snarled.

He stood there stock-still, taking in every word. *Take what you need and don't come back,* I ordered him in my mind. Nodding, the man grabbed a bucket and some sponges. "Now go and forget what you saw."

The janitor closed the door and I relaxed, running a hand down the back of my neck. I turned toward Gemma, who was putting her shirt on. "Hey . . . What are you doing?" I pinned her hands to the wall. "We're not done yet." I kissed her neck and she smiled, lacing her fingers with mine.

"You're going to drive me crazy, Evan James," she said softly, sliding her hands out of my grasp. "But now we'd better go to the game." She slipped away, leaving me with my hands on the wall.

"I should have killed him for interrupting us," I growled with annoyance.

"You wouldn't," Gemma said matter-of-factly.

I pulled on my shirt and drew her against me, this time tenderly. "For you, I'd kill anyone," I assured her, my eyes lingering on hers.

"Even if he didn't do anything?"

"He got between you and me. That's reason enough." I winked at her and grabbed her hand, pulling her out of the broom closet. "You okay? Your hand is scorching hot."

"It's nothing. It'll go back to normal in no time." My face darkened. *It was the power.*

Two girls in red uniforms stared at us, whispering to each other with smiles on their lips. Simon and Ginevra had told me how everyone at school had talked behind Gemma's back when they thought I'd abandoned her. If I could have followed my instinct I would have killed them all. But they'd already been taught their lesson. I smiled, listening to their whispers; now they were jealous of her. When one of them turned to look at us, I put my arm around Gemma's shoulder and pulled her to me. Gemma was special. But most importantly, she was mine. And I was all hers. Everyone needed to know that.

When we opened the doors to the Olympic Arena, a deafening roar hit us. The game was in full swing and the spectators were shouting and cheering on their teams. The stands were full of color because each class was wearing their team jersey. It was my first Winter Carnival at Lake Placid High but Gemma had explained everything to me with the enthusiasm of a child. It lasted two days, with all the high-school classes competing for points. On the third day they held the Snowball Hop, at which they announced the winning team and crowned the king and queen.

The senior players wore jerseys and shorts in yellow, matching the two streaks on their cheeks and their headbands. The same thing went for the juniors, though they wore red, the sophomores blue, and the freshmen green. The seniors scored a point and Gemma cheered, hurrying to reach the stands.

"Looks like it's almost over," I said. A moment later the referee called the end of the game. The stands exploded into cheers, including the rival teams. The Witches must have put on quite a show out there in the rink, dazzling everyone.

"So tell me, has that uniform always been so short?" I asked Gemma, jealous when I noticed how short her skirt was.

She blushed. "Nausyka did it. She altered the sweatshirt too, but I wore my spare." The oversized sweatshirt she wore was definitely cozier than the tight ones Anya, Nausyka, and Ginevra had on.

"Hey, what—what's going on?" Gemma asked, suddenly worried.

The spectators sat down again and a low murmur replaced the cheering. The senior women's team had gathered together opposite the senior men's team. I pricked my ears, canceling out every other sound around me. "The guys just challenged them," I told Gemma.

"What?!" She stood up, both frightened and excited. "That wasn't in the program!"

"It was Peter's idea. Brandon and Jake backed him up. What did you expect? Ginevra's team creamed their opponents."

The two senior teams, now opponents, went out onto the rink. The crowd stood up and cheered.

"If they think they can beat the girls playing like that, they've already lost." Gemma pointed to one of the male players. I laughed. He'd practically passed the orange ball straight to Anya.

"Hey, what the fuck are you doing?!" Brandon shoved the boy and his reproach could be heard all the way from our seats.

"Oh, nice. They're even fighting with each other," Gemma murmured.

"It's the Witches. That's the effect they have."

"You mean they're turning the boys against each other?"

"They're guys. With three girls that look like that in the rink they would have been at odds anyway, but yes, the presence of Witches triggers negative emotions in mortals."

The crowd cheered and Gemma stood up. "I don't believe it! Peter scored!" she cried, jumping up and down.

"Really?" I asked, scanning the rink for him.

The Witches' eyes glinted with defiance, but he stared back at them with more fighting spirit than I'd ever seen in him before. In the rink he knew his stuff. I'd always known he had it in him, but scoring against three Witch opponents was commendable. The entire men's team was fixated on their every movement, but he was focused on the game and wasn't letting himself be bedazzled. His love for Gemma must be so strong it left no room for little games of seduction.

Faith and Brandon were contending for the orange ball, gliding across the ice with their long sticks. He'd just about reached his opponents' goal when Jeneane blocked him, catching him off guard. The boy fell to the ice amid the crowd's shouts. Nausyka skidded to a halt beside him and held out her hand, but he got up on his own, scowling. The women's team was massacring them.

"It's not fair. The guys will never beat them," Gemma said.

The Witches moved gracefully, like seductive panthers. "Even when they aren't using magic, Witches are a thousand times stronger than mortals—not to mention the power they wield over their souls simply by being near them. This isn't a game; they're just having fun toying with the guys." Nausyka passed a boy and whispered something in his ear. They were playing dirty, and I wasn't happy about it. "But Peter's giving them a run for their money."

Just then, with Brandon backing him up, Peter managed to score another goal and the crowd went wild. "Way to go, Peter!" Gemma cheered. "You're right. I bet they weren't expecting this. The Witches can read the guys' minds and foresee their every move, but he's managed to score anyway."

"Funny, Peter's never been the unpredictable type. It must be the girls' strategy to avoid boring the crowd."

"I don't think so. Nausyka looks pretty pissed off," Gemma pointed out, suddenly worried. All at once she froze, her gaze unfocused. "There's something in the air. Can't you feel it too?"

I touched her hand to reassure her and a spark flew between us. Just then, in chorus, the spectators let out an *oooh* of concern. We looked around, but everyone had rushed down to the rink. I did the same, pulling Gemma by the hand, and leaned down to look. I had a bad feeling. A boy was stretched out in the middle of the ice, unmoving. My eyes scanned the rink. When Nausyka's eyes met mine, I slammed my fists against the railing and a growl of frustration escaped me. I knew what was going on but I wasn't going to let it happen. Grabbing hold of the railing, I leapt down and pushed through the crowd that had gathered around the boy. The coach held me back, but let me by after one fiery glance from me. I went up to the boy. His heartbeat was weak; the Witch was drawing him to her. Soon he would be dead. As I pretended to check his eyes, I rested a hand on his chest, counteracting Nausyka's efforts to take his soul. The boy shot bolt upright, avidly gulping in air, and an audible sigh of relief spread through the crowd.

I looked up at the Witch. *Don't try to mess with me again,* I threatened her mentally. I knew she could hear me. The coach knelt beside the boy and I stood up, leaving him to the others to take care of.

I followed the Witches into the dark hallway. "Sorry, Evan. I tried to stop her," Ginevra said softly. She'd also heard my thoughts and knew what I was capable of doing in order to keep Gemma safe.

I walked past her and stopped, my face inches from Nausyka's. "What did you think you were doing?!" I hissed.

She smiled contemptuously. "Was it against the rules? I'm new and not very familiar with your games . . ."

I punched the locker by her head, crumpling the metal. "You guys are here to protect Gemma," I reminded her sternly.

"No one told us we had to stop being what we are."

"*I'm* telling you."

"He was mine. I'd already claimed—"

"No souls," I said. She raised her chin, irritated. "Not in this school. Not when Gemma's around," I emphasized. We couldn't risk drawing in more Subterraneans.

"Evan." Gemma touched my arm and I pulled my fist away without taking my eyes off Nausyka.

"He's right," Anya insisted. "You seduced that boy's soul despite my objections. Why didn't you stop when we told you to?"

"Because I don't take orders from you," her Sister shot back.

"It wasn't an order," Ginevra intervened. "You can take his soul some other time. He's yours to claim."

"If he's stupid enough to listen to you again," I added, drawing looks from them.

"Right now," Ginevra went on, "our priority is protecting Gemma. I was wrong too, to let myself get wrapped up in the mortals' stupid game, but you crossed the line."

"Oh, come on, what did I do, anyway!? The kid's fine now, isn't he?"

"No thanks to you," I grumbled. "Anyway, let's get out of here before we attract too much attention." I put my arm around Gemma's neck and we all headed toward the door.

"You sure he'll be okay?" Gemma asked, watching the boy being loaded into an ambulance despite his protests.

"He'll be great," Nausyka interjected, passing me to get into the BMW. Ginevra and Anya got into the back. Ginevra had had a new light in her eyes ever since she'd started spending time with her Sisters, as though she'd rediscovered a part of herself.

"Gemma!" someone called as she was about to climb into the car. "Hey, guys! Wait up!"

We turned toward the voice. Faith was walking toward us, followed by Jeneane. "You disappeared. We were looking all over for you!" she exclaimed when she reached us.

"Great game! You guys were amazing!" Gemma cheered.

"I know!" Faith said excitedly. "It was unbelievable! I've never felt so charged up before, or so *strong*." Out of the corner of my eye I glanced at Nausyka, who was smiling to herself.

"The guys must have taken the defeat pretty hard," Gemma said with a grin.

"We'll be making fun of them literally forever!" Jeneane enthused, and all three of them laughed. From the car, Ginevra called to Gemma to hurry up.

"We're going to Saranac Lake tonight to see the Ice Castle. Coming with us?" Faith asked.

"I don't know . . ." Gemma said, looking at us questioningly.

"Why not?" I replied.

Jeneane cheered. "I heard they built a maze in it this year, too. It'll be so much fun!"

"Okay." Gemma smiled. "See you later, then."

"We'll go find the guys and let them know!" Faith said.

"And make fun of them!" her friend added as they hurried off.

I shook my head, grinning, but when I looked at Gemma I noticed she was smiling. It was nice that once in a while she could live the carefree life of an eighteen-year-old with her mortal friends, temporarily forgetting the fact that a horde of supernatural creatures was battling for her survival while the other half wanted her dead.

We got into our seats and I started the engine. Gemma turned on the stereo and *Thinking Out Loud* by Ed Sheeran filled the car. We exchanged glances, hiding a smile, both of us thinking of how we'd danced in her dream to the notes of that song.

"Hey, you two, hold off on the thoughts. We can hear them, you know," Nausyka groaned.

I smiled and took Gemma's hand. "So what? I'm not holding off on anything for you," I replied with a sneer. I raised Gemma's hand to my mouth and kissed her fingers, gazing into her eyes.

The Witch snorted in disgust. Though they'd already witnessed what had happened between Ginevra and Simon, they still couldn't stand the sight of a Witch and a Subterranean together. *Gemma isn't a Witch yet*, I reminded myself.

When we reached the driveway of our estate, I turned off the car as the gate was closing. "Gemma, going to school with you was fun. When can we do it again?" Anya asked, her voice eager.

"Never," I said sternly. "Not if you guys intend to cause trouble."

Gemma and Ginevra had arranged with the school principal for Ginevra's "cousins" to be able to attend class with us during their visit. Ginevra, whose powers of persuasion seemed unlimited when it came to the principal, had even gotten his permission for them to join in school sporting events like the Winter Carnival games.

"Come on, Evan!" Anya took my arm and walked beside me toward the front door. "Nausyka won't cause any more problems, you have my word. We want to go to the Ice Castle too!" she said enthusiastically.

How could these creatures be the same ones I'd met in Hell? They seemed like a group of silly adolescents with raging hormones. Yet I hadn't forgotten the time I'd spent with them in Hell: the torture, their filthy blood games. I hadn't forgotten they wanted to take Gemma away from me. No, there was nothing silly about them. I couldn't trust them. They were Witches. And I was a Subterranean.

"I've got a better idea," Nausyka said. "Why don't you stay here like a good little Soldier? We'll take care of protecting our Sister."

I rushed at her, but Anya stepped between us. "Calm down, she was only kidding," she said, casting a reproachful look at Nausyka, who was smirking, her long white hair blending in with the snowy background.

"All right, you can go, but I have no intention of babysitting you. You're not here for a guided tour—you're here to watch over Gemma."

"That's what we're going to do," Anya assured me happily.

I opened the front door and two panthers stopped to stare at us. I still had to get used to them. *No*, I thought. I never would.

Gemma leaned over to pet Irony, who'd waddled up to her, tail wagging. For some reason the big felines' presence didn't scare him. Maybe it was because Witches were in tune with nature and all its creatures bent to their will.

"Welcome back." Devina slunk down the stairs toward us.

Gemma was laughing with Anya and Ginevra, but her mood changed the second she saw her. "Well, well, if it isn't the Wicked Witch of the West," she said, dumping her backpack on the ground. "What were you doing upstairs? You don't have permission to go wandering around our rooms," she reproached her threateningly.

Without blinking an eye, Devina drew closer to me. "Oh, I only stayed in his bed for a little while . . . after he left." She looked at Gemma to provoke her and I clenched my fists. "Speaking of which, you left these in your room when you got dressed again." She rested her hand on my chest, her nails digging into me, but I didn't take what she held in it. I wasn't about to play along.

Gemma strode over to her and tore my boxers out of her hand. All at once something made her freeze, as though she'd gotten a shock. Her eyes became unfocused and for a second her pupils seemed to lengthen like a feline's. Devina smiled and moved her lips to Gemma's ear. "He's so sexy without them," she whispered.

A sconce on the wall exploded. Gemma tried to control her breathing. I'd never seen her like this before. She seemed to be trying to tame a demon raging inside her, like she was on the verge of making Devina's head explode through the power of her mind.

"Gemma . . ." I said, but her eyes remained locked on the Witch's, as if in communication with her. I noticed red drops dripping from her palms and went to her, breaking the dark spell between them. "You're hurt." I took her hands and ran my thumb over the cuts in her palms. She'd clenched her fists so hard her nails had pierced her flesh. I scowled at Devina. "You know, some bastards put collars on their dogs to make them stop barking. I'll get you one. I'm sure it would work on cats too."

"I'd be happy to wear it if you put it on me yourself. Electric shocks make everything more interesting," she replied mischievously.

"Devina, that's enough!" Ginevra broke in. "None of us likes staying under the same roof, but we've got to deal with it for as long as necessary, and you need to understand your place once and for all."

Devina cast her a haughty glance. "Who ever said I didn't like staying here?" She winked at me and walked away, leaving the door that led down to the dungeon open. She wanted us to watch her as she made her exit.

Ginevra closed it with a mental command, grumbling over her Sister's behavior. "It's hopeless. She'll never change."

"Was it just my imagination or did the little Witch make a lamp explode?" Nausyka asked. Gemma still looked shaken but her eyes had gone back to normal.

"Gemma . . ." I said.

She turned to look at me. "You undressed in front of Devina. I saw it," she hissed. I swallowed, shocked by her words. The dismay in her voice paralyzed me.

She hung her head and left me there, staring at nothing.

UNCONTROLLABLE INSTINCT

I had hurt her. I'd gotten undressed with Devina in the room, but only to make her suffer a little. Instead, I'd made Gemma suffer. Upstairs, my bedroom door slammed shut, snapping me out of my trance. With the eyes of all three Witches trained on me, I took the stairs three at a time to get to Gemma.

Outside my room, I froze. I could sense she was there, leaning against the door. I rested my palms on the wood, right where I knew hers were on the other side. I could hear her breathing. "Jamie . . ." I whispered. I was so connected to her soul that I could perceive her anywhere. This time, though, there was more than just a door between us—there was a painful silence I wished I could fill. A distance that was killing me. I made a fist and materialized behind her.

"Why did you do it?" she hissed, sensing my presence. She didn't turn around.

"It doesn't—"

"You undressed with her in the room!" She turned to face me and her hard glare turned me to ice.

"Nothing happened!" I assured her, angry at myself. Overwhelmed, I hit the desk with my fist.

"Getting undressed is already something. You shouldn't have done it, Evan! You know she wants you, and you go and provoke her?"

The shutters burst open. I went up to her and rested my fists on either side of her head. She was losing control and I had to bring her back. "Gemma, this is what Devina wants: to divide us. Don't let her do it." I grabbed her hands and looked her straight in the eye.

Her irises went back to normal, driving off the darkness. I kissed her fingers, never taking my eyes off hers, and she hugged me tight. Closing my eyes, I rubbed my head against hers.

For a few seconds I'd thought I'd lost her, and it had been terrible. The darkness was already extending its tentacles to take her from me, but I was going to hold her close.

"Forgive me, Evan," she murmured.

I stroked her hair. "It's my fault. I shouldn't have provoked that Witch. But believe me, the only thing I wanted to do to her was disintegrate her."

"I know. I've never doubted you or forgotten what she did to you. I never will forget it. Maybe that's why I lose control so easily when she's around. Sometimes, inside me, I know what I'm doing is wrong, but I can't control myself. I'm scared, Evan," she confessed.

I sighed and held her against me so she wouldn't see the fear on my face. How could I reassure her when I was terrified myself? The proximity to her Sisters was stimulating Gemma's powers. The Witch buried within her was awakening and we could do nothing to stop it.

But then again, it was often Devina who provoked it, and we could at least stand up to her. I cupped Gemma's face in my hands and looked her in the eye. "You can't let that Witch get the better of you."

She nodded as I brushed a tear from her cheek with my thumb. "Do you think it was her who showed me the vision?"

"No, it was you, but she triggered something in you that caused it—a spark that ignited your powers."

"Anger."

"Yeah. That's what they do, isn't it? Incite people to hatred and violence. Anger leads to more anger."

"I feel like Dr. Jekyll and Mr. Hyde. There's so much chaos inside me . . ."

"You must have chaos in you to give birth to a dancing star," I whispered.

"Friedrich Nietzsche."

"I was sure you would know that."

Gemma smiled.

"So what happened at school, then? In the broom closet, I also had a vision, at the same moment you did," I said.

"You mean it wasn't you?" I shook my head and she seemed to lose herself in a distant memory. "It's happened before," she murmured.

"When?"

"On the veranda." She pointed at the door. "The first time you brought me here. When you finally told me who you were. I touched your back and we saw the same thing in our minds. I projected the image into your head. I guess the same thing happened today at school."

"That must be what happens when a Subterranean desires a Witch— she can project into his mind what will happen if he follows his instinct."

"I *bewitched* you."

I smiled and stroked her ear with my nose. "You don't need any powers to do that," I murmured. "You do just fine all on your own."

Gemma laughed and held me away from her, both hands on my chest. "Be good. We need to dig deeper into what causes these visions. It was my nature that tried to seduce you, you see?"

Kissing her neck, I held her tight. "So there are positive aspects to your nature," I murmured, my lips on her skin.

"I need to learn how to control this desire effect," she said, deep in thought. "Let's try it again! Maybe I can project another image into your mind," she exclaimed, sounding determined.

But I was even more determined than she was. Following my urge, I lifted her up and sat her down on the desk. "I'd rather do it my way." I kissed her, pressing my hips against hers.

She bit my lip and squeezed her legs around my body to hold me tighter. "I'm afraid I'm not going to stop you," she moaned, giving in.

I pulled off her sweatshirt and undershirt at the same time, blinded by desire. Gemma pulled off my shirt, unbuttoned my jeans, and lowered them slightly. My hands made their way under her skirt, unable to resist as my desire pressed impetuously against her.

Just then her phone rang, vibrating inside the sweatshirt on the floor. "I should get that," Gemma said softly.

I clasped my hand around her bottom and pulled her tightly against me while caressing her back with the other. "It'll stop." I grabbed the back of her head and pressed my lips to her neck, making her moan. With a few tugs I got her out of her skirt. I couldn't stand to be separated from her by the stupid fabric any more. I wanted to touch her skin. I wanted to feel her against me.

The phone insisted, distracting her again. "It might be important," she mumbled.

I didn't stop. "I don't care."

"It might be my parents!" she exclaimed, jumping down and wriggling free from my grasp. I rested my hands on the desk, frustrated. "It's Faith," she told me.

I turned around and the sight of her left me breathless. *God, she was beautiful.* Why did she have that effect on me every time? I'd never experienced anything like it. My body, my senses, all of me felt overpowered by her. Her pearl-colored lingerie stood out against her golden skin: a lace bra and underwear that shouldn't have been legal. Gemma certainly knew how to drive me wild.

She'd taken the phone from her uniform on the floor and stood there in the middle of the room, focused on the message she was reading while I died with longing for her.

"She says they'll be here in half an hour." Gemma looked up. "I'm afraid we'll have to take a raincheck on our little chat. Hey, why are you looking at me like that?"

"Like *what?*" I moved closer, one eyebrow raised.

She stepped back, smiling. "Like someone who wants to eat me."

I trapped her against the wall and sniffed her neck. "Maybe because it's true. You're driving me wild—what can I do?" I whispered against her skin. I nibbled her shoulder and she trembled.

"Hey, you're not playing fair." Gemma rested her hands on my shoulders to calm me and smiled, her eyes still closed. "If we go to the Ice Castle in this state we'll be in danger of melting it all down."

"Then let's not go." I continued to kiss her. I loved to tease Gemma, to slowly drive her as wild as she drove me, kissing her everywhere, following the shivers I sent through her body. "Still want me to stop?"

"No," she whispered. "I don't want you to . . . But there's no time." She slipped away, pulling on her skirt and looking at me, a grin on her face. "Are you getting dressed or are you going like that?" She pointed at my bare chest. Gemma liked teasing me too. She couldn't even imagine what it triggered in me, the feelings I would have to overcome to manage to stay away from her. Quickly tying her hair up, she planted a kiss on my lips. "We've only got half an hour. I'm going to run and take a shower!" She left the room, carrying her clothes in a bundle.

I sighed, staring at the door that had just closed behind her. A sudden smile curved my lips. Did she really think she could slip away from me like that? I pricked my ears and heard the shower being turned on in the other room, the sound of the glass door closing, the melody she was humming to herself.

I took off my shoes, then my jeans, with the concentration of a wolf watching its prey from afar. The instant my boxers fell to the floor I disappeared and materialized behind her. Her eyes were closed and steam was billowing through the room, carrying with it the sound of that delicious melody. I would have liked to stand there watching her a little longer, but my hand moved on its own and rested on her back, slowly ascending.

She tensed slightly but immediately realized it was me and only turned her head. I moved closer behind her and took her hand. She half closed her eyes when I stroked her cheek with my nose.

"Did you really think I'd let you leave?" I whispered into her ear. I reached out and rested my hands on the wall in front of her, trapping her.

"I was hoping you wouldn't," she confessed. I kissed her earlobe, pressing my desire against her. Gemma turned and joined her lips to mine in a slow, hot kiss full of promises as her hand slid down my chest, lower and lower, and our tongues touched in a sensual, hypnotic dance.

A groan escaped me when Gemma stroked my erection. I felt like I was losing my mind. Gemma triggered unfamiliar instincts inside me. I was a Soldier of Death, but when she was around all that remained was a man.

I stepped across the shower and pressed her against the wall, my hands on the verge of pulverizing the rock from the emotions racing through me. I rested my forehead against hers, breaking off our kiss to try to regain control. Her big dark eyes probed mine and I swallowed, completely at the mercy of her power. I scooped up some lather and began to caress her, very slowly, running my hand up her back, over her shoulder, and then up her neck as she moved her head slowly, surrendering to my caresses. I followed the curve of her jaw and my thumb lingered on her lower lip. My hand descended to her collarbone, her breast, her waist . . . before slipping between her legs. Gemma reacted with a moan, sinking her nails into my biceps and pulling me closer. I felt undone by the sensations; the knot in my stomach her gaze provoked, the dizziness the touch of her hands on me triggered, the burning deep in my chest that begged me to meld with her.

I caressed her bottom and slid my hand down her thigh, which I lifted to make room for me between her legs. Gemma cried out my name but I almost didn't hear her, my mind clouded with passion as I entered her. I gripped her bottom, holding her tightly as I moved inside her. With my mouth I explored her neck, thirsty for her, her skin, her scent. I slowly sucked her earlobe as she moaned and twisted to mold her body to mine, to fuse with me, feeding off my own need. A fiery storm raged inside me. I grunted and clung to her, losing myself in her as I thrust harder and harder. Gemma's breathing grew more ragged. She again cried out my name and the storm exploded inside me. I sank my hand into her hair and kissed her chin as I climaxed inside her, slowing my movements.

I sucked Gemma's neck and she sank her nails into my back, groaning with pleasure, clinging to me, keeping me inside her. My hand slid between us, clasped her breast, and then went down to her belly, between her legs . . . I stroked Gemma's desire with my thumb and she cried out with pleasure, her muscles contracting and shivers running across her skin.

Gemma raised her eyes to mine, her breathing still uneven as the fog in her head lifted. I took her hand and raised it, holding it against the wall. I smiled at her and she squeezed it tightly. We'd just been to heaven and hell together, emerging from our own ashes. The fire that had enveloped us was so all-consuming it still burned in my chest.

"I don't want to lose you, Evan," she whispered unexpectedly.

"It's gratifying to hear that at moments like this," I said, grinning. I stroked her thumb and she turned to look at our joined hands. Resting my forehead against her temple, I kissed her cheekbone. "I won't let it happen," I whispered.

Gemma took a deep breath, her heart still racing. Her gaze was lost on the rings of our tattoos that together formed the infinity symbol, renewing our vow each time we joined hands.

Stay together. Fight together.

GEMMA

BLOCKS OF ICE

I got out of the shower and wrapped a towel around me, my cheeks aching from the huge smile that refused to leave my face. I let my hair down and opened the window a crack. The steam soon cleared and the mirror reflected my image. I ran a hand over my face, still grinning like a moron. It was bright red! Why did Evan inevitably have that effect on me?

Sweeping my hair to one side, I suddenly froze and leaned closer to my reflection, my hand on my neck. My eyes widened at the hickey Evan had left on me. Part of me was turned on by the sight of it—it reminded me of the electrifying moment when I'd felt his lips on me— yet I suspected a little part of him had done it because we were about to go out with Peter. By that point Evan should have realized he didn't need to leave his mark on me to know I was his. I still had butterflies in my stomach, thinking back to a few minutes earlier, to what had happened in the shower and how passionately he had desired me. I closed my eyes. I could still feel his hands on me, caressing my wet skin as the water slid down our bodies and the steam enveloped us. It was as though he possessed the code to activate all the sensors in my body. I saw myself stroking the tattoo on his arm. At my touch, a shiver had spread across his forearm, tracing the intricate design, his muscles flexing every time he thrust himself into me. I'd always been drawn by his mark. It aroused me and frightened me at the same time. Part of me wondered if it was because of what I was going to become—a Witch on the hunt for her Subterranean—but whenever that happened I reassured myself with a reminder that I'd never felt a similar attraction to the marks of other Subterraneans. My connection to Evan went beyond our roles, and love would overcome the dark power inside me. I would defeat the powers of evil—I wouldn't let them obliterate me. Though Evan was determined to find a solution that would prevent me from becoming a Witch, I was well aware that the darkness was inside me and only I could defeat it.

I'd already experienced what it meant to lose Evan and I wasn't willing to accept it again. I would respect the pact but would remain on Earth. I was more and more convinced I wouldn't change. It wasn't possible to erase the memories I'd built together with Evan. He couldn't be eradicated from my heart.

I ran my fingers over the hickey, remembering his mouth's fiery touch. Raising my eyes to the mirror, I found I was still smiling. Deep down, it warmed my heart that Evan felt the need to leave his mark on me, the need to make me his. He'd never stopped romancing me. We'd been through so much together, our relationship had evolved and our bond had strengthened, yet he was still the enamored and slightly crazy guy I'd always known. Even if I'd realized in time that he was giving me a hickey, I knew I would have let him do it, just like when he'd snuck into the shower even though the others were about to arrive. He was impulsive and stubborn—maybe even more than I was. After making love, we'd started fooling around again, and it had taken every ounce of my self-control to resist him and kick him out of the shower.

Downstairs, the front door closed and murmurs filled the living room. "Oh, *shit*," I murmured. They'd arrived. I dressed in a hurry, knowing I had to get downstairs, and fast, before Evan and Peter got into a fistfight in the living room. I hopped into the hallway, tugging my snow boots on, but something stopped me.

A sensation.

Slowly, I turned around as a shiver ran down my spine. The hallway was dark, illuminated only by a faint glow from one of the bedrooms. I felt a sudden gust of wind. Evan must have left his window open. I walked toward his room to close it, but my heart leapt in my chest from fright. Someone was staring at me through the crack in the door.

Blinking, I advanced cautiously, but the eyes were still there. It looked like a little boy. The door swung shut, closed by a puff of air, but I threw it open. Evan's sweatshirt swung back and forth on the doorknob. I heaved a sigh of relief. The room was empty and the window was, in fact, open, letting in the cold. I shivered, partly because of the draft and partly because of that nasty sensation.

"Hey, Gemma."

I jumped, my heart beating like crazy. "Simon," I said, still stunned.

"What are you doing here? Your friends are already downstairs. If I were you, I wouldn't leave Evan alone with Peter."

"Actually, you're right." I smiled at him. "Aren't you coming with us to the Ice Castle?"

"I'll catch up with you in a bit. First I'm going downstairs to make sure everything's under control."

"You mean the prisoners?"

"I mean the prisoners' *guards*. Better not to trust them too much."

I nodded. "Be careful," I warned him, serious.

He smiled and tousled my hair. "No need to worry. Everything's under control. Go have fun with your friends." I returned his smile and headed for the stairs. Casting a last glance at Evan's sweatshirt, I shook my head. I was getting paranoid.

"Here she is, finally!" Faith exclaimed as Jake pulled her against him, making her protest.

"Hey!" I said as I hurried down the stairs.

Peter was sprawled on the couch with Brandon, while Evan was drying his still-damp hair with a towel. I sighed with relief: no blood on the carpet. Peter had a strange look on his face. He seemed worried, or maybe confused—I couldn't tell. Irony had hopped into his lap, but Peter was focused on something else. When he saw me, though, his agitation vanished and he looked calm again.

"A little longer and nobody would have been able to drag these two off the couch," Jeneane exclaimed, climbing over Peter's legs to be closer to Brandon, who suddenly grabbed her hand and pulled.

"Hey!" she cried, toppling onto his lap. He laughed and held her tight.

"Sorry to keep you waiting. There was a slight holdup." Instinctively, my eyes sought Evan's. He smiled at me, making me blush. Faith and Jeneane must have noticed because they whispered something to each other. Peter glanced at me and then at Evan before looking away, irritated.

"I told you there wasn't time," I murmured, moving closer to Evan. I wished I could have avoided making a big entrance, with everyone's attention focused on me. They could read on my face what we'd just done.

He smiled, sensing my embarrassment, and moved his mouth to my ear. "Then you should choose your words more carefully. 'I'm going to take a shower' isn't the best way to get rid of me."

"I have the impression you wouldn't have given up no matter what I said," I teased, raising an eyebrow.

"You're right," he admitted. "And I'm sorry about *this*," he whispered, running his finger over the hickey.

I raised the neck of my sweatshirt and looked around. No one was paying attention to us, but Evan still had that saucy grin on his face. "You're completely insane," I said, grinning back at him.

"I know, that's what makes me irresistible." He winked at me, took me by the hand and pulled me away.

"Get your lazy asses off the sofa, it's time to go," Ginevra announced, coming down the stairs. I hadn't heard her upstairs. She must have been in the Copse, a little corner of Hell she'd recreated for her serpent in her bedroom—an area that was off limits for all of us. She opened the front door and motioned to us impatiently.

"For crying out loud," Brandon grumbled, still sunk into the couch, "why can't we stay here and watch the ga—" All at once he jumped in his seat, shocked, and pointed at the picture window in the kitchen, his eyes bulging. "Did you guys see that?! A black panther just walked by!" The others stared at him in silent disbelief as he clung to the couch, still scared. "It was there! You've got to believe me!"

Ginevra and I exchanged tense glances but then burst out laughing, followed immediately by the others. "I told you not to smoke that stuff, dude. It's too strong," Jake said, jeering.

Brandon composed himself, looking annoyed. "I saw it, okay?!" he insisted. Ginevra walked over to the window. He tried to stop her, more frightened than ever. "Are you crazy?! Get away from there!" he warned her, not bothering to hide the fear in his voice.

Ginevra ignored him and opened the window wide. Everyone held their breath. Peter had a grim look on his face again, like he felt he was in enemy territory, almost as if he suspected something. Evan and I exchanged looks. Maybe it hadn't been a good idea to invite a group of mortals to a house full of Witches, panthers, and imprisoned Executioners.

"There it is! It's right there! I can see its tail!" Brandon cried. "Close it, or—"

"She'll devour us all?" Ginevra turned to us, cradling a big black cat that flicked its tail in irritation. Everybody laughed and Brandon ran a hand up his neck, embarrassed but relieved.

"Maybe you really did overdo it with that stuff," Faith chided, one eyebrow raised.

"It was just a big, stupid cat," he muttered.

Ginevra held the cat up to his face and it hissed, making him pull back. "She must not have appreciated the word 'stupid.'"

"Come with me, champ." Jeneane grabbed Brandon by the shirt and pulled him away.

"Dude! Seriously? There are no panthers in the Adirondacks. At most it might've been a black bear!" Jake joked.

"I hate bears," Faith said. "They can rip your head off with a single blow."

"You've never seen what a panther can do to you," Ginevra said mischievously.

"There are no panthers around here," I repeated.

"You have to admit it's really big for a cat," Brandon insisted.

"Yeah, we will when you admit we destroyed you during the game!" Faith teased.

"You didn't *win*. The game wasn't over yet!" he said, annoyed.

The entire group started a heated discussion about how the game had gone and Evan took my hand, distracting me from the chatter. We exchanged a complicit glance. With our "slight holdup," we'd risked really messing things up, and Brandon had almost had a heart attack.

"Wait for me!" Nausyka ran out the door after us. She must have been the panther guarding the grounds. "You can't go to the Castle without me. I'm the main attraction!" she whined arrogantly, striding ahead of us. Actually, Nausyka did seem like an ice queen.

Evan rolled his eyes and both of us smiled. With all the Witches, supernatural creatures, and bloodthirsty Reaper Angels, one thing was certain: in that house, nobody ever got bored.

We arrived at the Ice Castle at dusk. The parade had already begun and the floats were making their way down the streets filled with music and groups of people wearing masks. After leaving the house, we'd gone to the North Elba toboggan run, where some middle-school students were still hanging out. They didn't take part in the Winter Carnival, so during the two days of competitions they would go sledding and have fun in the snow. Before leaving for the Ice Castle, we had some hot tea at my parents' diner.

In Saranac Lake they celebrated the Winter Carnival with two weeks full of events like the Ladies' Fry Pan Toss, musicals, great plays, and a parade complete with fireworks. But the most spectacular attraction was the Ice Castle on the shore of Lake Flower's Pontiac Bay. It was built out of two tons of ice blocks and had tunnels, mazes, and ever-changing surprises. I loved it. It was massive and majestic, one of the most magical parts of the Winter Carnival, and it made me feel like I was in a medieval fairy tale.

I took snapshots of the parade and my friends. Some of them complained because I was constantly taking pictures, but then they struck a pose, making funny faces for the camera.

Jeneane let out a sudden shriek and we all turned around, worried. "I can't wait to go inside!" she exclaimed, jumping up and down. She left us behind and slipped into the Castle with a huge smile.

"Wait for me!" Brandon broke away from the group to follow her.

"Relax," Evan whispered to me. He squeezed my hand and I took a deep breath. We were too tense. Ginevra and Simon also had serious looks on their faces. Anya, on the other hand, was looking around with her eyes full of enthusiasm while Nausyka was beaming and self-confident. On the way there, Evan had been very strict in reminding her that the only reason we were taking her with us was for my safety. She couldn't let the mortals' souls distract her. She was there to protect *me*. Evan had repeated it over and over again. Still, none of us were sure she would manage to restrain her instincts.

"What do we do, go track Jeneane down?" Faith asked, gesturing at the Ice Castle.

"I'm sure Brandon's checking the Castle for a cozy little room where he can be alone with her," Jake said.

"Not a bad idea," Nausyka said, her voice suddenly velvety. She rested her hand on Jake's shoulder and caressed his muscles. I looked at Faith. Her cheeks were practically purple, contrasting with her pale skin. Jake, on the other hand, paid no attention to Nausyka. The Witch suddenly turned to Peter and took his hand. "What do you say, want to go with me?"

"Nausyka, enough!" Ginevra said, stopping her and continuing the rest of the conversation mentally.

"Can't I have even a little bit of fun? I'm not doing anything wrong," she huffed. *"Besides, he's adorable!"* She pulled Peter closer, still holding him by the hand.

"Evan . . ." I murmured, worried. I turned to look at him but he was concentrating on something else.

"Don't worry. She won't tempt Peter's soul," he told me. Like Ginevra, he must have communicated telepathically with the Witch to remind her of the rules of the game.

"Okay," I said, though I still wasn't completely convinced she would abide by them. I'd noticed the constant glances she'd thrown at Peter during the game at school, and I wouldn't have had any objections if she'd been a mere mortal.

Peter readily accepted her attentions, though I saw caution in his eyes. He continued to hold her hand and from time to time even squeezed her waist, peeking in my direction. Chances were he was hoping to make me jealous, though that was impossible. My heart belonged to Evan and no one else. My only reaction to Nausyka's being so close to Peter was concern. Evil lurked inside her, and he didn't know it. The last thing I wanted was for Peter to lose his soul because of me.

"We're going to look for Brandon and Jeneane," Faith insisted, taking Jake by the arm. She was clearly doing everything she could to keep Nausyka away from him.

"We'll come with you." Peter glanced at Nausyka for confirmation. "Feel like it?"

"Go ahead," Evan told her in his mind, letting me listen in, *"but no tricks with the kid."*

"I don't take orders from you," she hissed as she passed him. They exchanged an icy glare and she grabbed hold of Peter's arm. The two of them headed toward the Castle.

I knew Nausyka's presence bothered Evan and he was probably happy to be rid of her. I went up to Anya, but there was no need for me to voice my concern out loud. *"Would you . . . ?"*

"Don't worry. I'll keep an eye on her." Anya smiled at me and followed her Sister into the Castle.

"Anyone else want to join their group?" Simon joked, irritated that the Witches hadn't stayed there to protect me.

"I'm just fine here with you guys," I said. He winked at me. Evan, Simon, and Ginevra were a more-than-capable surveillance team.

Nausyka could go ahead and have some fun in the world of the mortals ... just as long as it made her forget her Witch instincts.

I moved closer to Ginevra. "Gwen," I said in a low voice, "can we trust her?"

She'd already read the concern in my thoughts. "She won't claim Peter's soul—don't worry about that. Anya's there with them. Besides, I'll continue to keep an eye on their minds, if it makes you feel better."

I nodded, thankful for her help. I didn't want anyone else to pay the price for my destiny again. Drake's sacrifice was still a dagger piercing my stomach. We missed him every second of the day, and it was my fault. Protecting me had landed him in Hell.

"And thanks to that, he found his beloved Stella," Ginevra reproached me, listening to my thoughts. "Relax, Gemma. Nothing's going to happen to anyone today. We should all be like Nausyka. After all, we came here to have fun. The Executioners are all under lock and key, so we have nothing to worry about."

I took a deep breath, the cold air chilling my lungs. "You're right. I have no reason to be this nervous."

"Hear that, Evan?" Simon said. "Your girlfriend's really nervous. Why don't you warm her up a little?"

"Ooooh ... " Ginevra said, provoking me.

We'd been left on our own and all things considered, it was a good thing, because I felt more comfortable. In the past I would have found Simon's allusion embarrassing, but now we were all so close it was natural for us to tease each other in every situation. Evan, Simon, Ginevra, and I were a family—close-knit and inseparable.

"Hey, that was a private conversation." I punched Simon on the shoulder and clung to Evan's arm. "But he's not all wrong—it really is cold. I wouldn't mind a bit of your warmth."

Evan laughed. "Careful, I might take you at your word." He winked at me and we headed toward the Ice Castle. I fell behind to snap a few shots, and the others told me to hurry up. At the entrance, a big sign carved into the ice, lit up in blue lights, welcomed the visitors:

SARANAC LAKE
WINTER CARNIVAL

The air was even colder between the mighty walls of ice. I caught up with the group, snapping pictures of the amazing ice sculptures. There was a magnificent moose, a giant spider web, and even a motorcycle meticulously carved in the smallest detail. I turned the corner and found myself before a crystal carriage like the one I'd seen as a little girl. I couldn't help but remember the moment when I'd shared that memory with Evan and he'd created a prince and princess just for me on the frozen lake under the stars. The halls were full of incredible creations: a magnificent angel with unfurled wings, an archer with his bow pulled taut, and even a unicorn reared up on its hind legs. I turned another corner and found the sculpture of a ferocious beast in front of me. It was a wolf with its jaws open wide. A shiver ran down my back. I took a picture of it and realized I was all alone. Where had the others gone? I must have gotten too distracted. It was so easy to get lost while daydreaming in that enchanted kingdom. I turned around, still peering through the viewfinder, and a little boy's face filled the lens. I jumped in surprise. He seemed to have appeared out of nowhere. I smiled at him, but he continued to stare at me in silence. He must have been around four, and he was adorable, with eyes so blue they looked like ice. Instinctively I raised the lens to frame him. I had just snapped the picture when someone behind me grabbed me by the waist. "Boo!"

I whirled around, frightened. "So this is where you've been hiding." Evan's smile shone reassuringly but my heart was still pounding.

"Evan, you scared me to death."

"Relax, I was just teasing you. You shouldn't go wandering around all by yourself. Ginevra's keeping track of your thoughts, but even you know that sometimes your mind manages to block her."

"It's not my fault they designed a maze worthy of James Dashner this year."

"Who?"

"Nothing, never mind. I must have gotten lost," I said, gesticulating with the camera in my hand.

Evan grabbed it and took it from around my neck. "Maybe if you looked with your eyes and not through your viewfinder it would be easier for you to see where we're going." He pointed the lens at me as I held back a smile, pretending to pout. "You're beautiful," he said softly, snapping a couple of pictures.

"What are you doing?!" I protested.

"There's only one thing in this whole Castle worth immortalizing, and that's you."

"Cut it out!" I laughed and covered the lens with my hand. It was embarrassing to be on the other side of it. "Come on, give it back!"

"No, for today I'm holding it hostage." He pulled me into a secluded corner. "What do you say we melt a few blocks of ice?" he whispered into my hair.

I shivered. "What, is sneaking me into cramped spaces becoming your favorite pastime?"

"You're my favorite pastime." I closed my eyes in ecstasy as Evan's lips traced sweet kisses on my neck. "Kissing you," he went on, "touching you"—his hand slid up my thigh and came to rest on my bottom—"making love to you." He pulled me roughly against him and a moan escaped me.

"Evan, everybody will see us!"

"I can't do without it," he murmured against my skin, holding me tight.

"That's pretty obvious," I joked. He brushed his tongue over the hickey he'd left on me and I closed my eyes, tingles running through me. I clung to him and dug my fingers into his back. When he nibbled at my neck I broke free. "Evan, that tickles!"

He took my hand and his resonant laugh echoed through the tunnel as he backed away with a little smile on his lips. "Stay close to me or the next time you get lost I'll be forced to melt down the whole Castle to find you." I stuck my tongue out at him. "Try me if you don't believe it."

"I'd better not—I wouldn't want to spoil the fun for the whole town." I didn't dare challenge him. As stubborn as he was, there was a serious risk he would really do it.

Suddenly I remembered the little boy. "Wait a sec!" What if he'd gotten lost too? In that maze it wasn't hard to do. I turned around, but he was gone.

"What's wrong?" Evan asked, stopping to stare at me.

I walked back a few steps. He couldn't have gone far. I turned the corner and froze. It was a dead end. Where had the boy gone? Had he walked by us while we were fooling around?

"Gemma, what's worrying you?"

"I don't know where he went."

"Who?" Evan asked, puzzled.

"The little boy who was here with me."

"There was no boy when I got here."

"Yes there was—he was right there. I should've helped him. Maybe he was lost."

Evan drew me against him. "Relax. If he was, I'm sure he's already tracked down his parents."

I'd become hypersensitive when it came to children. Making it seem like a casual gesture, Evan touched his hand to my forehead. On the occasions when my power emerged, my body reacted with a high fever, more intense than any human being could bear. Sometimes just being near a Witch was enough to set it off. At first the fits had been so strong I'd passed out. With time I'd learned to control the power, especially once I'd accepted my true nature. Even my hair had grown darker recently.

"I saw him, Evan. I'm not seeing things!" I snapped, rage rising inside me. Why did everyone blame me whenever things weren't like they said they were?

"All right, all right! I didn't say anything. Calm down," Evan whispered, stroking my hair. He cupped my face in his hands and made me look at him.

Only when I'd begun to think clearly again did I realize I was trembling. I read the concern in his eyes and my anger vanished. "I'm sorry," I whispered, burying my face in his chest.

"Shh, everything's okay. It'll all be fine."

I wasn't so sure of that any more. If I already slipped toward evil so quickly without realizing it, how would I ever manage to resist the darkness once the serpent had sunk its fangs into me? With its venom in my bloodstream, rage and hatred would banish all the rest, just like everyone kept telling me. But I was stubborn. I'd convinced everyone it would be all right. Now doubts were starting to creep into my mind.

Evan took my hand. "Come on, let's catch up with the others."

I nodded, remaining silent. What if he'd been right all along? He didn't want to risk losing me in the transformation and was determined to find a solution that would release me from my promise to the Witches. Why did I never listen to him? I'd asked him to trust me when I didn't even trust myself. I had to rethink everything. I had to consider his idea. I had to trust Evan.

Simon and Ginevra were laughing, walking along cheerfully hand in hand. How I wished I could stop time, eliminate all the evil from our lives, bring back Drake and Stella, and let everyone live happily ever after. Unfortunately, we weren't living in a fairy tale and my destiny was more and more uncertain. All our destinies were. Yet they were still there, smiling as though our lives weren't about to change in a few months, as though we weren't in constant danger . . . because I wasn't the only one who had to escape death. Every day I was more aware of how much all of them were risking their lives to save me. When would they realize I wasn't worth it?

"Stop torturing yourself and take a picture of me and Simon." Ginevra tugged on my hair in an affectionate reproach and gave me my camera back.

"Sorry, I can't help it."

"Yes, you can! Enjoy the night, the hunk next to you, and your inseparable ball-breaking Sister who loves you." Ginevra hugged me from behind, resting her cheek against mine. *I loved her so much!*

"Hey, don't forget about me," Simon whined.

"You stay where you are—for today you're all mine." She winked at him and ran to hug him as I centered them in the frame. Ginevra was radiant with her long golden hair, dazzling smile, and sparkling green eyes. She definitely looked like an ice queen.

"Wait! I'll take one more. Hold it . . . Perfect."

"Let's go," Evan told us. "We should find the others before the fireworks start."

"Just a sec," I said, checking the pictures I'd taken of Simon and Ginevra. I smiled when I saw I'd managed to capture the light sparkling in Ginevra's eyes. I couldn't have been more satisfied. Clicking through the photos, I also found the ones Evan had taken of me. My colors were different from hers, but my big dark eyes stood out just as nicely against the white background, as did my cheeks, kissed by the blush only Evan could bring out in them.

The next shot was blank. I must have taken it by accident. I was about to delete it when I remembered and the smile died on my lips. It wasn't blank. It was the picture I'd taken of the little boy. What did it mean?

"Gemma, what is up with you today?" Simon groaned. "Do we have to drag you behind us on a sled?"

Meanwhile, Ginevra had already walked off. Evan squeezed me from behind and I forced myself to banish my concern. "It's nothing. I'm a little tired, that's all. It must be normal enough in my condition."

"Want me to carry you on my shoulders?" Evan joked.

I punched his arm. "I'm not a four-year-old."

"So what? I can still bear your weight . . . for the time being," he said, grinning.

"I'll dare you to do it when I'm a total blimp."

Evan laughed and held my hand. "I'll still carry you then."

I smiled at him but couldn't force down my nervousness for long. I kept thinking about the little boy.

I let go of Evan's hand and went back to looking at the pictures. He was right—there was no boy. Had I imagined him? Had he been another of my visions? What part of my subconscious had conjured him up? And why? Maybe it was because of my pregnancy . . . Could he be a projection of my future? Could he be my child? Who could say how far my powers might go?

A strange instinct tingled under my skin, the same one that had gripped me earlier. While before I hadn't wanted to give it any importance, now I was certain: it hadn't been the sweatshirt hanging from Evan's doorknob—I really had seen a little boy staring at me through the crack in the door.

I heard a whimper in the distance and slowed down, pricking my ears. It was coming from behind me. I turned and my heart contracted when I glimpsed the little boy disappear around the corner. I rushed through the maze after him, afraid he would disappear again. Instead, there he was, huddled on a slab of ice, crying. Just in case he was only in my imagination, I looked around to make sure no one could see me before asking, "Hey, everything okay? Are you lost?" He continued to cry. I moved closer and leaned over him. "What's your name? I'll take you to your mommy. Do you know where she is?"

"She died," a grim voice behind me said. "Two thousand years ago."

I spun around and found myself facing a little boy identical to the first. There were two of them. When I turned back, his brother slowly raised his head and his eyes of ice pierced me, shattering every doubt. "Soon you'll be dead too," he murmured with a crafty smile.

My heart twisted painfully in my chest. They were Subterraneans. And they were there to kill me.

FIREWORKS

"Evan!" I shouted. All at once a slab of ice fell from the ceiling behind the boy. I was trapped. Panicking, I tried to catch my breath, but it seemed an impossible task. Raising my hands to my throat, I crumpled to my knees.

"Gemma!" Evan's muffled shout reached me from outside my ice prison.

Evan!! I tried to scream but to my horror realized I couldn't. A drop of blood splashed onto the snow. *What . . . What are you doing to me?* My eyes shot to the two children as a sharp burning sensation spread through my body, making any movement impossible.

One of them smiled with an evil look in his eye. "Resisting is pointless." His voice didn't sound like a child's. It was deep, like a demon's.

Gwen! I shouted in my mind, *I'm here! Help me! I can't hold out much longer!*

The other boy walked slowly around me as I huddled on the ground, terrified, unable to move a muscle. "Don't bother trying to fight."

I gritted my teeth, trying to resist their power, but it was no use. My heartbeat began to slow inexorably as fire set the veins throughout my body ablaze.

Was everything truly about to end?

"Gemma!!" The desperate shout made its way through the walls as something hot trickled from my ears. I kept my eyes locked on the little boy as the world around me grew blurry, slowly fading. He smiled as craftily as a hungry wolf. Blood leaked from my nose and a crimson droplet splashed onto the snow, staining it red. I began to lose consciousness, barely noticing when my cheek struck the white ground. The pain had made me its own, gripping me in a vise of ice. *I was so tired . . .*

My eyelids blinked slowly and opened with effort. All I could think of were Evan and my baby, but their image grew ever fainter and more distant. Once they disappeared I knew I would lose them forever.

All at once the ground beneath me trembled, sending a shock through me. I opened my eyes but couldn't focus on anything. The cold stung my cheek. There was a burst of light and a loud noise that sounded like an explosion. The voices were close now, as though they were all around me, but there was something else: a chorus of shouts that filled the night, like a crazed crowd. A blond angel approached, hand outstretched. The children fell to their knees, powerless. Arms gently picked me up.

"Gemma, Gemma! Hang in there, stay with me." A hand brushed the hair from my face as a sweet warmth slowly spread through me. *Evan.* I struggled to focus on his face but lacked the strength. He cradled me in his arms. "We've got to get out of here. We've got to take her away!" he shouted, making my ears throb. I closed my eyes, amazed I could do it. Evan rested his forehead against mine. "You'll be fine. I'm here with you now," he whispered. I could sense the mix of emotions battling within him—anger, relief, and concern—while I felt as though I were enclosed in a bubble, separated from everyone else.

Evan kissed my forehead and an explosion of colors filled the sky. Then another . . . and another, coloring my world of confusion.

"You're in danger. Get out of here!"

Evan's gaze went to the Witch who'd just arrived—Zhora.

"You're late," Ginevra said.

"I'm sorry. I came as soon as I could."

"How the fuck could this have happened?" Evan burst out, furious. If more Subterraneans had shown up, it meant the Witches had killed at least one of their prisoners.

"Evan, calm down. We don't know what happened," said Simon.

"This is not good," grumbled Ginevra, who'd already read her Sister's mind. "We have to separate the prisoners. They're stronger together."

"Did they escape?" Simon asked.

"They committed suicide," Ginevra replied icily.

"Oh, great!" Evan fumed. "Just what we needed: kamikaze Subterraneans."

"But how could that happen?!"

"One of them sacrificed himself for the cause," Zhora explained. "He provoked our Dakor and got bitten on purpose. Another tried to do the same. We attempted to stop him, but were unable to . . . and he died. What happened here?" she asked, looking around.

"We showed up just in time. A few more minutes and they would have had her."

"How is she?" The Witch walked up to me. She stroked my cheek and kissed me on the mouth, leaving me dazed. A strange tingle filled me.

"She'll be okay," Evan replied, barely able to hide the bitterness in his voice. He gestured at the two unconscious children on the ice, guarded by Ginevra and Zhora's Dakor.

"For now we've stopped them. I'll take care of them later," Ginevra snarled. "Right now, let's get out of here." Evan nodded. I could see him more clearly now, as the fireworks lit up the night.

"Gemma! Gemma! Jesus! What happened to her?!" It was Peter.

I turned my head a little and smiled at him. "Pet . . ." I said, amazed I could speak again, though my voice was hoarse. "I'm fine. Don't worry."

"What happened?"

"We saw an explosion. The police blocked our way, but you guys were trapped in here!" Jeneane explained, shaken.

Faith covered her mouth with both hands as Jake gripped her shoulders. "My God! Who are those two little boys? We've got to get them to the hospital!" She moved closer but let out a shriek when she saw the serpents.

"Brandon, get the police!" Jeneane cried.

"Stop," Evan ordered, and Brandon stopped. "Everyone calm down," he continued, his voice grave as he crept into their minds. He was controlling them. *You guys split up from us and we didn't meet again. We left early because Gemma had a dizzy spell. It was a great night, but the Castle collapsed and you were all scared. Go home and get some sleep.*"

"C'mon, guys," Jake said. "You heard what the cops said, we can't hang around here."

The others nodded and walked toward their car. Brandon pulled Peter by the arm, but Peter yanked himself free. "Let go of me!" he barked, looking very concerned. "I have to call Gemma. Something happened, I can sense it," he muttered. He couldn't see me any more, yet Evan's words hadn't completely reassured him.

Evan and Simon exchanged a long look. Simon went over to Peter and rested a hand on his shoulder, looking at him intently.

He was about to use his power. I held my breath. Only a few times had I seen Simon erase someone's memory. It wasn't the same as the Subterraneans' ability to control people's minds. Evan had planted false memories in their minds, making them believe they'd had those experiences. Simon's power, on the other hand, went well beyond that. He acted on people's actual memory.

Don't worry. Evan's voice filled my head. *Simon will only erase his memory of us.*

"Why didn't he have to do that to the others, too?"

"Because Peter is so attached to you. My order only partially convinced him. He must have been too worried. It happens, sometimes."

I looked at Peter. The veins on his neck were turning black and flowing toward Simon's hand, as if Simon were sucking away the memories from that very spot.

"Will he be okay?" I said softly. I still felt very weak.

Evan nodded. "Tomorrow morning he'll have a bad headache, that's all." I smiled at him. Still filled with concern, his eyes never left mine.

"Guys!" Ginevra called, drawing our attention. "We have a problem."
A gasp escaped me. The little boys were gone.

GIFTS FROM HELL

"They're very strong," Ginevra noted as we entered the kitchen. "They almost killed Gemma—and kept us out at the same time."

During the trip home, I'd regained my strength and they'd explained what had happened. The two Subterraneans had frozen me in a sort of prison they'd created and had been draining me of my energy until Ginevra and Anya broke down their barriers and Evan shattered the Castle to pieces. Simon had managed to evacuate almost all the people inside, but many were injured.

They looked like little kids but it had taken two Subterraneans and two Witches to defeat them. Ginevra was right: they were very strong.

"But who are they?" Simon asked, frustrated.

"Could they be shapeshifters, like Drake?" I guessed. They must have taken advantage of my sensitivity toward children to lure me away from the others.

"No," stated a voice behind me. A black butterfly alighted on my hand. I shivered and turned around. *Sophìa.*

"Shit," Simon muttered.

The queen of darkness advanced. All the panthers bowed and the Witches around the table lowered their eyes as a sign of submission.

The devil incarnate was in our house. And she wanted me with her.

Ginevra froze, but didn't bow. She held her gaze until Sophìa approached me and took my chin in her fingers. Evan stepped forward, but Simon stopped him. I kept my gaze steadily on hers as her incredible lapis lazuli eyes probed mine, penetrating my soul. She was so close I could smell her scent. She smelled like flowers—an obscure, forbidden fragrance. She leaned in slowly and kissed me on the lips, leaving me dazed. A current of electricity branched through me, tingling under my skin. When Sophìa's lips left mine she smiled at me, inches from my face, but I couldn't move a muscle. In the room, silence had fallen.

"What did you do to her?!" Evan snarled, stepping in front of me.

"At ease, Spartan. I come in peace," Sophìa replied, her voice so charismatic and warm it made me quiver. "It was merely a greeting for my Naiad."

"She isn't yours," Evan growled.

Sophìa laughed. "Yes she is. It is only a matter of time."

"Why have you come?" Ginevra asked.

"Is this how you welcome me to your home?"

"You aren't welcome here," Simon reminded her.

"I was certain I understood there was a truce between us, Soldier. Is that no longer the case?" Sophìa stared at Simon.

He glared at her threateningly in turn. Ginevra intervened before things got out of hand. "Of course it is. We weren't expecting to see you here, that's all. What can we do for you, my lady?"

Sophìa smiled. Ginevra had subjugated herself to her, though her eyes burned with pride. Yet she didn't hate her—I could sense that. She was doing it out of fear for Simon. Still, there was another emotion. It was hidden deep down but I could sense it: nostalgia. Despite everything, she missed Sophìa.

"I am here to warn you. The two you saw are no ordinary Subterraneans."

"You mean they aren't Executioners who took on the appearance of children?" I asked.

"As I have already said, no. That is their true appearance. They are Asvins. They are not like you," she warned, speaking to the two Subterraneans in the room. "They are divinities. Celestial creatures. And they are very powerful. They never work together, but for you, Naiad, they seem to have made an exception."

"I've never heard anything of the kind," Simon murmured.

"They are Soldiers. Ferrymen of Souls, like you, but from a . . . *purer* species." A veiled insult glimmered in Sophìa's eyes.

"What does that mean?" Evan grunted. "And how do we kill them?" After what they'd done to me, he didn't even care about the fact that if we did so others would arrive.

"You can't," another voice said. We all turned to look at Devina, who'd just appeared in the living room. "My lady." Devina bowed to Sophìa, who gave her a long, sensual kiss on the lips.

Evan snorted, clearly disgusted. "Can we focus on the topic at hand or do you have to do that whenever you guys meet? If you want, we can leave the two of you alone."

Sophìa simply smiled, fixing her blue eyes on Evan. Her long, black, silver-tipped hair was tied up in a ponytail that reached her bottom, and the curves of her toned body were brought out by an extravagant gown in lace as black as her lipstick and pointy fingernails. She looked no older than twenty-five. No one would have guessed she was the devil.

"You can't kill them," Devina said again. "They're Deva twins, as old as time. They were among the first Subterraneans ever to exist and their name is legendary. They almost killed off two of us at the same time. They're very strong and have fun toying with Souls, terrorizing them before taking them away. For them *everything* is a game, but it's no laughing matter. They're immortal. Some legends say they obtained divine favor, while according to others their souls have been redeemed. Killing them is impossible. We've tried to subdue them several times," she admitted, "but since they're children, our seductive powers have no effect on them."

"However, I know a way to stop them," Sophìa concluded. "That is why I am here."

"We're listening," Evan said.

"There is only one thing that will keep them at bay. Your paltry underground prison will not be enough to trap them. You require something special: a cage forged of a substance as ancient as they are."

"Diamantea," Simon said under his breath.

I held back a smile. Sophìa herself had been imprisoned in a cage made of the divine stone.

"No," Sophìa said. "I have something better. Something more powerful." She opened her palm, showing us a tiny black crystal. I recognized it instantly. It was carbonado, the substance from Hell. She clasped it in her fist and the prism lengthened into a sharp stick that unfolded and changed shape, transforming in seconds into a cage of black diamond, impregnable and lethal. "Be careful, Subterraneans, not to cut yourselves on it unless you wish to pay us a visit in Hell. In that case, you are always welcome." She turned and winked at Simon. "The cage will deprive the Twins of all their powers. Including immortality." She smiled, her eyes flashing blue.

"We can't kill them," Simon spoke up, to calm Evan's anger. "Others would come. We can't risk it."

"In that case I will accept them as a gift when Naiad is safe . . . at my side." She fixed a sly smile on me before vanishing into the darkness.

"At least she was useful," Evan said sardonically.

"It was forged from Sophìa's venom, Simon. Don't touch it!" Ginevra warned, seeing that he'd moved closer to it than he should have. In the middle of the living room, the bars of the big black cage twisted like serpents, forming an intricate lattice that blocked much of the view of the inside.

"How do we move it?" I asked shyly, but no one answered. "You don't mean to leave it here, do you?"

"Why not?" Evan joked. "It's not bad. It goes with the rest of the furniture."

"Except that, unlike the rest of the furniture, it can kill you," Ginevra shot back.

"That would be such a loss . . ." Devina goaded him.

I glared at her, knowing she couldn't help but hope Evan cut himself on its poisoned edges, because if he did he would return to her in Hell. "Go lick your tail, you ugly bitch," I snarled at her.

Standing behind me, Evan rested his hands on my shoulders to calm me. Devina moved her face close to mine. "Or I could lick *him*," she whispered, touching my ear with her tongue. "He liked it so much last time . . ." Black rage boiled up within me and the light in the living room exploded.

Evan leaned over me and held me tight. "Shh . . ." he murmured in my hair. "Don't listen to her. Breathe." His soothing voice managed to keep the darkness from suffocating me.

Devina's eyes were locked on mine, the trace of a smile on her lips. "I wish I could transform right now just so I could tear you to shreds," I hissed at her.

"We'll see who you want to tear to shreds once you're one of us. My bet is I'll be your best friend." Devina cast a sly glance at Evan. "What role will *you* play, Evan?"

"That's enough, Devina!" Ginevra warned her. "This isn't a game. Get it through your head!"

"No matter what happens, I'll never play on your side, that's for sure," Evan told her contemptuously. Devina shrugged, pretending to let his remark slide. But it had been a fierce clash, and Evan hadn't come out of it unscathed. I took his hand and he forced a smile. I knew that what he most feared about the transformation was the chance that I might hate him. But that could never happen . . . or could it?

I wasn't so sure any more.

DANGEROUS NOSTALGIA

After Sophìa had left us, Simon and Evan received execution orders and went off on their missions. Meanwhile, Ginevra went downstairs with the other Witches to check on the remaining prisoners and make sure none of them had attempted suicide. Lying on the couch with one arm over my eyes, I distractedly petted Irony. The big cage was still there in the middle of the living room. It was so strange, being there all alone in its presence. It emanated a strange energy, as though it weren't just an object but a living being.

I felt someone staring at me and opened my eyes. A large panther rested its muzzle on my cushion and let out a low, vibrant growl. I smiled. It was Anya. Her jade-green eyes stared at me, inches from my own. I moved my head closer and she rubbed hers against me, purring. Just a year earlier if someone had tried to tell me something like that could happen I would have called them crazy. Instead, I was face to face with a large panther . . . *and I loved her so.* Recently my bond with Anya had grown stronger, partly because we'd been living together. It felt like I'd always known her. She nudged Irony over with her muzzle and curled up at the foot of the couch to guard me, though it wasn't necessary. The Deva twins had escaped, but they wouldn't attack me at our house. For a long time I stared at the cage, attracted by its power. How could a simple object be powerful enough to stop two immortal beings? Without realizing it, I had moved closer, driven by the urge to feel it beneath my fingers. I could sense Sophìa's power flowing though the carbonado and was drawn to it—helplessly.

I raised a hand to touch it and my fingers cautiously traced the curves of the bars. I could feel the blood racing beneath my skin. I took a deep breath, overwhelmed by the intensity of the energy, loving the sensation of strength it created in me. All at once the black stone came to life, slithering at my touch like serpents in a dark dance. The cage door opened and I held my breath, eager to enter it.

"What are you doing?" Ginevra burst into the room and I took a step back.

"Nothing," I said defensively. "Just admiring the cage."

Ginevra's face darkened and she glanced at the panther, secretly communicating with her. "We'd better take it down," she finally murmured to herself. "You know, it might be dangerous . . . for Evan and Simon." *I don't know what kind of power it might have over her.*

"Don't lie, Gwen. I heard you," I said.

"Your powers are growing stronger."

"It's inevitable, with all these Witches around."

Ginevra wrapped her hand around one of the carbonado bars and the cage folded up, collapsing into a prism of black diamond.

"How will it happen?" I asked her point-blank. I didn't need to say anything else for her to understand that I was referring to my transformation. "Will I have to . . . die?"

Anya leapt off the couch and left us alone. Ginevra smiled. "No, Gemma. That's not going to happen." I followed her up the stairs and into her room. "Our bodies don't die like a Subterranean's. They transform. It'll be a rebirth. The venom will flow through your veins, making your body stronger. Invincible. You'll have full power over yourself and your senses. And the energy that now controls you will become part of you. You'll be in control of it."

I sat down on her bed. "Will the others notice anything different? My parents, Peter . . . ?" I didn't want the change to take away my old life and the people I cared about.

"They'll all see you in a new light. No one will be able to say no to you any more. Your charm will dazzle them. There are four different kinds of pheromones and the Witches control them all. You'll have sway over mortals . . . and all the Subterraneans."

That was what unsettled me the most. "Gwen, do you think the love between Evan and me is tainted by my power?" It was clear there was a very specific explanation for the wild attraction I'd felt for Evan the first time I saw him—I just hadn't realized it yet.

"The feelings Evan has for you are pure, Gemma. You two didn't fall in love because of your nature. I've never had any doubt about it, and neither should you." When Evan had been in Hell, Devina had tried to convince him it was true. "Devina just wanted to separate him from you. That was her goal all along, but she never succeeded. The connection between you two doesn't depend on what's inside you—otherwise you would have felt the same thing for Simon, or for Drake. The same thing goes for Evan. He fell in love with your soul. I saw it. He was lost the moment he realized you were capable of seeing him. The only thing your power did was make it possible for you to meet."

I nodded, thankful for what she'd said. "Have you ever missed sleeping?"

"Are you kidding? There are so many things to do and learn that I can't even imagine wasting half my life doing nothing."

"Sleeping *isn't* doing nothing," I protested, getting a wink from her in response. "What else is going to change with my transformation?"

"I'll show you something you'll like." Ginevra raised her hand and a book flew into her palm. When she looked at it, it snapped open and the pages flipped over rapidly before her eyes, which now sparkled green. The book closed and she smiled at me. "Ask me what it's about."

My jaw dropped. "Don't tell me you—" She nodded. She'd read the entire book in seconds. "I've always wished I could do that—there are so many books out there!"

She looked at me affectionately and then grew serious, finally answering my question. "Lots of things will change with the transformation. Your skin will become impenetrable. Nothing will be able to scratch you—nothing human, at least. Your senses will sharpen, you'll smell more smells, hear more sounds, taste more tastes. You'll have a powerful relationship with food."

"More powerful than it already is?"

"Actually, I wouldn't count on it." She laughed. "Anyway, whatever substance you put into your body after the transformation will be burned off by the venom in your blood." Ginevra gazed at me. "And then, the powers, obviously. And your eyes . . ."

"What's going to happen to my eyes?"

"They'll still be the same, but they'll have a sparkle no one can resist. And whenever the power flows inside you, your pupils will lengthen, showing the animal souls that rule within you: the panther and your Dakor."

When the power possessed the Witches, their eyes glinted with energy like molten metal and their pupils took on the threatening shape of panthers' pupils or the lethal ones of venomous snakes. My eyes would transform like that too. The thought made me tremble, yet part of me was secretly excited.

"Tell me about the powers." *What will it be like to be able to read anyone's mind at any time?* I wondered.

"It's not always fun to know what people are thinking. It can be frustrating sometimes."

"You can't really believe that."

"Sure I can. You have no idea what it's like, hearing *every thought*, knowing *every emotion* of the people around you, even people who mean a lot to you."

"I thought it was the coolest part of all."

"No, it isn't. Everyone has something they'd rather keep to themselves, even out of politeness." A bitter smile escaped Ginevra. "But with me around, no one can do it. When you have an argument with someone you can decide to keep the nasty remarks to yourself, but you can't control your thoughts. And sometimes you don't want to hear them because they hurt more than words—they go straight to your heart." She sighed and sat down beside me. "I won't lie to you, Gemma. I don't want to tell you I don't like what I am, that you should stay away from my world and renounce your nature, because that's not how I feel. My connection to you is strong, and if the possibility you'll be able to transform without leaving us turns out to be true, then I couldn't be happier. But I don't want to lose you, Gemma, and the risk of that is high. The powers and everything else are extraordinary, but there's also a dark side you'll have to reckon with. Witches are spellbinding creatures who awaken the evil in every human on Earth. Sooner or later everyone faces their Temptation, and Witches are lying in wait, ready to creep into their consciences. They instill doubts, feed insecurities, pull out the dark side lurking in each mortal. They're corruptors of Souls. Some mortals, the weaker ones, can't resist, and the Witches work on them slowly. Others, the ones who are already too corrupt, are taken at once."

"I thought it was the Màsala who determined the time allotted to each mortal. Do Witches work on Death's behalf too?"

"Of course. If a Soul is corrupt, a Subterranean isn't assigned to it. The Witches decide how and when to deal with it, and it dies by the Witches' hand. Death has two faces: Subterraneans bring Radiant Death with them; Witches are Dark Death. The difference is that for the Children of Eve, killing and ferrying Souls is a duty while for the

Witches it's a pleasure. Gemma, you can't let yourself be dazzled by the desire for powers, even if it's difficult to resist. I have to admit I would never want to be a normal person, but only because I've already won my battle against the darkness. For me the worst is over, but you still have a world of challenges to face. I would give up my powers if it was enough to guarantee your redemption."

"Oh, Gwen . . ." I hugged her tight and a tear streaked my face.

Ginevra wiped it from my cheek and kissed me affectionately on the lips. A comforting warmth trembled in my heart. It wasn't a kiss like Sophia's, which had been one of possession, brimming with erotic undertones—it was a kiss of love. "I'll never let them hurt you."

"Thank you. Though I haven't transformed yet, you're a real Sister to me. You, Evan, and Simon are my whole world."

"Hey, don't forget about the baby." Ginevra stroked my belly and I smiled through my tears.

"I never could. He's a part of me." The thought of the baby brought to mind a more disturbing one. "How are we going to capture the Deva twins?" I asked. "What powers do they have?"

"We had our suspicions after they attacked you, but Devina confirmed it. As you know, all Subterraneans have powers that help them ferry mortal Souls and cause the natural death of their bodies. The twins have the power to paralyze. One of them can influence the muscles of the body and the other controls circulation. Generally one of them is enough to accomplish a mission, but—"

"But for me they sent both," I finished her sentence, and she nodded grimly.

I understood now. One of them had paralyzed my muscles while the other worked on my circulatory system. I'd bled from my nose and ears. When Evan healed me once we were back home, he'd been particularly careful to check whether they had damaged my internal organs.

"We'll get them," Ginevra reassured me. "We'll come up with a plan tomorrow. But now you need to rest. You're safe here—the house is protected. Take this." She held out her hand and put something into my palm. "You can keep it if it'll make you feel more at ease."

I opened my fist and stared in surprise at the black diamond. "Thanks. Though I already feel safe with all of you."

"Stay here in my room, if you want. I'm going down to have a snack. All this agitation has made me hungry. Want me to bring you something?"

I smiled. To Ginevra any excuse was a good excuse to eat, and I was becoming more and more like her. "I'm fine, thanks."

"If you change your mind . . ." Ginevra winked at me and walked out the door.

I got up from the bed. I would rather rest in Evan's room, where I could smell his scent. In the hallway I almost screamed with fright when a panther leapt down in front of me. A red splotch stood out on her right paw. *Devina.* "Hey, carrot top. Next time use the stairs." She bared her fangs and growled, the harsh noise echoing off the walls. I turned my back on her and walked toward Evan's room. It was horrifying to think that if I transformed, my mind would be connected to Devina's. I didn't want to read her thoughts. If there was one person I hated most in the world, it was her. Not even Sophia made me feel such deep hatred.

Turning the knob on his bedroom door, a strange nostalgia suddenly gripped me. I hadn't read *Jane Eyre* in months, and in the state of tension I was in, the thought that I could hide away in its yellowed pages was comforting. In the margins were notes I'd written when my life had been normal, when Witches, Heaven, and Hell existed only in novels.

I kept walking. I missed my Rochester, especially now that Evan was gone. I climbed the narrow ladder that led to the attic, where Evan had stored all the things I'd brought from my parents' house. I had no idea when he would be back from his mission. No matter how many crushes I'd had during my lifelong career as an avid reader, no book boyfriend could hold a candle to Evan, as far as I was concerned.

With effort, I pushed open the wooden door in the ceiling, climbed through it and immediately turned on the yellow lightbulb hanging in the middle of the room. A gust of wind crept in through the round window. I shivered and hurried to close it. Outside it was dark and had started to snow. I rubbed my arms from the cold and examined the large storage boxes. I had so much stuff in there! I closed my eyes and let myself be enveloped by the smell of the books, the paper, the ink . . . the smell of stories. The most wonderful fragrance in the world. I knelt down and looked through a few of the boxes, reliving with a smile the memories the old books' covers conjured up in me.

Something behind me moved.

I spun around, my heart leaping in my chest, but the attic was deserted and surprisingly eerie. I filled my lungs with courage. There was nothing for me to worry about. Kneeling down again, I went back to rummaging around and finally found the old Charlotte Brontë book when a sudden noise made me start. I jumped to my feet. Something was moving in the corner. A box. I fought the urge to flee and reached out to see what it was hiding.

A gray squirrel chattered with fright and I let out the breath I'd been holding. "What are you doing up here, huh?" The squirrel hid in the corner, clawing the wall as though wanting to dig a hole in it. I reached out to pick it up and the window banged open, letting in a gust of snow.

"Ow!" The squirrel bit me and I yanked my hand back. "Hey, what did I ever do to you?" I grumbled. The wind made the lightbulb sway on its cord, illuminating the squirrel's face intermittently.

I tried again, lowering my voice. "C'mere. I'm not going to hurt you." I picked it up and found it was trembling. "Don't worry, little fella. You know, when I was a little girl they used to call me Squirrelicue? Actually, they still do, though I can't stand it." I stroked its head and something dampened my fingers. When I stared at my trembling hand, my eyes went wide. It was blood. It wasn't the finger it had bitten— there was too much of it. It was the squirrel, bleeding from the ears. Its gray fur was matted with red. I gagged as the squirrel squeaked in pain, and a terrible suspicion took root in me.

The light flickered and went out. I whirled around and the little boy of death stared at me, his eyes of ice glinting in the darkness. With a shriek I threw the squirrel at him and bolted, but his twin materialized in front of me, blocking my way.

"Want to see who can run faster?" he asked in his demon's voice. I grabbed the black diamond from my pocket and jammed it into the shoulder of the Deva behind me, taking him by surprise. Howling with pain, an inhuman sound that gave me goosebumps, he fell to the floor. With a shocked look on his face, he watched the blood gush from the wound, then raised his hate-filled eyes to me as he yanked the sharp prism out of his flesh. His brother raised his hand at me and I fell to my knees, paralyzed. Though I struggled to move my muscles, it was no use. The wounded Deva hurled the black stone away and laughed in the darkness as a drop of blood slid from my nose.

Just then a roar made the attic walls tremble and a panther landed on the Deva who was paralyzing my body. "Gemma!" Ginevra rushed into the room with two other panthers. In seconds their snarls filled the air. I wasn't strong enough to move, though the twins had released their grip. One of them was on the floor, grappling with a panther. The wounded Deva tried to escape, but Ginevra stopped him.

She summoned the black crystal to her and hurled it at his feet. He stared at the stone, at a loss, fear in his eyes for perhaps the first time in his entire existence. The carbonado came to life, unfolding around the Devas . . . and me. The panther bounded out before the cage door could close. One of the twins tried to rush out but the panthers snarled and he retreated.

"Gemma! Get out of there! *Now!*" Ginevra screamed.

I didn't move. The cage sealed itself up . . . with me inside.

THE DARKNESS SUMMONS

Though I knew I was no longer the victim of the Devas' power, since they—like me—were trapped in the cage, I felt a strange force inside me. Lying on the floor of the cage, my disheveled hair covering my face, I was trying to understand what it was when I heard a low growl. The twins backed up. I hid a smile because the sound had come from me.

And I liked it.

"What the fuck?" Simon gasped, but I barely heard him. I wanted to focus only on myself.

"It's the carbonado's power. It's awakened the evil inside her."

I could hear them, hear them all. It was like I was everywhere. They were holding their breath. Slowly, I raised my eyes to look at the Devas and terror spread across their childlike faces. They were powerless inside the cage. I, however, felt invincible. I crept toward them. One of the twins tried to attack me but my power hurled him away before he could even come close. *I had done it.* I felt the power flow through me like black lava. It burned but it made me stronger.

"Gemma, what are you doing? Get out of there!" Ginevra shouted. She opened the cage and tried to draw me to her with magic, but I blocked it and the barred door slammed shut.

"Go away! Go away, all of you!" I screamed. I didn't want to leave. I didn't want to give up that sensation, give up the *power*. The power was irresistible. The power satiated me. Someone shrieked and I spun around. It was Anya, who had just covered her mouth with both hands. I tilted my head because all at once I realized I was seeing her upside down. Somehow I had ended up on all fours on the ceiling of the cage. I leapt down to the floor as the cage door flew open and someone rushed inside and grabbed me by the waist.

"No! NO!" I shrieked, and my voice seemed to come straight from Hell. Strong arms dragged me away against my will. I clung to the cage with all my might, making my abductor scream in pain, but I continued to kick and struggle.

"Evan, get her out of there!"

I heard a grunt of effort and fell on top of someone. My body quivered. Hands clasped my face. My eyes met Evan's, and then . . . nothing.

"She's coming to."

I blinked and slowly opened my eyes. A small crowd was leaning over me. There were Subterraneans and Witches, but Ginevra told them all to move back so I could breathe.

"Evan . . ." I murmured. I tried to get up from the couch but felt drained.

"Good," Simon snorted irritably. "Now she can explain what the fuck happened!"

Evan stood up straight and faced his brother. "Hey, what's your problem?"

"We'd better call in an exorcist. We can't handle this kind of stuff," Simon hissed, his voice hard. My eyes widened. His comment had cut me to the quick.

"Simon!" Ginevra said reproachfully. "That's enough. Calm down, both of you."

Simon ran a hand over his face. "You're right. I don't even know why I said it. I'm sorry, Gemma. I've never even thought anything like that."

I happened to catch sight of my reflection in the mirror and my heart skipped a beat. My eyes . . . They were completely black, without whites. "It's my fault," I said in a tiny voice.

Evan immediately leaned over me. "What are you saying? None of this is your fault."

"Yes it is. Simon reacted that way because of me. Didn't he, Gwen?"

"Probably," she admitted regretfully.

But I *knew* it was because of me. I had felt the evil spread from me to Simon. I'd tried to stop it but couldn't. He'd said those nasty things because I'd generated a negative energy in him. Was that what was in store for me? Wasn't it enough for evil to darken my life? Did it also have to affect the lives of the people I loved? I didn't want to drag everyone else into my own darkness.

"Sophia's kiss must have awakened your power and the cage brought it out."

"That bitch!" Evan snarled. The panthers growled, advancing threateningly.

"Enough!" Ginevra stopped them. "You're not here to fight."

"He cannot insult the Empress in front of us."

"Then leave. If you stay here only to fight you're not helping."

I swallowed, dejected. I'd heard Ginevra speaking with Devina in her panther form. It was already happening. Every day I was closer to my transformation.

The panthers departed angrily, closing the door leading to the dungeon behind them. I let my head drop and breathed deeply. "I'm sorry, Simon. I didn't mean to influence you."

"It's not your fault," he reassured me. He'd come back from his mission just in time to see Evan pull me out of the cage.

"Tell me what happened," I said.

"The twins paralyzed you. We managed to stop them and hit them with the fragment of carbonado, which turned back into a cage, trapping you inside it too," Ginevra told me. "When they lost their powers you wouldn't come out. We tried to pull you out with magic, but you fought us off. You even injured Devina."

My eyes bulged. "I remember. Now I remember everything. I was the one who did those things."

"You weren't yourself. You were possessed, Gemma. Possessed by evil. Even I had never seen anything like it. Your voice was . . . different. You put the twins out of action. You hung them upside down inside the cage and came close to killing them. Fortunately Evan arrived in time."

Evan. I remembered him grunting with pain as he tried to drag me away. "You're hurt!" I exclaimed, taking his hand in mine.

He squeezed it tight. "It's nothing. All that matters is that you're safe now."

"That's not true. You risked your life for me! You could have died!"

"I could have lost you, which is worse."

"If you'd cut yourself on the black diamond, I—"

"But I didn't," he said, his eyes probing mine.

"How did you manage to get me out?"

"Not even we Witches were able to do that with our magic," Ginevra admitted. "Evan came back from his mission and when he saw you in the cage, he rushed in without thinking twice. He didn't have his powers in there and had to sling you over his shoulder against your will, but the poisonous bars left burns on him when you struggled to break free."

"Gin, why are you telling her this?"

"She needs to know. There can't be secrets among us."

I covered my face with my hands. "Forgive me, Evan."

"Everything's okay. It's going to be fine, I promise."

"Is this what's going to happen to me, Gwen?"

"No," said Anya, the only other Sister who'd stayed in the room. "It's the darkness trapped inside you that's possessing you. Once you accept the transformation, you'll set it free. You'll control it."

"I saw my eyes in the mirror." I shuddered at the memory of those big black pools staring back at me. "I looked possessed by the devil."

"You were—it's just that the devil is a part of you."

"My eyes aren't like yours. Why not?"

"For the same reason, I suppose." This time it was Ginevra who spoke. "You haven't undergone the transformation yet. What's happening to you is new for us too. Your closeness to our world jumpstarted the process. Your Dakor's venom will complete it, when Sophìa baptizes it. At that point your eyes will be his eyes and you'll have a single heartbeat."

That was why I'd seen fear on Anya's face. A tear slid down my cheek. "Evan, how can you—" I couldn't find the words. I'd even frightened myself when I saw my reflection.

"It wasn't the first time I'd seen you like that."

"What are you talking about?" I asked, shocked.

"I've seen that darkness in your eyes before," he admitted.

"It happens whenever the power summons you," Ginevra said.

"Why didn't you tell me about it?"

"There was no point in scaring you," Simon explained.

"So you let me be around other people and risk being seen?!" I shouted. "Are you trying to ruin my life?! How could you do that to me?!"

Evan took my face in his hands and his eyes focused on mine. When I looked into them, so deep and intense, a knot formed in my throat. *I was about to lose control again.* How could it be happening so soon?

A river of tears filled my eyes and I let them flow. "I'm sorry," I sobbed. "How can you still bear to be near me? You should lock me up in a cage too. I'm a monster!"

All of them filed out of the room, leaving me alone with Evan. "Don't say that," he whispered. He laced his fingers with mine and our tattoos joined, forming the infinity symbol. "Remember? Stay together. Fight together. I'll never give you up."

I clung to him, unable to hold back the sobs, and he held me tight until I fell asleep.

The lake shore shimmered amber. The sun was setting, kissing its surface in a warm farewell. Evan emerged from the lake, as handsome as a god. Beaded water sparkled on his golden skin. The mark of the Children of Eve stood out on his left forearm. With my finger I beckoned to him, on my lips a seductive smile.

Evan rested his palms on the sand and locked eyes with me. He pressed his wet lips against mine, coaxing them open. I did as he wished and our tongues touched. Still kissing me, he made his way between my legs, pressing his erection against me, and I came alive with desire. I took him by the shoulders, swiftly pushed him to the ground, and straddled him, staring at him with a provocative look on my face. He grabbed my bottom to pull me closer, but I pinned his hands against the sand. I moved my mouth close to his, without touching it, savoring his yearning for me. Provoking him gave me intense pleasure. My hand slid down his arm. I felt the veins in his flexed muscles, my nails sharp on the tattoo of the Subterraneans. Moving very slowly, I ran my tongue over his lips. He couldn't hold back any longer. Moaning with pleasure, he took my lower lip lightly between his teeth. I was *so* aroused, I wanted him. I wanted him inside me, to feel he was mine.

"Can I join your little party?" My head shot up. Evan came out of the lake house and walked up to me with a saucy little smile on his face.

If he was there, who was I . . . I looked at the Evan lying beneath me: he was still smiling at me but began to fade like a puff of smoke. The real Evan sat down beside me and I smoothed my hair, unable to meet his sly gaze. "So this is what you dream about when I'm not around." He grinned.

My cheeks burned. *It was a dream.* And he'd seen everything. "You looked a lot better shirtless."

"I can always take it off," he teased.

"You know, you shouldn't spy on my dreams like that," I reproached him, embarrassed. "Besides, why did it take you so long to show up? I mean, while I was making out with the other you."

"You fell asleep—I picked you up and carried you to bed. But you didn't waste any time." He raised an eyebrow. "And for the record, I wasn't spying. I came to visit you and you were with that guy. If you want I can leave you two alone. I saw how you came onto him. Maybe I should be jealous."

"*That guy* was you. Or better," I stammered, "it was you as my imagination sees you."

A sexy smile appeared on Evan's face. "I'm really here now. What do you say we pick up from where you two left off?" he suggested, his voice provocative.

I laughed and punched him on the shoulder. "Stop teasing me!"

"I'm serious!" Evan protested, but I was still too embarrassed to consider his proposal. When Evan burst into my dreams, the line between reality and make-believe disappeared and everything became possible. It was just that he could read every emotion, every mood, so not only had he seen my attempt to seduce him on the beach, he must have also perceived my desperate need for him, to have him inside me. I blushed again.

"So I'm dreaming," I said, to break the tension. "At least I realize it now."

"Well, don't go running away," he warned, smiling. The last time I'd realized we were in a dream, I'd seized my chance to play around with him by hiding behind the doors of my mind. He'd found me. He always did.

"I would never run away from you," I whispered.

Evan's face suddenly darkened. "I wish I could believe that."

Strangely, though he was the custodian of dreams, I'd always been able to read Evan's soul almost as well as he could read mine. Who knew, maybe it was another one of the lethal secrets in my Witch nature. What I did know for sure was that Evan was afraid, and right then I could sense it. "You know, there's something I really miss, something I'm sure I'll never stop missing."

"What?" he asked.

He turned to look at me but I continued to stare straight ahead at the water. "Heaven." I took a deep breath, letting my heart warm at my only memory of Eden. It had been an incredible journey full of comforting sensations. Never again had I felt like I had there: complete and at peace. It was an amazing gift Evan had wanted to give me so I would be part of his world. Back then I hadn't known that evil lurked inside me. My presence there had given us away, though, and Evan had paid the price. I was a Witch, and my world would soon be Hell. There was no place for me in Heaven. Yet the longing for it was part of our punishment—mine and my Sisters'.

Evan squeezed my hand and stroked my palm with his thumb. "We can still go there."

I whipped my head around. What was he talking about? "Sure, if we want to enrage the celestial forces." I smiled. "More than we already have, that is."

Evan remained serious. "Come with me."

"What are you doing? Stop, this is crazy!"

He took my hands and rested his forehead against mine, giving me a smile. "We're not going to unleash any celestial forces. Trust me." I smiled back and nodded. The world all around us disappeared.

POETRY IN THE SKY

"Evan, where are we?" I looked around, breathless. The familiar sights of our little lake had disappeared and now, spread out before us, was a seemingly endless landscape. We were high up on a snow-covered mountain. The night concealed the ocean but its song reached us nonetheless.

"What place is this?" I insisted as he savored the infinite sensations filling me.

"We're in Norway," he finally answered, casting me an enquiring glance.

"In Norway? You brought me to *Norway*?!" I exclaimed in disbelief.

"Well, technically *you* brought me *here*, given that we're in your dream," Evan joked, but then became serious. "It's the closest place to Heaven there is on Earth. Look."

I looked away from him and my eyes filled with the magic that lit up the sky. "Oh my God . . ." I murmured. Above us, the colors of the aurora borealis danced in the dark night like rays of hope. The darkness was a theater curtain that lifted to reveal the display of lights performed just for us, like a poem recited by the sky.

"They call it the dance of the northern lights. I've always wanted to bring you here," Evan confessed. "Isn't it amazing?"

"Divine," I said, because there was no other word to describe it.

Pleased, Evan smiled. "Subterraneans love to come here. All the legends about us began in Norway. People can't see us, obviously, but some of them with slightly sharper senses can feel our presence. Coming here is a way to ease the burden of our punishment. It's not Heaven, but we can pretend it is. Though the Souls we've ferried aren't here, we can at least meet up with other Subterraneans." Evan laughed. "It's a lie I like to tell myself."

I took his hand and squeezed it, looking up at the sky again. "You're right. It's not Heaven. It's much more, because we're here together. Thank you for showing it to me."

Evan leaned over and brushed my ear with his lips. "It can be our Heaven," he whispered, and a shiver tickled my neck.

"I love you, Evan. I love you like I've never loved anyone." I rested my forehead against his and he closed his eyes.

"Say it again."

"I love you," I whispered against his mouth. I kissed him and a tear dampened our lips.

"*Samam*." As do I. Evan slowly pushed my hair from my face, his fingers lingering to caress it. "Being away from you is like having a noose around my heart: it hurts, but I know you'll always show up to loosen it. If I lost you now, the noose would turn to barbed wire and my heart would bleed for eternity."

"No, Evan." I shook my head, tears filling my eyes.

"For me, there can be no worse punishment than losing you."

"You're not going to lose me," I assured him.

"You can't be certain, Gemma. You saw what happens to you when the power controls you."

"Only because 1 haven't transformed yet. At that point *I'll* be controlling *it*. I'm not going to leave you, Evan. I'll never leave you."

"I wish I could believe you, but I can't. Even if you don't forget all about me, how will you renounce Sophìa? Who says she'll let you go?"

"Our agreement is that I transform. I never said I would live in Hell with them."

"Once the Bond is established, nothing will be more important to you."

I shook my head. What he was saying was unacceptable. "You and the baby are everything to me, do you understand that?"

"It's true now, but the venom will erase us from your heart."

"That's impossible. No power could ever erase you from my heart."

"Yes it can, if you don't remember us." Evan clenched his fists and growled with frustration. "Gemma, I've lived with Simon for a long time and I know what I'm talking about. Lots of times I've seen what happens when a memory is erased. The heart and mind are connected. If a memory is removed from the mind, no trace is left of the emotion it was connected to. You're deluding yourself."

"Ginevra believes in me. Why can't you? She's been through it herself!" If Ginevra thought I could do it, transform without the old me disappearing, there was hope. It wasn't just a delusion. I would become a Witch, and Evan and I would live on Earth together with our child. With Simon and Ginevra. Maybe one day we could even find a way to bring back Drake and Stella and then we would be a family again. A tear emerged, streaking my face, and at the same time, a doubt: what if Ginevra's confidence was influenced by her desire to have me as a Sister? No, that couldn't be. She would lose me too, in that case. I couldn't give in to doubt or I wouldn't be able to do it. I would respect the pact, but would do so by my own rules.

Evan cupped my face in his hands. "Things don't necessarily have to go that way. I'm begging you, at least consider my proposal."

"Drink Ambrosia?" I asked. He nodded. "Don't you realize how risky that would be for you? I won't let you fight my battles for me any more. Last time you paid far too high a price." I rubbed his shoulders. Beneath the fabric he still bore the marks of Hell, where he'd been captured and tortured over and over. I couldn't let that happen again. The very thought was unbearable.

"I don't care about the risks if I know you're safe. Ambrosia will eradicate the evil inside you. It'll purify you."

"But you can't be sure, can you? Your plan doesn't give us any guarantee that I'll be able to escape the transformation either. It might unleash even worse forces against us."

"How could it get any worse than it already is?!" Evan raged. Frustrated, he ran his hand over his face. "I don't want to lose you."

"You won't. I'll always love you, Evan. It's inconceivable that that would ever change. No spell will ever take me away from you." I looked him steadily in the eye and he swallowed. "I made a promise and I'm going to keep it—that way I'll be immortal and we can stay together forever."

Evan hid from me in grim silence, his mind filled with the demons that tortured him. Ever since he'd discovered my true nature, something in him had changed. There was no longer fear in his eyes when he battled the other Soldiers of Death. He was fierce and self-confident. The only thing that frightened him now was my transformation.

I raised my head, drawn by a sudden new gleam in the sky. The green of the aurora slowly faded to red, like a dark omen. Evan stared at it for a long while and his voice dropped to a melancholy whisper: *"In nocturnal skies a blood-red light glows / with dark, livid rays that stream through the air / whilst languish, uncertain, 'neath veils of rose / all seven suns of the frigid Great Bear."*

"That's beautiful," I said softly, my eyes captivated by the tongues of fire that pierced the darkness. The sight was magnificent yet also frightening, like the second life that had been granted to me—a destiny that sooner or later would be tinged the color of my blood, just like the red in the sky that night.

"A poet wrote it in 1870," Evan explained, to banish the dismal thoughts from my heart. "Red northern lights are the rarest kind. They appear every ten years, sometimes even less frequently. The color is caused by the gases present in the atmosphere, their electrical state, and the energy of the particles that strike them."

"What causes the color red?"

"Molecular oxygen. Atomic oxygen, on the other hand, causes the color green."

"Blue is my favorite," I admitted. *Because it reminds me of your eyes.*

"Blue isn't as rare as red, but not as common as green, either. It's caused by nitrogen."

I covered my belly with my hand and Evan rested his hand on mine. He sat down behind me and continued to hold me while in the sky coronas and brilliant rays of light moved like a huge veil that painted the night. *What color would our baby's eyes be?*

"Evan . . ." I laced my fingers with his. How I wished I knew what would become of us and the baby I carried. "Do you ever wonder what he'll be like?"

"Every day."

"And?"

"It's not important if he's a Subterranean or a simple mortal. He's the living proof of our great love—that's all that matters." I squeezed his hand tighter, listening to the sounds of the northern lights. "Hear that?" he said softly, behind me. Distant whispers drifted through the air. When Evan's lips brushed my ear I closed my eyes. "That's the auroral chorus. You can't imagine how many incredible legends it's inspired."

"Tell me one," I encouraged him, knowing how much mythology fascinated him. I thought back to the night we'd spent beneath the stars, long ago, when I was still oblivious to the terrible fate in store for me and he was preparing to say goodbye forever. It felt like centuries had passed since then.

"I don't know any," he said.

I smiled. "Liar," I accused him, but he remained serious.

"There are lots of different beliefs. Some indigenous tribes, for example, thought the lights were reflections of a 'dance of fire' performed by sprites. To the Inuit in Greenland they were the spirits of children who had died violent deaths or on their birthdays. The Vikings, on the other hand, thought it was the work of the Valkyries who rode through the sky in shining armor on their steeds."

That was why he didn't want to talk to me about it. "So it's my fault, is it? Well, my Sisters', I mean, of course," I said with a grin, but the comment seemed to hit Evan hard. "I'm sorry. That was a lame joke."

"Don't worry," he reassured me, holding me tighter. "You know there are people who go aurora hunting? They wait up for nights on end to see them and then race over the snow following them."

"I guess it must be worth it. Seeing them has been such an exciting experience."

"For me too." Evan stood up and held out his hand. "Come on, I want to introduce you to someone."

I frowned but took his hand without questioning him. We walked down a hill and I smiled in amazement when I saw what awaited us. "What's this?!" I asked, electrified.

"Your carriage, my lady." Evan smiled and let go of my hand.

I went toward the five exquisite white wolves in front of the little sled. Fascinated, I approached them cautiously. Their eyes were as clear as ice, as if they too were Subterraneans, their fur snow-white streaked with gray. As I neared them, the wolves bowed to me. I knelt down and they came closer. At first they sniffed me, but then began to lick my face. I laughed as they rubbed against me.

"What should we call them? We have to give them names!" When Evan saw my enthusiasm his laughter filled the night. In my dreams, my emotions became his, because he could perceive them. "Hey, champ," I whispered to the lead wolf. "I bet you're the bravest. I'll call you Balto."

"Like one of the dogs that brought diphtheria serum to Nome, Alaska during the epidemic of winter 1925." I nodded, even though

Evan hadn't really posed it as a question. He'd probably been there when those people died, but I didn't dare ask.

"'Endurance, fidelity, intelligence,'" I said, quoting from the inscription dedicated to the dog in New York's Central Park. They'd even made a cartoon about him, and it had made me cry rivers of tears. "Yes, it's decided: I'm calling you Balto," I repeated, stroking his thick fur. Another wolf licked me. It tickled. He had eyes so clear they looked like crystal. "And you'll be White Fang."

Evan stared at me inquisitively. "Another hero of the ice?"

I smiled to myself. Evan wasn't as well-versed in fictional characters as he was in historical ones. "In a way, yeah. He's the title character of a Jack London book. When I was four, my mother would read it to me every night." Maybe that was why I had become so passionate about reading.

"We have to go," Evan said. "Come on. Want to take a spin?"

I smiled and took the hand he was holding out to me. He raised mine to his lips, turned it over and kissed my palm, his gray eyes locked on mine, then walked me to the sled and bowed gallantly.

I laughed. "Do I sit here?" I pointed at a tiny seat big enough for only one person.

"No, stay close to me." He raised an eyebrow, inviting me to join him on the footboards. "The view is better from here. Careful." He showed me where to put my feet and I took hold of the handlebar in front of me. Evan took his place behind me and wrapped his arms around me, resting his hands on top of mine. "Ready?" I nodded, my eyes sparkling with joy. "Hold on tight. We're going to chase the aurora."

Evan perceived my thoughts and held me tighter, breathing against my neck. "Cold?"

I shook my head. "I grew up in the Adirondacks. I'm used to the cold."

"The cold in Scandinavia is different, though."

"We're in my dream," I reminded him. "You're all I need to keep warm." Evan laughed, tickling my skin. He nibbled at my neck, sending a wave of tingles through my body. "Evan, stop it!"

"Stop what?" His teeth tickled me again. He was smiling.

"You're teasing me."

"I would never!" he cried.

"Just warn me if you plan to make this thing fly at some point."

Evan burst out laughing. "Who do you think I am, Santa Claus?"

The wolves stopped beside a wooden cabin half-buried in the snow. Evan looked at the cabin and then at me, confused. I smiled and took him by the hand, leading him inside.

"I wasn't expecting this, but it's an excellent change of plans," he said, pleased.

"After all, it's *my* dream, isn't it?"

"I agree. Let's let it end the way it began." He took me in his arms and the door closed behind us. I laughed as he opened it a second later only to hang out a do-not-disturb sign.

"There's a little stardust in each of us, but you must have more of it than other people," Evan whispered against my neck.

I closed my eyes as the shiver lingered against my skin. "Do you think we'll ever find this kind of peace in our waking life?" I asked as we listened to the fire crackle. I would gladly remain asleep if it meant I could stay there, embracing Evan in our dreams. Only there could we find peace. As soon as I woke up, harsh reality always returned to overwhelm us.

"That's what we're fighting for. As long as we're together, there's hope."

I stroked his Subterranean tattoo, running my fingers along the lines that marked his muscles, and Evan kissed my forehead. We were naked, on the floor, the fire burning in a stone brazier in the middle of the room. We had made love as though it were our last night together and then started all over again. I didn't know how much of the night we had left, but I wanted it to be endless.

"Will you always love me, Evan?"

"Yes, my love."

"Until when?"

"Beyond death."

I breathed in against his chest and closed my eyes, my hands clasped around his dog tag.

STAY WITH ME

"A sleigh drawn by white wolves!" I laughed, thinking back to the magical night I'd spent with Evan just hours earlier. "How'd you come up with the idea, anyway?"

Evan walked beside me down the school hallway, where the walls, lockers, and even the floors were decked out for the Winter Carnival. On the floor, wide strips of tape in yellow, red, green, and blue indicated the various teams while decorations and streamers in the same colors hung from the ceiling—though a sign on the wall read:

> Yellow, red, green, or blue,
> whatever color you choose,
> we all represent our high school!

"You sure seemed to enjoy it . . . judging from the reward you gave me," Evan said with a sly smile.

"Shh! Do you want someone to hear?" I reproached him, looking around. I blushed and chewed on the sleeve of my yellow sweatshirt. But it was true—it had been so romantic that in the end I'd practically pounced on him.

"I bet I know what you're thinking about," he teased me, one eyebrow raised.

"Why, you . . . !" I shot back, punching his shoulder. "I was just saying that knowing *you,* I would have expected a snowmobile instead."

"But I know *you* and knew you wouldn't be able to resist a pack of pure-white wolves." He smiled.

He was right, though I wished I could wipe that mischievous little smile off his face. Evan was the real wolf—and I was his prey.

"Anyway, there's something I was going to ask you last night. Who knows why I forg—Would you stop smirking?!" Evan laughed out loud. "Okay, okay. I know why I forgot. Happy?"

"Very," he replied, pleased.

The memory of his hands on me, his mouth on every inch of my skin, our naked bodies entwined in front of the fire made me lose my train of thought for a second. The mental image left my blood boiling.

"Well? What is it you wanted to ask?"

"Huh?" I blinked. Evan had stopped, leaning his shoulder against my locker. "Oh, yeah, right. Your birthday. You've never told me what day it is."

He smiled and shook his head. "I'm not telling you."

"Aw, come on! You know I won't stop asking until you do!"

"I have all the time in the world."

"Then I won't let you touch me until you've told me," I threatened.

Evan grabbed me by the shirt and pulled me against him. "You sure you'll be able to resist me?" he murmured, inches from my face. He touched his nose to mine and I felt butterflies in my stomach. I was lost to him. The problem was that he knew it. The wonderful thing was that he felt the same about me. I was about to kiss him when he smiled against my lips. "I would have bet." He was being so cheeky I could have hit him, but he pressed me back against the lockers and kissed me passionately. "Sorry. I can't resist you either," he admitted.

"So will you tell me when your birthday is?"

"No."

"Damn it!"

"It might even have been last night. What difference does it make?"

My eyes opened wide. "Was it last night? If it was you *have to* tell me."

"If it was, it means you've already given me a gift. More than one, actually." He laughed. "In any case, no. It wasn't last night."

"Promise me you'll tell me some time, at least. I know you're just doing this to spite me."

Evan laughed again. How he loved teasing me. After all the time we'd spent together, that had never changed. I groaned in exasperation. I was stubborn, but he was unbeatable. "Any chance I could sweet-talk it out of you?" I raised an eyebrow and stroked his chest to provoke him.

He took my hand and kissed my thumb. Gazing into my eyes, he brushed it with his tongue. "Alas, I fear you would only forget the question yet again, m'lady," he replied, his voice sensual but his eyes glinting with mockery.

Pouting, I pulled back my hand. "What if an Executioner suddenly popped out of nowhere and offed me? You'd let me die without knowing when your birthday is?"

"First, I would kill him before he could even get close to you. Second, we're not going to see any more Subterraneans around here for quite some time."

"Right." That was what I hoped, and the others seemed convinced of it too. While Evan and I had been fooling around in the mountain cabin the night before, Ginevra and the other Witches had reinforced the security measures. After the suicides of the two Angels of Death and the attack of the twin Devas, no precaution was too much.

"Hey." Evan took both my hands and rested his forehead on mine. "You're safe now," he whispered. I nodded. "This is an important time, your last year of school, and our baby is growing inside you." He rested his hand on my belly. "I mean to spend every minute with you. No Subterranean is going to cheat me of any more time with you or he'll be dead before he's even given his orders."

I smiled and Evan stroked my lip with his thumb while keeping his other hand protectively over my belly. Just then, we felt a movement. Our jaws dropped. *The baby had kicked.* "Did you feel that?" Evan asked, a look of wonderment on his face.

I nodded, my eyes glistening. A silent tear slid down my face and Evan wiped it away with his thumb and hugged me, both of us smiling.

"Hey guys!"

"Jeneane at three o'clock," Evan warned me.

I quickly tried to dry my tears before she could see them, but it was too late. "Hey, what's up?" She hurried over and took me by the shoulders, then shot a reproachful glance at Evan. "If I find out you hurt her, you're going to have to answer to me, Mr. Hunk," she told him. Evan raised his hands defensively, hiding a smile.

I laughed and the tears returned to fill my eyes. "Don't worry, Jeneane, they're tears of joy. The baby just kicked for the first time."

"Oh my God!" she squealed, holding me tight. "No way! Let me feel . . ." She rested a hand on my belly but nothing happened.

"Sorry, I can't control it."

"No problem." She hugged me again. "And here I figured the pregnancy was just an excuse for you to get out of class once in a while!"

"What?" I gasped, confused.

"Come on, I'm not the only one! There are even bets being made around school. Tons of people don't believe you're really pregnant. You're in better shape than my mom."

"Oh, thanks. You mean that as a compliment?"

"Hello! My mother's a knockout. I work up a sweat trying to keep up with her. You eat like an elephant and you've only gained, what, five pounds? I gain weight just by looking at food. So yeah, it was totally a compliment."

Everything considered, Jeneane was right. In my ample sweatshirt for the games, no one would have imagined I was expecting a baby. "I've got a fast metabolism. It's true, my belly hasn't grown much, but he's right here." I touched my middle. "And today he let us feel his presence for the first time."

Just then, Faith, Brandon, and Jake came walking up behind her. "The baby kicked!" Jeneane told them before they could even say hi.

"Perfect," I grumbled to Evan. "Pretty soon the whole school's going to know."

"Don't worry, it's wonderful."

"Okay, but the two of us aren't through talking about your birthday." Evan laughed.

"Dude, cool!" Jake exclaimed, moving closer.

"Out of my way, I want to feel it too!" Brandon exclaimed. "Can we?" A moment later the two huge jocks were leaning over my belly, listening.

"Move it, champs. You look like a couple of little girls!" Jeneane teased, pushing them aside.

"Hey, you two." Evan stared at them. "I think that's enough. Keep your hands to yourself."

"Okay, okay," I said, moving away from the little group gathered around me. "That's enough for now."

"But I haven't felt it yet!" Jeneane protested. She sighed. "I want to have a baby in my belly too."

"I can put one there for you if you want," Brandon said, seizing the moment as he raised an eyebrow.

"Pervert!" she snapped, hitting him on the head.

"Ow! You said you wanted one! I was just offering to help. You should be thanking me!" Jeneane hit him again. "Ow! What did I say?!" The whole group laughed as he rubbed his head.

Jeneane took his hand. "Come on, the dodgeball game starts in half an hour. If we beat our opponents, maybe afterwards I'll show you my boobs." A broad smile spread over Brandon's face and he waggled his eyebrows at us as she dragged him away. "Gemma, bathroom in five minutes," Jeneane ordered me before disappearing into the crowd.

"What an asshat!" Jake sneered. "We'd better go keep an eye on them. He would get himself embalmed for that girl."

"Coming with us?" Faith asked, her long red ponytail contrasting with her Winter Carnival outfit. Yellow was definitely her color.

"You guys go on ahead," I said. "We'll meet up in the bathroom in five."

"Okay—I wouldn't miss it for anything in the world," Jake said.

"You're not invited."

"Here you are." Ginevra turned the corner just then. She was with Camelia, the most eccentric and sensual of the Sisters. In her altered uniform she was stunning. Someone had snitched on them to the principal, who had come charging out of his office to explain to them that it was against the rules. Needless to say, he'd forgotten all about it the second he'd seen them approach.

"Just in time for the war paint."

"Sounds interesting," Camelia exclaimed. "What are we waiting for?" Anya and Nausyka had stayed to guard the Subterraneans and the Twins, but Camelia had wanted to come with me. She and Nausyka together would have been too much.

"War paint?" Evan asked, looking amused.

"That's what Jeneane calls it. Why do you think she's waiting for us in the bathroom? Stay here. She's liable to paint you too," I warned him, giving him a peck on the lips.

"I'll take your advice, then. See you later!"

"And don't forget your promise!"

Evan smiled. "What promise?"

I headed to the bathroom with Ginevra and Camelia. Everyone turned as we walked by, astounded by the magnetism the two Witches emanated. Of course, their close-fitting outfits and tall boots helped. Even I had a hard time taking my eyes off them. Part of me was secretly electrified about becoming like them, about mastering my sensuality like they did and finally feeling more confident.

"Look out," Camelia said to a boy a moment before he ran smack dab into an open locker. She shrugged, a sexy smile on her lips. "I warned him." I laughed with my Sisters as he touched his forehead, still unable to take his eyes off us.

My Sisters. It was strange how easily I managed to think of them that way. Though I hadn't transformed yet, I could already feel the power connecting us. Ginevra said it was because of the Bond—the mystical connection that would be cemented by a bite from my Dakor—and I already sensed its power. Being with them made me feel good, and I could tell the same thing went for Ginevra. She'd been beaming lately, ever since they'd started fighting together to protect me. And I was happy it was because of me. I'd given her back part of her old world.

"I heard people are getting ready for a war here." Camelia walked into the girls' room, drawing the attention of Faith and Jeneane, who was painting yellow lines on her face.

"Not the kind you're thinking of," Ginevra communicated telepathically to rein her in. I stared at her, shocked. I'd heard her!

"Relax, little Sister. I just want to have some fun."

"As long as you remember your place. This isn't the Hunt, after all."

"What do you mean, the hunt?" I thought, and they both turned to look at me.

"A more exciting kind of competition." Camelia winked at me, tacitly promising I would soon find out once I was in Hell. "Well? Is it my turn yet?" she asked, this time aloud.

"Get in line, Miss America. I'm going first," Jeneane replied, intent on doing up her face in the mirror. The big yellow pencil slipped in her hand, leaving a broad smear across her cheek all the way up to her ear.

"Now is it my turn?" Camelia asked, a little smile on her lips. Faith laughed but tried to hide it from her friend. Jeneane couldn't have known it was the Witch who'd made her mess it up, but she shot her a deadly glare all the same.

"C'mon, hand it over," I said, stepping forward and taking the pencil out of her hand. I had to be careful around Camelia. Though they all did their best to control themselves, they weren't accustomed to interacting with mortals, and Jeneane might end up paying a serious price. Wiping off the smear, I made a new mark and colored her lips yellow while Faith drew little flowers on her temples. That morning the two of them, like almost all the girls in school, had dyed one or more locks of their hair yellow to imitate Camelia. With her orange hair streaked with yellow, her head looked like a sunset. I was sure she was proud of how she'd influenced my friends . . . and the rest of the school.

"I'm used to it."

"Huh?" Jeneane asked.

"Nothing," I quickly answered for Camelia, casting a reproachful glance at my Sister for responding to my thoughts out loud. She laughed, not caring in the least.

"Do you have only one pencil?" I asked as I finished touching up Faith's face.

"We gave the other one to the guys."

I did Ginevra's face and then started on Camelia. She stared me straight in the eye the whole time and I felt a strange energy filling me. That always happened with them. They looked at me like someone would look at a lover.

"Your turn," she murmured, her voice hypnotic. I gave the pencil to Ginevra so she could do me but Camelia snatched it out of her hand. "Leave it to me."

I blinked. She was so close I almost felt embarrassed. She drew on my face and then leaned over me.

"*Don't.*" Ginevra's voice burst into our minds. I shook myself free of Camelia's spell. She ran her thumb over my lip, staring at me with a slight smile, her eyes gray and sensual.

"Hey, is your friend a lesbian?" I held my breath at Jeneane's remark, afraid of how Camelia might react, but she just laughed and moved closer to her.

"Never say never." Sliding her hand from Jeneane's neck to her chest, she whispered against her lips, "Want to try something new, little mortal?" Captivated by Camelia's lips, Jeneane didn't reply.

"*Gwen!*"

"*That's enough, Camelia! You can't bewitch the girls. You can't do it to* anyone. *We've already talked about this,*" Ginevra ordered her in her mind.

Faith walked out of one of the stalls and stared at them, confused. "Um, what's going on?"

Reluctantly, Camelia moved away from Jeneane. "Nothing fun, it seems," the Witch complained.

"Where's Peter?" I asked, to change the subject.

"Oh, I think I heard he was with a girl," Faith said.

"Wow! Peter, with a girl? Anyone I know?" I asked excitedly.

"She's a friend of yours. The one who was with you yesterday," Jeneane said.

"We aren't friends. We're Sisters," Camelia replied contemptuously. I barely heard her. My happiness had been shattered by Jeneane's words. I looked at Ginevra, who shrugged.

"Sorry, I don't know anything about it. I thought she was guarding the prisoners."

"Gwen, you've got to tell Nausyka to stay away from him. What does she want from him, anyway?"

"Calm down. I'll talk to her."

I was able to communicate mentally with Ginevra more regularly now. My powers were growing stronger. Or could it have been my anger that intensified them?

"Hey, Gemma, what's wrong?" Faith asked, bringing me back to them. She rested her hand on my shoulder and I realized I was shaking.

"Nothing. Nothing's wrong," I replied, trying to calm myself.

"You're jealous!" Jeneane exclaimed. "What have I always told you, little Joey? Why choose between Dawson and Pacey when you can have them both?"

"That's what I always say! I underestimated you," Camelia chimed in, "even if I don't know who those people are."

"You're crazy, Jeneane. Evan, Peter, and I have never been a triangle and we never will be. Get that through your head once and for all. I'm expecting Evan's baby!"

"So what? What are you going to do? Get married? Live happily ever after? Sooner or later you might want a little diversion."

"What the—"

"Chill, okay? I was only kidding! There's never been a more lopsided triangle than yours. Nobody could come between you two. Romeo and Juliet! You're disgustingly inseparable. Still . . . you're really not jealous about Peter? Not even a little?"

"Not even a little. I'm just a bit worried about him. We grew up together and I care about him. You don't know Nausyka. She can be a real witch."

"Speaking of witches, who was the redhead at your place last night? She seemed like a total bitch."

Camelia stepped in front of her, her expression threatening. "Don't you dare say that again. Devina is my Sister."

"I could've guessed that," Jeneane shot back sardonically. "What'd they feed you when you were babies?" *All as pretty as they are bitchy,* she thought.

"Okay, time to go!" I exclaimed before things got ugly.

"Hey, Gemma, how are you?" Faith asked as we walked out the door. "After your dizzy spell at the Ice Castle, I mean."

"Fine. Evan just took me home. Why, did you stop by to see me?" I asked, suddenly remembering that Evan had ordered them to go home.

"We were on our way home, but Peter was really worried about you. He wanted to make sure you were okay."

"He didn't mention it. He texted me this morning but didn't say anything about you guys stopping by."

"Because that girl wouldn't let us in. She practically kicked us out." Faith laughed, but I was thinking of Peter. His brain had obeyed Simon's order, but his love for me was so deep that he'd stopped by to see me first. He couldn't get near Nausyka. I had to protect him because there was only one thing that Witch wanted from him: his soul.

"I can't believe the baby kicked and I wasn't there to feel it!" Ginevra whined as we headed toward the gym. We'd stopped off at our lockers so Jeneane could put away the makeup, while I'd picked up my camera and—just in case—the novel about aliens I hadn't finished yet. "I'm not leaving your side until I've felt it too."

"Don't worry. It'll happen again, Gwen."

"Have you chosen a name yet?"

"Yes, but don't go rummaging through my brain because I have no intention of letting you find out what it is."

"Oh, come on! I didn't teach you to block your mind so you could use it against *me*. We're Sisters. There shouldn't be secrets between us."

I smiled. I'd inadvertently given Ginevra a challenge and I knew she wouldn't give in until she'd won. "We're not Sisters with a capital S yet."

"Yes we are. You and I always have been."

"You'll find out the name when the time is right."

"But—"

I slipped into the gym before she could try to persuade me. A murmur filled the large room, peppered with the squeal of the players' sneakers as they warmed up on the court. The dodgeball game was about to begin and the stands were filling up fast, taking on the colors of the various teams. We were about to battle the sophomores.

"Root for us, Gemma!" Faith exclaimed, to sugarcoat the pill. She knew how much I loved dodgeball and the Winter Carnival in general. I'd always been athletic. Competition exhilarated me and when I went out onto the field, the rest of the world disappeared.

"I bet you won't need it." With Camelia and Ginevra playing, their opponents didn't have a chance. "Hit them all!"

"Come on, I can't wait to try out this new game!" Camelia exclaimed excitedly as she strode onto the court.

"Don't worry, Gemma. I'll keep an eye on her. She's just here to have fun."

"Nausyka was too, but you saw what happened at the game yesterday, didn't you?"

"Relax. It won't happen this time. I'll keep her under control."

"Okay, I trust you." All my friends were there in the building, people I'd grown up with and cared a lot about. I didn't want any of their souls to be compromised purely on a whim.

"I said relax!" Ginevra insisted, following my train of thought. I looked around, searching for Camelia, and spotted Peter. He was already on the court with Brandon and Jake. No sign of Nausyka. *Thank Heaven.*

The referee gave them instructions as they got ready. I'd already explained the rules of the game to Ginevra and Camelia, and they'd found them pretty funny. I was sorry I couldn't play too, but when I thought of the little kick I'd felt earlier, my disappointment disappeared. I stroked my belly and smiled.

The referee blew his whistle to alert the players and I rushed to the sideline to snap a few shots for the yearbook. Along the central line—the dead zone—a number of balls were lined up. The rival teams were positioned on opposite sides behind the end lines, ready to race to the center and grab as many balls as possible for their own team.

When the referee blew his whistle again, officially starting the first game, the players charged toward the balls and hurried back to their respective fields. Seconds later, a full-fledged war broke out on the court.

I took some snapshots: players on the ground, doubled over laughing, others flying through the air with funny looks on their faces as they dodged a ball just about to hit them. I even managed to capture the moment a player was taken out by enemy fire, the ball frozen on his chest and his eyes bulging. The players could defend themselves only by warding off an attack with a ball. Those hit directly by a ball were "killed" and had to leave the court until one of their teammates brought them back in by catching one of their adversaries' balls. By the end of the games, there would be a few bruises and lots of laughs.

Ginevra and Camelia were having loads of fun. It was easier for them to catch the balls and at times they even helped out members of our team. Peter hit the last of our remaining adversaries and the referee blew the whistle, announcing the end of the first game.

The players traded sides and the balls were once again placed mid-court. We had to win seven three-minute games to win the entire match. I zoomed in on Faith in her starting position and focused on her lily-white face, green eyes, and freckled nose. She could have been a Witch, she was so pretty.

I got ready to steal a few more shots when someone grabbed me by the waist. "Hiding from me?" Evan whispered in my ear, pressing up against me so tightly I couldn't turn around. A quiver ran down my back.

"There's no place on Earth I could hide from you. And I would never want to anyway," I assured him, smiling.

"Hey, you two, that's not a sporting event we practice on my court. Back to the stands," the gym teacher told us.

"Come with me." Evan took my hand and I blushed, seeing that the teacher was watching us.

"Where? The stands are over there."

"We'll hide together." The sexy smile I couldn't say no to appeared on his lips and he winked at me before pulling me toward the boys' locker rooms.

"Evan, no! I can't come in here!" I protested, embarrassed.

He took the camera from around my neck and put it on a bench together with my book. "Yes you can, if you're with me." Pushing me against the wall, he began to kiss me with burning desire, drawing me into his whirlwind of passion.

"Oh, Evan, stop," I panted as his lips touched my neck to then nibble my shoulder and his warm hands explored my body. *Oh, Evan, please don't stop,* I thought, consumed by the fire he'd ignited. "Someone might come in. The match is almost over."

His hands slid under my skirt and I moaned. Unable to hold back, I took off his shirt and stroked his bare shoulders as he devoured me with kisses. In a flash he'd freed me of my sweatshirt. I arched my back, dying to feel him closer, to feel him inside me, and he pushed me against the wall, pressing his erection against me.

"Oh, Jamie," he whispered as I melted.

"What's going on here?!" The gym teacher's voice boomed through the locker room and Evan pulled away from me to face him, his expression suddenly violent.

"Get. Out. Now," he warned, his face an inch away from the man's. "Gemma went home. You gave her a permission slip. Stop looking for her."

The teacher glanced at me and blinked, deep in thought. I sheepishly covered my chest with my arms. Nature hadn't been generous with me as far as that went, but recently I'd been spilling out of my bra. He left the room. A crowd of boys walked in on his heels and my eyes widened.

"Put your shirt on," Evan ordered me. I quickly slipped it on, but one of the boys spotted me in the process and whistled. Evan rushed him and slammed him against the wall before the boy knew what had hit him. "Don't even look at her," he threatened.

"Calm down, bro. I didn't do anything." The boy raised his hands, scared. No one in the room dared get close to Evan.

The locker room door opened and Peter walked in. His smile of victory died the moment he saw me there. "Gemma, what are you doing in here? What's up with your—" He moved closer, studying my eyes. I blinked, afraid the darkness had returned, and he pulled back, confused.

"Pet, I'm fine. Don't worry. We were just leaving."

Evan let go of the boy and picked his shirt up from the floor. "Yeah," Peter replied, staring at Evan's bare chest, "I can see that."

"Let's go, Gemma." Evan took my hand and I squeezed his with both of mine.

"Talk to you later," I told Peter as we left the locker room. Looking deflated, he nodded and disappeared behind the door as it closed after me.

"But it isn't over yet! I have to take pictures for the yearbook. What was all that about a permission slip?" I asked Evan, following him down the hall.

"I'm taking you away. They'll survive."

"Away? But where?"

"Where no one can disturb us." Evan stopped and pulled me against him. "I want to be alone with you," he whispered in my ear. "I can't stay away from you any longer."

My knees trembled from the desire his warm, sensual voice aroused in me. "Okay," I murmured, at the mercy of his spell.

He let me get my things from my locker before dragging me out of the school, where he took my hand again and led me to his car. I got into the big BMW, my heart pounding. I had made love with Evan a thousand times, but the desire I could see in his eyes sent an electric current through me, melting me. Two fires were poised to merge and spread, and the anticipation was as scorching hot as the air separating them. *When I Was Your Man* by Bruno Mars was playing on the radio. As we drove off, Evan lifted my hand and kissed my palm, taking his eyes off the road to look at me. It was one of the gestures I'd missed most when he was in Hell, and a smile spontaneously blossomed on my lips.

"Now would you mind telling me what got into you back there in the locker room?" I'd felt the wall shudder when Evan slammed the boy against it. I hoped someone had taken him to the nurse's office.

Evan looked at me and kissed my palm again. "You're mine," he said, looking me in the eye.

"I think everyone already knows that," I joked. After all, the guy hadn't done anything wrong. Evan's reaction had been a bit harsh, and yet part of me was smiling at how he'd defended my honor. He'd been jealous because I was stripped down to my bra in front of a bunch of other boys. I recalled how his back muscles had tautened when he was holding the kid against the wall, and for a second I got lost in the memory.

"Hey." I shook myself out of my thoughts and realized Evan was staring at me. "You with me?"

"What is it?" I asked, worried, quickly lowering the visor to check my face in the mirror. "Are my eyes okay? Is something wrong with me again?"

Evan laughed. "No, Gemma. There's nothing wrong, believe me." His eyes slid down my body, stopping on my miniskirt. I was wearing over-the-knee socks, but my thighs were bare. "I was just admiring how sexy you are in that outfit. I'm jealous of my own eyes, because they can explore you while my poor hands are forced to stay on the wheel."

His impatience made me smile. "We're almost there, Evan. In a matter of minutes they'll be able to touch me all they want."

He rested his hand between my thighs and when I slowly opened them he slipped it beneath my skirt and stroked my underwear with his thumb. I held my breath, my heart skipping a beat, and a wave of heat flowed like lava to the spot where he was touching me.

"I'm going to do a lot more than that," he said, his gaze brimming with promises.

My body trembled. When he stared at me, Evan never hid his desire for me. *He wanted me.* He wanted me to be his. At every moment. He never got enough. Neither did I. We were hungry for each other's vital essence.

The car stopped outside our hideaway, the house on the lake. I reached over to open the door, but Evan put out a hand and stopped me. "Aren't we going in?" I asked, confused.

"No, it's snowing. Let's stay here. Have some alone time." Evan raised an eyebrow and leaned in to kiss me. His lips still on mine, he climbed over the gearshift and sat down beside me on my seat. He was so close it made me tremble. I slipped my knee between his legs to entwine mine with his. Evan gazed at me tenderly, the creases under his eyes driving me wild, and swept the hair off my face. My lips were so close to his I could smell the scent of his breath.

"People seem to interrupt us nonstop," I murmured, impulsively raising my chin to kiss his lips.

"No one will do it here," he assured me. He kissed me back, gently brushing his tongue against mine.

Just months ago, I'd been afraid an Angel could never succumb to his carnal desires, that it was forbidden to him. Even if that had been true, it wouldn't have mattered to Evan. Together we had explored the universe, losing ourselves and rediscovering the light. Every time.

"Evan, will you ever get tired of risking everything for me?"

"I've already broken all the rules I know of to be with you, and if I discover more I'll break those too."

"Will it always be true? Even if I—" He rested his finger on my lips, keeping me from going on, but I took his hand and lowered it. "Even if I get lost during the transformation?"

He swallowed and looked me straight in the eye. "Then I'll find you and bring you back." He slid his hand down my nape and rested his forehead against mine. I knew his outer confidence was only a mask and that just beneath the surface hid the fear it might actually happen.

"I'm afraid I was what set you off in the locker room," I confessed bitterly.

Evan chuckled and stroked my hair. "The only fault you have is being so beautiful it made me lose my mind. Your power didn't drive me to go at the kid, Gemma. If it had, I would know it. I've *always* felt the urge to kill anyone who gets close to you. You don't know how many times I've been on the verge of doing it. Especially with your friend Peter. I'm an Angel of Death, Gemma. It's an innate impulse. When those guys walked in and saw you half-naked, I . . . I lost it. Forgive me."

"Don't feel bad." I smiled and kissed him, holding him tight. "I like it when you fight for me," I admitted as the radio whispered the notes of *Young and Beautiful* by Lana Del Rey. I thought back to when I'd heard it in that same car on the way home from the long journey that had given me back my great love. After all the hardships and challenges, he was still there, supporting me, protecting me. *Loving me*. My future was uncertain, but there was one thing I had no doubt about: he would always be there.

"Think it's wise to skip school to be here?" he asked me suddenly.

"In my future there are Witches, a horde of celestial creatures dead set on killing me, and it's highly likely I'm going to become a plague to humanity. I don't care if it isn't wise to be here."

Evan leaned over and buried his nose in my hair, speaking in my ear. "I meant being here with me."

"I'm not afraid of you. I never have been."

"I'm the one who's afraid of me and what I might do to you, if you only . . ." he whispered, staring steadily at my lips.

"You don't need my permission," I replied, at the mercy of my emotions, and Evan kissed me passionately.

"It's cramped in here. Are you comfortable?"

"I'm fine," I murmured. He shifted and straddled me to leave me more room. "Do you ever think about your Ferrari?" I asked out of the blue. It had ended up in the water below the bridge after our accident. Ginevra could have gotten it back or given him a new one, but he didn't want her to. "You know, I have to admit I do miss it myself sometimes."

"Me too. But then I remember we couldn't do this in it." He reached out and the seat swung back. I laughed from fright and rested a hand on Evan's chest as he laughed too. A silence fell between us and my eyes found his. How was it possible to love someone so much? To the point that my heart ached every time I looked at him? Like this, with him on top of me, his arms extended to avoid crushing me and the dog tag dangling from his neck, he was more handsome than ever. Suddenly the distance felt unbearable. I wanted to have him closer, to meld with him. I pulled him to me as the notes of *All of Me* filled the car.

Recognizing the song, he looked at me and smiled, whispering the words against my skin like he'd done in my dream when we'd made love immersed in the magic of the colorful paints. *What would I do without your smart mouth? Drawing me in, and you kicking me out. You've got my head spinning, no kidding, I can't pin you down. What's going on in that beautiful mind? I'm your magical mystery ride. And I'm so dizzy, don't know what hit me, but I'll be all right. My head's underwater but I'm breathing fine. You're crazy and I'm out of my mind.* His hands slid down me, slowly exploring my body, his voice caressing my neck. I closed my eyes, swept away by emotion, and his lips touched my ear, sending a thousand shivers through me.

Give your all to me. I'll give my all to you. You're my end and my beginning, even when I lose I'm winning. I wrapped my arms around his neck and pulled him against me, erasing the distance between us. My hands made their way under his shirt and pushed it up to caress every muscle in his firm abdomen. He straightened up, grabbed it behind his head and pulled it off, refocusing his attention on me. Taking off my sweatshirt, he swiftly unhooked my bra. My heart pounded at the touch of his hot body against mine, skin against skin, as the snowflakes brushed against the car windows, peeking in at us.

"Want to make love with me?" he whispered against my skin.

"Every second," I said softly.

His hand slipped beneath my skirt. Suddenly it was very hot, and not because the heater was on. I unbuttoned his jeans and lowered them, grabbing his behind to move him closer. He held me tight and rubbed his erection against me, making me melt.

"Oh, Evan . . ." I whispered, intoxicated.

He pulled off my underwear. "Say it again," he whispered in ecstasy. "Say my name. Tell me you want me."

"I want you, Evan. I want you inside me." I slid my hands into his boxers, pushed them down and clasped his firm buttocks. He parted my legs with his knee and I arched my back, offering myself to him. Sensing my need, he entered me, drawing a moan from me and then another as he kissed my neck, my shoulder, my breast. I surrendered to him completely, to his lips that sent hot tingles all through my body, to his ragged breathing that mingled with mine, to the heat, all our own, as the forest all around us turned white.

His hand gripped my arm, his fingers grasping my hair tie and pulling it tight as though wanting to tear it off me. I sank my nails into his skin and he accelerated his pace, thrusting harder to fuse with me, filling my entire being with quivers.

"Stay with me, Jamie," he begged, rubbing his forehead, damp with perspiration, against my chin.

"Forever," I promised. No transformation would stifle our love. Evan gripped me tighter and his heat flooded my body as he climaxed inside me. He kissed me passionately and trapped my lip between his teeth. I moaned against his mouth, reaching ecstasy, and our breathing became one.

Evan rested his cheek against mine and cradled me in his arms as I wrapped my legs around his waist to stay connected to him. "Stay inside me, Evan," I begged, demanding from him a promise I desperately hoped I would be able to keep myself. Whatever his answer was, though, it would be a lie, because the choice wasn't up to him. Still, it was a lie we both needed.

He looked at me, his dark eyes probing mine, and swept the hair from my face. "Forever."

A SOLDIER OF DEATH

"April thirteenth," Evan whispered in my ear as I drew a heart on the fogged-up glass.

"Huh?" I turned to look at him, confused.

"My birthday. It's April thirteenth."

"Oh, so that explains it." I pretended not to be interested in the fact that, after my countless requests, he'd finally told me.

"Explains what, pray tell?"

I shrugged, keeping him in suspense. "You're an Aries."

"If we consider Western astrology, yes, I am an Aries. So what? Does that tell you anything?"

"It tells me everything!" I burst out, amused.

"I didn't know you believed in astrology."

I laughed. "Actually, I don't. I was just kidding."

"Ah, all right. And, just out of curiosity, what are Aries normally like?"

I ran my hand down his arm to his tattoo. "Brave . . . romantic, and also very protective," I stated, still drawing the heart on the glass with my other hand.

Evan reached out and finished my drawing, writing our combined name in it.

Gevan.

"I don't need a horoscope to know you're all those things and much more," he whispered when he was done.

"Yours is a fire sign," I continued. I, on the other hand, was an earth sign, which was why I was so pensive.

"All good qualities, basically." He raised an eyebrow, looking cocky.

"Don't get your hopes up. Aries are also very hotheaded and incredibly stubborn."

"Me? Hotheaded?"

"Says the guy who just beat up another guy for merely looking at his girlfriend."

"He would always be possessive of her because she was his."

"She was," I said softly, looking into his eyes, "and forever would be."

Evan's hungry gaze slid down my bare body as he touched me with his fingertips. "She couldn't blame him. She was naked in that locker room and no one else had permission to look at her."

"She didn't want anyone except him to look at her."

Evan rested his forehead against mine and sighed. "And yet he was desperate," he confessed, his voice trembling.

"Why?" I asked. I slid my hand into his hair and made him look at me.

"Because he was desperately in love with her. I have a desperate need of you, Jamie."

I closed my eyes and kissed his lips, losing myself in him. I knew what was hidden in his sweet declaration: fear. It continued to surface, haunting us like a ghost. Deep in my heart I hoped our love—born and raised amid trials and tribulations—could also survive this, the hardest of all ordeals. "No one can tell us what the future holds. Day after day, we need to live in the present, always hoping we'll have another tomorrow together," I murmured, quoting something Evan had said to me some time before.

He recognized it and chuckled. "Wait." He pulled his phone out of his jeans pocket. "I want to take a picture of this moment." Sliding his arm under my neck, he put his face next to mine and gazed at me for a moment, then snapped the shot. Eternal moments of fleeting bliss.

Evan and I stayed there in each other's arms for hours, listening to music as snow drifted through the branches like little sprites who'd come down from the sky to spy on us. We talked about our baby, about the Witches who'd invaded our everyday lives, about Devina who'd never stopped longing to claim Evan's soul. We talked about Peter and my parents, who continued to worry about me.

At first my father had been against my living with Evan, but no human will could resist the power of a Witch like Ginevra, and she'd convinced him that letting me live with him was the best solution, especially for the baby. My mother was overjoyed to see me smiling again thanks to Evan. She was fine with my going to live with him on the condition that I stopped by to see them or called them every day. And that I finished high school, naturally. I lived up to my word and studied hard, though when I did my homework Evan often came to distract me from my obligations and I could never resist him for long.

"What are you thinking about?" Evan asked, noticing my smile.

"How stubborn you are."

"Again with the horoscope? And for the record, I didn't beat up that kid. I just threatened him a little."

"Lucky him. If you'd punched him, I doubt we'd be here talking about it. He'd be in the morgue and you'd be locked up."

"Only you can put me in chains." He winked at me and I punched him on the shoulder.

Evan climbed back into the driver's seat and got dressed, a smile on his lips. I'd promised my folks I would stop by the diner to see them, and judging from the noises my stomach was making, it had gotten late. Evan had yellow streaks on his forehead and along his cheekbones, and I couldn't help but giggle.

"What is it?" he asked, realizing I was laughing at him.

"You'd better clean up your face or my dad might get pissed off at you."

"More than usual?" Evan joked, not even glancing in the mirror as he put the car into reverse. He knew what I was talking about but didn't care.

"What were you just saying about not being stubborn?" I reached out and wiped his cheeks with my fingers. "Besides, my dad likes you. I know he doesn't show it, but that's only because he's always been really protective of me. Despite that, he gave you his blessing."

"I'm afraid he's going to change his mind about me if you show up looking like this." He flipped down the mirror in front of me so I could see myself.

"Oh my God." My eyes bulged and I covered my cheeks with both hands. My cheeks were red, my hair was one big tangle, and the yellow makeup was smeared ear to ear. What had happened between us was practically written all over my face. As Evan set off, I quickly cleaned myself up, combed my hair, and put it up in a ponytail with the hair tie I kept around my arm.

"You still wear it," he murmured, a fiery sadness in his eyes. Ever since we'd discovered why I never parted from my hair tie, Evan had looked at it angrily. I'd noticed how he'd clung to it while we were making love, though.

"I can't help it," I admitted. Putting it on was an unconscious response to my connection to my Dakor. Now that I knew that, I should have stopped wearing it, but it was hard. Looking at Evan, I rested my hand on his and changed the subject. "Can we stop by Adirondack Popcorn? I've got an incredible craving for Moose Crunch."

He relaxed and smiled. "Weren't you drooling over the thought of your mom's potato puff a second ago? Didn't you ask her to make it for you?"

"Sure. I'll eat that too. Why wouldn't I?"

Evan smiled. "Right. Why did I bother asking?"

"Hey, what are you insinuating?" I said, frowning. "It's not my fault I have a healthy appetite!"

"Anyone would already have gained sixty pounds with all you eat," he exclaimed with a grin.

"Shut up. I'm so hungry I could eat you too," I warned, giving him a dirty look.

He pulled up outside the popcorn shop at 2520 Main Street. Next to it was the Cabin Grill, and at the thought of French fries my stomach growled again. I lowered the window and the smell of caramel corn wafted over to me in the car. "Mmm . . . What sweet torture," I said, breathing it in deeply. "Hurry up or I'll make good on my threat."

Evan laughed and got out of the car. I watched him walk into the shop with its wooden façade and display window filled with treats. He came back minutes later with various bags of my favorite flavors of popcorn: peanut, caramel, and chocolate; maple, bourbon, and bacon; and toasted hazelnut.

"You're my angel." I almost ripped them out of his hands and stuffed my mouth like a glutton. "Oh my God," I whispered, closing my eyes. "I'm in heaven." Evan shook his head and chuckled. "Laugh at me all you want—it doesn't matter. I've got these." I clasped the bags to my chest and wolfed down more popcorn as the car headed toward my parents' diner.

"Wait. You've got some crumbs here." He leaned toward me and touched my lip with his thumb. Then he moved closer to kiss me, lingering as though tasting me. "Your mouth is like the nectar of the gods. It goes straight to my head."

"It's the popcorn. I told you it was good." Evan laughed again but then his expression slowly turned grim. "What is it?" I asked, worried I'd upset him somehow. "Sorry, I really am being a glutton."

"You're adorable," he reassured me.

"Then why do you look so serious? Is something the matter?"

"No, it's nothing. I was just concentrating, that's all." He looked at me with a little smile. "Mind if we take a quick detour?" He turned right, heading away from the diner.

"Why?" I asked with alarm. "Has something happened?"

"Nothing you need to worry about." The car came to a sudden halt. Evan turned to look at me and his eyes turned a silvery gray. A shiver ran down my back. He'd transformed.

"I'll be back in a sec."

I nodded and watched him get out of the car. He walked around to the other side, his eyes on me the whole time. No one on the street could see him in his angelic form, but I could. He stopped on the front walk of a house, took one last look at me, and disappeared.

I raised more caramel corn to my mouth, one piece after another, completely on edge. I didn't want to know where he'd gone. With me he was always so sweet, which made it hard to accept that inside him was a Soldier of Death.

Suddenly, Evan materialized in the driver's seat, making me jump. "That was fast," I said. He pressed his lips together, still serious. As he started the engine, someone inside the house screamed and I whipped my head in that direction. Evan switched on the radio so I wouldn't hear. A shiver turned my blood to ice as I realized what had happened. "You just killed someone," I murmured, petrified.

"Sorry," he said sadly. "For some orders we have very little advance notice. I didn't have time to drop you off and come back, and I didn't want to leave you alone. If it's any consolation, he was elderly and passed on quickly."

I nodded and blinked, shaken. For him it was so normal, but I still hadn't gotten used to his dark side. How could Evan accept mine? Maybe he wouldn't be able to either. I leaned back in my seat and an icy silence fell over us.

HEAVEN AND HELL

"Here you are at last!" My mom came up to me and gave me a big hug. "I hope my Squirrelicue is hungry, because I made her favorite dishes!"

"I could eat a horse," I assured her. The funny part was that it was true.

"Hello, Evan. Please have a seat." My mom took him by the arm and led him to his chair, casting me a look of approval. She'd always liked Evan in spite of everything. "Give me a second. I'll be right back."

"I'll come with you," I said. "That way I can say hi to Dad."

"I'll wait for you here," Evan said.

I followed my mom into the back and gave my dad a hug. "Careful, you'll get custard all over you," he warned, but I didn't care. "You here alone?" he asked warily.

"I'm with Evan, and our friends will be here any minute."

Dad grumbled something as Mom burst with enthusiasm. "Great! I'll go get the tables ready." She adored not only Ginevra but also her Sisters.

Our Sisters, suggested a voice inside me, but I instantly banished the thought. I helped Mom take out the food she'd made for Evan and me. She didn't know he didn't eat our food, but I would polish off all of it before she even noticed.

"Oh, the redheaded girl is already here," Mom told me.

Strange, I hadn't told Faith we'd be there. I looked up, but instead of Faith I saw Devina. *"Get away from him now,"* I ordered her telepathically. She turned toward me and smiled, resting her arm on Evan's shoulder.

"Why is it that Ginevra's cousin is so attached to Evan? Are they related?"

"No, she's a bitch, that's all," I grunted. The dish in my hands trembled. My mother shot me a concerned look; I didn't usually talk like that in front of her. A couple near me suddenly raised their voices and the girl slapped her boyfriend across the face. *It was my fault.* My anger had extended to them. I had to be more careful. I risked losing control.

"Don't worry, Squirrelicue. Evan only has eyes for you," Mom reassured me. "I have to go help your father, but I'll be back soon."

I took a deep breath to calm my nerves and went to sit next to Evan, but he grabbed me and made me sit on his lap. "You'll be more comfy here," he whispered, completely ignoring Devina. I rubbed my head against him and inside me clear skies returned. Evan was my beacon. He always managed to guide me through the darkness.

"You two are disgusting," Devina complained, leaning back in her chair.

"Either that, or you're dying of jealousy," I said insolently.

She snorted. "Don't delude yourself. I'm only here for the food. Your mother's cooking is divine."

"You have powers. Use them to cook for yourself."

"I like being served."

"Then here. Feed your face with this." I rudely shoved a dish at her and focused on Evan, kissing him sensually. Without objecting, he kissed me back as Devina watched. In her presence, Evan was always very affectionate with me—partly to reassure me, partly to make her understand that he was all mine.

"A-hem . . ." *My father.* "Let's not overdo it, okay?"

Devina smiled. She must have lured him out front. I shot her a lethal look and pulled away from Evan. "Sorry, Dad," I murmured, sitting in my seat.

"I brought you fries with black pepper, just how you like them."

"Thanks! You're the best." I got up to kiss his cheek and he calmed down.

"You're still my little girl. Don't forget it."

"I won't." I squeezed his arm affectionately and he disappeared into the back.

Just then, Ginevra and Simon appeared in the door along with four Witches: Safria, who had amazing violet-blue eyes that stood out against her black skin; Nausyka, with her silver hair and eyes of ice; Zhora—whom many of the Sisters called Suri—with her short mahogany-colored hair and incredible emerald-green eyes; and finally Camelia, who on that occasion was showing off both light- and dark-blue hair.

It must have been strange for them to be there, keeping their instincts under control. Maybe they considered it a game, a challenge to themselves that they didn't want to lose. And yet I saw the way their eyes caressed the other customers as though they were all potential prey. Everyone around us was fascinated by our group. If they'd been normal people dressed in the Witches' sexy, extravagant outfits, there would have been an outbreak of gossip in our town, but they charmed everyone. They were breathtakingly beautiful.

The Witches praised my mom's cooking, polishing it off as though they hadn't eaten for months, and she was so enthusiastic she kept filling up their plates, proud of their constant compliments. Once again, Ginevra assured me her Sisters wouldn't put the mortals' lives at risk. They were only there to spend some time with us and protect me if need be. Some of the Drusas, in the form of panthers, had stayed to watch over the prisoners in the dungeons, while other Witches had stayed with Sophìa because, like it or not, the evil in the world couldn't take a vacation. Their work had to go on.

"Gemma, you absolutely have to try this," Camelia told me. "It's *divine!*"

Her excitement made me smile. "It's all yours. I grew up with my mom's potato puff. I know what it tastes like."

"Don't you want even a little bit?" she asked sadly, almost as though I'd told her I didn't want to be her friend.

"Okay, I'll take some." A radiant smile lit up her face and I couldn't help but return it.

Ginevra squeezed my hand under the table and for a moment it felt like it was just her and me in the room. I knew exactly what she was feeling. She was happy to be there with her Sisters. *With me.* It must have been so hard for her to choose to leave them. I felt the bond and I hadn't even transformed yet. They already treated me like a Sister. People were spellbound by them. They looked at them, their eyes brimming with admiration, as though they were princesses. And maybe they actually were—they were princesses of darkness. And soon I would be one of them. A part of me that I tried to keep hidden wanted to be part of it, but then I remembered that the price was being separated from Evan. I would never be willing to pay that price.

The line between good and evil had grown so tenuous it was hard to tell them apart. The Witches were evil . . . yet they wanted to protect me. The Màsala, on the other hand, had done nothing but try to kill me. Where was my place? Who was I supposed to defend myself from? Sometimes I no longer knew.

And then there was Evan, there were Simon, Ginevra . . . and Drake. They were sacrificing everything for me. They'd protected me from the Subterraneans and the Witches, from both warring factions. It had always been a battle for souls between them, and now they both wanted mine—the Màsala, to send it to Heaven, where Evan and I would never be able to see each other again, and the Witches, to send it to Hell, where *maybe* there was still a chance for us.

Noticing I was in a daze, Evan squeezed my hand. I looked into his eyes and every doubt vanished. We were caught at the midpoint of the battle between good and evil. That was where our love was. Nothing else mattered.

The candles cast quivering lights and shadows that danced across the walls. The water in the tub was hot and the little cascade flowed from the rock with a sound that soothed my spirit.

Evan had gone on a mission to the other side of the world. I'd gone home with Simon and Ginevra, but then he too had been called to duty. Even with everything happening around us, they were Soldiers and their orders came before everything else . . . except me.

I smiled, thinking of how affectionately Evan and Simon protected me. Two Soldiers of Death battling for a mortal soul. A soul everyone was vying for. When it was all over, who would it belong to?

To me, I promised myself. That was the only way I could stay together with Evan. I moved closer to the little waterfall and let the water run over my head, filling me with its warmth, relaxing my every muscle. I moved my head to the right, then to the left. Suddenly I sensed a presence in the room and my eyes shot open.

"You going to stand there watching me?" I asked provocatively without turning around, my eyes on the rock wall.

Evan came over and rested his hands on the tub. "That was one of my options." I turned and looked into his eyes, which were as gray as the storm of desire that I knew raged inside him. God . . . Why did he stare at me like that? It drove me wild.

I moved closer and raised myself slightly, dangerously close to his face. "Or," I whispered against his mouth, "we could explore the other options."

Evan swallowed and his hand stroked my wet side. "I agree," he whispered, mesmerized by my lips. I grazed them just barely against his, igniting his desire, but instantly pulled back, toying with him. "Option one: I stand here and watch you take a bath for me," he murmured.

"The idea sounds enticing," I said playfully, still provoking him. I'd realized that I loved arousing him.

"Option two: I get undressed and take a bath with you. It *has* been a long day, you know . . ." He raised an eyebrow, his expression telling.

"I think I'll choose option three."

"Which is . . . ?"

I smiled and grabbed him by the shirt. "The one where I pull you in still dressed!"

"Wait, stop!" But it was too late. He emerged from the water, a saucy smile on his lips, and slicked back his hair. "You're getting mischievous! You want war?"

I shrieked when Evan lunged at me, splattering the floor. I tried to escape, but he grabbed me by the waist and pinned me down beneath him. "Now you're my prisoner."

I challenged his eyes of ice. "And what will you do with me?" I teased him again, moving my lips closer and then pulling them back.

Evan cupped my head in his hand and kissed my chin passionately. "I'll take you to heaven."

I moaned when he nibbled my shoulder, sending an electric charge surging through my entire body. Clinging to him, I hurriedly pulled off his wet shirt and unbuttoned his jeans, flinging them to the floor. We were naked, immersed in the hot water, one against the other. His hands moved over me, leaving shivers on my skin. All the while devouring me with kisses, he grabbed me by the bottom and pulled me astride him. My core throbbed with desire; I squeezed my legs around Evan's hips to feel his erection against me. Lifting me up slightly, he penetrated me, staying motionless, holding me tight. "Oh, Jamie. Why do you do this to me?" he whispered, clasping one of my breasts in his strong, warm hand. He stroked my nipple with his thumb and I felt it stiffen at his touch. He kissed it and rested his head on my chest. "You break down all my defenses," he murmured in desperation.

I cupped his face in my hands and kissed it, taking my fill of him. He was inside me, satiating me, completing me, like he always did. Grabbing the hair at the nape of his neck, I moved against him, pursuing the pleasure only he could give me.

"You'll take me to hell," he grunted, letting desire overwhelm him. He grabbed my buttocks and squeezed me tighter, thrusting with tender force. Our cheeks brushed together, our foreheads touched, our lips sought each other. We were in another world, a bubble all our own, intoxicated by the love that united us. It inundated us, touching our souls.

He bit my lip, panting in my ear, and a quiver made my heart tremble. I clung to Evan and a cry escaped me as I peaked. Evan gripped my bottom tighter and climaxed inside me with a groan roughened by desire. He held me tight, rubbing his cheek against mine. "You are my goddess," he whispered, his lips brushing my ear.

I smiled and kissed his shoulder. "Didn't you just say I would take you to hell?" I left more kisses on his neck, moving down to his chest, following the scars.

Evan nodded. "But I promised you heaven, remember?"

"You kept your promise, then, because I was just there."

DUSTY MEMORIES

"Why didn't you tell me right away when your birthday was?" I asked Evan. We were still in the tub, the soft light barely illuminating the room. He was behind me, stroking my back with a sponge, immersed in a cloud of white foam.

"It wasn't important," he replied, his voice suddenly sad. "So much time has gone by since I celebrated it that I barely remembered it."

"Tell the truth, Evan."

He remained silent, running the sponge over my neck before answering. "That was also the day my mother died." He dropped the sponge and caressed my arms, soothing the shiver that his confession had triggered. "There was a chance for me to see her," he continued in a whisper, "to say goodbye to her the way I hadn't been able to before I died. But I was out on a mission. Her soul left her body and I could have spoken to her, but I wasn't there. And so she passed to the other side. I missed my only chance."

"I'm sorry," I murmured in a tiny voice. A tear slid down my face. I should have realized there had to be a reason he hadn't wanted to tell me. My stubbornness had hurt him.

"You couldn't have known. Besides, like I said, it's been a long time. It's not important any more." I turned to look at him and nodded. He wiped a tear from my face and smiled. "I don't want to see you cry," he warned me. "Let's think of the present. It's much more . . . comforting." He raised an eyebrow and pulled me back against him, kissing me tenderly, then took some shampoo and applied it to my hair, his strong fingers gently massaging my scalp.

I closed my eyes, surrendering to the pleasurable sensation. "I like taking baths with you."

"I'm better than a spa," he boasted. "Full service." He winked at me and smiled.

"Will you visit me tonight?" I looked at him hopefully. Every time his gray eyes probed mine, I lost myself.

"I don't think I can. I'm going on a mission and won't be back in time. Sorry."

"Oh . . . " A bitter sigh escaped me. "So you'll be gone all night long?"

"And all day too, I think."

"I'll have nightmares." That always happened when he was gone. When he was in my dreams, he drove off all my demons.

Evan tucked my hair behind my ear. "I'll ask Ginevra to stay with you."

"No, there's no need. I'm safe now. I can handle a bad dream. Let's let her enjoy a little free time."

He nodded, though I wasn't sure he would listen to me, and asked, "Is there something I can do for you?"

I already had the answer to that. "Actually, there is."

"I'm all ears."

"Would you go up to the attic with me?"

Evan looked puzzled. The twins were in the attic, still imprisoned in the carbonado cage.

"I don't want to do anything rash," I reassured him.

"Of course not. Otherwise you wouldn't need to ask—you would have just gone and done it."

"Very funny."

"What's so important up there?"

"Something I wanted to get yesterday, but then they attacked me and—"

"When you say 'something' you mean a book, I presume."

I shrugged, holding back a smile. "You know me well."

"Don't you have two of them on the nightstand?" Evan was probably a little scared to take me there—not because of what the twins might do to me but because of what the carbonado might awaken in me.

"I've already finished those," I said, thinking about the series on aliens that I'd left in Evan's room. I bit my lip and batted my eyelashes.

"All right, I'll take you up there. Otherwise, knowing you, you'll probably go on your own."

I clapped my hands happily. I couldn't wait to have my *Jane Eyre* back. If I had to be alone that night, Rochester would keep me company.

We climbed out of the tub and got dressed. A big black panther was guarding the door and I smiled when I saw the red patch on its paw. It was Devina and she must have heard everything. Picking up on that thought, she flicked her tail at me and walked off with a low growl. *He was mine.* Sooner or later she would get it through her head.

Oblivious to our little battle to mark our territory, Evan took my hand and led me to the trapdoor that went to the attic. He opened it, went up the ladder first, and peered into the darkness. Pulling himself up, he offered me his hand to help me up. The lightbulb was gone—I'd made it explode—and outside a cold darkness had already fallen. Evan opened his palm and a sphere of light came to life, dimly illuminating the room. *Angel fire.* I stood there staring at it, almost hypnotized by its silvery glow. How could I be so fascinated by something that was such a serious danger to me? Once I transformed, that fire—so pure and radiant—would be the only weapon capable of killing me.

My heart beat faster. No. The energy making me quiver was coming from elsewhere. I followed my instinct and turned toward the cage at the far end of the attic. The two children were sitting on the floor, leaning back against the bars with their heads lolling forward as though sleeping . . . or dead. I truly hoped that wasn't the case. That cage was our only hope of living a peaceful life during our last remaining months. As though he'd sensed my thoughts, Evan squeezed my hand. "Well? Where do we start looking?"

"I-it should be over here," I stammered. "I don't understand. It was right here." Evan stepped forward and helped me look through the storage boxes as the energy that filled the room continued to prickle me. Maybe going up there hadn't been such a good idea. Fighting the instinct to turn toward the cage, I continued to rummage around.

"Looking for this?" asked two hoarse voices.

"Don't turn around," Evan warned me between clenched teeth.

"It must be important if you came all the way up here to get it," one of the Devas continued. Pages rustled and I turned around. The little boy stared at me. *He had my book.*

"Give it back." I slowly stood up and looked him in the eye.

"Why don't you come get it?" he challenged me, his voice eerie. I moved a step closer.

"Gemma, no!" Evan blocked my way, facing me. I remained calm. "I'll take care of this." He raised his hand, bending the air to his will . . . but nothing happened. He frowned with frustration and the Deva grinned, clutching my book in his hands. Evan's power couldn't go past the barrier.

"I'm bored in here. Maybe I'll tear out some pages. It might be fun."

I clenched my fists.

"Gemma, forget about it. Let's get out of here!"

The little boy ripped the corner of one of the pages and Evan shot across the room. "I wouldn't provoke her if I were you," he warned, but the boy boldly ripped out the rest of the page.

"No!" I screamed. My dark power hit him full force, slamming him back against the bars. The sound of the paper being ripped had torn my heart.

"Gemma, that's enough," Evan shouted, rushing back to me. "I have it. I've got the book." He showed me the volume and the torn page, and I blinked, finally breathing again. The Deva fell to the floor of the cage with a thud and didn't get up.

"Let's get out of here." Evan put his arm around my shoulder and kissed my forehead. I nodded and looked around. It looked like a hurricane had torn through the room. Had I done that? A shudder of terror ran through me at the thought that such a destructive power lurked inside me.

We reached the trapdoor, where the panther with a red splotch on its paw awaited us. If she'd been in her human form just then she would have had a smug smile on her face. But I didn't want to be like that. Like her. *Like them.* I didn't want to destroy things . . . or people, by stealing their souls. I held Evan's hand tight, less and less sure I would remain myself.

"Why does this book mean so much to you?" Evan asked me as I tried to carefully tape the page back in. He stopped me and without saying a word used his powers to repair it. I stared at him, amazed, and he winked at me. "Well? Why is it so important? Was it a present from an admirer?" he joked, but I remained serious, clutching the book to my chest.

"My grandmother gave it to me. See?" I opened it and showed him the first page, which had her name on it. *Gemma.*

"Oh, I thought that was you," Evan said.

"It is, but not only. We wrote it together when I was eight. She said that that way the book would be ours. The margins are full of notes, reflections, questions, thoughts . . ."

"Now I understand."

"There are two kinds of books: ones you can't wait to finish and ones you wish would never end."

Seeing how much I loved the story, Evan had once given me his copy of *Jane Eyre*, a first edition from 1847, which I took special care of. Nevertheless, not even that priceless volume was as precious to me as my own copy, which was irreplaceable.

"Thank you for fixing it."

"Well, you were the one who got it back," Evan joked, but a second later his expression darkened. "You're getting stronger and stronger."

"Does it scare you?"

"The only thing that scares me is the thought of losing you."

"That's not going to happen," I promised, taking his hand to reunite our tattoo. "*Samvicaranam,*" I whispered, and he rested his forehead against mine.

"*Samyodhanam,*" he murmured against my lips.

Stay together. Fight together.

"I'll find myself and you'll be there too. I swear it."

Evan looked at me. He wanted to believe me, wanted to with all his heart, yet part of him couldn't. So how could I be so sure?

"I have to go now," he said softly, and I nodded, still shaken by all those emotions. "Promise me you won't go back up there."

"I wouldn't even think of it," I reassured him.

"A whole day without you. How will I live?"

"How will I not die?"

Evan hugged me to him again, his dark eyes transforming, turning to ice. Giving me a kiss on the lips that sent a tingle through me, he vanished, leaving me alone in the silence.

"I wouldn't even think of it," I repeated to myself. But the demon I feared wasn't in the attic.

It was trapped inside me.

PARALLEL WORLDS

I wandered through the trees of the snowy forest, wrapped in my long red cloak that stood out against the pure white snow like a drop of blood. Its broad hood covered my head. It was chilly and the night was preparing to slice the air with its sickle of darkness, bringing with it cold and death, because not far away one of its Executioners would claim a soul. Evan was on a mission and wouldn't be there to protect me. I wrapped the cloak around me more tightly, though the devastating cold was not around me but inside me.

The tree trunks stood like silent soldiers, and yet there was something eerie in the air, a sinister shiver that followed me everywhere, as though death were passing by me time and time again.

Someone grabbed my wrist all of a sudden. "You lost, Little Red Riding Hood?" I spun around and Evan was in front of me, his silvery gray eyes shining in the darkness like a wolf's.

"Evan!" I sighed with relief. "What are you doing here? Didn't you have to go on a mission?"

He smiled. "I couldn't stay away from you." He kissed my neck and moved toward me, forcing me to take a step back.

"Orders come first—isn't that your motto?"

"*You* come first—that's my motto." I laughed and returned his insistent kisses.

He pulled back and took me by the hand. "Let's go."

"Where?"

"Someplace warmer, so I can take off your clothes." I laughed and ran with him through the trees. As we passed, the forest shed its white mantle and the lake showed us its shimmering waters. I turned around. Winter had disappeared, leaving in its place a crisp spring night. "Come here, Gemma. It's fun," Evan called out.

My gaze found him on Peninsula Trail, a path that crossed the lake. It was so nice to stroll along it, surrounded by the calm waters. It was like being at the ends of the earth.

"Come back!" I shouted to him. "The water's freezing."

"Come get me!" he dared me.

Sometimes Evan was worse than a little boy. I laughed and took off my shoes, pulled up the hem of my cloak and dress, and walked down the path barefoot. It was the long dress Ginevra had lent me for my journey through Hell, though I couldn't remember putting it on . . .

The water rose to my ankles, the current tickling my skin. "Here I am! I made it! Happy?"

Evan grabbed my waist and smiled. "I'm always happy to see you, Peachskin."

"What?" Why had he called me that? I looked up and found myself staring into Ahrec's ink-black eyes. The Unholy Soul smiled at me, his tiny teeth jagged like a shark's. *Was I in Hell?* I backed up, frightened, but my foot slipped on the mossy rocks and I fell into the shallow water.

"Come. I'll help you cross the river." *The river.* I had to follow the river to find Evan. Ahrec held out his hand but I let out a scream and backed away. I struggled to my feet and the current pulled off my cloak, sweeping it away from the shore.

I turned back, running barefoot along the path. Ahrec suddenly appeared right in front of me. Unable to come to a halt, I tumbled onto him. He tried to restrain me, but I broke free and scratched him hard. Blood splattered my face but instead of stopping I continued to tear at his flesh. My nails were as sharp as a panther's. I slashed open his chest and with a suffocated gurgle Ahrec fell to his knees.

His eyes had gone back to normal. "Well done, Peachskin." He fell face-down into the water. A dark red pool spread out around his body and the current dragged him away. I thought of my cloak and stared at my hands, trembling. They were covered with his blood but it wasn't black, like the blood of the Damned. It was red. I washed them obsessively in the river, getting my long dress wet. What had I done? I ran away without turning back, wanting to return to the car, but I couldn't remember where I'd parked it.

I spotted the hideaway in the distance and my heart leapt with joy. As I looked over my shoulder, frightened by a dark presence I continued to sense, I crashed into someone. I looked up, dazed by the impact. It was Evan. "It's you!" I threw my arms around him.

"Hey, calm down. Why are you so on edge?"

"Where have you been?"

"On a mission. I told you I had an execution order. But I'm here now." He stroked my head and I let myself breathe. I looked at our hideaway on the shore. Through the window I glimpsed the glow of the fireplace, defying the darkness. Smoke rose from the chimney. I'd thought he was alone there, but from the house came the roar of a group of panthers that pierced the night.

"Aren't we going inside?" I asked Evan, puzzled.

He kissed me on the lips. "No. Let's spend some alone time," he murmured, stroking my cheek. "Just you, me, and Devina." I leapt back, my heart pounding in my chest, but bumped into someone behind me. I spun around, panting.

Devina smiled and leaned in to kiss me. "He'll be all mine," she whispered against my lips. Her honey-colored eyes challenged me, as narrow as a panther's.

"No!" I shouted, taking another step back and continuing to stare at them. Evan took her hand and led her to our hideaway. A tear slid down my face when the door closed, leaving me all alone.

I turned and started running, hoping the darkness would ease my pain, but I felt a strange presence at my heels. Soon the air was full of hostile, deafening hisses. I stopped, exhausted, as the air all around me shimmered and took shape. It was then that I recognized it.

A Pariah.

I knew I couldn't pay attention to it or it would absorb my soul, but I couldn't help it. Its evanescent figure hypnotized me, circling me slowly, as though in a dance. Whispers filled my head. It wasn't alone. I looked around and a group of them emerged from the thick of the forest. Though I tried to resist their call, I was mesmerized, at the mercy of some dark power. The first Pariah quivered, excited by my interest. My yearning overpowered me and I reached out my hand.

"DON'T TOUCH IT!"

I woke with a start, Ginevra's voice still echoing through my mind. Raising my hands to my head, I took a deep breath, still shaken. *Just another bad dream.* Another horribly bad dream.

The house was quiet. I looked around. Through the half-opened door came a shaft of light that barely illuminated the darkness. In the hall, a panther stood guard outside the door.

Everything was normal. *Except for the fact that my life was a horror movie,* I thought. I pushed off the heavy covers and headed to the bathroom. Evan hadn't come back yet. I went to the sink and rinsed my face. Suddenly I had a strange sensation: I felt drawn to the mirror and slowly raised my face. In the reflection, my eyes captivated me. They were dark and powerful . . . as though they weren't mine. My heart skipped a beat. There was no trace of their whites—they were two deep pools summoning me, the eyes of the demon within me. Suddenly I wanted to free it. I wanted to touch it. I wanted to *be it* and absorb its power. I reached out, rested my fingers on the mirror . . . and they sank into it. Looking at them, confused, I noticed that the black eyes in the mirror continued to stare at me as dark bulgy streaks slithered across my face like snakes. It was the demon absorbing *me,* absorbing my energy. Frightened, I tried to pull my hand back but couldn't. Something was blocking me. The darkness wanted me for its own. The streaks on my reflection grew darker and darker. It was going to annihilate me!

Panicking, I tried once more to pull back my hand and the mirror cracked. I tugged on my wrist with my other hand and finally jerked my hand free, shattering the mirror into a thousand pieces. As I stared at my bloody fingers, a voice hissed through the silence: *"You cannot escape me."*

My body went cold. *It was my voice.* I spun around. In front of me was another me, in flesh and blood. Terror trapped the air in my lungs. "I'm you," she hissed, her black eyes pools of evil.

"No!" I screamed.

A slow smile spread over her lips. "It's too late. He's inside you. *He's growing!"* A hiss broke the silence and a serpent slithered out of her mouth. I jumped back, but the animal darted forward and lunged at me.

My eyes shot open. It had only been a nightmare. It was already daytime. Outside, the sunlight reflecting off the pure white snow was blinding. My heart still beating fast, I suddenly realized my arm was raised, suspended in the air and swaying like a snake hypnotized by a snake charmer. I pulled it down, bewildered, and sat up in bed.

A large panther put its head around the door. It was Anya, with her marvelous eyes of jade. I smiled at her. "Good morning." She gave a little bow, came over, and rubbed her head against my legs. I stroked her and she rose onto her hind legs, trapping me on the bed. She licked my face, which tickled, and I giggled like a little girl when she didn't stop.

"I get it! I get it! It's a good morning for you too." The panther purred and I petted her some more. The sun was already high in the sky. How long had I slept? It didn't really matter. It was Saturday and I wouldn't have to worry about school. Anya walked back to the door and flicked her tail. She wanted me to follow her, but first I had to get ready.

I let her out, closed the door, and headed to the bathroom, avoiding the mirror. All of a sudden I was afraid to look at myself, afraid of the darkness . . . *I was afraid of myself.* It had been a spine-chilling sensation, staring into my own evil-filled eyes. Fear was starting to become a reality and my unconscious was sending me signals. What if I really didn't manage to stay myself? More and more often I'd seen evil possess me and had done nothing to stop it. The power that flowed through me was exhilarating. Evan had always been the one to pull me out of the clutches of darkness. But I could no longer ignore the doubt that had begun to hound me: what if evil really did manage to obliterate me?

I dried my face and looked at myself in the mirror, my heart pounding. My eyes were normal. I sighed with relief. What had I expected to see? In an automatic gesture I let down my hair and put the hair tie around my upper arm. A shudder raised goosebumps on my arms as I remembered the serpent that had crawled out of my mouth. It had been shiny and as black as night.

He's inside you. He's growing, my voice had said.

I touched the scar on my belly and it throbbed. My fingers felt wet and I looked at them. *They were bloody.* Like in my dream. Nervous, I checked the wound. A stream of scarlet trickled from it. I hurriedly cleaned it with some washcloths, opened the medicine cabinet, and took out some cotton, pressing it against my skin until the bleeding stopped. I leaned against the sink, still shaken. Where would all this take me?

I closed the cabinet and jumped at the sight of my reflection. And yet it was just me—not the demon inside me. Was I actually afraid of *myself* now? I brushed my hair, never taking my eyes off my reflection. I needed to overcome my insecurity, otherwise I would never manage to face my future—it would be too frightening. But the more I stared at my eyes, the more I sank into their depths, as if they no longer belonged to me. Suddenly I thought I saw my lips curve in a little smirk of power. My heart skipped a beat.

"Gemma, everything okay?" Ginevra's voice shook me out of those thoughts. "Breakfast is ready. You'd better hurry if you want to find anything left. They're polishing everything off down here!"

"Coming!" I put down my brush, casting a last glance in the mirror. I'd battled Subterraneans and Witches. I'd even battled death. I was strong. But that meant that so was *she*, the other me. Which of the two of us would prevail? The answer wasn't so easy to see any more.

The aromas reached the stairs. Festive chatter filled the living room. Simon wasn't there. He must have been away on a mission too. There were only women in the house. *Witches*, I corrected myself. "What is this, a pajama party?" I asked, joining them in the kitchen. Irony trotted over to me, wagging his tail, and I leaned down to pet him.

"Gemma!" Anya called to me. "Have a seat. We were waiting for you."

I looked at the girls, whose mouths were all full. "That's clear to see," I joked, making them freeze and stare at me with guilty expressions. "Don't worry, I was just kidding. Don't let me stop you."

Anya laughed. "We're definitely not short on food," she assured me. "There's all you could want."

"Oh, fries!" Only Witches would think of having them for breakfast. I immediately ate one, chewing with delight. "Say what you want, but to me this is heaven. It's still a mystery how you guys don't gain an ounce, given everything you eat."

"Look who's talking." Nausyka winked at me. "You should be a blimp by now, given everything *you* eat, but you're still in good shape for someone who's expecting a baby."

I blushed. It was a huge compliment, coming from one of them. "You're one of us, Sister," Camelia said in response to my thoughts. I smiled at her. It was really nice to have them around. They were so closely knit that, in spite of myself, I felt flattered by the thought of being part of their group.

Ginevra picked up on my thought and smiled at me. If I transformed, would I love them all as much as I loved Ginevra? The answer was obvious. *It was already happening.* But I wasn't going to follow them into Hell. So would separating from them be painful?

The answer to that was also clear: never as much as separating from Evan and Ginevra would be.

"Did I miss anything?" Just then, Simon appeared behind me, reminding me that he was also on my list. I would miss him at least as much as I did Drake. I smiled at him and banished my thoughts before the Witches discovered them.

"Take a seat, if you can get near them, but I'm warning you: be careful. They're pretty dangerous when someone eyes their food."

"More dangerous than normal?" Simon joked, pulling his beloved Ginevra to him. "I missed you," he whispered to her, resting his forehead on hers.

I looked away to give them some privacy. A pang in my heart reminded me Evan wouldn't be back until that evening. Who knew where he was or what he was doing? Was he in some distant corner of the world or only miles away? What kind of Souls did he need to help that it was taking him so long? Whoever they were, I was jealous of the time Evan was spending with them instead of me. He was mine and I wanted him all to myself.

"He will be, once you claim him," someone whispered in my ear. I looked at Zhora, surprised she'd heard my thought. Something trembled in my chest. *Desire.* Deep down, I found the idea enticing.

The Witch smiled at me and winked, but Devina, at the back of the room, glared icily at both of us. "Evan will always be *free* to love me," I told Zhora adamantly. "I would never want him to be subjugated to me."

The Witch laughed. Did she not believe it, perhaps? For Simon and Ginevra it had worked. "Hey, Gemma," Simon put in just then, "I ran into Evan last night. He wanted me to give you this." He held out a piece of paper folded in two. I took it, trembling with emotion as I opened it.

I miss you.
E.

I sighed, butterflies fluttering in my stomach over those three little words that meant the world to me. I missed him to death. My soul was so entwined with his that being apart was always painful.

"Couldn't he have texted you?" Devina said, rolling her eyes. "Did he forget this is the twenty-first century?"

"I think it's so romantic!" Camelia sighed, earning a glare from Devina. "What did I say?!" she protested.

Ignoring them both, I went into the living room, clutching the note to my chest, and stared out the window, where everything was covered with white. It was only one day. What was one day? Still, I missed him terribly. I kept telling myself it would all work out, but actually I was quivering inside. Our future was more uncertain than ever. We had only a few months left. What would become of us?

"Simon, are you going to see him again?" I asked, hoping I could reply to his note.

"Sorry, I don't think so, but he'll be back tonight. Don't tell him I told you, but he was pretty excited about your big date," he admitted, winking at me.

I smiled. Some time before, at the lakeshore, Evan had asked me to the Snowball Hop and I had accepted, despite having less-than-fond memories of the last school dance I'd gone to. The Winter Carnival games were over, and that night we would crown a king and queen who would officially kick off the dance.

Simon rested his hands on my shoulders. "Everything will go fine. And I don't just mean tonight," he reassured me, reading on my face the fears that tormented me.

"Thanks for being a snitch, then. I'll keep your secret."

He gave me a peck on the forehead and stroked my belly. As he did, the baby kicked. Simon pulled away, his eyes going wide and his face lighting up with joy. "Did you feel that?"

I laughed. "Yes, I felt it. He doesn't do that for everyone, you know—you're one of the privileged few. If you ask me, he already loves you a lot."

"I hope so!" he exclaimed happily. "I intend to teach him all sorts of little tricks."

"Um, what exactly do you have in mind?"

"Being an anxious mother already? Parents can't always know everything," he said, teasing me.

I thought about the little Subterranean boys locked up in the attic and couldn't help but wonder what would become of my son. Would he have to serve Death, like them? Or would he be human? Would good claim him, or evil? Would he even be able to choose between the two? Only time would tell.

Simon's voice interrupted my musings. "Can I ask you something? Why did you ask the Witches for three days after the baby's birth? Why not five—or seven, for that matter?"

"I figured that by then we would have come up with a plan to prevent the transformation. I couldn't ask for months—that would have been too long. Once the baby was born and taken to safety, three days seemed like more than enough time to put our plan into action. Besides, Ariel managed!"

"Who?"

"The Little Mermaid. In three days she got her voice back, defeated the evil witch, and won the prince's love."

"You're forgetting that your evil witch is the devil and you aren't in a Disney movie."

"Right." I sighed with resignation. "I'm more like an episode of *Final Destination*," I joked, a bitter smile on my face.

"Gemma. I want you to know I've never thought what I said the other night. I was being controlled by some power that *forced* me to say it."

"It was me." I looked down. "That power came from me. I'm sorry. I didn't want to hurt you, Simon. I should run away, but I'm not brave enough."

"You could never hide from us."

"Sure I could." A tear slid down my face. If I were dead, they would never be able to find me and they would all be safe.

"Don't even think that." Simon hugged me, stroking my head.

"No one else should suffer because of me. I'm not worth it."

"Do you really not see how special you are? The forces of Heaven and Hell have mobilized to claim you. It's not all your fault I said those things. It's partly mine too."

"What do you mean?"

"I admit that your bond with Ginevra scares me a little. She's very protective of you."

"You all are."

"I know. That's not what I meant. Something in her has changed since she found out about your nature. She feels *the Bond.*" A shudder ran through my body. "And I'm a little jealous."

"What are you talking about, Simon? For her, you come before everything else."

"What if that wasn't true any more?"

"That's crazy." The love between Simon and Ginevra was my benchmark, the rock to which I clung to convince myself the transformation wouldn't drag me away.

"I know. I'm sorry. I'm just afraid of losing her."

I stroked his arm. I'd never seen him so vulnerable before. "That'll never happen," I reassured him.

"That's probably true. What I'm saying is that your power wouldn't have had any influence on me if I didn't feel the way I feel."

"You're in love, and everything around us is changing. We can't know what's going to happen, but the one thing I'm sure of is that you two are going to stay together. Nothing can break the bond between you," I stated without a shadow of doubt. "It's normal for you to have thoughts like that, but *I* made them come out. It's all my fault. Don't be mad at me for what I am."

Simon hugged me. "You shouldn't be mad at yourself either. We'll get through this." I nodded and sank into his hug.

"Sorry if I'm interrupting." Nausyka came over and Simon left us alone. "Gemma, I just wanted to let you know your friend Peter asked me to go to the dance with him."

"What did you tell him?" I asked, upset.

"I accepted, of course."

"You *what*?! You can't go to the dance with him! Call him and tell him you changed your mind."

Nausyka turned her back on me, her expression pleased. "I wasn't asking for your permission. It was just an FYI."

I felt steam coming out of my ears. "What do you want from him?" I growled at her.

"I just told you: I want to go to the dance with him."

I clenched my fists, overcome with anger. "No. You won't. He's like a brother to me. Leave him alone." The window exploded and an icy wind blew into the room. I could feel myself rising off the floor, my fiery eyes locked on the Witch's.

In the blink of an eye she was right there in front of me. "Think these little tricks scare me?" she hissed, her ice-colored eyes transforming into those of her Dakor. "You have no idea who you're dealing with." The serpent materialized from her flesh and hissed in my face.

"That's enough!" Anya shouted. The wind stopped blowing and my feet touched the floor. I looked at Anya and she shot me a complicit look. "Nausyka, I challenge you. Choose your competition. The prize will be the boy." I opened my mouth to protest but she interrupted me. "Only for tonight, that is. If you win, you can take him to the dance. Otherwise he'll go with me."

"Don't worry," Ginevra whispered in my ear. "Nausyka's a wimp compared to Anya. Whatever challenge she proposes, she has zero chance of beating her."

I looked at Anya and my heart warmed at how she'd come to my rescue. I smiled at her and she smiled back. I would never have managed to convince Nausyka to change her mind, whereas Anya had been shrewd. I was certain that if Nausyka had gone out with Peter that night, she would have somehow jeopardized his soul, and sooner or later she would have returned to claim it. Anya, on the other hand, I trusted. I knew Peter's soul would be safe with her.

"Coming upstairs with me?" Ginevra asked me.

"Aren't we going to watch the competition?"

Ginevra laughed. "I strongly advise against it."

"Oh." I followed her up the stairs, watching Nausyka and Anya turn and walk away, both in panther form. "Where are they going?"

"The workout room," Ginevra told me after reading her Sisters' minds. "Nausyka chose a pretty cool simulation scenario. I bet Peter wouldn't mind being there with them."

"And I bet that's all I should know about it."

Ginevra laughed and opened the door to her room. "You win that bet."

"But wait, in the workout room? Aren't the prisoners there?"

"No. They're on another level. That's how the simulation scenarios work, like parallel realities."

"Like a multiverse."

"In a way." Ginevra stopped to look at me. "Have you thought about what to do with your Dakor? Even if the transformation doesn't obliterate you, he'll be part of you."

"I'm willing to destroy him," I said confidently.

"That won't be so simple. Besides, it's not like you need to. In any case, you can take your time and decide. Meanwhile, there's a safe place where you can set him free." Ginevra deactivated the vault door's locking mechanism and I gaped.

"What are you doing, Gwen?"

She turned to me and smiled. "Taking you into my own personal Hell."

Hesitantly, I took the hand she held out to me and followed her. "That's not very reassuring, as far as invitations go."

"Were you expecting a welcome mat?" she shot back as we made our way into the Copse. The door thudded closed behind us and I spun around. "It's safer this way," she explained.

Of course. We couldn't leave a door to Hell open—not with Simon around. The atmosphere was grim and eerie, like a haunted forest at twilight. Roots twisted on the ground and, farther in, a strange trunk was bent over on itself, its boughs so thick they formed an impenetrable cocoon. Only when I drew close to it did I realize it was a nest: her Dakor's lair. The last time I'd gone into Ginevra's secret hiding place the Dakor had been in a glass case, but she must have transformed it. Now the animal was trapped in the tree, but its forked tongue flickered through the branches, making me shiver. Ginevra stood in front of him. When he saw her he froze, as though hypnotized. They stared into each other's eyes for a long moment and suddenly the branches retreated.

I took a step back, shuddering at the thought of the dream I'd had the night before. The serpent sensed my nervousness and hissed at me, but Ginevra reached her right hand out to him and he penetrated her palm. She let her head fall back, on her face an expression of pain mixed with intense pleasure. When she looked at me again, her eyes were different. They were like her Dakor's. The pupils had lengthened and the green of her irises seemed to come to life. It moved, as brilliant as liquid jade, spreading over the whites like claws about to seize it.

I stared at her, as fascinated as though seeing it for the first time. But now there was also another feeling: fear. I raised my hand to my belly, where my scar was. Soon my body would also spawn a Dakor and he and I would be one.

Just then, Ginevra extended her left hand toward me and the serpent emerged, ripping her flesh. I stared at it in shock. "Don't be afraid," she said softly.

In spite of everything, I found her Dakor irresistibly attractive. I wanted to touch him. I wanted to feel him on me, absorb his power. As if he'd heard my thought, the serpent moved toward me and coiled around my arm. I closed my eyes, exhilarated, and let him slither over me, going up my arm, wrapping around my neck and creeping into my shirt, moving down between my breasts . . . to my belly, right where my scar was. A hiss of excitement shook the serpent, who knew what was lurking there: my Dakor. And yet my baby was there too. The thought snapped me out of it.

"Gwen." My eyes flew to hers and, sensing my concern, she summoned her serpent with her mind. What if he didn't manage to control his instincts? What if he'd detected Evan's genes in my baby?

Cautiously, Ginevra slipped her hand under my shirt as I stood still. The serpent coiled around her arm and slithered up to her neck, staring at me intently. "Don't worry. The baby isn't running any risk," she assured me, but I'd already forgotten every concern as my eyes fused with the animal's. They were so hypnotic and powerful, as though they hid some dark, fascinating, mysterious energy, the door to a magical place full of promises.

I was burning up. "That's enough for today," Ginevra said softly.

I looked at her, still dazed but free from the Dakor's spell. "Why did you bring me here?" I asked.

She put her Dakor back into his nest and the branches sealed up around him. "There's too much power in you, Gemma. You might be able to learn to control it, though, a little at a time. I'll help you."

"Do you think it'll make it easier to resist the transformation? That it won't obliterate me?"

"It's possible. We can at least try. Your body is slowly getting accustomed to it. You used to end up unconscious for days when the Witches established contact, and now your fever doesn't run nearly as high as it used to. Maybe your mind can get used to it too."

She was right. I nodded, grateful for her precious help. "What was your transformation like?" I asked.

"I wasn't so attached to my life. I wanted to slaughter everyone. Back then, my power awoke on Earth and the Sisters sensed it. They began to invade my dreams, tempting me with their promises, and I was happy to listen to them. When the time for my transformation came, I had no doubt about the choice I would make. I wanted to be like them, to be with them. And that was what happened, just like it had with all the others, one every five hundred years. With you, though, everything was different right from the start. The process began long before it was expected to. Your proximity to me and to the Subterraneans awakened your power. When you ingested the poison to kill the guy we thought was Drake, the transformation began and things got worse and worse. We all changed from mortals into Witches in a single night, whereas you're transforming slowly. And with every passing day you grow more powerful."

"You think that might help me avoid losing myself, don't you?"

"A gradual process might be less invasive than a more drastic one, but that's just my hope."

"What effect will the Bond have on me?"

"The Bond is an unbreakable force that will connect you to the Sisters. It compels you to protect and defend them. It's all of you against the world, and nothing can break it." Ginevra still suffered from being away from her Sisters.

"Where are we going?" I asked, following her up a hill.

"Let's stay here for a while, if you don't have other plans." She helped me climb onto a rock and a huge valley opened up before us, taking my breath away.

"No plans," I whispered, hypnotized by the incredible landscape. Ginevra laughed and motioned for me to join her, sitting on the summit of the peak and leaning back against a large tree. It seemed like the whole world was spread out below us.

"What do you think?" she asked excitedly.

"It's breathtaking."

Something moved in the distance, approaching us. A big black bird. No, it wasn't a bird. I jumped to my feet with a mix of surprise and excitement. "Argas!" I exclaimed, a lump in my throat.

Ginevra smiled. "I knew you'd be happy to see him again."

Ginevra's Saurus landed on the peak, folding his big black wings, and came toward me. I ran over and threw my arms around him. He whinnied and rubbed his head against mine. "I can't believe he's here." I'd missed him so much! I could never have survived Hell without him. Though he was Ginevra's steed, a connection had formed instantly between us. He'd also defended Evan from the Damned.

I sat down again and he curled up at Ginevra's feet, his giant head on her lap. I looked at Ginevra and saw a tear slide down her face. "Gwen

. . ." I whispered, surprised. She stroked her animal, her eyes veiled with sorrow.

Only then did I understand. "This isn't the real Hell." Ginevra shook her head, still stroking Argas. "And he isn't real," I murmured. "So that's why you lock yourself up in here so often. Not only to train, but—"

"To remember. It's not easy to eradicate such an important part of you."

Ginevra had recreated a corner of Hell and hidden it behind the bars of her "forbidden door." She'd done so not only to give her Dakor a safe place to stay, but also to have a memory in which to seek refuge. I'd always believed it was a door that led to a little portion of her world. Only now did I realize it wasn't true. It was a lie she told herself to hide the pain. She missed her world terribly. "So this is just another artificial scenario?"

"Yes."

"And he's not really here," I said, this time louder. "He's just an illusion?"

"Yes." Her voice was sad.

I sighed. "You'd like to see him again, wouldn't you?"

"More than anything in the world."

I sighed again and stared at the valley that stretched beyond the mountains with their waterfalls and lush vegetation. "I really admire you for the decision you made," I said. "I can tell how much it makes you suffer, but despite that you chose Simon."

"He counts more than anything else," she stated without hesitation. And yet, though hundreds of years had passed, her connection to her world was still deeply rooted in her and the distance made her suffer. I too remembered the feeling of belonging I'd had once I was there.

"I wish I had half your courage," I admitted. If I were as strong as she was, maybe I would be able to avoid letting the transformation obliterate me.

Ginevra laughed and looked at me with affection. "If courage were enough, you'd have nothing to fear from the transformation. You're the bravest person I know."

"That's not true. I'm always filled with doubt, I never know what the right thing to do is, and most importantly . . . I'm afraid, Gwen. I'm even afraid of myself."

"*Fear* makes us strong. Every time you face it, you win a battle with yourself. And you're the strongest warrior I've ever seen."

A tear slid down my cheek.

"You faced Death with your head held high when it came to take you. You took the poison, knowing it would kill you. You even went all the way to Hell for your love. Without help. Without powers. Just you and the immense strength you have in your heart. You mean to tell me that isn't courage?"

I smiled through my tears. "Thanks, Gwen." I rested my head on her shoulder and she hugged me.

"I'm happy you're here with me," she suddenly said. "I can never go back to Hell, and this is the only way we can be there together."

"I'm not going there either," I assured her.

She squeezed my hand. "I hope not. I don't want to lose you, Gemma."

"That's not going to happen. I'm not giving up." I wasn't going to let evil obliterate me. I risked losing so much, *too* much. I wasn't willing to give in.

Argas whinnied and I trembled. Of all the challenges I'd faced, the hardest one was yet to come: the battle against myself.

THE SNOWBALL HOP

"Were we gone so long?!" I exclaimed as we came out through the vault door. I couldn't believe it was dark out already.

"Time flies when you're with a Sister."

I smiled at her affectionately. The bond between us wasn't because of my nature—it had grown strong long before. "What happened to Nausyka and Anya?" I asked, curious, hoping Ginevra would track down their minds wherever they were in the house.

"We can find out later. First let's eat something. I'm famished," she protested, walking down the stairs.

"You're always famished."

"Look who's talking!"

I stuck my tongue out at her and she shoved something in my mouth. My eyes bulged and I took a bite out of a chocolate muffin. It was delicious. Ginevra had used an effective argument to come out of the conversation a winner. The table in the living room was piled high with food, but we were so hungry that in minutes there was almost nothing left.

"Aren't you two ready yet?"

Sprawled on the couch, our bellies about to burst—at least mine—Ginevra and I turned toward Anya, who'd just appeared in the living room. I usually jumped whenever one of them popped up out of the blue, but I was too full to do even that. The Witches didn't gradually appear and disappear, like Subterraneans—they went *poof.*

I struggled to my feet, surprised to see how stunning Anya looked in her luxurious gown. A big smile spread across her face. "You like it?" She twirled around. With her long, green, Venetian dress and her curly hair, she looked like a princess. She was all set for the Snowball Hop, while I still had to get ready—and there was no sign of Evan.

"Mmm . . . Pizza!" Nausyka took a slice and savored it voluptuously, as though making love to it. I cast a questioning glance at Anya: Nausyka was also dressed for the dance. She wore an elegant black gown with a plunging neckline and a mermaid train. Her white hair was plaited in a long braid that hung over one shoulder. Its tip looked like it had been dipped in black ink. She looked like an evil, sexy twin of Elsa from *Frozen*. I didn't dare imagine the reaction she would get in a room full of mortals ready to fall at her feet. One of them, however, worried me more than the others.

"Are you going to tell your friend about the change of plans or do you want to give me his number?" Anya winked at me and smiled. She'd won! *Thank you*, I mouthed to her. Nausyka glared at me icily. "But now, what are we waiting for? I don't want to miss the coronation!" Anya took me by the hand and pulled me up the stairs.

"Wait for me!" shouted Ginevra, hurrying after us.

"Don't take too long," Nausyka grumbled. "I'm tired of being cooped up in this house."

Anya pushed me into a chair and started to put makeup on me while Ginevra styled my hair. Strangely, I didn't feel like a rag doll in their hands—I felt like a princess with her ladies-in-waiting. I felt loved.

"Was it easy to snatch Nausyka's date away from her?" I asked Anya.

"I have to admit she gave it her best shot."

"What does she want from Peter? Why is she obsessed with him?"

"She's not going to compromise his soul," Ginevra said. "Trust me."

"It's her I don't trust. I want her to stay away from him. I'm a lot happier that he's going to the dance with Anya."

She smiled, continuing to put eye shadow on me. "To tell you the truth, you shouldn't be wondering what she wants from him, but what *he* wants from *her*."

"What do you mean?"

"Your friend's a really bright kid—above all, he's very curious."

"We've known that for a while now," Ginevra said, grinning. Peter had always pried into their business, but I was sure he did it to protect me. "He only wanted to go out with Nausyka because he thinks he may uncover something strange. He's not the least bit interested in her, aside from the physical attraction . . . which she has every intention of satisfying."

"Yeah, I can imagine," I said.

"But you don't have to worry about it any more. With me around, she'll stay away from him and I can assure you I won't seduce him."

"Anya, I know he's just a mortal Soul to you, but I don't want him *not* to have a good time. With you he can. You have my blessing."

Anya stopped, a black eyeliner pencil poised near my eyes. "That's really kind of you. I know how close you two are."

"That's true, but I don't think about him like *that*, so it's okay if he goes to the dance with you and has fun. Who knows? Maybe you and he could deepen your new *friendship*." I looked at Anya with a mischievous air.

"You mean you wouldn't be even a little jealous?"

"Not even a little," I said confidently. "I would be happy if Peter found someone who deserved him."

"That someone can't be me," Anya reminded me. She was only there temporarily. Once her mission was finished, she would return to Hell with her Sisters.

"I know," I admitted a little sadly, "but it certainly can't be Nausyka. If Peter has to have a good time, I'd rather he have it with you."

"It's natural for you to want to protect him," Ginevra said, busy braiding my hair.

"*Et voilà!* Mission accomplished," Anya exclaimed excitedly. Ginevra looked at me and for a second seemed shocked.

"Gwen, everything okay?" I asked with concern.

She smiled at me, banishing my fears. "Yes. You're spellbinding." She helped me put on the voluminous Victorian gown and laced up the back. "Remember when we bought these dresses?" she asked affectionately.

"When *you* bought them," I reminded her. "I didn't even want to try mine on!"

"Turns out they came in handy, didn't they?"

"Yeah, and I'm sure you had nothing to do with it."

"I don't know what you mean." Ginevra shot me a sidelong glance, hiding a smile. My dress was red, the color of blood. We'd bought it in New York during a day trip. Back then we hadn't known what the theme for the Winter Carnival dance would be, but I suspected Ginevra had had a hand in the decision.

"All done. Now you can look," she said as Anya gazed at me with delight.

I raised the hem of my skirt just above my ankles and walked over to the mirror, where I slowly raised my eyes, almost fearfully. I instantly realized why Ginevra seemed so shaken. *I looked like one of them.*

"You look divine," Anya whispered behind me, squeezing my shoulders. I blinked, astonished. Mascara enhanced my long lashes and eyeliner as black as my eye shadow brought out the curve of my eyes. The line continued to my temples, creating a design. It almost looked like an elegant mask—no, not a mask. *Butterfly wings.* My gaze had become deep and incredibly magnetic, and my hair was gathered into a soft wave of curls that flowed over one shoulder. Peeking out here and there were little braids that held the hairstyle in place. I couldn't believe it was me.

"That dress is perfect. I would never be able to tell you're expecting a baby," Anya said.

I touched my abdomen. She was right. With that dress, my belly wasn't noticeable at all. There were girls at school who looked more pregnant than I did—even though they weren't. Though I didn't know why, it really was hard to tell on me. Now I just hoped Evan got back in time. When he'd asked me to the dance I wasn't sure whether it was a good idea, but then, like a little girl, I'd let excitement wash over me. It was our first dance together. The first dance to which someone other than Peter had invited me. And I was crazy in love with my date. I had a bad feeling, though. Something inside me told me he wasn't coming.

"He'll come," Anya reassured me, though there was no way she could be sure.

"Knowing him, he'll be there in time to kill every guy who checks out your cleavage," Ginevra added. I burst out laughing. "I wouldn't laugh if I were you. Believe me, it'll be a slaughter." She smiled, pointing at the plunging neckline that brought out the curve of my breasts.

"I say he'll be the one to die—the minute he lays eyes on you. You're going to be the prettiest girl at the dance. After me, naturally." Anya winked at me and I smiled. Evan had captured my heart and held it tight, but I knew it was safe in his hands.

The doorbell rang but before I could wonder who it was they already knew. "It's Peter," said Anya. "We'd better go down before Nausyka seizes her chance."

"You two finish getting ready. I'll take care of it," I offered. I hurried down the stairs but the bell rang again and Nausyka opened it.

"Hi," I heard Peter say to her.

"Thanks, Nausyka. I've got it," I exclaimed before she could try anything on him. *"You lost your bet, remember?"* I told her in my mind.

"It won't be the last one," she replied, glancing at me before walking off. Peter watched her leave, confused, and then his eyes rested on me.

"Hi," I said, but he seemed to have lost his power of speech. "Change of plans. Nausyka isn't going with you any more." For a second his eyes lit up.

"Anya's going with you," I hurried to add before he got any ideas.

"It doesn't matter," he replied, his eyes fixed on mine. "She wasn't my first choice anyway."

I looked away, embarrassed. "Come on in. Anya will be down in a minute."

Peter walked into the living room. He looked handsome in his elegant nineteenth-century suit: a black waistcoat over a blue silk shirt and, for the first time, a tie. It wasn't just the clothes—there was also something different in his bearing. He was becoming a man.

"You're not wearing your hair tie on your arm," he noticed.

I'd forgotten how attentive he was when it came to me. "I can go without it tonight," I said. The truth was that the dream I'd had the night before had upset me so much that I'd started to be afraid of myself, of what I would become. The hair tie had always been part of me, but as a response to the summons of evil. Just for one night I wanted to escape the darkness. I hoped it wouldn't pursue me.

"Funny," Peter exclaimed. "I think I've only seen you without it a few times."

"Lots of things about me have changed lately, Pet."

His eyes fell to the tattoo on my hand. It hadn't escaped him that Evan had one just like it. "Right, everything's different. Strange, don't you think? This is our first dance *not* together." *Finally, he'd said it.* Naturally it had occurred to him too. Peter gave me an affectionate smile. It made me realize one thing hadn't changed: despite everything, he would always be my best friend.

"Yeah." I smiled back. "It really is strange." He and I had always gone to school dances together, from the Halloween dance to the Snowball Hop to Prom. Every year, every event.

"Where's your date?"

"Oh, Evan's meeting me later on . . . I hope. He had an important commitment."

"More important than you?" he asked, suddenly annoyed. He'd never stopped being protective.

"He'll turn up in no time, really."

"Tell the truth, Gemma," Devina said, magically appearing behind him. "You're not even sure he's coming. Why don't you go to the dance with your friend here?"

"Is what she says true?" Peter blurted.

"No, she's only saying it to make me angry." I shot her an icy glare. There were times I wished I could transform just so I could take her on in a battle to the death.

"Seriously, Gemma." Peter took my hand. "If Evan's not here you can go with me. As friends. Like we've always done."

I freed myself from his grip, trying not to hurt his feelings. "I'm sure he's coming. Besides, you can't bail on Anya, can you?"

"He certainly can't. He's my knight in shining armor!" Anya said, making her entrance. She curtsied and Peter, acting the gentleman, kissed the back of her hand, but secretly continued to stare at me. Was he becoming bolder?

"It's not his fault. You're breathtaking tonight," Ginevra whispered in my thoughts. I turned and she winked at me with a broad smile as she walked down the stairs. She was radiant in her white-and-gold gown, like a sun goddess. Her blond hair was gathered back, a small braid crossing her forehead like a diadem. She had once explained that Witches had the habit of braiding their hair, and that a braid across the forehead was like a symbol of the Sisterhood.

"Look who's talking," I whispered to her when she approached me.

"I'm not kidding," she insisted. "You have an aura of power around you. I can feel it. Your body is producing loads of pheromones." My mouth dropped open in concern. That was why Peter couldn't take his eyes off me. Ginevra nodded, picking up on my thought. "It must have been your visit to the Copse. It made you stronger."

"We're going in Peter's car," Anya broke in. "See you there!"

"We'd better get going too," Ginevra said, changing the subject. "Don't worry. Relax and enjoy the dance. Everything will go fine, you'll see." I nodded, hoping with all my heart that Evan would show up soon to make sure of it. I always felt safer when he was with me.

"Well?" Camelia appeared in the room in a dreamy powder-blue gown. "Are we going to the dance or aren't we?" She'd dyed her hair the same color, leaving the roots darker. Her outfit was complete with a delightful little pink hat. Her enthusiasm made me smile, but the mischief in her eyes worried me. "I missed these dresses so much!" she exclaimed, twirling around.

"I didn't, not one bit." Simon appeared behind Ginevra and kissed her bare neck, pulling her against him. She turned and kissed him passionately. "I think I'm going to get rid of it, and fast," he whispered, his hands on her hips.

She bit his lip. "I'm not sure I can wait that long."

"Hey, we're still here, you know," I warned them. They smiled at each other, taming the fire that consumed them.

"Okay, if you're so scandalized . . ." Ginevra told me, a sly grin on her face.

Actually, I was missing Evan terribly. "Gwen, I have a bad feeling about this. Maybe we shouldn't go without Evan."

"He's just on a mission, Gemma."

"Do you really think he'll get there in time?" I asked as we opened the garage door.

"I don't know," she admitted, taking my hand, "but whatever happens, we're going to have fun." I returned her smile and got into the back between Camelia and Nausyka. Simon sat down behind the wheel, with Ginevra in the passenger seat.

I put on my iPod earbuds to shut myself off from the group for a moment. My mind continued to return to Evan. I picked out an Avril Lavigne song, *When You're Gone*. I'd always liked listening to songs that matched my mood. Music was like a good friend: it understood me, no matter what. And I missed Evan so much . . . The fear of losing him through the transformation seemed more real when he was gone, because I knew no one else was capable of pulling me out of the darkness.

We reached the Crowne Plaza Resort in no time. The atmosphere inside was magical. All the students from the high school looked so elegant, and the Victorian theme had been implemented to perfection, with draperies and fabrics from that era, big candelabras, and even an area for the orchestra with a piano and various instruments. Some of the boys wore hats and carried canes while others even had fake mustaches or beards. It was really like being in the nineteenth century.

Peter was at the back of the room with Anya. He took her hand when the coronation was announced.

"Just in time!" Nausyka exclaimed.

"Don't get your hopes up. The queen can only be chosen from among the seniors, and you're a little bit older," I teased her. "Besides, you're not even enrolled in this school."

"Oh yeah?" she replied, annoyed. "If I want to, I can get myself crowned this very—"

"Faith Nichols!" the principal announced.

"Aw, too late," I said, one eyebrow raised.

"You did that on purpose. You distracted me!" she said, stunned. Surprisingly, there was no trace of anger in her voice. In fact, she seemed to find it funny. "You're learning," she admitted, realizing I'd done it intentionally. Knowing that Nausyka wanted to make the principal say her name, I'd stolen that little victory from her.

I searched the crowd for my friend Faith. She was climbing the steps to the dais that had been set up for the occasion. I forgot about Nausyka and smiled. I was so happy Faith had won the title of Winter Carnival Queen. I'd voted for her myself a few days before. Though she tried to hide it by wearing her magnificent red hair in a tight bun or always staying in Jeneane's shadow, her beauty hadn't gone unnoticed. The truth was that Faith didn't like to have everyone's eyes on her—too much attention made her uncomfortable. She preferred to be with the horses on her family's ranch. I'd seen her with her mare, Hope. Together they seemed invincible. That night, like it or not, everyone had noticed her. She'd worn her copper-red hair down and it flowed over her peach-colored dress. She was gorgeous. I'd always known she was. She went to sit on the throne that had been prepared, waiting for them to announce the king.

" . . . and the Winter Carnival King is . . ." the principal continued. Brandon stepped toward the stairs. "Peter Turner!" the man announced in a booming voice.

I gaped, ecstatic, as Peter rubbed his neck, embarrassed. He hadn't been expecting it. He looked at me from across the room and I clapped for him. *It was the tie*, I mimed. He laughed and walked toward the dais. As he passed Brandon he slapped him on the shoulder. "Next time, dude," he joked, regaining his confidence. Brandon reached out to give him a playful punch on the shoulder, but Peter dodged it.

He thanked everyone, as Faith had done, and went to sit on the throne beside her, but the principal asked them to open the dance. Peter held his hand out to her and she let him guide her to the middle of the room, where they began to dance.

"My knight has become a king!" Anya exclaimed, joining us.

"That doesn't make you a queen," said Nausyka, who hadn't yet gotten over her defeat.

"At least I *have* a knight."

"*Had*," the Witch pointed out, gesturing at Peter and Faith, who were dancing close together.

"You could be his secret lover," Camelia suggested, looking amused.

I shook my head and went off in search of the punch, hoping no one had spiked it. "Want something to drink?" I asked the three of them, but they paid no attention to me.

Ginevra and Simon danced by to the rhythm of a Venetian rondo. Simon wore a white-and-gold suit, probably an original. Everyone's eyes were on them. They really did look like a knight with his princess. He stood out with his dark allure, a blond Angel of Death dressed in white. He looked like an officer—and, come to think of it, he was. I'd read in Ginevra's diary that before they met Simon had been a soldier in the Swedish forces. *General Adrian Simeone Dahlberg*. The girls from school weren't used to seeing him and he left them dazzled.

Faith and Peter also danced by as I was sipping my punch. I raised my glass to toast them and Faith smiled at me cheerfully. They danced off, but a moment later Jake asked to cut in and Peter relinquished Faith, taking off the crown and giving it to his friend. It wasn't a secret to anyone that Jake was in love with her and that Faith loved him back. The mystery was why they weren't together. Peter came over to me and I smiled at him.

"Congratulations," I told him. "Winter Carnival King! Who would have guessed?"

"Was it that unlikely?" he asked, pretending to be offended, but two dimples soon appeared in his cheeks.

"No, not at all. You look great tonight."

"So you do."

The silence grew awkward.

"Those two are perfect together," I said, nodding toward Faith and Jake.

Peter laughed. "He's nervous. He's about to ask her to be his girlfriend."

"Finally! Let's hope it happens."

"Your date's not here yet?"

"Ahem . . . Here you are!" Anya emerged from the crowd and linked her arm in his. "Gemma, do you mind if I steal him for a moment?"

"Of course not," I said as she led him away.

She looked back and winked at me. "So tell me all about the coronation . . . Speaking of which, where's your crown? Have they dethroned you already?"

I laughed as they walked off. I wasn't sure Peter would be able to handle her Witch's exuberance. Still, they were cute together. Watching them as they moved across the dance floor, I knew for certain that I wouldn't mind if something romantic started between them. Maybe my friendship with Peter would go back to what it had once been. I smiled. Yes, I liked the idea.

All at once, a sharp pain in my abdomen made me double over. Unable to breathe, I gripped the tablecloth in one hand. Glasses of punch crashed to the floor, spilling their contents. I looked at the crowd dancing and the room started to spin.

I'd do anything to go out with him.

I'm going to get back at that bitch.

Please, kiss me. Go on, kiss me.

What I would give to get her into bed.

If I find out they hooked up it's over between us.

I gasped for air. Where were all those voices coming from? People's faces passed me like ghosts and their laughs jumbled together, filling my head. I closed my eyes and everything stopped. In the darkness I could hear only my breathing; all the other sounds had faded away. Even the pain was gone. When I opened my eyes I found myself in the center of the room. A couple in front of me was arguing.

"You've been staring at him all night. I saw you!"

"That's not true! I don't even know who you're talking about!"

I walked around the boy. Though I didn't know him well, I suddenly felt attracted to him. I wanted to see him from closer up. As I moved nearer, his breathing accelerated and he shouted at the girl, his eyes bulging, "Don't lie!" He was on the verge of losing control.

"I'm not lying! I swear, I only care about you." A tear streaked the girl's face and he wavered. I couldn't tolerate it.

"She wants to go to bed with him," I whispered in his ear.

"You want to go to bed with him!" the boy repeated. A sensation of immense power surged through me. "It's the truth, isn't it?"

"Maybe she's already cheated on you."

"Or you already cheated on me," he continued. He pulled his hand back and slapped his girlfriend across the face. She fell to the floor and everyone turned to stare at them. I smiled, but something distracted me: a distant voice.

"Gemma? Hey, Gemma, you okay?" I felt myself being dragged away as though at the mercy of a raging river, the frenzied beating of my heart returning to drown out all the other sounds. My eyes shot open and the voice became clear. It was Jeneane. I looked at my hands clutching the paper tablecloth, now torn, and felt my heartbeat slowing down. "Hey, do you feel okay?" she asked again, worried.

I struggled to my feet and saw the couple fighting, but . . . they were on the other side of the room. What had just happened? My head spun faster and I felt like I was falling.

"Gemma!"

"Step aside, people. I'm a doctor." It was Simon. His warm hands raised my head and in the background I heard Ginevra and Anya coaxing the crowd to stay back.

"Gemma!" Peter said, resisting their efforts. "What's wrong with her? Is she okay? Let me through!"

"She just had a dizzy spell. It's natural when you're expecting a baby. Give her a moment," they told him.

Someone loosened my bodice and I started breathing again. I slowly opened my eyes to see Simon gazing at me. "Welcome back." He smiled. I stared back at him, unsmiling, as a silent tear slid down my cheek. What had just happened? I knew the answer. It had been me. I'd incited that boy to slap his girlfriend, even though she hadn't done anything. How could it be?

"Calm down now," Simon whispered, using his healing power on me. The only problem was that what was wrong with me couldn't be healed. "Think you can stand up?" I nodded, letting him help me. He walked me to the hallway and the Witches followed us.

"What happened?" I asked, exasperated and frightened. No one answered. *"What just happened?"* I insisted.

"Gemma." Anya rested her hands on my shoulders. She'd read the guilt in my mind. "It's nothing. Calm down. This isn't good for the baby."

"How can you say it's nothing? It was me! *I* made that guy hit her. It might not be a big deal to you, but to me it's a *very* big deal."

"You'd better get used to it," Nausyka replied curtly.

"What?" I turned to face her.

"That's enough. You guys can't mean to argue here, I hope," Ginevra intervened.

"I refuse to console her," her Sister insisted.

"She's upset."

"She has no reason to be. What's going to happen later?"

"She's still a mortal. Her soul isn't ready yet," Ginevra hissed.

"It's her nature and she's going to have to deal with it."

I covered my ears and Nausyka went back into the ballroom, Camelia at her side.

"I'm going too," Anya whispered. "I'd better keep an eye on them."

Ginevra put her arm around my shoulders and tried to look me in the eye. I stared into space, though, lost in the darkness lurking inside me. "There were two of me," I murmured in shock. Ginevra let out a long sigh.

I'd had an out-of-body experience. "Tell me I imagined it, Gwen. Tell me it wasn't me who caused their fight."

"It wasn't you." I looked at her, in my eyes a hope that faded the second they met hers. "You didn't cause their fight, but you heard it and . . . you fanned the flames." Ginevra put a hand to her forehead, remorseful. "It's my fault. It's all my fault. I was wrong. Taking you to see my Dakor wasn't a good idea—it just made things worse." My eyes widened. She was right: taking me into her world had exposed me to evil, and my soul had absorbed it, accelerating the process.

"But I split in two. How could that be?"

"Your soul felt drawn to their argument and went to it. Your body isn't yet ready for power like that, so you passed out. It's my fault. I'm sorry."

I touched the mark on my belly that was still throbbing. I'd felt a knife plunge into my flesh there. That mark belonged to the devil, as did I. I'd already sworn, but suddenly I wanted to take it all back. I didn't want to transform any more. I didn't want to risk turning into a monster. Evan was right—I couldn't control the darkness. It would force me to remain there, watching, feeding off me as I lost everything. As I lost Evan.

I remembered everything about the fight between the couple. Every crude, appealing sensation. The scary thing was that during it I hadn't remembered anything about myself. All I'd wanted was to continue to feel that power.

I'd been deluding myself. I would never manage to battle the evil inside me, because I wouldn't want to battle it any more. My doubts dissolved, leaving way for a terrible certainty: the transformation would obliterate me. I'd been all wrong and everyone else had been right—most of all Evan, who had never accepted the thought of my transforming and was desperately looking for another solution. I'd always thought he didn't trust in us, in our love, but he was just afraid of losing me. He didn't want to risk it. He understood that no matter how strong our love was, it didn't depend on us—only on me. I never listened to him and always complicated everything. But this time I couldn't be wrong again, because everything was at stake. Not even I wanted to risk it any more. I wasn't going to transform.

"Guys . . . " Ginevra's whisper shook me from my thoughts as a shiver ran down my spine.

Simon and I leaned toward her, worried. Ginevra looked like she'd seen a ghost. "Gwen, what's wrong?"

Distraught, her eyes met mine. "It's your Dakor," she said, her voice low and frozen from shock. "His heart has started beating."

A shudder of fear chilled me to the bone.

THE FIRST DANCE

"Want to go home?" Ginevra asked me, worried. I hadn't said a word since she'd revealed the terrible truth: my Dakor had awakened. With every passing day, I was closer and closer to the transformation. How would I manage to prevent it? Whenever I wondered that, I felt a knot in my throat. I was afraid. I didn't want to lose everything.

"We can leave, if you want," she insisted.

"No. I want to stay."

"It doesn't look like Evan is going to make it after all," Simon told us. It was strange he hadn't shown up yet, and by now it was clear he wasn't coming.

"I'm sure his mission delayed him," Ginevra said. "Let's go home, Gemma. You're still upset."

"I said no." I wiped my tears with my hand. "You guys got all dressed up for me. I don't want to ruin the party. Nausyka would never forgive me."

"We didn't get dressed up like this just for you," Ginevra said, looking at me out of the corner of her eye. I smiled. She loved that dress.

"We'll stay if she wants to," Simon spoke up, "but on one condition."

"Which is . . . ?" I looked at Simon, curious.

"That you'll do me the honor of granting me the next dance."

"What?" Simon had gotten a smile out of me. "You don't have to do that for me, really."

"I don't have to, but you do. You have to do it for me."

"Why would our dancing be a favor to you?"

Simon took my hand in his white-gloved one and kissed the back of it with a bow. "Because I come from a distant time in which a lady wasn't permitted to leave a ball without having first danced with at least one gentleman."

Smiling at his sweetness, I looked at Ginevra and she nodded her approval. I squeezed Simon's hand and walked at his side to the center of the ballroom. "But we're not in your time," I finally said.

"Let's pretend we are, shall we?" He bowed slightly, without taking his eyes off mine, and I curtsied to him.

Everyone was lined up, ready to begin the magical dance. I was sorry Evan wasn't with me, but at least having Simon there was a consolation. I cared about him so much. He'd protected me, risking his life so many times. I'd never forgotten how afraid I'd been at the sight of Desdemona pointing that gun at his head. He could have decided from that point on to abandon me, but he never had. He'd been at my side physically and morally, and I loved him for it. Not like I loved Evan or my baby, but with a deep, fraternal love, as though we shared the same blood.

The music began and Simon smiled at me. "Ready?"

"I promise not to step on your toes."

We moved to the rhythm of the violins, executing the dance steps. Stepping toward each other, we pressed our palms together before taking a step back. Simon twirled me around and knelt down like all the other boys, while the other girls and I circled them. Another step forward and another back. Then we both raised our right hands, palms facing without touching, and made a full circle, looking each other in the eye. We smiled the whole time, but when the circle was finished the line of boys moved down and I found myself facing another dance partner. He bowed, I nodded, and the dance began again. I danced with a boy I didn't know and then with Jake, who was surprisingly gallant. Next came Brandon, who ogled my neckline the whole time. I had to give him a slap on the back of the head when he knelt down. I tried not to let the others notice, but he yelped and clutched his head, making the whole line of dancers grin.

Then it was Peter's turn. "Hi," I said.

He bowed before replying. "Hi." We came together and he looked me in the eye. "You okay?" We joined palms and took a step back.

"It was just a dizzy spell," I assured him. He smiled, kneeling in front of me. "You going to ask for your crown back?"

"That kind of stuff isn't for me. I'm more the trophy type."

"Right." I laughed. Peter was a jock and in his room he had a collection of cups and medals.

He stood up and we looked each other in the eye, following the choreography. "I'm happy I got to dance with you."

"Even if just a little," I reminded him.

"Even if just a little," he said, laughing before growing serious again and bowing to his new dance partner. I curtsied to the boy in front of me and jumped when I saw it was the boy from the fight. A tumult of emotions rose within me and I felt like running away. I tried to control my breathing and overcome my fear. The boy took my hand and turned me around, but then let go. Had he recognized me too? Impossible. In fact, a second later I felt him take my hand again while my back was still to him. I completed the circle and my heart skipped a beat.

"My lady," Evan said, smiling. He was right there in front of me, my hand in his. He bowed and I circled him, my heart pounding. He'd sent the boy away and taken his place. Evan looked so dashing in his Victorian clothes that it felt like I was lost in an ancient dream. He wore a white silk shirt beneath a black jacket from that era. A filmy neckerchief in black silk completed the look. We joined palms and when we neared each other he interlaced his fingers with mine. "I missed you," he whispered, touching my forehead with his.

Tears filled my eyes, releasing all my tension. "I missed you too," I said. I raised my right hand and he stroked it as we turned around, gazing intently into each other's eyes. He wasn't supposed to touch my hand but the energy between us wouldn't allow that distance, so our fingers touched and then parted, like two secret lovers who feared being exposed.

The circle finished and we changed dance partners again, but the whole time his eyes never left mine, nor mine his. Before the time came for us to move down to another partner, Evan grabbed my hand and pulled me away.

"Hey!" my new partner protested, but Evan paid no attention to him. Putting his arms around my waist, he led me in a dance all our own. Far from the others. Far from the world.

The music stopped and the hall burst into applause. We took refuge in a secluded corner at the back of the room. A slow song came on, met by a chorus of approval. Evan took both my hands and placed them around his neck. Holding me by the waist, he stared at me intensely. We hadn't seen each other for a whole day and I'd missed him as if he were oxygen; I needed him to breathe. "Oh, Evan. I thought you weren't coming."

He rested his forehead against mine. "I wouldn't have missed this for anything in the world. I was hoping to get here in time for the first dance, but the mission took longer than expected."

"You made it. That was my first dance."

"But I wasn't your first partner."

"You were the last one—that's all that matters. Just for your information, Simon was the first."

He smiled. "Remind me to thank him. Did you get my note?"

"Yes, it made me so happy, thanks. Now I know you're thinking of me too when you're on a mission."

Evan brushed a lock of hair off my forehead. "I can go to the ends of the earth, but my heart stays here with you." He gently took my hand and placed it on his chest. "Hear that? There's only silence here. Now listen." He took my hand again and this time placed it on my chest. My heart was beating powerfully. "Your heart beats for us both."

I shook my head. "No, Evan. You shouldn't say that." I knew the message hidden in those words. If I died, he wouldn't go on living without me. I couldn't accept that. I needed to know he would be safe. "Take back your heart. If it means you would die without me, I don't want it." A tear streaked my face. Now more than ever I felt the end was near—the end of everything.

Evan wiped the tear from my cheek. "Hey, why are you crying? What's going on?"

How could I tell him that everything I'd believed was wrong? That he was right and the transformation would be the end of everything? That it would be the end of us . . . "I'm scared, Evan."

He clasped my face in his hands and looked into my eyes. "I'm here now. I'm not leaving you."

I shook my head. "I can't control it. You were right. The power is going to annihilate me."

Evan's eyes widened. I could see he was shocked by my confession, torn. For such a long time I'd been saying just the opposite, and now, for the first time, I was casting doubt on everything. My life was in his hands. It depended on his decisions.

"Help me, Evan. I don't want to transform. I don't want to forget you forever."

Evan held me tight. "I won't let it happen. I would never have let it happen," he told me. "I'm taking you with me to Heaven and you're eating of the Tree. No matter what."

I rested my forehead against his. "Are you with me?" he whispered in my ear.

"No matter what," I repeated. For once, I would listen to Evan and go along with his plan. It was our only chance. The divine nectar would rid me of the evil inside me. I had to cling to that certainty.

"I wouldn't have given up anyway, but I'm thankful you finally changed your mind," Evan admitted.

"I should have listened to you before."

"One way or the other I would have convinced you. I wouldn't have let you go, Gemma. I was *desperate*." I looked him straight in the eye. On his face I could read his fear of losing me. "Because I'm desperately in love with you," he continued in a whisper.

I pressed my lips to his and he kissed me tenderly, brushing my tongue with his softly one moment and passionately the next. His hand slid into my hair to hold me closer as our mouths sought each other, hot from our forbidden love. The world around us disappeared. It was just me and Evan, locked in an embrace.

"Marry me, Jamie." He gazed at me intently, our breath mingling.

"I've already said yes. I will marry you, Evan."

He shook his head, still resting on mine. "I mean here. Now. Marry me, Gemma," he whispered against my lips.

My heart skipped a beat. "But how—"

"We'll do it in secret. Just us. Simon will perform the ceremony, if you'll agree to do it here. I don't want to wait a second longer." I closed my eyes, my heart ready to burst with emotion. "Say yes, Gemma. Be mine."

"I'm already yours," I whispered, and kissed him.

"It's you and me. We don't need anything else."

I looked at him. "My mother's going to kill me."

"She won't know. No one will know," Evan whispered, smiling. "We'll have a big ceremony once all this is over. Until then"—he took my hands and stroked the ring I wore on my finger—"only we will know. It'll be our secret. So is that a yes?"

I smiled and he didn't take his eyes off mine as his voice filled my head: *"Simon, you need to come here."* My heart began to pound. Were we really about to do it? Yes, yes, and again yes. I wanted to marry Evan. I wanted to join my soul with his; that was where it belonged.

Simon soon reached us. "What's going on?" he asked, worried. Anya and Ginevra turned up a second later and let out a cry of surprise when they mentally read our intentions.

I smiled at Simon, the only one who still didn't know what was happening. "Would you marry us?" I asked him point-blank.

Unsurprised, he smiled back at me. "It would be an honor."

"We don't have rings, though," I pointed out.

"There's no need for anything new. Do you have something here with you that can serve as a testament to your love?"

Without thinking twice, Evan grabbed his dog tag and pulled it over his head, laying it in Simon's open palm. I took off my butterfly necklace and handed it to him. We couldn't have found anything more symbolic. Both chains had been with us from the start: I never took mine off, even at night, and he never went without his either. They'd been there for our first kiss, when Evan had come into my dream to say goodbye forever; they'd been there when he'd declared his love and engraved our names on them; when we'd made love for the first time . . . and all the other times after that. They'd been there when he asked me to marry him and when I'd followed him all the way to Hell to give his dog tag back to him and we'd made love in the dungeon cell. Those chains were the emblems of our great love. I didn't need anything else.

Simon held them and began to recite an ancient litany I imagined was in Sanskrit. I gazed at Evan. He held my hands, his dark eyes lost in mine, as mine were in his.

Simon held out our keepsakes, now consecrated. "Repeat after me: *Tavātmānam upadhehi. ahaμ taμ saμdadhe.*"

Evan took my chain from Simon's palm and, without taking his eyes from mine, whispered: "Entrust to me your soul and I will watch over it."

"I entrust my soul to you," I said softly. Evan put the necklace around my neck and smiled. I took the dog tag from Simon's palm and noticed there was another engraving on the back of it now, beside our names.

अत्यन्तम्

"Tavātmānam upadhehi. ahaμ taμ saμdadhe," I went on, this time in Sanskrit. *Entrust to me your soul and I will watch over it.*

"*Tubhyaɱ mamātmānam upadadhe.* I entrust my soul to you," Evan replied. He leaned down slightly to let me slip the chain over his head and took my hands. My heart was beating so hard I was sure he could hear it. "*Mamātmā mari, yati tvayā saha.* My spirit will die with you and rise again with you." He stroked my palm and a sigh of love filled my chest.

"*Mamātmā mari, yati tvayā saha,*" I repeated, enchanted. The whole time his eyes had never once left mine.

"*Atyantam,*" Simon decreed. "Your souls are united. Now and forever."

"Now and forever," Evan whispered before kissing me. I rested my forehead against his and he held me tightly around the waist.

"Now and forever," I repeated, smiling against his lips.

In the background, the lake watched us through the picture window, a silent witness. No one in the ballroom had noticed anything. They'd all been dancing while we joined our souls right before their eyes.

I had become his wife.

"Hey, make way for the maid of honor," Ginevra exclaimed. "I need to congratulate the bride!" She came up to me and gave me a big, strong hug.

"Congratulations, brother." Simon shook Evan's hand and gave him a friendly slap on the shoulder before hugging him.

"You didn't know anything about this?" I asked Ginevra, thinking she might have read Evan's mind.

"I knew he wanted to marry you, but I didn't think he'd be crazy enough to do it here."

"What does it matter where they did it?" Anya spoke up. "It was so romantic!" She hugged me and I returned the gesture. "Congratulations. I'm rooting for you," she said, wiping a tear from her eye.

"I love you, Anya."

"Oh, if you knew how much I love you!" She squeezed me so long I started to laugh.

"Okay, she gets how much you care about her," Evan remarked, reclaiming my attention, "but now the bride's coming with me." He took me by the hand and led me away as violins played the notes of *Odissea Veneziana.*

"Hey!" the girls grumbled, while Simon laughed.

"Wait, where are we going?" I exclaimed, raising the hem of my long gown with one hand.

Evan opened the front door and nodded at his motorcycle parked outside. "On our honeymoon," he said with a sly smile. I smiled and followed him. He took off his jacket and offered it to me. I slipped it on and closed it snugly, though I knew he would warm the air around us so I wouldn't be cold, the way he always did. He offered me a hand to help me onto the bike while holding the handlebar with the other.

Ginevra and Anya watched from the door, smiling, and I waved goodbye. "Wait!" I took off the red lace garter that matched my dress and climbed on, holding him tight. The engine started up with a roar that filled the night. Evan gunned the accelerator and set off as I tossed the garter behind me. I saw Anya catch it.

I hugged Evan, my heart warming at the thought of what had just happened. We had just secretly wed. He was my husband and I was his bride. Nothing could deprive us of that certainty. For the first time, I felt like everything would be okay. The Ambrosia would purify me and the nightmare would be over, replaced by our dreams. As though he'd heard my thoughts, Evan accelerated, racing toward that new hope, toward a new world where he and I would be together . . . this time forever.

Atyantam.

EVAN

WAITING

I gazed at Gemma, who lay on the bed in my room as I played the violin. Five months had gone by since the night of our wedding, and it had been the most wonderful time of my entire life.

"Don't stop. Keep playing for me, Evan."

"As you wish," I whispered. I tucked the violin back under my chin, my damp hair falling over my forehead. My eyes were prisoners to hers as my melody filled the room, pursuing our eternal love. I couldn't stop staring at Gemma as she lay there, relaxed, her cheeks flushed after we'd made love. The sun had just risen but the summer light was already streaming into the room. The song came to an end and I walked over to her.

"There's nothing sexier than a handsome, bare-chested man playing the violin while gazing into your eyes."

". . . Said the woman who had bewitched him." I touched the bow to her neck ever so slightly. "Will that suffice or would you have more, my lady?" She smiled at me, raising her arms over her head as the bow moved across her skin, sliding down to her breasts. It rose again and pushed the bra strap off her shoulder.

"I could watch you play for hours," she said. It had become her favorite thing, asking me for a song after we made love. She would lie there gazing at me while I poured my love for her into the strings, playing brand-new notes.

"That last song reminded me of an old movie I used to adore. *Canone Inverso: Making Love.*"

"I've never seen it, but we could watch it together."

"It's really touching. I'm afraid I would cry more than usual. We'd better wait until after the baby's born. You can listen to the soundtrack, if you like. It's by Ennio Morricone."

"Speaking of the baby, do you still feel nothing different? I mean, he should've been born by now." Over the last few weeks my tension had grown with each passing day as the time drew near for the big moment . . . and for Sophìa to claim Gemma's soul. No other Subterraneans had attacked us, and Gemma was safe, but the baby was overdue and it worried me not to know why.

Gemma smiled. Unlike me, she was calm. "I told you, Evan. It's normal in my family. My mother had a really long pregnancy too."

"And you're special," I said without thinking.

"Does that mean you think he will be too?" she asked. That seemed to be the only thing that still upset her. We didn't know if the baby would be human or if he would have powers. Ginevra had tried using magic to find out more, but the baby was protected by an impenetrable shell.

"We'll find out soon enough," I reassured her, and she nodded. I was happy Gemma had agreed to follow my plan and not transform. It had been hard to keep the secret all those months. The Witches continued to stay at the house, but Gemma had gotten good at keeping them from reading her mind. I'd helped her perfect the technique and together we'd hidden our true intentions, letting them believe Gemma intended to keep up her side of the pact with Sophìa. Not even Simon and Ginevra knew. We did it to protect them—both from the Witches, who were always prowling around, and from the consequences of our decision.

Once the baby was born, I would take Gemma to Heaven and she would eat of the Tree, casting evil out of her heart forever. In recent months, our plan had helped her stay strong whenever the darkness spread its tentacles around her. The closer the time to transform drew, the more strongly the power of evil writhed within her, threatening to tear her away. But soon it would all be over.

"There's something you haven't told me."

"What?" she asked.

"Why did you ask the Witches for three days after the birth?"

"Funny, Simon asked me the same thing."

"Really? What did you tell him?"

"That's how they do it in Disney movies."

I laughed. "Is that the real reason?"

"Well, not only that."

"Tell me the rest," I encouraged her, pushing the hair from her forehead. I sought her eyes until she raised them and looked at me. "I wanted to spend time with the baby. No matter what happened, I wanted us to be a family, at least for a little while."

Her answer left me wordless. I held her close and kissed her head. "We will be. And not for three days, but forever."

She pressed her lips to mine to seal the vow. "A while ago you said you'd gotten orders?"

I bit her lip. "I only take orders from you," I whispered.

Gemma laughed. "At ease, Soldier. We can't spend the whole day in this room making love."

"You're right." My hand slid down to her hip. "There's the spa and the living room . . . and the kitchen. What about the garage?"

She punched my shoulder and broke free from my embrace. "We've already done it in the garage, remember? And in the workout room and the swimming pool and the music room." She leaned in again to tease me, which she loved doing so much. "But the part I love most is when you steal into my dreams," she admitted.

"Why?" I asked, curious.

"Because that way we can be together all the time, day and night. I don't want to waste even one minute."

She kissed me sweetly and I took a deep breath, preparing to leave her. "Speaking of which . . ."

"You have to go," she finished for me. "You have a mission and you can't stay, I know. Orders come first. What's wrong, Evan? Why that look? With Anya and Ginevra here I'll be fine."

"No, not this time." She stared at me, puzzled. It was hard to give her the bad news. "I never thought I'd say this, but you need to spend some time with your friend Peter. I'm going over to take his father."

"No . . ." she gasped in shock. "Mr. Turner . . ."

"I'm sorry. I have to follow orders. His time has come."

Gemma blinked and a tear slid down her face. "Can I at least say goodbye to him?" I nodded. "How much time does he have left?"

"I'll be at his house in an hour."

She leapt out of bed and pulled on her clothes. "Take the car. I won't be needing it," I told her.

"Thank you," she said softly. I knew she was talking not about the car but the fact that I was giving her the chance to say goodbye. She kissed me on the lips and left the room. I heard her run down the stairs, open and shut the front door, and start the car. It couldn't have been easy for her. She'd grown up with Peter and had known Mr. Turner since she was a little girl; it was right that she be there for her friend, though the thought of the two of them together put me on edge. To avoid upsetting her too much, I'd waited until the last minute to break the bad news to her, but the time had come. I went downstairs to the living room.

"Everything okay?" Simon asked. "I saw Gemma run out the door. She all right?"

"Yeah, she's fine. She went to Peter's. In a little while I've got an appointment at his house."

"I see. The mother?"

"Father. I gave Gemma the chance to say goodbye. Besides, the kid's going to need her."

"That was a nice thing to do. I know how hard it is for you."

"Yeah."

"The baby? Any news?"

"Nothing yet. I wonder if his being overdue has anything to do with his nature," I told him, worried.

"We've already talked about that. There's no way we can know until he's born. In any case, Gemma ingested the poison and the baby survived anyway. That should give us hope. It means he's immune to the poison and he's not a Subterranean. Besides, Gemma conceived him as a mortal. Maybe he'll be a baby like all the others."

"We can't say that for sure." Ginevra appeared in the room. "Evil was already rooted inside her. Maybe your genes combined to generate something unique. His powers might prove to be immense. He has the blood of a Subterranean and the blood of a Witch."

"You know what that means?" Simon asked her, without actually expecting an answer. "It might put an end to the feud that has shed blood on both sides for centuries."

"Or it might trigger a war," Ginevra said. "The bloodiest, most ferocious one ever seen."

I clenched my fists. If there was one thing that was sure, it was that no one was going to take my son from me.

"The day is coming, Evan," Simon reminded me. "Gemma could give birth at any moment. Have you thought of how you're going to face the Witches if she really does manage to go through the transformation without being obliterated? Do you really think they'll agree to let her go without a fight?"

Ginevra gave me a hard look. "She's not going to transform, is she?" I frowned in frustration. Distracted, I'd let a bit of my concern show and Ginevra had picked up on it.

"What's she talking about?" Simon asked, surprised.

"We'll talk it over when I get back. Right now I have to go."

"Evan!" Ginevra called after me as I disappeared. But it was too late.

A SAD FAREWELL

I materialized at the Turner home. They were all in the living room—
Peter, his parents, and Gemma. When I arrived she flinched, but
instantly realized from my gray eyes that she was the only one who
could see me, so she tried to hide her emotions as best she could. We
stared at each other for a few seconds and then I nodded my head. Her
lips tightened and her eyes filled with sadness because the time had
come. I was there for Mr. Turner and soon I would take his soul.

"Get him out of here," I told her with my mind.

She took Peter by the arm and pulled him up from the sofa. "Why
don't you show me your latest drawing?"

Peter was instantly enthusiastic. Gemma knew how to handle the guy.
"You're going to like it. It's in my room. Come upstairs with me."

They turned to go but before leaving the living room, Gemma
stopped. "Mr. Turner?"

"Yes, sweetheart?" he replied. He was a tall, broad-shouldered man
with gray hair and a slight paunch. His son didn't much resemble him;
he'd inherited his mother's traits.

"I'm happy you decided not to move to Europe."

The man's face lit up. "Fortunately, that good-for-nothing brother-in-
law of mine came to his senses."

"My uncle took over Grandpa's business so we didn't need to
relocate any more," Peter said.

"Last year we were on the verge of packing our bags who knows how
many times," his mother said. "My brother wouldn't hear of working in
the fields and we couldn't let everything fall apart. Still, my father isn't
as strong as he used to be and needed help."

"I understand, Mrs. Turner. You're Italian, right?"

"Yes, I'm from a small town in Tuscany."

"Peter told me about it. It must be a wonderful place."

"Oh, you can't imagine!"

"Let them go, dear. You can tell them all about it some other time," her husband said, as though he had a more pressing need.

"In any case, thank you," Gemma concluded. "It's great that you stayed here."

"You're such a sweet girl," he replied.

Gemma shot me one last glance before leaving the room with Peter. I went over to the man, who had started chatting with his wife, believing they were alone. He had no idea I was there for him. No one knew it, except Gemma. I found the thought a bit disorienting. It was strange to carry out orders knowing she was there in the house with me.

"It's such a shame Gemma got pregnant by another boy."

"What are you saying, Matthew?"

"I know my son. He'll never give up on that girl, and with a baby on the way it'll be harder for him to win her over." I clenched my fists, tempted to put an immediate end to the conversation.

"Gemma's a fine girl, but she's with another boy now and they're about to have a baby together. I'm sure Peter has already gotten over it and that one day he'll find someone more fitting for him."

"What, are you blind? Can't you see how he looks at her? He's not going to give up until he gets her, Angela. Either that or he'll suffer in silence for the rest of his life. Between the two alternatives, I prefer the first."

"What do you want him to do?"

"I don't want him to suffer. I hope Gemma has a change of heart and finally recognizes what there is between them."

"Do you really want Peter to raise someone else's child?"

"Why not? I did it." My eyes bulged with surprise. So he wasn't Peter's real father?

"Shh . . . Do you want him to hear you?"

"You're the one who never wanted to tell him. I never had a problem with it. He's my son, as far as I'm concerned."

"He's not ready yet," the mother said softly, tears in her eyes. "He'll find out when the time is right. The truth might upset him now."

"Or it might give him the strength to—Ah!" Mr. Turner raised a hand to his head. His coffee cup fell to the ground.

"Matthew! Matthew, what's wrong?!" His wife knelt in front of him.

"My head!" he groaned between gritted teeth. "It feels like it's been split in two with an ax. It . . . hurts."

His wife jumped to her feet, grabbed her phone, and called 911. "Help! My husband needs help! Hurry!" She gave them the address and went back to comforting him, trembling. He was on his knees now, his elbow propped on the sofa. I clenched my fists tighter to finish what I'd begun. The man gave a cry of pain and crumpled to the floor.

"Matthew!" Angela screamed, bursting into tears. "Peter! Peter, come here! Hurry!"

"What's wrong?" he shouted, rushing into the room. Seeing his father lying there, Peter stood paralyzed in the doorway for a moment. "Dad . . ." he murmured.

In tears, his mother looked at her husband. "They're on their way," she said, stroking his face. "Everything will be just fine. You're going to be just fine." She'd rested her husband's head on her lap, tears streaming down her cheeks.

Peter ran across the room and knelt before his father. "Dad!" he said anxiously. I looked up and met Gemma's eyes. She'd never seen me during a mission and she hadn't taken her eyes off me for a second. Was she afraid of me? What was she thinking? Was all she saw a Soldier of Death who'd come to tear away the soul of her friend's father? Or did she realize it was still me?

"You don't have to watch this, you know," my voice touched her mind. I didn't want her to see the darkness that lurked in me. She shook her head slowly. She was going to stay put.

"Dad!" Peter's voice broke the connection between us. We both looked at the boy, who was leaning over his dying father. "Don't worry, they're coming." He didn't cry, but his voice was distraught.

His father, who'd realized his time had come, shook his head and motioned him closer. "Take care of your mother. You're the man of the house now. Understood?"

A tear slid down Peter's face. "Don't say that, Dad! You're going to get better."

"There's something you should know."

"Matthew . . ." His wife tried to stop him but her sobs prevented it.

"Your mother was already pregnant when I met her. I . . . ." Suddenly he let out another cry of pain.

"Don't talk, Dad. Don't talk . . . They're on their way."

"No. You need to know. I'm not . . . I'm not your father," he confessed, his eyes filling with tears.

"Yes. Yes, you are. I've always known, but I've never cared. You *are* my father." The man's eyes wavered with surprise and his heart beat faster for a moment before going forever silent. "Dad!" Peter cried, but the man's gaze was already lost and his hand dropped out of the boy's.

The mother bit her fist, unable to hold back a grief-stricken sob. She hugged her husband, shaking him through her tears. I looked at Gemma, who was standing in the doorway, a hand clasped over her mouth and her eyes full of tears.

"I'm sorry," I whispered to her mind. Why had I thought bringing her there was a good idea? I knew the answer: she would never have forgiven me if I hadn't told her.

Something behind me drew her attention. The sorrow vanished from her eyes, replaced by astonishment. I turned to find Peter's father's soul standing beside me, his gaze locked on his family. I looked back at Gemma, stunned. *She could see him.* A shiver crept through me as I lost myself in her eyes. They were turning black.

"Gemma, stay with me," I whispered in her mind. What the hell had I been thinking, bringing her there?! *"Jamie, Peter is suffering. Your friend needs you."* My words managed to break through to her heart, driving the darkness away. Gemma knelt beside Peter and held his hand without saying a word.

"Have you come for me?" Mr. Turner stared at me, waiting. "Thank you," he said quietly. "I never would have been able to tell him any other way."

I nodded. He'd suffered so much about not being Peter's biological father that he'd only been able to tell him with his last breath. If he'd found the courage to do so sooner, he would have realized it didn't matter much to Peter. Mr. Turner's soul was now free of remorse and fear. The confession had liberated him and his soul was at peace.

"Can she see us?" His question snapped me out of my meditative trance. I stared at Gemma, still shaken, and she immediately looked away.

"No. None of them can," I lied.

He took a closer look at me. "I know you. You're—"

"You're mistaken. You've never seen me before."

"I've never seen you before. Who are you?" he asked, influenced by what I'd said.

"It doesn't matter. Your time here is over. Take my hand and you'll finally be free."

The man looked one last time at his family. "Will I see them again?"

"One day, perhaps." I didn't want to lie to him again. I didn't know if there would be Subterraneans waiting for them when their time came. If they gave in to Temptation, they would find a Witch waiting for them instead.

The man reached out and took my hand, slowly vanishing. My eyes went to Gemma's. She'd seen the whole thing. I had no idea what she was thinking or how she saw me just then. I was Death. Had she truly understood that before? The ambulance's siren announced its pointless arrival. Gemma hugged Peter, staring at me over his shoulder. *"Stay with him for a while,"* I suggested in her mind, *"but then come back to me."* She nodded slightly, her big dark eyes fixed on mine as I disappeared.

DISAGREEMENTS

"Well?" Ginevra snapped the second I reappeared in the living room. "What's going on? And why have you kept us out of the loop?"

I walked past her and went to pour myself a bourbon, which I tossed back in a single gulp before pouring another one. "I did it to protect you. It's not safe with them here," I growled, nodding at the door leading down to the dungeon. The Witches were still underfoot. It would be easier for them to discover the truth if all of us knew about it.

"What are you planning, Evan?" Simon admonished me, grabbing me by the arm.

"I'm going to have Gemma eat of the Tree. She's already agreed."

Simon stepped back, gripping his hair in his hands. "You're out of your mind. We already discarded that idea, remember?"

"We said we'd talk about it one day, but we never did."

"I thought you'd gotten a hold on yourself! Damn it, you never think of the consequences."

"Well, you think about them too much."

"Because everything is at stake!" he yelled.

"I'm not going to sit around while she transforms and erases me from her heart completely. You and Ginevra were enemies once—you should know what it means."

"This is different. Everything is different! Gemma isn't going to erase you from her heart."

"We can't know that for sure, and I don't want to lose her. I'm willing to lose myself. I'm even willing to lose you two if you're not with me on this. I'm sorry, but not her—I can't lose her."

"Evan," Ginevra said. Reading the desperation in my thoughts had calmed her. "There's a good chance it won't happen. I wouldn't tell you that if I didn't believe it. Gemma is strong and can withstand evil."

"But she doesn't want to go through with it," I snarled. "She's afraid. She's afraid of herself; I can feel it. Every night in her dreams I feel the terror consuming her. She doesn't want to undergo the transformation any longer because she's afraid she can't do it. I've seen how powerfully evil possesses her—you two have seen it for yourselves."

"That's because she hasn't transformed yet. Once she has, she'll be capable of controlling all that power, but she can't do it as long as she's still human. Evil is like a beast trapped inside her."

"And I'm not willing to set it free. Not if it means Gemma could become my enemy. I'm sorry."

"She made a deal with the devil herself, Evan. There's no turning back."

"Ambrosia will free her."

"That's insane!" my brother roared.

"Why don't you ever agree with me?!" I groaned in frustration.

"Because you're reckless," Simon retorted, "and because your love for Gemma is making you desperate."

"I'm not crazy and I'll prove it to you."

"Evan, think about this." Simon struggled to stay calm, hoping I would listen to him. "If making Gemma drink Ambrosia was enough to prevent her from becoming a Witch, don't you think the Màsala would have done that already—not only with her, but with all the other Sisters?!"

"The Màsala can't go against what God Himself has decreed. The Witches are His gift to Sophìa. One every five hundred years. He made a promise," Ginevra put in.

"But they also decided to intervene by trying to kill her before she could transform, and who has to pay the consequences for their dirty tricks? We do!" I shouted, beside myself. "A random accident that happens to a soon-to-be Witch goes unnoticed, whereas purifying her with the Divine Fruit would expose them, revealing their treachery, which would mean another Witch might get called in to replace Gemma and they'd be back at square one. For the Màsala, nothing would change. For me, everything would."

"Purification didn't work on Sophìa," Ginevra reminded me. "Not even the Diamantea cage eradicated evil from her heart."

"Gemma isn't the devil. It might work on her."

"But then what happens?" Simon asked. "You don't know."

"You're still in time to reconsider," Ginevra added. "Maybe Gemma can undergo the transformation without losing herself. There's still hope."

"Hope isn't enough for me, Gin. I need to do something."

Simon shook his head. "I can't let you. It's too big a risk for you."

"She's already agreed. If you want to prevent it, you'll have to go through me." I stared at Simon, my eyes brimming with defiance.

"Fine, if it'll knock some sense into you." Simon took off his shirt and I did the same, assuming a defensive stance. He materialized behind me and grabbed me by the shoulders, but I warded off his attack and tried to shove him off balance.

"My mind's made up," I said resolutely.

He threw a punch but I blocked his arm and knocked him to the floor. He deftly dragged me down with him and the battle ensued amid broken glass and shattered stones. I grabbed Simon and slammed him against a wall, which cracked under the blow.

"That's enough!" Ginevra yelled.

But with a snarl Simon struck me full in the chest, sending me flying backwards, gritting my teeth from the pain. I fell to my knees, panting. He'd burned me with white fire. "You bastard," I murmured.

"I can't believe this. You're like two little kids. We've got to stick together! You even agreed to join forces with the Witches and now you're fighting each other?"

Simon held out his hand to help me up and I took it, groaning from the pain. "Sorry, bro," he said, nodding at the scorch marks the fire had left on my chest.

"You play dirty," I said reproachfully.

"I did it for you. I can't let you do something so crazy." He rested his hand on my shoulder and the burns slowly healed.

"Sorry, but there's no talking me out of it. Not this time." When I'd fallen in love with Gemma, my only fear had been that she would be afraid of me, but now I had a bigger fear: that she would see me as an enemy.

"It's not up to us to decide, unfortunately," Ginevra said. There was a hint of sorrow in her eyes. I knew that deep down, a small part of her wanted Gemma to transform. "Is that really what she wants?"

"Yes."

"She did a good job hiding it. She had a good teacher." Ginevra looked at me sharply.

"No one's better than me at keeping you out, remember? I've thought a lot about the possible consequences, believe me. I know there may be a high price to pay, but my mind's made up: once the baby is born, Gemma is going to drink Ambrosia."

"Making a decision is always an act of courage," Ginevra said softly.

"Sometimes courage lies in backing down," Simon countered, still far from convinced. He turned to me. "What makes you think she won't transform all the same?"

"I *need* this hope. Don't take it away from me. It's all I've got. Some risks are worth fighting for."

"Such vehemence in your eyes." I jumped at Devina's voice and glanced at Ginevra. How much of our conversation had she overheard? I could see Ginevra looking at Devina, searching her mind. She looked at me and shook her head.

Devina circled me, stroking my bare chest. "Aw, did my Champion get wounded in battle?" She gazed at me with tender eyes while I glowered back at her. I grabbed her wrists roughly, taking her hands off me.

She smiled. "You always did know how to turn me on."

"I'm not your Champion."

"Not yet. Hope springs eternal." With a wink, she turned her back on me and cracked her whip.

I need this hope. The words I'd just said a minute ago whirled through my head. What if Devina was capable of hiding the truth from Ginevra too? No. She couldn't have overheard our conversation. My sister would have realized it.

"Don't you knock before *appearing*?" Simon asked her curtly.

Devina looked him over from head to toe. "You're not so bad yourself," she said provocatively. "We could have a nice party here, just the four of us. What do you say?" She winked at Simon.

Ginevra stepped in front of her. "Why don't we have one, just you and me?" she challenged, her eyes burning into Devina's.

"Okay, blondie, don't get all worked up."

Anya walked through the door leading downstairs. "What's going on? Haven't you told them yet?"

"I was just about to," Devina said.

"Told us what?"

"We're going to have a problem pretty soon. The Subterraneans are fading because they haven't eaten of the Tree for such a long time."

"So soon?" I asked, worried. "It's only been a few months."

"It's our poison. The blood we give them and the magic we use to keep them under control saps their energy. That's why we think they're going to fade away soon. I don't know how much longer they have. The baby should have been born by now. We didn't expect things to go on this long. Soon they'll begin to disappear into Oblivion."

"What a waste!" Devina groaned. "Let's at least claim their souls before they disappear—that way they'll end up in Hell instead of vanishing. Some of them have even begged me: 'Please, I don't want to end up in Oblivion!' Cowards! Still, it's been torture, not being able to give in to their wishes."

"Cut it out, Dev," Anya told her. "That's not the problem. If the prisoners die . . ."

"Others will come," Simon thought aloud.

"So we fight them," I continued, resolute. I was prepared to do anything. No one was going to stop me.

THE FOREST AWAKENS

"Is Gemma still with Peter?" Simon asked me as he walked into the workout room.

The punching bag was still swinging from my blows. I stopped it with my forearm. "Yeah. It's a rough moment for him. He needs her."

"How's Gemma handling it?"

"She's strong. She'll manage to help him through it."

"Not that." Simon sent me a knowing look.

Gemma had watched me carry out an order. The sight of her eyes filling with darkness had shaken me, but I didn't tell Simon about that. I grabbed a long steel staff and began practicing with it, twirling it in front of me. "It wasn't the first time it had happened, actually. She'd already seen Drake take somebody right before the accident in my Ferrari," I said, mostly trying to reassure myself. I spun the stick and shifted it from hand to hand.

"That's not the same thing," Simon insisted.

"What do you want me to say, that I'm scared? Yeah, I am. Happy now?" I exclaimed in exasperation. "I took that man's life right in front of her eyes and I have no idea how she's going to see me from now on."

Simon removed his shirt and started punching the bag that hung from the ceiling, glancing at me from over his rear fist. "Why don't you ask her?"

I stopped, the staff slamming to a halt in my palm. "You're right. It's been hours. I'd better get Gemma some lunch."

"Otherwise she might eat some of her friends," Simon joked. I shot him a dirty look, holding back a grin, then focused on Gemma. A second later, I frowned.

"What's up?" he asked, seeing my expression suddenly go grave.

"I can't find her," I said, worried.

"What do you mean you can't find her?" He too tried to search for Gemma's soul, but a second later his eyes met mine. "You're right. I can't sense her aura."

I searched for Peter's soul and quickly found it: he was with his mother, but Gemma wasn't there. "What the fuck is going on? Where did she go?" I materialized upstairs in the living room and Simon followed me. "Gwen, try to find Gemma. I can't."

"What do you mean, you can't?"

"I mean you have to track down her thoughts, damn it!" I snapped, out of my mind with worry.

Ginevra stood there listening, combing the whole town in search of Gemma's mind. She stared into space for a moment before finally turning to me, disheartened. She couldn't find her either. I grabbed my hair in desperation.

"Calm down, Evan. It doesn't mean anything," Simon reassured me.

A surge of rage filled my chest. I struck the glass coffee table with my fist, shattering it into a thousand pieces, furious at myself for having been so careless. "I shouldn't have let her go! We can't find Gemma. How can you think I could possibly calm down?! Do you know what this means? She might even be dead!" I shouted in despair.

"Evan, you know that's not the only possible explanation," Ginevra said. "Evil has probably taken her over. That's been happening more and more often lately."

I tried to calm myself. She was right. Gemma couldn't be dead—the Subterraneans were all under lock and key. She wasn't running any risks. But then where was she? Her experience with Peter's father must have brought back the darkness. When her mind was possessed, not even the Witches could sense her. She disappeared as though she no longer existed. At Peter's house I'd seen her eyes transform. I shouldn't have left her alone. What a fool I'd been!

"She's in the forest," Devina said, materializing next to us.

I rushed at her and squeezed my hand around her neck, shoving her against the wall. "How do you know that? Did you take her there?" Her serpent burst through her skin, poised to attack me, its fiery eyes defiant.

"Enough! You're losing control," Ginevra shouted, stepping between us. "Evan, you need to calm down. Devina knows where Gemma is. That's a good thing." Devina smiled at me, her catlike eyes locked on mine.

"And you, try to be clearer and tell us exactly where Gemma is," her Sister said.

"Only when the Spartan gets over his urge to kill me."

"Then we'll never know," I snarled through clenched teeth. "Put your serpent away," I warned her.

She smiled, her gaze provocative. "Why don't you take yours out? Please?"

"Tell me where Gemma is!" I slammed my palms against the wall on either side of her head, cracking it.

"She's in the forest," Ginevra said, reading the Witch's mind, "near the Peninsula Trail by the old Howard Johnson."

"I know where that is." We'd been there a thousand times before, alone or with her friends. But why had Gemma gone there?

"We'll come with you," Simon was quick to offer.

"No," I said. "I'm going alone. I'll contact you if I need you." He nodded, realizing that after what had happened at Peter's house I needed to talk to Gemma alone.

I vanished and rematerialized in the forest, unsure exactly where Gemma was—I still couldn't sense her soul. I wandered through the trees, calling her name, but there was no sign of her. A boat was making its way across the river. There seemed to be injured people on board but I didn't have time to look into it. Gemma wasn't with them.

Then I saw her.

"Gemma . . ." I murmured, my heart in turmoil. She was curled up on the ground, head down. "Gemma!" I cried as I rushed to her. She heard me and raised her head. A second later I was holding her in my arms. She clung to me as though afraid she would sink into the earth.

"Evan," she sobbed.

"My love, what happened? I was going out of my mind."

She clung to me harder and wept, shattering my heart into a million pieces. "It was terrible," she whispered. "I don't want to be like this. Save me, Evan, I'm begging you."

I stroked her hair and closed my eyes. How could I even think of letting her transform? "It's over. I'm here now," I said softly. Feeling the desperate need to keep her with me, I held her close. There was dirt under her fingernails. She must have sunk her hands into the ground as she abandoned herself to the tears. "Tell me what happened."

"I don't even know where to start."

"What were you doing here?"

She shook her head, drying her tears. "I don't know. I found myself here. The other night I dreamed of the Peninsula Trail—maybe that's why. I felt this shooting pain in my temples and suddenly my mind was filled with the thoughts of people I didn't know. Prayers, desires. My head was about to explode. And then I heard your voice. It was you, guiding me through the darkness."

"It wasn't me."

"I know, but at the moment I believed it was. I must have imagined it."

"Or maybe not." Gemma looked at me and frowned, seeing the fire in my eyes. "Did you happen to see Devina while you were coming here?"

"No, but . . . You're right. Now I remember clearly. I thought it was you, but it wasn't really your voice. It was hers. She was telling me to follow my instinct."

"I'm going to kill that bitch!" I snarled, gritting my teeth.

Gemma took my hands and I tried to remain calm. "You can't hold it against her. They want me with them—they've never made a secret of that. It's my fault. It's what I am," she murmured, distraught.

"No it isn't, and it never will be," I said with conviction. I wouldn't let evil drag her away. I couldn't bear to see her like this, defenseless. I would offer myself in her place if it meant saving her from the darkness.

Gemma stared at her hands, still trembling. "Evil is inside me. I can feel it growing every day." I clenched my jaw. At that moment—more than ever before—I longed to have her drink the nectar of the Divine Fruit. I didn't care what Simon thought. I didn't care what the consequences would be. "Maybe there's no hope for me any more. The darkness is consuming me," she whispered, tears in her eyes.

"Don't say that. Please don't."

Gemma looked at me. The sorrow in her eyes was a knife driven into my heart. "You don't understand," she murmured in a barely audible voice. "I killed him."

My eyes widened. "What are you talking about, Gemma? Who did you kill?"

Gemma wasn't listening to me. She seemed lost in the memory. "I wanted his soul." An icy shiver crept over me, trapping my breath in my lungs. She continued: "It was so easy. I saw a boat. On it, a dog was whimpering. Someone had hit it. Blind rage flooded me and I felt I couldn't allow it. A second later there I was, on board with them. Not my body, just my soul. My dark, dangerous soul. The owner of the dog had rushed the guy and I told him not to stop. *'Hit him! He's a filthy bastard!'* And so he hit him.

"Their wives were screaming, trying to get them to stop, but the two kept fighting and the boat rocked on the current. Then the guy fell and the dog's owner grabbed him, glaring at him with bloodshot eyes. He held the guy's head over the side of the boat, blinded by the rage that I was fueling. 'Stop it!' the women screamed. But he didn't stop, because I didn't want him to. I wanted him to keep going. I wanted him to kill the guy.

"'Not so tough when you're the one getting beat up, are you, asshole?' he shouted, repeating the words I put into his head. He slammed the man's head against the boat. The dog was barking. The women were crying. I was electrified by his energy.

"'Okay, you win,' the other man said, pleading. 'I shouldn't have hit your dog. I'm sorry.' His teeth were covered with blood and he could barely breathe. The dog's owner loosened his grip, so I went up to him. *'Kill him. Otherwise he might do it again. He deserves to be punished,'* I whispered in his ear.

"He shouted, 'Fuck you, you ugly bastard.' 'Richard, no!' his friend's wife begged. But it was too late. He slammed his head harder against the boat and the women shrieked at the sight of the blood. Then a force pulled me back and I was here again." Gemma stared at her hands, as though they were drenched in blood.

I hugged her and she burst into tears. "I killed him! He hadn't done anything and I killed him. Evan, I don't want to be this way. Save me, please!"

I cupped her face in my hands, wiped away her tears, and rested my forehead against hers. "Look at me, Gemma. You didn't kill him. You got that?" She frowned. I had her full attention. "I saw the boat just before I found you. Someone was injured but no one was dead," I reassured her.

She gaped at me. "It was you. You brought me back." She hugged me tight. "Only you can drag me out of the darkness. Be my light, Evan. Don't leave me in the shadows."

"I won't." I kissed her forehead. "I never will. Forgive me—it was all my fault."

"What do you mean?"

"You came into contact with a Soul. I showed you his passing. It reawakened the Witch buried in you," I admitted. "It was all my fault."

Gemma shook her head, seeing how guilty I felt. "Don't say that. You did something wonderful, letting me be there for my friend. I'm the one who always ruins everything."

"You mean you don't see me differently now?"

"What? Why should I?"

"Because you saw the Executioner. You saw me when I killed a mortal and took his soul. That's why I told you to leave. I didn't want you to see the darkness in me," I admitted wearily.

Gemma looked at me, her expression calm again. "You've seen mine and you haven't run away. Why would I do it to you?"

"I'm Death, Gemma."

"You're still you, Evan. And to me you're everything," she said, looking me steadily in the eye.

"I realize that part of me has always scared you, and today I showed it to you. We're going to stop the evil inside you, but no one can ever change what I am: I'm a Soldier and I bring death with me. I took your friend's father, whom you also cared for. How can you not hate me?"

"Hate you? Seeing you in action was *magnificent*," she confessed.

"Magnificent? I killed that man right in front of your eyes, Gemma. Weren't you even a little afraid for him? You knew I was there, that he was about to die."

"How is it you don't understand? You saved him."

"I understand that. I'm just amazed you do too." We Subterraneans were clear about our mission: to liberate Souls from their bodies and guide them to eternal peace. It was mortals who usually didn't understand death. "What else did you feel?" I asked, eager to know her emotions.

"I saw how you convinced Mr. Turner I couldn't see the two of you. I almost believed it myself. It was weird . . . and exciting."

"Exciting," I repeated, laughing.

"Don't make fun of me!" Gemma punched me on the shoulder.

"You're right. This is no time to kid around. How's Peter?"

"Shaken, but he's trying to be strong for his mom. I was with him all morning. Jeneane, Brandon, Jake, and Faith came over too."

I nodded. Jake and Faith had finally become a couple and were inseparable. It had happened at the dance: he'd kissed her, and seeing how eagerly she'd kissed him back, he wouldn't take no for an answer. "Where's Peter now?"

"Running errands. He had to help his mom make all the arrangements, so we left. She's devastated and needs him right now, poor thing. The funeral is tomorrow."

"I'm sorry."

"Me too."

I stood up and held out my hand. "What do you say I get you something to eat?"

Gemma smiled. "What were you planning to get for me here in the forest, hmm?"

"Fish, birds . . . how about a little squirrel meat?"

She took my hand, stood up, and punched me on the shoulder again. "I don't eat squirrels!"

I laughed. "I know. I was only kidding—though I bet right now you could eat a horse. I heard your stomach growl a couple times."

"Moron!" Gemma walked past me, pouting.

"Only joking! But you really should eat something. Our hideaway isn't far from here. I could ask Ginevra to bring you something."

"All right, but I'm not a bottomless pit. I don't know why you guys always say that."

"If you say so." I shrugged, hiding a smile.

"Oh, all right, I admit it. Happy? I like food. I could eat a—Ahhh!"

I flinched, petrified by her scream. She doubled over, her hands on her belly. "Gemma, what's wrong?" I asked anxiously.

She cried out again, this time louder. "It's the baby," she managed to say, gritting her teeth against the pain. "He's coming."

"What? Here? *Now*?"

"Ahhh!"

I looked around. What was I supposed to do? I didn't have the faintest idea! I'd seen many lives come into the world, but I'd never felt so nervous before. Our baby was about to be born. It was both exciting and frightening.

"Evan!" Gemma's shout brought me back to reality.

"Hold on to me," I told her. "I'll take you to the hideaway. It's not far." I took her in my arms and she cried out even louder.

"No. No! Put me down!" she cried, panting. "Here. We need to do it here."

"All right." I gently rested her on the ground and she clung tightly to my arm.

"Don't leave me, Evan. I'm afraid."

"I'm here." I took her hand and kissed it, looking into her eyes. Gemma needed me; there was no room for doubt. I had to give her strength now. "Stay calm and breathe normally. I'll help you. You're safe with me," I whispered.

She nodded, clenching her teeth against another contraction. I took off my shirt and used it to cushion her head. "You trying to turn me on? Because this is not the time," she joked.

"What a shame—I was hoping it would work as a distraction." I winked at her and she laughed. "Now you need to focus, Gemma. Don't worry. Everything's going to be fine." She nodded several times and let me spread her legs apart.

"Gin! Simon! I need you, now!" I shouted in my mind. Removing Gemma's underwear, I saw it was drenched with amniotic fluid. The impenetrable shell that had protected our son for all those months had broken. I knelt there, perfectly still, a shiver running down my spine. For the first time, I could sense my son's soul. The emotion threatened to overwhelm me.

"Is everything all right? What is it?" she asked, concerned by my expression.

"It's our baby. The time has come to meet him. It's time, my love. Now you have to help him come out, okay? Here, let me help you. When you feel the pain, just—"

She squeezed my hand in a death grip. "Ahhh . . ." The earth shook beneath us. I looked up. All at once, clouds gathered in the sky and the forest came to life. Leaves whirled through the air, driven by a dark force. It was as though Gemma and I were in the eye of a hurricane that raged all around us. The lake churned, the water rising into giant waves. Nature was witnessing an extraordinary event; never before had a Witch given birth.

"What's happening, Evan?"

"It's nothing. Just focus on the baby. Here he comes! I see his head!" I exclaimed, my hands trembling. "You're doing great. One more push. We're almost there! That's it!"

The forest howled around us as though Gemma's energy had transferred itself to the trees. I let go of her hand, preparing to catch the baby. She screeched between clenched teeth and bore down in one final, exhausting push.

I caught the baby and cradled him in my arms. The forest filled with his cries. The leaves trembled and the wind howled even more fiercely, like a wolf acknowledging its leader. All the elements seemed to awaken at the force of his life's shriek. A flock of birds rose in flight and filled the air. I raised the baby to my chest. He looked at me and the wind stopped howling. The clouds dispersed and sunlight streamed down on us as my soul touched my son's. Tears flooded my eyes and I had to squeeze them shut and open them several times to make out his face.

"Evan . . ." Gemma murmured, breathless. She was exhausted. "Quickly, I want to see him," she begged me, in tears. I cut the umbilical cord, healed the end of it, and rested him, still covered with blood, in Gemma's arms. "It's a boy," I whispered. "Just like you always said."

She clasped him to her chest and wept. I couldn't stop staring at him. He had big, blue, slightly almond-shaped eyes and thick, curly, dark hair. And those tiny hands . . . I felt a primordial need to protect him. I healed Gemma's wounds, sat down behind her, and held her close as together we admired our little miracle, with only the forest as witness.

"Thank you," she said softly. "I couldn't have done it without you."

"I wouldn't have missed it for anything in the world." I kissed her.

The baby wailed. "See that, Evan? He's looking at us."

"He recognizes you," I said as mother and child gazed at one another.

She smiled. "Hello, sweetheart. Welcome to the world," she whispered.

"Do you already have a name for him?"

Gemma nodded. "He's always had one. His name is Daniel Liam James."

My eyes went wide. "Daniel. Like Danielle, my mother."

"And Liam from William, like his father. For us he'll just be Liam."

"What do you say we also add Drake, after his uncle?"

"I bet he would call him Double D." Gemma laughed through her tears and then gazed at the baby again. "Drake Daniel Liam James. It's a bit long, but I like it."

I kissed the baby on the forehead. "Liam," I repeated.

Gemma caressed his face. "Hold me tight, Evan."

"I'm right here," I whispered behind her.

A tear trickled down her cheek. "I . . . I don't want to leave him. I don't want the Witches to take me away from you."

"I'll never allow it. We'll follow our plan and everything will go fine, I promise. No one's going to separate us."

Gemma went back to stroking the baby. "Don't worry," she whispered to him. "We'll protect you."

"Guys, where the hell are you?!" I called out in my mind. A second later, Simon and Ginevra appeared behind Gemma. "You guys missed one hell of a show," I exclaimed.

"Oh my God!" Ginevra saw Gemma on the ground and rushed to her side.

"There's someone who wants to meet you," she said.

"Shit." Simon quickly took off his shirt and wrapped it around the baby, who was still in Gemma's arms.

"Hey, would you wait a few days before teaching him swear words?" she joked.

"How did it happen? Why didn't you call us earlier?" Ginevra asked me reproachfully. "I can't believe I missed it!"

"Don't worry, you'll be spending a lot of time together," Gemma assured her.

"I did. I tried calling you. I figured you were in the workout room."

"No, we didn't want be out of reach."

"So why didn't we hear you?" Simon asked me.

Ginevra's eyes shot to mine. We were both thinking the same thing. *It must have been Gemma.* During the birth, it was as though Gemma's energy had exploded all around us. Her power must have interfered with my thoughts, preventing them from reaching the others.

"Can I hold him?" Ginevra asked. Gemma smiled and let her take him out of her arms. "Of all the forms of magic, this is the most extraordinary one," she whispered, cradling the baby.

Simon leaned over and kissed the child on the forehead. "He's adorable. Have you chosen a name?"

"More than one, actually: Drake Daniel Liam James, but to us he'll just be Liam."

"Liam," Ginevra repeated. "You're one of us now."

"He's perfect," Simon told us.

"Simon, bring the baby here," I said. Gin, take care of Gemma."

"Evan, don't leave me," Gemma begged.

"I'm not going anywhere. I just need to get a little water, okay? I'll be back in a second." She nodded and let Ginevra clean her up.

I went to the edge of the lake with Simon, who knelt beside me holding the baby. I raised my palm over the water and it rose up in a gurgling arc. With the heat of my fire I sterilized it, then cooled it enough so Simon could bathe Liam and wrap him in his shirt again.

"Congratulations," he told me, slapping my shoulder. "You're a father now."

"Yeah." I smiled. It was strange to actually hear it said.

"How do you feel?"

"Never been happier," I said.

"As we all are."

"Come on, let's take them someplace more comfortable. Gemma needs to rest." Simon nodded, cradling the baby. I picked Gemma up in my arms and we walked toward our lake house, which wasn't far away.

"We have to tell my parents," Gemma exclaimed when we arrived.

"Simon, would you?" I laid Gemma on the sofa. The sun was still high and sunshine was coming in through the windows, lighting up the room.

"Liam must be hungry," Ginevra said. "I'll get him some milk."

"No," Gemma said. "I want to feed him myself."

Simon handed her the baby and turned to give them some privacy as he phoned Gemma's parents. She bared her breast and snuggled Liam against her. The baby opened his eyes and gazed at his mother for a long moment. He nuzzled her skin, finally found her breast, and began to suckle. Gemma held her breath with emotion and a tear slid down her face. I couldn't imagine her feelings as she fed him.

Our lives were hanging by a thread, held together by an unacceptable oath. The baby was born. We had three days before the Witches returned to claim Gemma. But I wasn't going to let it happen. I was going to take her hand and together, we would let that thread snap and fall into the void—wherever we ended up.

LIGHT AND DARKNESS

Gemma's parents were overjoyed by the news of the birth. They closed the diner and hurried over to the lake house. It took a bit longer than expected to convince them there was no need to take Gemma and the baby to the hospital. To reassure them, we made them believe Simon—who everyone believed was a doctor—had delivered Gemma's baby there because there hadn't been time. The two of them couldn't stop thanking him. They had no idea that the baby had been born in the middle of the forest and that I was the one who had delivered him.

Peter's father's funeral was the next morning. We promised we would stop by to see Gemma's parents the next afternoon before leaving town. We'd used a little persuasive mind control to make Gemma's parents believe—and accept—the idea that we were going on a vacation once the baby was born. It was a necessary lie, given that we didn't know what the future had in store for us. They accepted our decision, though reluctantly, and insisted that upon our "return" we get married. They didn't know we already had.

Anya was also with us all afternoon, along with two panthers that prowled the room nervously. Fortunately, the panthers had waited for Gemma's parents to leave before making their appearance. The time was drawing near and the thought was making me nervous. Having them around was risky. At any moment they might discover our plans and ruin everything.

When the sun finally set the visitors left, leaving us alone to admire our son. I was a father. It made me so proud, I could think of nothing else. To Liam I would be the father I'd never had. I would love him, protect him. And maybe one day he would look up to me.

I gazed at Gemma. She'd slept peacefully on the sofa for most of the night, the baby nestled in her arm. She couldn't bear the thought of being separated from him.

Simon and Ginevra had finally come around. It was important for us to have them as allies in our war against the Witches.

"Look, Evan. He woke up," Ginevra whispered. I slowly went up to Liam and took him in my arms, rocking him beside the fireplace. "He looks so sweet, and so human," Ginevra said, caressing him.

"Sure does," Simon added at her side.

"What's he thinking?" I asked Ginevra.

"He's too young. He doesn't have actual thoughts yet, but he's processing everything around him, the images, the sounds . . . I can interpret his sensations."

"How does he feel right now?"

"He feels safe."

"You're my son," I whispered as he studied my face.

"A son born from the union between good and evil, light and darkness," Simon added solemnly. "Whatever his nature is, he's the emblem of that balance."

Ginevra leaned in for a closer look. "And the whole world will kneel to him."

"Liam . . ." Gemma mumbled, waking up.

"He's here," I said reassuringly, going over to her.

"Do you think he's eaten enough?"

"I think so, but maybe you should eat something now. You need to regain your strength."

"I already have," she assured me, "though I'd gladly have some pizza anyway." She cast a hopeful glance at Ginevra.

"You've got an appetite—that's a good sign." She winked at Gemma and pointed at the kitchen table where the pizza was waiting for her. Gemma made a beeline for the food. She was wearing a white nightgown and her long black hair flowed over her shoulders. Her figure was fantastic. No one would have imagined she'd just given birth to a seven-pound bundle of joy. Everyone had been worried that she'd barely gained weight and the pregnancy had lasted so long, but we knew it was because of her nature. Now that the baby was born, there was no longer any sign of the pregnancy, and after the delivery I'd healed all her wounds.

"Simon, would you mind holding Liam?"

"Of course not. We're already best friends," he said.

"Mmm . . . This pizza's delicious. Evan, you brought your violin!" Gemma exclaimed, beaming.

I smiled. "I thought the baby might like a little music." I rested the instrument on my shoulder and played a new melody, sweet and slow, like a soothing lullaby. Liam stared at me attentively, filling my heart with emotions I'd never experienced before. Pride, mostly. His eyelids soon drooped and he surrendered to sleep. I smiled and walked toward his mother, moving the bow over the strings as I looked into Gemma's eyes. Notes from the mahogany piano joined mine. I didn't need to look to know it was Simon accompanying me.

"It's beautiful," Gemma said softly when the music stopped.

"It's for you." I took her hand and kissed her palm, gazing into her eyes. "The love I feel is captured in its notes."

"If Drake were here right now, I bet he'd be grousing about all this lovey-dovey stuff," Ginevra said, grinning.

"She's right, bro. You've completely lost it," Simon added with a smile. He stroked Liam, who was in Ginevra's arms. "But with a miracle like this, I would too."

"We'll all raise him together," Gemma said. "After all, he's also a little bit yours. If it hadn't been for the two of you he wouldn't be here today."

I smiled at Gemma and squeezed her hand. "Come on. Feel like taking a walk?"

"Outside?" She looked at the baby, her expression apprehensive.

"Don't worry, he's in good hands."

"I know." She relaxed, went over to Liam, and stroked his head. After tenderly kissing his forehead, she joined me by the door. "It's strange not to have him inside me any more," she admitted.

It was still dark out, but the sun was preparing to rise, slightly illuminating the sky.

"I feel an emptiness inside. It's like I miss him. I can't stop looking at him."

"Yeah, I know what you mean. But you kept him all to yourself for long enough. It's my turn to get to know him." I winked at her and she laughed as we neared the lake shore, barefoot.

"You're right. I can't imagine being separated from him, that's all."

"No one is going to separate you from him . . . or from me. We're a family now, and soon we'll make sure no supernatural force will ever threaten to divide us again." I rested my forehead against hers and took a deep breath, the water lapping at my ankles. "Sometimes I think it's all my fault," I admitted.

"What are you talking about, Evan?"

"If you hadn't gone to get me in Hell, you wouldn't have been forced to swear loyalty to the Witches, and you and the baby would be able to live normal lives."

"There's nothing normal about my life, Evan. This is my fate. Without you, I'd be lost in the darkness. I made the pact with the Witches because I knew your love would keep me here. There's hope only if you're here at my side."

"No, hope isn't enough for me. We'll do it my way."

"I know, we've already agreed."

I hugged Gemma around the waist. "What are we waiting for, then? Let's do it now. I don't want to waste another second."

"We still have two days before the Witches come to force me to make good on my promise. Let's at least wait a few hours."

"Why? You and the baby are fine. There's no reason to wait any longer."

"I . . . I'm afraid, Evan. We don't know what the consequences of our decision will be, and I'm not ready to part from Liam yet. Just a few more hours, okay? For just a little while let's pretend everything's normal."

I held her tight and stroked her head, breathing in the scent of her hair. "Everything's going to be fine, Jamie."

"I know. As long as you're with me, I won't be afraid."

"Want to go inside?"

"No, let's stay here a little longer." Gemma took my hands and waded into the lake, her eyes never leaving mine. She immersed herself and the morning light made the beaded water on her face sparkle like diamonds. I stroked her cheek and my thumb lingered on her lip.

She gazed at me provocatively and guided my hand to her breast, her stiffened nipples peeking through her transparent nightgown. She looked like a water nymph who'd come to bewitch me. I drew her to me and breathed against her neck. "Why are you doing this to me?" I whispered, pressing my arousal against her.

Gemma bit her lip, smiling. "I want to make sure you still desire me."

"I desire you more than ever now that you've given me a son," I whispered against her mouth before kissing her passionately.

"You'll have to keep your distance for a while, I'm afraid."

"It'll be sheer hell." I kissed her again and she laughed, resting her hands on my chest. The dog tag had grown cold beneath my wet shirt. Or maybe it was the contrast with the fire racing through my veins.

"We'd better get back," Gemma whispered. How she loved to tease me.

I blocked her path and lifted her up by the thighs, drawing her against me. "Where do you think you're going?" I raised an eyebrow and my mouth traced the curve of her chin.

"It's almost day, Evan."

"No it isn't. It's night. The stars are out."

Gemma looked up at the sky and laughed. "Where do you see any? There are no stars."

I sought her hand beneath the water and squeezed it, gazing into her beautiful eyes. "You're wrong, because I'm looking at two of them right now." I kissed her tenderly on the mouth and she responded, biting my lip.

"I wish I could make love with you," she whispered, lighting the fire that dominated me. I pulled her hips against mine and felt the heat of her desire. I kissed her more ardently, mingling our breath.

"Hey, little mermaid!" Ginevra called out. "The baby woke up and is demanding breakfast. And you, Adonis, behave yourself! Can't you even wait one day? By Lilith! The woman just gave birth!" She went back inside, muttering, and Gemma and I burst out laughing.

"Looks like the little guy is going to have what I can't," I joked, fondling one of her breasts. "He's already one step ahead of me."

Gemma laughed. "I'm sure you'll teach him all sorts of things, *Adonis*. As for the two of us, later on we'll pick up this conversation where we left off. But now, Soldier, at ease."

I raised her hand to my mouth and kissed her palm, looking her in the eye. "As you wish." I waded toward the shore, Gemma behind me.

"I'd better put something dry on before nursing the baby," she thought aloud.

"No problem. Ginevra can get you a change of clothes." I emerged from the lake and shook the water from my hair, wetting her even more.

"Evan!" I smiled. I couldn't help it. I had no idea why, but I loved teasing her. Sometimes it made her mad, but she never held a grudge for long. "Wait!" Gemma called out. I turned around and saw her leaning over, searching for something on the lakebed. "How on earth . . .? My necklace fell off. Ah, there it is!" she exclaimed, relieved.

Just then Liam's wails reached us. "As impatient as his mother when it comes to food. I'll go on ahead," I told her as she groped through the sand for her chain. I strode to the door of the hideaway where Ginevra smiled at me, my son in her arms.

"Got it!" Gemma exclaimed, still in the water. I turned to look at her as she stood up, the necklace clasped in her hand and a smile on her lips.

A sudden hiss pierced the air.

Too fast.

Too unexpected.

"Gemmaaa!!!" Her eyes locked onto mine. Then they moved down to the large arrow lodged in her chest. I raced toward her but a cold wind pushed me back, turning my heart to ice. "Gemmaaa!!!" I screamed, my chest splintering into shards of pain.

"Fuck, no!" Simon shouted. "Gin, don't leave Liam!" He joined me and together we tried to break through the barrier. Gemma raised her eyes and stared at me, devastated. I knew that look—I'd seen it a million times on the faces of mortals about to die. *No. Not Gemma, no!*

A tear slid down her cheek. "Liam," her lips murmured as a patch of red spread out around the arrow. She fell to her knees, her eyes trained on mine. Everything around me vanished as I drowned in the chaos inside my mind. All I could hear was the sound of her heartbeat that grew slower and slower.

"Gemmaaa!" I screamed.

A man appeared behind her, a bow in his hand. "Die, Witch." He grasped her head and snapped her neck. Gemma's eyes wavered and went blank.

"Noooo!" I screamed at the top of my lungs.

Anya appeared beside me and froze. Shaking herself out of it, she rushed at the man, but the barrier repelled her. The man raised his eyes, looked at me with a sneer, and disappeared. I raced into the water to Gemma, who was floating face down with the arrow sticking out of her back. Her heart had stopped beating.

I turned her over and dragged her to shore as Simon and Anya rushed to us. "Simon, help me! We've got to heal her!" I snapped the arrow in two and pulled it out of her body. It had pierced her heart. "No, Gemma, no! Don't leave me now, of all times." I tried to close up the wound but she didn't respond. "Come on, Gemma! Fight!" I screamed.

"No! This wasn't supposed to happen!" Anya said, leaning over Gemma.

Simon rested his hand on my shoulder. "Evan, stop."

"Don't tell me to stop!" I shouted. "Keep healing her, Simon! Don't give up!"

"She's dead, Evan."

"We'll bring her back. We've done it before. Where's her soul? Why isn't her soul here?!" Simon stared at me, devastated, and I covered my face with my bloody hands.

"Gemma!" Ginevra ran to her and threw herself to her knees. "Gemma, no! How could this happen?" she screamed at her Sister who'd had the task of watching over the Subterranean prisoners.

"I don't know. The Subterraneans are all still there. They're fading, but none of them has died. I don't understand."

"Then why did another Executioner show up?"

"That wasn't just any Executioner. I recognized him," Anya said. "That was Gareth Kreihn. We call him Absolon, which in our language means . . ."

"Witch hunter," Ginevra murmured, turning pale.

"How is that even possible? He died centuries ago," I exclaimed.

"It seems not." Ginevra grabbed the arrow and sniffed it. "This is poisoned."

I clenched my fists. "Why didn't he take her? Why didn't he help her cross over?"

"It's too late for her soul. Evil has claimed her. By dying, Gemma will now be a Soul damned to wander Hell."

"It can't end this way!" I snarled. I had denied Gemma Heaven, denied her immortality with her Sisters, and now she would be nothing but another of the Damned in Hell? Was this the future I'd promised her? I'd been such an egotist! My love for her had destroyed her.

I couldn't accept it. "Transform her." I looked at Anya, determined.

"What did you say?"

"Transform her," I repeated firmly. There was still a chance. I had to act fast.

"Evan, think this through," Simon warned me.

"Shut up! She can't die like this! Not now!"

Anya and Ginevra exchanged glances. "Simon, take the baby," Ginevra told him. "Take him away. Go back home."

"I'm not leaving you here."

"Yes, you are! Take him away, now! You have to keep him safe." She shot him a pointed look and he nodded. She leaned over and tore open Gemma's nightgown. A knot formed in my throat at the sight of Gemma so defenseless, with a hole in her chest. I bit my fist to fight back the pain.

"Evan, move back," Ginevra ordered. "Move back, I told you!"

I took a step backward as they tried to summon Gemma's Dakor so it could bite her. Her heart wasn't beating any more and her soul was lost somewhere in the darkness. There was no choice. I would rather she transform than be dead. Maybe the transformation wouldn't obliterate her after all. Maybe there was still a chance she would choose me.

"It's not working!" Ginevra growled.

"What do you mean, it's not working? Try again, damn it!"

"She has to be alive to transform," Anya said sadly.

"This shouldn't have happened," Ginevra murmured, leaning over Gemma's body.

I crumpled to my knees as my soul slowly died. No. It couldn't actually have happened. I dug my fingers into the earth and a scream tore my chest in two: "LILITH! You can't let her die! I'm begging you!"

A burst of lightning streaked through the sky and Devina materialized in front of us. "Sophia is preparing to wage war. The Màsala will regret what they've done to Gemma."

"No," Ginevra gasped.

I clenched my fists. "Take me with you. I want to fight."

"Evan, what are you talking about?" Ginevra exclaimed. "A war against the Màsala won't accomplish anything. It won't bring Gemma back!"

"She's right," Anya said. "It'll be a massacre. The battlefield will be Earth. Many will die."

"I don't care," I shot back icily. Gemma had died and my humanity had died with her, leaving behind only the Executioner. I wanted revenge. For months we'd fought to protect my love. Now it was time for me to hunt.

"Evan, listen to me!" Ginevra shouted. Her voice was distant, as though she were speaking from some faraway place, but she was right there. It was me who was lost. "You're blinded by rage! Think of the baby. Who's going to protect Liam? He's your son. He needs you." I eased my grip, my fists loosening. Ginevra had managed to penetrate the black shroud around my heart. "Wait. Devina isn't here just to tell us that—are you?" Ginevra added, picking up on her Sister's thoughts.

"There's still a way to prevent war."

"She's right," Anya said in a low voice, her expression focused as she read her Sister's thoughts. "Maybe we still have a chance to save Gemma." She stared at Devina, who laughed to herself.

"The Empress gave me *this* for her. She tore it off her finger before my very eyes. You'd better hope it works." Devina showed us a small object, black and sharp.

"What is it?" I asked.

"The Devil's Claw."

"Will it work?" Ginevra asked anxiously.

"We have to try," Anya said.

"Try what? What's going on?" I asked, apprehensive.

Anya looked at me. "Ginevra and I can't awaken Gemma's Dakôr . . ."

"Only the devil can bring the dead back from Hell," Devina added.

"Well? What are you waiting for? Do something!" I yelled. Anya slowly looked up at me. What did that look mean?

"Evan, Sophìa's poison will cancel every last trace of Gemma," Ginevra warned me, voicing her Sister's thoughts. "There's no chance she'll still be herself. Are you sure you want this?"

I looked at her. "Do it." Ginevra nodded and Devina smirked at me.

"I'm sorry," Anya said softly, looking at me regretfully.

Devina went up to Gemma, holding Sophìa's claw. She took her wrist and carved the mark of the Witches into her skin while murmuring an ancient litany whose meaning I couldn't understand. *"Treh. Immuaarimet. Lohe. Keh. Kuta Sih."*

"Treh. Immuaarimet. Lohe. Keh. Kuta Sih," Ginevra and Anya echoed. *"Treh. Immuaarimet. Lohe. Keh. Kuta Sih."*

The mark sizzled like seared flesh and Gemma's outstretched body levitated into the air. The water in the lake churned; the wind blew fiercely. Something rested on my shoulder: a black butterfly. No, not one. They were everywhere, filling the sky, a vortex created by a dark force. All the windows in the lake house exploded. I took a step back as a burst of lightning lit up the sky. Gemma's head jerked back as though her neck had snapped again. Her eyes were pure black, wide open, and trained on me as they changed form. The darkness retreated from their whites and her pupils lengthened like a serpent's before returning to normal. A myriad of water droplets rose from the lake and hovered until another stroke of lightning pierced the sky and they crashed down like an explosion. A shriek of pain burst from Gemma's mouth. I rushed toward her but someone held me back. It was Devina. For once she was right: I couldn't interfere.

The wind was so strong it threatened to drag me away as Gemma continued to shriek. Something stirred in her belly, creeping beneath her skin, finally rupturing it to emerge. *Her Dakor.*

"It's black," Ginevra whispered to her Sisters, as though that were something unusual for them. The serpent slithered across Gemma's belly and she stopped screaming. Aroused by the power, the animal moved swiftly, longing to feed, longing to be part of Gemma. It opened its fangs and sank them into her wrist. She seemed struck by a jolt of exhilaration mixed with anguish as the serpent penetrated her arm and disappeared inside her once again.

The wound disappeared. Gemma straightened and stood, keeping her head down for a moment as she avidly gulped in the air. We all held our breath. She slowly raised her head and fixed her gaze on me, her eyes lengthening like her serpent's and glittering like carbonado.

"Gemma," I whispered, and part of me died forever when I realized it was no longer her. Her black eyes, streaked with purple, remained fixed on mine as a challenging sneer spread across her face. She was still disoriented, but one thing was clear: she saw me as her enemy. The new beginning for Gemma was the end for us.

Anya rested her hands on Gemma's shoulders, looking sadly at my lost expression. "We have to go," she said, turning to Devina. "We have a war to prevent." I looked at Gemma one last time as she disappeared before my eyes, leaving me petrified with pain.

They had used Sophia's own poison to awaken Gemma's Dakor. While before we'd had some hope Gemma might transform yet remain herself, that hope was now gone.

Ginevra looked at me, in her eyes her sorrow over the undeniable verdict. "We've lost her."

GEMMA

THE AWAKENING

I felt my heart beat wildly as a powerful energy flooded me. My first instinct was to fight it, but instead I surrendered to its power and let it fill me. A hot shiver ran through my body. I opened my eyes. Light was all around me, while shadows gathered inside me.

My head bowed, I tried to control my breathing and with it, the energy surging within me. I smiled, enraptured by the power I felt flowing through my veins like lava, regenerating me. It was dark and magnificent. I slowly raised my eyes and was instantly drawn to the Soul before me. It was unlike the other three; instinct urged me to annihilate it. I had no idea where I was or even who I was. My gaze remained locked on the young man's gray eyes while inside me violent impulses raged.

A young woman with green eyes rested her hands on my shoulders, preventing me from unleashing my fury on him. "We have to go. We have a war to prevent."

Before I could stop her, the man vanished. The journey lasted only a moment. When I looked around, we were in a different place. "Who are you?" I asked warily. "Where are we? Why have you brought me here?"

The green-eyed woman looked closely at me and took my hand. "I'm Anya. Don't you remember?" Should I have? She looked at me as though I should, or at least as though she hoped I would, but I had no idea what was going on.

The redhead beside her laughed. "Of course she doesn't remember. It erased everything. Absolutely *everything*." She seemed pleased by it. Should I be too?

"It was Sophia's poison that awakened her. How could she remember?"

"I know. I was just hoping."

"Hoping for what?"

I stared at them, bewildered. I'd heard their voices, but neither of them had opened their mouths. Had I only imagined it? The redhead took me by the hand and led me away from the other woman. "Come, dear. Someone is expecting you."

I looked back, where Anya still stood. She had a look of irritation on her face, as though she were angry at the redhead. Someone clapped their hands and the sound filled the large circular hall. There were windows everywhere that reached to the ceiling, letting in the twilight.

Then I saw her. A woman sat on a majestic black throne. She wore a long gown with a V-shaped neckline that plunged to her navel. The powerful energy she emanated drew me to her. My heart began to beat harder. I wanted to go to her, to touch her.

As though she'd heard my thoughts, the woman with the gaze of ice smiled at me and stood. Her waist-long hair was black at the roots, gradually fading to gray, until it became white at the tips, like a splendid partial eclipse of the moon. At her feet, two big black panthers watched my every movement.

I had no idea who the women were or where I was, but for some reason I didn't care. I felt at home. The two women at my side bowed to her and I did the same, but she raised my chin. Her eyes were such an intense shade of blue it took my breath away. Her long lashes stood out against her fair skin and her lips, painted black, bewitched me. They were so perfectly contoured they seemed magical. I felt as though I were a bee and she was my queen. That was all I knew. Moving her lips close to mine, she kissed me, sending an electric charge through my body. "Welcome," she said, her voice captivating. "Do you know who I am?"

I looked into her eyes. "No." I neither knew nor cared. Whoever she was, I was hers.

She smiled. "Do not worry. Soon you will know all." She seemed so pleased to see me. "You will blossom, my little chrysalis. You will spread your wings and become a magnificent black butterfly. Your arrival changes many things. It was good of your Sisters to bring you home."

My Sisters. So that was why I felt that energy between us.

The woman turned and the panthers watched her as she walked back to them and seated herself again on her throne. "Prepare her. Later there is to be a great celebration."

"Yes, my Empress," both women replied.

She smiled at me and suddenly burst into an explosion of black butterflies that rose into the air. I watched them, fascinated, as they disappeared through a hole in the ceiling, then dropped my eyes again to the now-empty throne. She had transformed. I should have been afraid, but instead I was exhilarated.

"Where are they going?" I asked, but a pain gripped my head, doubling me over.

"She asks so many questions . . ."

"I have to find a way to . . ."

"Did you see? She's here . . ."

I clapped my hands over my ears and looked around, confused. Where were all those voices coming from? They were in my head. That was why it ached so badly.

". . . on me . . ." Anya was trying to speak to me. ". . . other voices." I didn't understand. What was she saying? "Gemma, listen to me!" Her voice rose above the chorus of others in my mind. "Focus on me . . . Good, that's it. Breathe and watch my lips moving."

I did as she said and managed to isolate the sound, banishing the other voices. "What's happening to me?" I asked in alarm.

Anya smiled. "It's perfectly normal. You'll get used to it soon. Come. I'll take you to your chambers."

"I'll stay here," the other Sister said, "in case any new prisoners to play with show up."

"As you like," Anya replied. "See you at the celebration."

"Gemma, I'm happy you're finally home." The redhead smiled at me and I nodded.

"Thank you," I said before Anya led me away.

We went through several rooms and I understood almost immediately that we were in a castle. There were lots of people, mainly women in combat outfits. I wore a white nightgown that was torn and bloodied. What could possibly have happened to me?

"Don't worry about that," Anya said, as though she'd read my mind. "We'll bring you some suitable clothes in time for the festivities."

"What festivities?" I asked hesitantly.

She beamed. "The ones in your honor, the Welcome Ceremony. All of us have one."

"All of you? How many of you are there?"

"Oh, you'll find out soon enough. You're very confused, I know, but you'll like it here with us, Gemma. I guarantee it." I stared at Anya.

Gemma. She kept saying that. It seemed to be my name. Why couldn't I remember it? "Come on, let me show you something fun." She pulled me into a small hallway where voices filled my head:

"What gorgeous hair!"

"And look at that complexion!"

"Hands down, she's the most beautiful of all the Sisters."

"What is this place?" I asked, confused.

"The Hall of Flattery. Each of us hears what we'd like to hear. It boosts your self-esteem. Not that any of us need it, but compliments can't hurt, and most of us can't go without them. If you like this, wait till you see the Chamber of Mirrors."

We reached a large wooden door at the end of the hall. Anya opened it and showed me the room. It had a high, high ceiling where black butterflies fluttered. The walls were almost entirely covered with mirrors. A large fireplace set into one wall lit up the room while another wall had a window framing a clear sky at twilight. In the center of the room stood a big black bed with blood-red silk sheets. All the walls were black—as were the ceiling and floor—and made of a material that sparkled like a dark diamond.

Two young women bowed to me and smiled. "We've been expecting you, my lady," another one said, ushering me inside.

"Who are you?"

"They're Mizhyas."

"Are they my Sisters too?" I asked, though I didn't feel the same connection to them that I did to Anya.

"No, but you can consider them your handmaids. They're very loyal and are always at your service."

The three women bowed. I realized I could perceive their emotions: veneration mixed with fear. One of them kissed my hand. "I am Emayn and I will be honored to serve you." I stepped back, studying her carefully. She had olive skin and a sensual gaze. An artistic tattoo on her right hand made its way up her arm.

Another, her skin snow-white, stepped forward and lowered her eyes fearfully. "My name is Meryall. Ask of me what you will and I will do it." I raised her chin and looked into her big blue eyes.

The last of them had remained in reverential silence. I approached her. She had a small face and a sharp expression. Her eyes showed no fear—only caution. "And what is your name?"

"Freia, my lady. At your service."

I studied them from head to toe. All three wore leather ankle boots and sexy, close-fitting, brown uniforms, and their hair was braided, like the other women I'd seen in the Castle. Each had a band tattooed on her arm in a different shape, like a distinctive marking. Their bodies were toned and muscular and they looked like battle-trained Amazons.

"Actually, they are," Anya replied.

I turned to her, surprised. Now there was no doubt about it. "You can read my mind?"

She smiled. "Cool, isn't it? Pretty soon you'll be doing it too. And that's nothing!"

"I have powers?" The idea thrilled me.

"Of course you do. You have a great power buried inside you. We're going to teach you to control it."

"Who am I?" I asked, sensing that the answer was the key to everything.

"You're one of us." Anya hugged me. "And you're finally home."

BLOOD BOND

The Castle was abuzz. Everyone seemed excited about the party. From time to time Mizhyas came to peek into the room. Anya had directed me to put on a special gown, the same one they'd all worn the day of their ceremony. It consisted of black leather shorts with a fluffy, full-length train that looked like it was made of interwoven butterfly wings, black knee-high boots, and leather laces that crisscrossed up my thighs.

My maidservants had given me a long, hot bath and a massage before carefully doing up my eyes with black shadow, enhancing them greatly. Now Anya was giving my hair a final touch-up, gathering a few locks and braiding the style into place.

"Why don't I remember anything about my past?"

"Because you were generated by Earth to join us."

"You mean I didn't have a life before this one?"

Anya hesitated, as if choosing her words carefully. "You did, but you swore loyalty to us."

"Did I know it would make me lose my memory?"

"Yes."

My life must have been horrible if I'd wanted to run away from it. This place, on the other hand, made me feel strong.

"Your life begins now." Anya looked me in the eye. "With us. You're special, Gemma. Only one mortal every five hundred years receives this gift."

"What gift?"

"The power. Immortality. Sisterhood. We're Witches, Gemma."

Witches. A quiver of pleasure ran beneath my skin. "Who was that man with the gray eyes in the forest?"

"Your greatest enemy: a Subterranean," said the redhead, who'd just appeared. So that was why I'd felt such hostility toward him.

"Devina, are you already tired of waiting for new prisoners? Why don't you go out and find some yourself?"

"No, stay here," I told her. "Please." I felt a strong affinity toward her. I had the impression she had much to teach me. She emanated power and I wanted to absorb every drop.

Devina smiled at me. "Of course, with great pleasure."

The two Sisters looked at each other challengingly. I was sure they were having a mental conversation without including me. A constant murmur filled my mind but I couldn't distinguish the voices. "Will I always have these voices in my head?"

"You'll get used to it. Focus on your own thoughts and everything else will fade into the background."

"When will I start understanding your thoughts too?" I asked, frustrated by their silent conversation.

"After your Dakor's baptism, once you've sealed the Bond with us. Sophìa will officially unite you to us and the transformation will be complete."

"Sophìa is the woman who was on the throne, isn't she?"

"She's our Great Sister," Devina replied. "A Witch, just like you and me."

"But she's also our Empress, although Devina sometimes forgets it."

"Can we do what she did when she disintegrated?" For some reason, I'd been bewitched by her butterflies.

"No. Only when we die—but that's a remote possibility."

"Each time it's like a tiny death for her," Devina added. "It's just that she can't die."

"She's the queen of darkness. Death belongs to her."

"But it's the only thing she can't have herself. That's why she likes it so much."

"You're ready," Anya said.

I looked into a large mirror and smiled at my reflection. I didn't know who I'd been before, but what I saw now pleased me. I was pretty. And soon I would become very dangerous.

Anya turned to her Sister. "What do you think?"

"I think she's missing something." Devina smiled and turned around. "Follow me."

I obeyed, letting her guide me down a long hallway that took us to a huge courtyard where a grim twilight ruled. The place was in commotion, with Amazons running in and out of it.

"Are there only women here?" I asked.

A half-smile appeared on Devina's face. "No, but we keep the men out of our way. We don't need them. If anything, they're the ones who need us. Depending on a man is a sign of weakness, but making him depend on you is an indicator of power. Every man you see in the Castle subjugated himself to us of his own free will . . . either that or he's our prisoner." I smiled. It was an interesting topic.

I followed her down broad staircases leading to an underground door. When Devina opened it, a flame ran along the stone walls, lighting them up. "Here. This is it."

"What is this place?"

"This is where we keep a few of our toys." I looked around and my jaw dropped. "This is the weapons room. You can't go to the ceremony without having chosen a weapon."

"Have I ever battled before?"

"You have it in your blood. For you, it'll be like breathing."

All the walls were entirely covered with weapons. There were so many of them! "How do I choose?"

"You can use all the weapons you want, whenever you want, naturally, but each of us has a special one we always keep with us."

"What's yours?"

Devina brought her hand to her thigh and a second later a whip cracked through the air. The sound was so sharp its echo filled the room. "Once you have your toy, you can personalize it with symbols of your battles. I perfected my *Magnificent* with Molock skin."

"What's a Molock?"

"It's a creature from Hell—one of the fiercest. It was fun to see the terror in its eyes while I was flaying it. You'll have fun too, I'm sure of it."

"You chose the perfect name. It really is magnificent," I admitted, staring at the whip in her hand. "How will I find mine?"

"It'll find you. When you touch it, its energy will come to life and you'll be able to feel the power that unites you."

"What are we waiting for, then? Let's start right away!" I smiled at her and began to look around. There were weapons of all kinds, eras, and sizes. I picked up a sword and weighed it in my hand. It was incredible how confidently I handled it. I spun it around in one hand as Devina watched me with a proud look on her face. Putting it back, I grabbed a long iron staff. I followed my instinct and the staff moved in my hands as though we were one. I made a feint at Devina, who nimbly dodged it and pinned me to the wall.

She smiled, pleased. "You're a natural, but you still have a lot to learn."

"When?" I asked impatiently. I felt strong. I wanted to become invincible.

"Soon. Very soon," she promised. "Have you found what you were looking for?"

I was about to say no when my eyes fell on a pedestal at the back of the room. A crossbow sat atop it, a beautiful black crossbow that begged me to come closer. "There it is," I murmured to myself, heeding its call.

"Excellent choice," Devina said, a touch of admiration in her eyes.

After a moment's hesitation, I reached out and picked up the crossbow, almost with deference. It adapted perfectly to my grip and I felt its lethal power flow into me. It looked like it had been carved from a black diamond, the same stone the Castle was made from. Looking at the crossbow, I noticed there was a tattoo on my hand. It was composed of strange symbols, but somehow I knew what it meant: *stay together*. It must have had something to do with my Sisters.

"It's a rare object," Devina said, pulling me out of my thoughts. "Sophìa forged it centuries and centuries ago. No one has touched it since, but I was there when she made it. I saw the power it possesses." She picked up a small, all-black arrow and showed it to me. "Its arrows are unstoppable and deadly. You'll have to be careful how you use it, because it's a weapon that takes no prisoners."

I smiled, my eyes locked on my new weapon. *"Khalida,"* I whispered. *Unstoppable.* The language that had suddenly filled my mind was unfamiliar to me, but suddenly I could speak it.

Devina nodded with satisfaction. "I think it's perfect."

"I want to try it," I said excitedly.

"We'll do that soon. Right now we need to go to the ceremony. You're the guest of honor, so you can't be late." She winked at me and motioned for me to follow her.

I strapped on a sling and hung the crossbow on my back. I was about to follow Devina, but something stopped me. "Wait!" I picked up two daggers with crescent-shaped blades, spun them around, and tucked them into the strips of leather laced around my thighs. "I'm taking these too."

Devina smiled. I liked that room. I would have to go back soon. Outside, I looked around the empty courtyard. "Where did everybody go?"

"They're in the Pantheon. The ceremony is about to begin." Devina led me inside the Castle to a massive door of carved black stone. "Ready?"

I nodded and the door slowly opened at her command. We were once again in the throne room, only this time everyone was there, clad in long golden cloaks with broad hoods, their eyes trained on me. I raised my chin and made my way into the room with my head held high, gazing steadily at the Empress. It was as though I was bound to her by some mystical connection. As I passed, everyone around me bowed: women, men, and majestic black panthers. I stopped only when I reached the throne.

Silence reigned supreme. A tongue of fire ran along the walls, casting lights and shadows on my Sisters' beautiful faces. A flock of black butterflies circled through the air and alit on the throne, drawn by its power, but my eyes didn't waver.

Sophìa smiled, her expression radiant. As she stood, everyone held their breath. A black serpent slithered around her neck. *Dakor*, my instinct said. His incredible lapis lazuli eyes peered at me from close up, hypnotic. They were identical to Sophìa's. She glanced at my crossbow and nodded, as though satisfied with my choice. All at once, her voice filled my head.

"Naiad. I have waited so long for you, my little warrior."

"I am yours, my Empress," I said resolutely, bowing my head.

She slowly spread her arms and proclaimed, "May the ceremony begin!" A chorus of drums and shouts filled the room. "Come," she said, holding my hand. "Take your place. It is time for you to unite with your Sisters." She walked me to a throne next to hers. It was smaller but just as majestic. At its sides, two panthers bowed to me. There was something familiar about one of them . . . It must have been the color of its eyes—jade green. A moment later it changed form and I realized why I had had that sensation: it was Anya. I stared at her, amazed. The other panther also took on a human form, but I'd never seen her before.

I sat on the throne and Sophìa took her place at my side. "Today is a great day," she proclaimed as the crowd listened, ecstatic. Once again she wore a gown that appeared to be made of black butterflies, but the design was different, as if it were molding itself to her body. "After five hundred long years, one of our Sisters has awakened from Earth to join us. She has been given to us and we welcome her as blood of our blood, now and for eternity." The crowd cheered and stamped their feet. "And now introduce yourselves, Sisters! Let us present Naiad's new family to her."

Anya knelt before me. "She is Anya," Sophìa said, "but I know you have already met her. She is loyal and wise. She will be a good Sister to you."

My new Sister stood. Her hair flowed over her shoulders in soft chestnut-brown curls with a contrasting blond streak that crossed through them like a shaft of light. She gazed at me for a moment, the serpent coiled around her arm peering at me with the same incredible green eyes, then kissed me on the lips. "Welcome," she whispered before winking at me and stepping back. She stopped before the throne at the edge of a red symbol on the floor, the symbol that represented us. No one had explained that to me but somehow I knew it.

"Devina. The first Sister . . . and my Specter," Sophìa announced. "She has the spirit of a warrior and will guide you in your ascent."

Devina made a little bow without taking her eyes off mine and kissed me. Her kiss wasn't tender like Anya's, but electrifying and sensual. Her lips were painted red, the same color as her hair. Even her eyes seemed to be made of fire.

Then came Bathsheeva, whom the Sisters simply called Sheeva. She had a long ponytail that reached her ankles, caramel-colored skin, and eyes of molten gold. She too knelt before me and kissed me on the lips to welcome me. Next was Zafirah—Safria to the Sisters. Her blue eyes with their hints of purple stood out against her black skin and crown of braided black hair. Kreeshna, also dark-skinned, had a long braid that hung over her shoulder. Zhora followed, with very short, bright, mahogany hair and emerald-green eyes that glowed like those of the Dakor wrapped around her wrist. Nerea was next. She had long blond hair with speckled tips and incredible yellow eyes; then Camelia, as sensual as a siren with her big gray eyes, fair skin, and pastel-pink hair that turned lilac at the tips. Last of all came Nausyka. Her hair was platinum blond and her blue eyes sparkled like pole stars. They each wore a lock of braided hair across their foreheads like a diadem. I counted nine of them, plus Sophìa and me. Though I'd never seen most of them before, I felt the strong connection uniting us. They were my Sisters and I was one of them. A Witch. Each had her own serpent, some coiled around arms, others around necks, still others around thighs.

They stood there waiting until the Empress spoke again. "The time has come," she announced solemnly. The entire audience knelt as Sophìa stood and offered me her hand. She led me to the center of the circle of Witches where the symbol was carved into the black stone. A maidservant appeared carrying a black chalice covered with a red silk cloth, which Sophìa removed. The Mizhya took it, bowed, and retreated, joining a long line of maidservants. The Witches' serpents hissed. Only they stirred inside the hall. Everyone else held their breath.

Sophìa approached Devina and offered her the chalice. As Devina looked at me, her eyes as ardent as fire, her serpent opened his jaws and bit her wrist, disappearing inside her. Her irises expanded like tentacles, filling the whites of her eyes, and her pupils lengthened. Devina held out her wrist and let a drop of her blood fall into Sophìa's cup. Anya did the same, and all the other Sisters followed suit. When the last drop of blood had been offered, Sophìa came to me and handed me the cup. I took it and her serpent hissed, fixing his eyes on mine before opening his jaws, striking, and then slithering into his mistress. The Empress's blue eyes glittered for a moment, becoming just like her Dakor's, as her blood dripped into the cup, sizzling. "This is the blood of your Sisters," she recited in an ancient tongue that I was able to understand. "Drink it and receive them inside you."

I raised the cup to my lips, looking at the Witches one by one. They looked back at me with respect and anticipation. I allowed their blood to flow onto my tongue and its aroma enraptured me down to my soul. The Mizhya returned and carried the cup away. My head was spinning.

Sophìa took my wrist and slid her long black nails over my skin, cutting my palm. "Though everywhere he is forced to crawl, in this his realm he rules over all." My heart was thumping and I felt like I'd taken a powerful drug. "Come to me," Sophìa whispered.

Then it happened. A serpent, like those of my Sisters, slowly emerged from my palm. He was black—completely black. I stood there staring at him as he slithered up my wrist. He hissed, gazing at me intently. His black eyes were streaked with violet and I instantly felt he was part of me.

A murmur swept through the crowd.

"Do you see that? It's black."

"It can't be . . ."

"It's just like the Empress's . . ."

They were right. My serpent wasn't green, like my other Sisters'.

Sophìa looked at me and smiled. "You are not only one of us," she said, her voice solemn. "You are the thirteenth Witch and I have been awaiting you a long, long time." She took my hand and raised it to her lips, kissing my bloody palm. "Offer your blood to the Sisterhood to seal the Bond." I went around the circle of Witches and one by one they leaned in to drink from my palm. "It is time," Sophìa announced.

All the Witches, including the Empress, held hands, closing the circle around me. *"Kaameh. Tika nun kàa. Saeth rith,"* they chanted as one. The serpents crept out of their bodies as the prayer grew more rhythmic and intense. It was Kahatmunì, the Witches' secret, ancient code. And I understood it.

The Bond has now been consecrated and cannot be eradicated.
"Kaameh. Tika nun kàa. Saeth rith."
"Kaameh. Tika nun kàa. Saeth rith."

All their Dakor came to me, slithering across the floor and encircling me. My serpent was excited, responding to their call. The crowd began to stamp their feet in a hypnotic rhythm, faster and faster.

"Blossom, my little chrysalis."

Silence filled the room once more as my Dakor opened his jaws and sank his fangs into my wrist, penetrating me. The train of my dress exploded into a myriad of black butterflies and I threw back my head, overwhelmed by a mix of pain and pure pleasure. My eyes burned as he fused with me and the butterflies whirled around me. I felt his heart beat and synchronize with mine. I heard his hiss whisper inside my head and sensed his soul bond to mine. We were one.

"You will have the strength of a panther. The shrewdness of a serpent. The grace of a butterfly," Sophìa proclaimed.

"She's magnificent," one of the Sisters was thinking.

"A worthy warrior."

"I'll teach her everything," Devina added.

"I must protect her," Anya thought.

They were inside my mind, all of them. I was a Witch. The transformation was complete.

When the tingling stopped, I turned to look at Sophìa, who awaited me, beaming. She moved closer and pressed her lips to mine in a long, sensual kiss. "You are officially one of us now. Nothing can break our bond."

"Yes, my Empress."

The Witches cheered and lifted me onto their shoulders, letting out a battle cry. I smiled, letting their enthusiasm infect me. I remembered nothing about my past, but I was certain I'd never been so happy before.

A NEW WORLD

"Where are we going?" I asked them telepathically. The ceremony was over and the Witches were carrying me out of the Castle, tossing me into the air from time to time and letting out war whoops.

"This is when the real party starts!" Devina told me.

I could hear their every smallest thought. The voices of the other people present also filled my mind, and if I concentrated, I could make out one or another, but with the Witches it was different. Their voices were loud and clear, as if we were all a single, inseparable being.

They led me to what looked like an amphitheater. There were already lots of people looking out from the balconies of the surrounding buildings, in the stands, in the center of the arena. Bare-chested men beat drums while others performed an acrobatic tribal dance that was crude and incredibly sexy. The Witches put me down and Devina rested her hand on my shoulder. "Here, try this." She offered me a chalice containing a clear liquid and I gulped it down.

My eyes went wide and my throat burned. "What is it?!" I exclaimed, but a second later the liquid warmed my stomach and spread through my entire body, causing a quiver of pleasure. I savored the sensation and longed for more.

Devina smiled. "It's poison. Something exquisite."

I looked around and saw that everyone was having fun. "It's really strong!" I exclaimed, tipsy.

"Cider is lethal, but not for us."

Beside me, a bare-chested man belted back the contents of a glass. "Not for them either, I see."

"What they're drinking is different from ours. Small amounts of our blood filtered of its poison is a delight, if properly distilled."

"They're drinking our blood?"

"Only a few drops. There are certain Souls—Apothecaries—who are in great demand because they're skilled at preparing a special blend. Here they call it Elixir. Our blood is the most powerful drug that has ever existed."

I watched the bare-chested men as they danced, feeling incredibly drawn to their good looks and virility. My Sister looked at me with a twinkle in her eye. "Wait till you see them in the Arena. *There's nothing sexier than two warriors battling to the death for you.*"

"Who are they?" I asked, curious.

Devina laughed and took the cup from my hands. "Don't overdo it your first time or you'll get a headache. Those are Subterraneans," she explained, bringing to my mind the distant memory of the young man with gray eyes.

"I thought they were our enemies."

"Not here in the Castle. On Earth, the Children of Eve hinder our mission and must be stopped. Every Subterranean you see here, on the other hand, has chosen to subjugate himself to us." Devina stopped beside one of the men and kissed him. He took her by the hips and squeezed her bottom, but she slid her finger down his neck and sank her nail in, leaving a line of blood. The Subterranean fell to his knees.

"You can have as many as you want at your command. I'll bring you the finest Soldiers from which to choose. It's your party—tonight you should have company," Devina promised.

I looked at the Subterranean and smiled, arousal growing inside me. But something else she'd said had caught my attention. "What's our mission?"

"Souls," she replied, a light in her eye. "There are many of them on Earth and the number continues to grow. Over the last century there's been a dangerous decline in the perception of evil. Dangerous for them, naturally, not for us. Our task is to bring them here."

"How?"

"With our power. It's still early for you. First you'll have to train. But when the time comes, you'll feed off that power. You won't be able to do without it. You'll wonder how you ever managed to live without it." I listened to her, fascinated. I wanted that day to come as soon as possible. "It will come," she promised, reading my mind. "Meanwhile, let's enjoy the party." Devina picked up two cups of poison and offered me one. I smiled at her, drank the liquid in a single gulp, and let out a whoop.

"There you are," Sophìa exclaimed, coming over to us. Everyone bowed as she passed and so did I, but she stopped me, raising my chin. "Please, Naiad. This is your party. It is I who should bow to you. Your presence here brings me immense joy. It has been centuries since I was as excited over something as I am over your arrival."

"I am honored, my Empress."

Suddenly I couldn't hear Devina's thoughts any more. I looked in her direction, but she was still there, staring at Sophìa. With a cross expression, she turned and walked away.

"Where is she going?" I asked, but no one replied.

"Come. I wish to give you a gift," Sophìa said.

I followed her across the courtyard, through the crowd. I recognized two of my Sisters, Zhora and Sheeva, who were battling some Mizhyas. A small circle had gathered around them. I felt a strong urge to join them, and Sophìa smiled.

"You will have much time to fight. Soon your training will begin. I am certain you will prove to be an excellent warrior. The strength of your soul is extraordinary. Never before had I seen a fire like yours in a mortal."

"Are the maidservants mortal?" I asked. My eyes could see their strength, but my spirit detected their weakness. Not even the Subterraneans were as strong as us—at least the ones there at the Castle—yet I had perceived in them the flame of immortality.

"Mizhyas are nothing but Damned Souls brought in to serve us."

Just then, Sheeva slit one of their throats and the crowd cheered. Black liquid gushed from the wound until she fell to the ground and disappeared in a cloud of dust. "We train them to fight for our entertainment, but none of them last long. Nevertheless, they are happy to serve us. Being with us is a fine way to go. Outside our walls it is true 'Hell' for them compared to this." Sophìa smiled, her blue eyes glittering in the twilight.

Her words piqued my interest. "When may I leave the Castle?"

"Whenever you like. That is why we are here."

"May I ask a question?"

"There is no need. I already know what you wish to ask."

I frowned. I felt the need to ask her out loud. "During the ceremony you said I was the thirteenth Witch, but there were only eleven Sisters, counting you and me. Where are the other two?"

Sophìa looked at me, deep sorrow clouding her eyes. All at once her voice filled my mind: *In the past we lost two Sisters and the pain over their loss still flows strong in the blood of each of us.*

"What were their names?"

"Tamaya and . . . Ginevra." The names echoed in my mind. I didn't know them, but somehow I felt the pain in my heart as well.

"We have arrived. After you," Sophia said, this time aloud. We'd reached the top of a tall tower that rose up, challenging the sky. I stepped out onto its broad terrace and the crisp air hit me. I closed my eyes and breathed in deeply. I felt so free . . . and happy.

A whinny drew my attention. I looked around and for the first time noticed there were covered stalls on the roof of the circular tower. Yes, now I could hear it: their breathing. There were creatures inside the stalls and they had to be enormous.

"Where are we?" I asked, surprised.

"The stables. This is where you are to receive your gift, a Saurus."

A chorus of whinnies filled the twilight as, all around us, magnificent steeds spread their wings and bowed to the Empress. Excitement filled my chest. "These Sauruses belong to your Sisters, but tonight a new creature will rise from the darkness to serve you . . . and protect you."

One of them whinnied and pawed the ground, awakening in me the desire to move closer. I stroked his nose and he relaxed. He was majestic, strong, and graceful—a perfect warrior of the shadows.

Argas. The name burst into my thoughts. I didn't know where it had come from, but suddenly I was sure it was his. "Argas," I whispered, following my instinct. He whinnied and nuzzled me. "I want him," I said, resolute. It was a selfish thought. The creature belonged to one of my Sisters, but I didn't care. I felt a deep connection to him the second I touched him.

"So be it," Sophìa granted.

"I'm willing to fight for him." A fire burned in me: the yearning to excel, even at my Sisters' expense.

Sophìa smiled. "That will not be necessary . . . this time. He lost his Witch centuries ago." I stroked his coat. It was soft, though it looked as hard as armor. Argas rubbed his head against me, tickling me. "It would seem that it is he who has chosen you. Here." She tossed something to me and I caught it. It was a small whistle made of carbonado. It was old, and one end of it was chipped, but I loved it. I stroked it, wondering what its story was.

"Thank you," I murmured. "It's the most beautiful gift you could have given me. Along with the rest, naturally."

"What are you waiting for, then?" she asked with a big smile. "Your new world awaits you." I smiled excitedly and mounted Argas, who whinnied and reared before galloping to the end of the terrace, where he plunged off the edge and swooped through the air.

Sophia's voice filled my head. *"Spread your wings, my butterfly, and* soar.*"*

QUEEN OF THE SKIES

"Yahooo!" The wind swallowed up my shout as we rose into the sky, exploring my new world. I felt strong and full of life. This place was my home; I could feel it in every fiber of my being. Argas kicked out his hind legs and whinnied to catch my attention. He was also happy to be there with me. I laughed, filling the air with the wonderful sound, and leaned down to stroke him as he carried me higher. Spreading my arms, I closed my eyes, the air whipping at my face. I held the world in my hands and power flowed through me like an electric charge as I inhaled the scent of the twilight—the scent of home.

Suddenly my eyes stung. They were transforming. I opened them, an evil grin on my lips. My Dakor was inside me—I could feel him. His poison was powerful, intoxicating. "Yah!" I spurred Argas and he responded at once by plunging downward. The sight below us was breathtaking. The river twisted and turned between the valleys; the volcano erupted, celebrating my presence; Mount Nhubii, with its waterfalls, watched me in silent reverence. And then, the Castle: a majestic, menacing needle pointed at the sky. Sensing my need to return there, Argas beat his mighty black wings and headed toward the tall tower so swiftly I feared we would crash into it, but at the last moment he pulled up, his claws brushing the black wall. I could hear and see everything, even the smallest creature running to hide from me. I spotted the torches at the celebration and circled the courtyard. The crowd saw me and cheered, raising their cups in my honor. I swooped down to be closer to my Sisters, who let out war cries. Flying past them, I joined my voice with theirs. Suddenly, whistles filled the air and huge shadows clouded the sky. I looked up in time to see a magnificent flock of Sauruses beating their wings and racing toward us.

"The Kryadon!" Anya shouted, jumping onto her own. All our Sisters echoed her, their shouts filling my head. Even Sophia joined them.

Hers was the only Saurus with shades of gray. All the others were black.

"What's the Kryadon?" I asked of no one in particular. Their Sauruses all rose into the sky to join Argas.

"Get ready for the Games, princess," Devina replied.

I spurred my Saurus on and flew alongside her. "What games? I don't know the rules."

A grin spread across her face before she angled her Saurus downward. *"There's only one rule that counts: kill."* I smiled and plunged after her.

A group of Souls raced across the ground as fast as their legs could carry them, seeking shelter. Devina's Saurus rushed at them and captured one. The Soul tried to kick free, but her whip was wrapped around his neck. She charged back into the sky, tearing his head off.

"What a cruel game," I murmured to myself, feeling a smile emerge. "I like it."

"Gemma, this one's all yours," Zhora shouted. She rushed at an escaping Soul and grabbed him, hurling him head-first into a tree. I instinctively whipped out my crossbow and nocked an arrow, shooting him in the throat. The Soul disintegrated on the spot and my Sisters cheered. I smiled as a powerful energy grew inside me. The arrow dislodged itself from the tree and returned to me on its own. I caught it and let out a whoop, brandishing it like a trophy.

"So this is the Kryadon?" I asked.

"No, we're just warming up." Nausyka smiled. "Hone your weapons! It's time to have fun!"

I leaned low over Argas's back as he flew into a narrow tunnel. Seconds later he burst out the other side, a swarm of black butterflies following us and a magnificent cascade tumbling down beneath us. Argas followed it straight down, continuing along the river.

"Gemma, come here. We've found a village." The voice was Anya's.

I spurred my Saurus and joined the other Sisters circling a village carved into the rock. From the looks of the square it seemed deserted, but Sheeva shot a flaming arrow into one of the grottos and a Soul rushed out, screaming and consumed by flames. He was soon followed by many others. Panic ensued as they began to turn to ash. I did as my Sisters did, spreading chaos and death. In Sophìa's thoughts I could sense her pride that I'd learned so quickly. She was proud of me. And I would have done anything to please her.

I plunged down toward a little house hidden among the rocks and summoned the power of darkness. I felt it grow inside me, pervading me with its incredible energy. Focusing on my target, I sent a burst of light crashing into it, destroying everything. The other Witches cheered, struck by my boldness. I felt as though I'd been reborn. Anya's Saurus flew up alongside mine. "Is this how you have fun here?" I asked.

She smiled at me. "Do you like it?"

"I don't think I can do without it any more!" I exclaimed, the poison setting my veins on fire.

"I told you you'd be happy here with us," she said with a smile before challenging the wind.

"Catch me!" shouted another Sister. I turned to the right. It was Camelia. She'd stood up on her Saurus's back and spread her arms. Before I could even wonder what she was doing, she let herself fall backwards into the void. I spurred Argas and swooped down beneath her. Everyone's laughter filled my mind. Grinning, Camelia did a backflip and landed on my Saurus.

"You guys are all insane!" I exclaimed in my mind.

"Then welcome to the madhouse." Camelia winked at me and jumped into the void again. A moment later she was back on her Saurus, which passed me as it ascended. "Thanks for the ride!" she shouted to me, smiling. I shook my head.

"There aren't any here," Devina told the group.

"What are we looking for?" I asked.

"Recruits," Anya said.

"Recruits for what?"

"For the Opalion, naturally. This is the Kryadon. We call it the Hunt. It's the preparation for the Games."

"Look, over there!" Nerea shouted. Suddenly something gripped my shoulders and head while my skin felt like it had been stroked with a paintbrush dipped in ink. I touched my body, surprised. Armor had appeared on me, but I wasn't the only one. All the Sisters were now clad in strange armored helmets with antennas like a butterfly's, and tattoos had appeared on their faces. While earlier my Sisters had looked like Amazons, now they were fierce knights.

"Hold on tight!" Anya told me.

A second later my Saurus did a nosedive, following his companions. He hit the ground at a gallop and entered a cave. I could hear the cries of Souls running away, as well as their thoughts, a confused jumble of fear. It was too dark for the Damned to see, whereas our eyesight was perfect. I could even make out the color of their eyes as we rushed alongside them. "Gotcha!" Nausyka exclaimed, and emitted a strange cry. We emerged from the tunnel and I saw a Soul hanging from her Saurus, his feet bound.

"There are two more!" Sophia alerted us, scanning the crowd, but I didn't understand which Souls in particular she was talking about. Sheeva charged one of the Damned but Devina unsaddled her with her Saurus. With a snap of Devina's whip, the Soul fell to the ground, screaming in pain. She flew up, dragging him into the air until he disintegrated.

I heard another strange shout, and another still. I flew over to Anya, who'd just caught another Soul. "Who are they?"

"First-Echelon Sane Souls," she explained. "They're prized fighters for the Opalion because they're particularly aggressive. They've survived years of trials and tribulations without joining the ranks of the Insane, that is, without losing their minds. It's a perfect combination in a combatant: strong but also controllable. They hide among the Lucid—the ones we killed in the cave. The Lucid have no hope of serving evil, though we occasionally toss a few of them into the Arena to amuse the crowds. But Kreeshna's outdone us. She caught a Subterranean. He'll be useful, and he's worth twice as much."

I looked at Kreeshna's prisoner. When she'd captured him, her victory cry had been different from the others. It must have been a signal. The prisoner was a young black man with a strange tattoo that branched out on his right arm. His silvery gray eyes shone through the darkness like those of all the other men I'd seen at the celebration. Like those of the young man in the forest.

"Subterraneans are better at hiding from us because they're not afraid," Anya went on.

"How do you find the Sane?"

"By attacking villages and killing everyone we come across," Nausyka replied, flying alongside us with a satisfied smile on her lips.

"I mean, how do you distinguish them from the rest of the Damned?"

"You probe their minds. It takes practice, though. You need to learn to understand Souls in order to discover their fears. It'll get easier for you after your first Reaping."

"Look, there's one down there," Anya said, pointing. "Each Soul is worth one point. Whoever returns to the Castle with three wins." She plunged downward.

"I didn't know it was a contest!"

"Everything's a contest!" she called back.

Two Sisters were already contending for the prey, but Anya swooped down between them, clearing the way for me. I turned to look at her and she winked. *"Go ahead! Don't aim at the throat!"* she called out in my mind.

Beside me, Nerea and Safria also rushed at the Sane Soul, so I clung to Argas and spurred him on. When I was close to the Soul, I grabbed the two curved daggers strapped to my thighs and threw them, pinning him to a tree by the shoulders.

Argas landed at a gallop and reared in front of our prey. I leapt off his back and summoned the knives with magic. I liked their threatening shape. The sharp blades flew back to me as obediently as boomerangs. The Soul fell to his knees. I licked one of the blades, cleaning the black blood off it, and spat it in his face. He glared at me defiantly, the affront sending a powerful anger surging through me. I raised my foot and smashed it into his face, sending him sprawling. The Soul gurgled . . . and burst into a cloud of ashes. I looked around, confused, as my Sisters galloped over to me.

"What a shame," Nerea said. "He could at least have been mine."

"I only kicked him. I didn't think it would reduce him to ashes," I protested, defending my actions.

Sophìa smiled, her eyes glinting with satisfaction. "The Hunt is in your blood. I am not surprised. Yet you must use the proper amount of force."

"I couldn't control myself," I said in my defense. It hadn't been my fault.

"You will learn."

"Where's Devina?" I asked, noticing she wasn't with us.

"She went hunting for ferocious beasts. Those are worth three points." Sophìa grinned, seeing me burn with curiosity.

"So one of them is enough . . . What's the reward for the winner of the Hunt?"

"She becomes the prize of the Opalion and initiates the Games." Sophìa mounted her majestic Saurus and took flight. Fascinated, I watched her ascend into the sky. My Sisters followed her like bees behind their queen.

"Sheathe your weapons because the Opalion has its queen," Devina said in our minds. She'd caught one. A moment later she emerged from behind a mountain with a big, odd-looking creature dangling from her Saurus. A single catch and she'd won the competition.

"When can I take part in the Reaping?" I asked, anxious to win. I had to learn to recognize Souls' fears as quickly as possible.

"You must first prepare for it, but do not fear. Your training will begin today," Sophìa promised. Her laughter tickled my mind. She knew my most intimate thoughts, and there was only one thing I could think about: at the next Opalion, *I* would be the queen.

EVAN

PROMISES

"That way, Simon!" The motorcycle slid beneath me as the flaming arrow intended for my brother lodged in the asphalt. I drove around it and set off again, rising onto my back wheel while Simon and Ginevra dodged the attacks of the bastard who'd been chasing us for weeks. I'd had enough of him. I prepared a fireball as the roar of our engines filled the night. *"Simon, get ready!"* I shouted to him in my mind.

He positioned himself behind me, waiting for our target to reappear, while Ginevra, who knew what I was about to do, conjured a vacuum sphere around her. When our adversary materialized on the road in front of us, I threw my fireball and Simon manipulated the air so its flames branched out, surrounding us in a protective bubble that moved at the same speed as the bikes.

I stared into the Hunter's dark eyes as we approached. He didn't move—only his dark-brown ponytail stirred in the wind. In his brown leather clothes, he looked like a warrior who'd escaped from another era.

The Executioner ran toward us, breaching the barrier. "What the fuck?" Simon muttered. In a flash Absolon was in front of me. He grabbed my handlebars, swung himself up from the ground and landed behind me on the seat, putting me in a stranglehold with his bow.

I lost control of the bike, which leaned to the side and slid across the asphalt, sparks flying, dragging me with it. I struggled against the Subterranean, but he was strong—stronger than anyone I'd ever encountered. Simon reared up and zoomed toward us, but Absolon was prepared: setting an arrow against his mighty bow, he released it. It lodged in the bike's gas tank, which exploded. The arrows were dipped in poison, like the one that had killed Gemma, and the fire spread instantly. I searched for Simon among the flames while fighting off the

Hunter. Fortunately, he'd already materialized on Ginevra's motorcycle.

"He's mine!" she shouted. Her wheels squealed against the asphalt and the bike skidded to a halt scant yards from us. Ginevra moved swiftly, her green Witch eyes slicing through the night.

"No!" Simon shouted, but it was too late. Ginevra's serpent emerged from her flesh and lunged at the Subterranean. In a split second Absolon turned and, to our astonishment, grabbed the serpent by the head.

"Shit, no!" I exclaimed in shock.

Ginevra's eyes bulged as the creature wriggled in his grip. All the Hunter had to do was crush its skull . . . and Ginevra would die. Terrified, Simon didn't hesitate. With a barbaric shriek he reared up on his bike and shot toward the Hunter, but before he could reach him Absolon vanished, letting the serpent fall to the ground. Simon hit the brakes, confused.

I stared at the Dakor. It was battling the same enemy as I was, but did that mean there was a truce between us? The serpent hissed and approached me threateningly. "Guess not," I muttered. Ginevra summoned her Dakor. It went back to her and disappeared under her skin.

"What the hell just happened?" Simon snapped before letting out a string of curses. He kicked the bike, making it slide across the ground, and turned to face Ginevra. "Damn it, he was *this close* to killing you! Do you realize that?" he screamed in her face.

"Did you expect me to stand around and watch him kill Evan? His arrows are poisoned!"

"I told you to stay out of it!"

"Gin, he wouldn't have killed me and you know it. It's you he wants. He's a Witch Hunter. You have to let me protect you," I reminded her, backing Simon up.

"You were really risking it," he added.

"How could I know he'd catch my Dakor in midair?"

"That's true," I agreed. "I've never met anyone who could do that. He's really strong and he could have killed you in the blink of an eye. So why didn't he?" I picked up my bike. It was falling apart. A surge of rage overtook me and I slammed it to the ground again.

"The bikes are totaled," Simon remarked.

"I'll take care of them," Ginevra said. "They'll be as good as new."

"I don't give a shit about the bikes!" I growled. My tension was mounting. The Subterranean who'd killed Gemma had been hunting us down relentlessly for weeks, stalking us like mice. I grabbed my hair in my fists and howled at the night, overwhelmed with exasperation.

It had been three months since the Witches had taken Gemma and there hadn't been a sign of her since. I was losing my mind. Beyond all logic, I'd even started dreaming. I dreamed of touching her, of brushing my lips across hers . . . but every night those images turned into terrifying nightmares.

Ginevra took my hands in hers. "Evan, calm down. You can't lose it now, of all times. Liam needs you." I forced myself to look at her and filled my lungs with air. The thought of my son was the only thing that could make me think clearly again. "Let's go home," she murmured, "before that bastard Hunter comes back."

I nodded. Ginevra was right. Her life was in danger. I couldn't let anger cloud my judgment. She needed me and I had to protect her. I owed it to Simon—he'd protected Gemma while I was gone, and now they both needed my help . . . and my focus. I had to stay lucid and fight, though what consumed me more than the fire of a thousand Hunters was the terrible awareness that I had lost Gemma.

"And so the princess saved her prince from the castle in which he was imprisoned and—" Anya stopped when she sensed our thoughts. She raised her eyes and gave me a sad smile.

"Thanks, Anya," Ginevra told her. "I knew I could count on you."

She gently rested Liam in his crib. "He just fell asleep. Don't make any noise."

I went over to look at him and every shadow disappeared from my mind. His big, almond-shaped eyes were closed, his cheeks flushed from sleep, and his hair curled on his forehead. Whenever I got lost, he had the power to bring me back.

"Why has that Subterranean got it in for us?" Simon hissed. "Wasn't Gemma enough for him?"

"He's not a Subterranean like the others—he's a Witch Hunter, and Ginevra's the only Witch dwelling on Earth now. It's her he wants," said Anya, who knew him well.

"I know how dangerous it is for you to come here," I told her, "and I'm grateful for your help." The Witch nodded. A painful silence developed between us. "How is she?" I asked. I knew she wasn't allowed to talk to me about Gemma, but if I didn't find out I might lose my mind.

"She's fine," was the only answer I got.

"Is there any trace of us left in her?" Even a little would be enough for me: a memory, an image that had resisted the transformation.

"None, sorry." I clenched my fists, letting my defenses down in front of her. "The Devil's Claw wiped away every last feeling in her. There's only room for the Bond."

"I don't believe it," I said, my voice tight with frustration. "I—I can't accept it. It's been three months! Why hasn't she set foot on Earth again?"

"She's finishing her training. That's how it works."

"No, that's not true. You're trying to keep her away from me."

"Evan . . ." Ginevra tried to calm me down, but it was a lost cause.

"How can I hope to win her back if I don't even get to see her?"

"Actually, you can't. She made her choice, Evan."

"No she didn't," I snapped.

Anya gaped as she read the truth in my mind: Gemma had decided to drink Ambrosia. She locked eyes with me. "Sophìa would never have let you two go. In any case, things turned out differently. You yourself asked me to transform her. You yourself invoked Sophìa. It was the only way to save her life."

"Give her this." Anya stared at the diary in Ginevra's hands. In it were hidden Gemma's deepest thoughts. "It might help her remember," Ginevra said quietly.

"I doubt it," she replied, looking sorry, "but I can try."

"Wait." I went to Anya and pulled out a letter. I'd written it for Gemma months earlier, just in case she ended up transforming. She looked at it for a moment and slipped it into the diary.

"Take care of her, please," Ginevra begged her.

"I'll try, though Devina has taken her under her wing." Ginevra's eyes widened. "Gemma trusts her and there's not much I can do about it."

"That bitch!" I snarled.

"Don't worry. I'll keep looking out for her."

I nodded my thanks and she disappeared. Simon and Ginevra also left, closing the door behind them softly. I wasn't sure Gemma's diary or my letter would help much, but at least it was something, though not what I hoped for: I wanted to see her. I needed her and knew that deep in her heart Gemma also needed me and our baby. Maybe I'd done everything wrong. Maybe I should have let Gemma pass on rather than allowing her transformation. I'd battled Subterraneans who wanted to take her away from me, I'd battled the Màsala who had condemned her to death, but I'd been self-centered. I'd spent all that time keeping her from dying so I wouldn't lose her, but by doing so I'd denied her the peace of Eden. Now all that awaited her was eternity in Hell. And there was no guarantee she would come back to me.

Her eyes looked out at me from a snapshot of us together. I'd taken it on a snowy day after we'd made love in my car. Beside the framed picture on the dresser were Gemma's ring and necklace. I'd picked them up from the lakeside when she'd disappeared. I turned the pendant over and read the inscription on the back of it.

Gevan. Forever.

The little diamond sparkled as I turned it in my fingers. When she'd transformed, the diamond had absorbed her dark essence and become carbonado. I'd stared at it for a moment as the sun rose over the lake, mocking me. Like Gemma, the diamond had lost its light, surrendering to the darkness. Moments later, though, it had begun to sparkle again. I gripped the pendant in my fist until my palm ached. No, it wasn't the end. I couldn't accept it. I would never give up. Like the diamond, Gemma would also find her light again.

Liam wailed and I went over to the crib. He looked at me with his deep, curious, blue eyes. I was sure he missed his mother too. "I'll bring her back to us," I promised, stroking his cheek. He smiled at me. I picked up the violin and played the song I'd composed for him and Gemma the day of his birth. A lullaby. Liam loved it. The sound of the violin calmed him, so every night I would play it for him.

We were alone, the two of us. A father with his wonderful child. If only I'd purified Gemma immediately after the birth . . . Waiting had been a mistake. But how could I have imagined I would lose her? My whole world had changed in a single night . . . in a single instant.

Ginevra was leaning against the door, listening. She often did that. I continued to play. She was suffering too. I let the final note linger, sighing as the room fell back into silence. Ginevra waited a moment and then walked away. I looked at Liam, who'd fallen asleep.

Physiologically, he was completely normal. Despite our expectations, he was human. He was the sweetest baby in the world and looking at him made my heart ache because everything about him reminded me of Gemma. I had promised to protect him. That was my mission now, the most important one I would ever carry out.

There was only one way to keep my promise to the very end: find Gemma and bring her back. At all costs.

GEMMA

DANGEROUS TEMPTATIONS

I dodged Nausyka's staff as Sheeva attacked me from behind in the form of a panther. I saw her just in time, did a backflip, landed behind her, and looked up at my Sisters. "I'm afraid you're too old for me," I provoked them smugly.

"Don't count on it, newbie. You've still got a lot to learn."

"You've taught me everything there is to know. When can I come with you to the Reaping?" I groaned.

"Sophìa will be the one to decide. You can't contend with Subterraneans unless you're adequately trained—otherwise you'll get yourself killed by their fire."

"I didn't ask to go on Recon. It's mortal Souls I'm interested in," I insisted.

"That would be even more dangerous, because you'd be running not into fledgling Subterraneans but Soldiers of Death prepared to battle for the soul of whomever you want to take possession of."

"I'm ready. I can face them if I need to."

"We'll see," Nausyka said.

I raised the staff using the power of my mind and spun it through the air challengingly. My Sister looked me straight in the eye and snatched it. I turned and leapt high into the air, climbing barehanded up the black stone of the Castle until I reached the floor where my rooms were. I wanted to take a hot bath. I was dirty and the training had been more grueling than usual. Still, I couldn't complain—I'd been the one to push myself beyond the limit. I felt like a caged lion. I wanted to fight. I wanted to face our enemies. But more than anything else, I wanted to take part in the Reaping. I *thirsted* for Souls. It was a desire that had grown in me day after day to the point of being unbearable.

The moment I arrived at the entrance to my chambers, I froze: the door was ajar. Someone was inside. I blocked off my thoughts and peeked through the gap. Anya and Devina were there. The former was holding a book with embossing on its blue cover. She held it tight, as though it were something important.

"She's forgotten him! Get over it!" Using magic, Devina whisked the book out of her hands and set fire to it. It burst into flames and fell to the floor in a pile of ash.

"No!" Anya gasped, leaning over it. "What have you done?!" She was furious. Her green panther eyes flashed and her Dakor hissed.

"Do you want to challenge me, by chance?" Devina asked, facing up to her. "Or do you want me to tell Sophìa that instead of working on the Reaping you were playing nanny to a Subterranean's son?"

What was going on between them? What were they talking about? Why were they behaving like that?

"He's her son too."

"That's not important any more."

"She might want him here."

I burst into the room, flinging the door open wide. "What's going on?"

They turned to look at me, stunned, probably mystified as to why they hadn't sensed my arrival. I was able to block off my thoughts almost all the time, something that continued to surprise them. They certainly hadn't taught me how; closing off your mind to the other Sisters was forbidden. Not officially, of course. It was more of an unwritten law. Nevertheless, I couldn't help it. It was an innate gift, one that not all of them possessed. It was as if I'd learned how to do it in my past life.

Devina smiled at me as though nothing had happened. "You're back. We were waiting for you." She came over and put her arm around my waist. "How did training go today?"

"As usual. I beat Zhora, Nausyka, and even Bathsheeva. I think I'm ready for the Reaping."

"I agree with you. Come, let's go to the spas. You can take a nice hot bath and then we'll convince Sophìa you're ready." She turned to look at Anya. "If I promise to go along and keep an eye on you, she'll listen to me."

"That's the greatest thing you could do for me!" I exclaimed excitedly.

"I'm your Sister. You know that we help each other out."

"Anya, are you coming with us?" I turned toward her and noticed she was staring at us with a fiery gaze.

"I'll catch up with you."

Why was she acting that way? Was she jealous of my relationship with Devina? Like me, she too often blocked her thoughts, so I had no way of knowing what was going through her mind. Devina, on the other hand, was more transparent. Her thoughts weren't always commendable, but at least she didn't hide them. She'd been my role model ever since I arrived at the Castle. I wanted to be like Devina.

The heat could already be felt in the hallways. When Devina and I made our entrance in the Spa Parlor every head turned. Devina was respected in the Castle—almost as much as Sophìa. I admired her for that, though I had to admit I was jealous of her power. I wanted it to be mine . . . and one day it would be. The Subterraneans bowed to us and let us through. I watched them, attracted to their well-trained bodies. They weren't simple Children of Eve like all the others; visiting the Spa Parlor was a privilege granted exclusively to Champions. Almost all the Witches had one, and maybe soon I would have my own.

Emayn, my Mizhya, knelt at my feet and undid the laces wrapped around my high-heeled boots. Then she stood up to undress me, but Devina grabbed her hand. *"Get lost,"* she hissed, then turned to smile at me. "I'll take care of you."

The maidservant bowed and retreated rapidly, cringing, afraid Devina would kill her. That happened often, even for far less. I was growing fond of my maids but Devina considered them chattel, and when she tired of hers she would slay them brutally. I knew that for her the only bond that counted was the one with her Sisters. Maybe she was right, like she was about everything else. I smiled back at her and let her unlace my brown bodice. It fell to the floor, freeing my breasts. Devina also got undressed, revealing her generous bosom.

We sank into the tub. Devina slowly moved toward me and our breasts touched. She picked up a pitcher and poured scalding hot water over my neck as I melted in its heat. I looked into her amber eyes, hiding a smile. I knew what she was doing. The others' Champions were watching and she wanted to arouse them. I enjoyed feeling desired; it turned me on. Playing along, I slowly ran a sponge over her shoulders and down to her breasts as she closed her eyes, letting me touch her.

"Come on. Let's give them a little show," she whispered in my mind. I leaned over and kissed her sensually on the lips. "Choose one."

"What?" I asked.

"Choose a Champion. Which one do you want to be with?"

"But they belong to my Sisters. It's against the rules."

"I'll take care of them, don't worry. It's my gift to you for completing your training." Devina moved her lips to my ear and her voice became a murmur: "Come on, don't tell me you're not tempted. Choose one. Which one excites you the most?" I studied the Subterraneans. Their thoughts were a tangle of arousal. "I could give you mine . . . or would you prefer Anya's?"

My eyes lingered on a dark-skinned Subterranean. He had a penetrating gaze and sexy creases below his eyes. "Careful, princess—that's Sophìa's Champion. None of us can touch him. But if you want him, I can arrange for a secret encounter."

"What's going on here?" Anya hissed with irritation. I pulled away from Devina. How much had Anya overheard? I wasn't sure how far I could trust her. Loyalty to Sophìa counted a lot for all the Sisters . . . a little less for Devina.

"We were just relaxing a bit," Devina replied. She slid into the water, immersing her shoulders. "You should too. You could really use it," she said to provoke her.

"Do you want to take a bath with us?" I asked.

"There's no time. I came to tell you I spoke with Sophìa about your training. I proposed taking you with me to the Reaping."

"Really?" I jumped to my feet, excited by the news. "When can we start?"

Her lips curved in a smile. Anya's smile was always sweet and affectionate, unlike Devina's, which was sharp and most times full of contempt. "You're ready," Anya said. "Even today, if you like. But first the Empress wishes to see you."

I got out of the tub and my Mizhyas ran over to dry me. "Well? What are we waiting for?"

"Hang on," Devina said. "I said I was going to speak to her on Gemma's behalf. That was my prerogative."

"Gemma isn't your property. She's as much my Sister as yours."

"What difference does it make who takes me to the Reaping? All that matters to me is going. There's no need to fight over this. In fact, why don't you both come?"

"That sounds like an excellent idea," Devina exclaimed, her amber eyes locked on Anya's.

"Let's go," she said, annoyed. "The Empress awaits us."

"Let's not keep her waiting," Devina replied, winking at me.

I sheathed my daggers and crossbow and followed them, casting one last glance at Sophia's Champion. I'd just discovered something important about myself: I was drawn to things that were forbidden.

30

THE WHISPER OF EVIL

"No." Sophìa stopped us at the entrance to the Pantheon. "Only Naiad." Anya and Devina looked at each other. I couldn't take my eyes off the Empress. Her beauty was spellbinding. None of us could hold a candle to her. "Come now. Come forward," she said.

I walked toward her and my Sisters stayed behind. Sophìa rose from her throne and I bowed. It was then that a panther attacked me from behind. I leapt back just in time as another two crept toward me, on their guard. *She was challenging me.*

I smiled: challenge accepted.

All three panthers lunged at once, but I managed to avoid their claws and counterattack. In a few quick moves I sent two of them—Nerea and Kreeshna—to the ground. That left only Bathsheeva, who watched me with her golden eyes. I channeled my power and unleashed it on her, generating a shock wave that struck all three panthers, hurling them away. The force of my attack even made Sophìa's hair fly back.

It was clear what was happening: Sophìa wanted to see with her own eyes how far along I was with my training. It was a test, and I had every intention of passing it. I materialized behind Sophìa and attacked her. She blocked the blow in time and smiled at me, her gaze captivating. If she wanted war, she would have it. The Sisters were shocked.

"What's she doing?"

"She's challenging the Empress?"

"Is she out of her mind?"

"Go on, Gemma. Show her all you've got." It was Devina, backing me up.

Smiling, I drew my daggers and tried to strike Sophìa. She was very agile, and stronger than anyone I'd ever fought before, but I wasn't about to give up. The entire hall became our battleground, our rapid attacks a dark dance. Sophìa smiled, cast me an amused glance, and with a single blow sent me crashing into the wall. The impact was so powerful it felt like it had come from a sledgehammer. I sank to my knees, feeling like every bone in my body was broken. She hadn't even used her powers—only her physical strength. I saw Sophìa's feet approach and stop in front of me. "You are ready."

I raised my head, surprised, and she smiled at me and held out her hand. I took it, looking into her blue eyes. "You mean I can take part in the Reaping?"

"We train for two purposes: attacking Subterraneans when we are on Reconnaissance and defending ourselves from Subterraneans during the Reaping. This is the most difficult, most dangerous part. The Children of Eve do not always hinder our work, but when they do we must know how to defend ourselves, and you have proven you are capable of at least trying to do so. It was brave of you to challenge me. I admit I expected it from you—you have war in your blood. I would be a fool to force you to suppress it any longer."

"I've been waiting for this for a long time."

"Anya and Devina will go along to protect you."

I looked at my Sisters, who had joined us. "I don't need to be protected." I fixed my eyes on hers to emphasize my confidence.

"You are very skilled. Not even Devina learned so quickly," Sophìa said.

"Thank you, my Empress." I bowed to her. Though I sensed Devina's thoughts were in turmoil because of the provocation, I couldn't decipher them. The competition among us Sisters was always fierce. Sophìa said challenges brought us to life, which was why she constantly stirred up rivalries among us. Despite it all, the Bond among us was solid. Nothing was stronger.

My Sisters had taught me everything. Every day they trained me in the field and helped me practice using magic. Sophìa had revealed the secrets of the world to me and finally I was ready to discover it with my own eyes.

Anya rested her hand on my chest and my brown clothing changed, wrapping around me like the skin of a serpent—a black serpent, just like my Dakor. I'd already seen the outfit on my Sisters. It was what they wore to the Reaping. It was exciting to finally be able to wear it. My eyes were aflame, burning with poison. In my mouth I could almost taste the flavor of the Souls I would make mine.

"Have a good Reaping, my wicked little butterflies," Sophìa told us. "Show mercy only to yourselves and to the thirst of your Dakor." We bowed to the Empress. She leapt up and disintegrated into a hundred black butterflies that disappeared through the hole in the ceiling.

Someone took my hand and I turned around to find Anya giving me an encouraging smile. I nodded to let her know I was ready, then took Devina's hand as darkness engulfed us. *"Follow your instinct,"* Devina told me in her mind.

The chaos lasted only seconds. When the light returned, we were no longer in the Castle. I looked around. I was in a cluttered apartment. Anya and Devina weren't at my side any more, but even though I couldn't see them I knew they were there with me. I felt the power of the Bond. However, something just as powerful was summoning me, clouding everything else. An intoxicating sensation. No—perhaps it was a scent. It was nothing and everything, together. The pure essence of evil. I felt it flowing inside me and my blood boiled at its call. I focused on that sweet song and swiftly reached them: a young married couple fighting in the kitchen.

It was my first Temptation, yet I knew perfectly what to do. My instinct cried out for me to do as it wished. I moved closer and studied them. Within seconds I knew everything. I knew their dirtiest secrets. She looked desperate, her eyes red from crying and her face covered with bruises. She'd waited up all night for him and when he'd gotten home he'd beaten her.

"I told you I had a meeting!"

"He's lying," I whispered to the woman. *"You smell perfume on him. He was with another woman."*

"A meeting with your whore! Liar!"

"You're crazy. Tomorrow I'm sending you back to your mother's!" he shouted.

I fed the woman's suspicions: *"So he'll be free to go to her."*

"So you'll be free to go to her, right? Answer me!"

I looked into the man's eyes. I was enjoying the game more and more. *"Is that how you let a woman treat you? Put her in her place!"*

"Shut up, bitch!" He smacked her face so hard it sent her flying to the ground. She crawled across the floor in tears and I returned to fan the flames inside her.

"I bet this is how you fuck her, huh?! You used to love doing it with me on the floor. Or do you two do it on your desk?"

"Don't hide," I whispered to the man. *"You're in charge here and she has to accept it. Tell her how it was. Tell her how hard she made you come."*

"You wanna know how we did it? We did it on the floor and on the couch and in the bathroom and in every corner of my office. While you were here at home I was making her ride me. I fucked her every single day. Happy?"

I felt her heart break and reach the point of no return. *"He fucked her every single day. He's just a filthy son of a bitch. Make him pay!"* The woman shot to her feet, grabbed a knife, and rushed at him with a shriek of rage, but the man stopped her in time and disarmed her, wounding her in the belly in the process. They stared at each other for a long moment. Her eyes were full of fear now. The man's were bloodshot. He'd lost all control.

I smiled and whispered my Temptation: *"Kill her. Kill her or for you it'll be the end."*

"No! Wait!" the woman begged, in tears.

"Stab her. It's too late to back out now. She's just an obstacle. She'll leave you and press charges. You'll lose everything. Your life will be over."

"I can't lose everything," he hissed to himself. Raising the knife, he plunged it into her body again and again, venting all his anger on her. The woman's eyes opened wide with terror and then went blank. I slipped out of the man's mind.

As though emptied, he stood there, perfectly still. He looked at the bloody knife in his hand and flung it to the floor. "What have I done?" he gasped in horror. "Nadine! Nadine!" He tried to revive the woman, but it was useless. The man straightened up, wiping a tear from his eyes, his cheek smeared with the woman's blood. "Why wouldn't she believe me? I didn't do anything with that woman! Nadine . . . I shouldn't have provoked her like that! I wanted to reassure her and instead I killed her! I'm a monster!"

Now that I wasn't clouding his conscience, guilt was consuming him. He stared at the knife for a long moment, then leaned over, picked it up, and plunged it into his heart. His soul came out of his body and looked me straight in the eye. "Who are you?"

"I'm the evil inside you," I whispered.

The man's eyes bulged and his soul was sucked back into his body, which fell to its knees in a puddle of blood. Something stirred in his mouth. I smiled smugly as a black butterfly forced his lips open and crawled out—his now-damned Soul. I leaned over and picked it up, watching it wriggle between my fingers.

A powerful energy surged through me like lava, setting my veins aflame. The exhilaration went to my head more strongly than pure poison. How had I ever managed to exist without that sensation before? My Dakor slithered beneath my skin, broke through it near my collarbone, and hissed at the Soul. I could feel my serpent's heart beat faster. I could sense his thirst. Guided by instinct, he opened his fangs wide and devoured the butterfly.

The Reaping had begun.

INSATIABLE THIRST

I closed my eyes as my Dakor devoured the man's damned soul and dark energy flooded through me, leaving me in bliss. Everything I'd done up to that point, all the incredible sensations I'd experienced since I'd been in Hell, were suddenly *nothing* compared to the power surging through me. Not the Hunt, not the Opalion, not all the fun I'd had with my Sisters . . . nothing had quenched my thirst. It was as though I'd been awaiting that moment forever. I realized it was my calling: Souls—leading them to perdition was pure pleasure. I wanted to seduce them. I wanted to make them mine and quench my thirst.

All at once, something tore me away from those thoughts. Someone was there with me. I turned and found the woman's soul staring at me, perfectly still. She was frightened—I could feel it. No Witch had corrupted her over the course of her life, though she'd faced Temptation many times.

Just then, a Subterranean appeared for her. "Hello there," I said, my voice provocative. My Dakor hissed uneasily.

"Who are you two? What do you want from me?" the woman asked, trying unsuccessfully to conceal her terror.

"Come with me. Can't you see what he did to you?" I showed her her body on the floor, lying in a pool of blood. "I'll take you to him so you can get your revenge."

"Where is he? Where have you taken him?"

"Come with me and I'll show you."

"Don't listen to her!" the Subterranean boomed, glaring at me with fiery eyes. The woman, however, was tempted. "If you follow me, I can save you from the darkness. I'll show you the light and you'll find peace," the Subterranean went on.

"There is no peace without revenge," I whispered to her. "Deep down, what do you want?"

"I . . . I want to make him pay," she murmured to herself. She looked up, determined. "Take me to him." With those words, her soul was sucked back into her body and regurgitated as a splendid black butterfly.

Well done, little mortal. There's a bit of Witch in each of you. I smiled at the Subterranean. "Step aside, ferryman. Her soul is mine."

"Her soul isn't yours to take! I was sent here for her!"

"Oops, did I ruin your mission?" I goaded him.

He shot me a piercing look and my eyes burned with poison. I wasn't afraid of him. Devina and Anya appeared just then and he backed up in fright before disappearing, still furious. My Dakor opened its fangs and devoured the woman's soul.

Looking around, my Sisters stepped over the two bodies. "Not bad for her first time," Devina said. "She even managed to corrupt the woman after she'd been entrusted to a Subterranean. See that, Anya? She's a fast learner."

"Faster than you, it would seem," Anya returned, repeating the Empress's words. "Why didn't you leave after you took the man's Soul?" she asked me reproachfully.

"I took the woman's too. Aren't you pleased?"

"Of course, but there was a Subterranean. A battle over Souls is too dangerous for you."

"She worked it out just fine," Devina said in my defense.

"What's the problem? I won and I took her Soul."

"It could have ended badly."

"But it didn't. The situation was under control."

"Only because we showed up."

"Then next time stay out of it. That way I can prove you wrong. You're not my babysitter."

"Oh, you're going to break her heart," Devina said, smirking. "Babysitting is becoming her favorite pastime. Isn't it, Anya?" She sent her a look I couldn't decipher. What were they saying in their minds? And why weren't they including me in it?

"I don't understand why you can't be proud of me like Devina," I grumbled.

Anya came closer. "You're wrong—I'm very proud of you, really. I care about you more than you can imagine. That's why I worry about you." I nodded. I could tell her affection for me was sincere. It wasn't only because of the Bond. "How do you feel?" she asked.

"Intoxicated," I replied.

"Do you want to go home now? I know how draining the first time can be."

The power that had surged through me was fierce, but it hadn't slaked my thirst—it had intensified it. "Not at all. We've only just begun."

"Why not just one little glass? Go on, drink it!"

"Marcos, cut it out. Justin has to drive!" A redheaded girl took the glass out of his hands. She was drunk. "This stuff's too strong for him. It's better off in my stomach than his. Otherwise who's going to take me home?"

The statement hurt the boy, who had a crush on her. He hated that she was treating him like a chauffeur, a little boy she could put in a corner and take advantage of whenever she liked. He felt left out but didn't have the courage to do anything about it. I was going to give him that courage.

I stepped forward, stoking the anger secretly smoldering inside the boy. *She doesn't think you have the guts to do it. Pick up that glass. Show her you're brave too. Show her you're no coward."*

"Screw it, Sara! Hand me that glass!" Justin knocked the drink back in one gulp. The girl cheered excitedly and dragged him through the crowd.

"Time to go home, people. Party's over." An adult had come into the room. The kids all moaned. "Come on, out you go. Which of you is the designated driver?"

"That would be me," Justin replied, slurring his words. That single drink had been enough to dull his senses.

The kid's drunk. Maybe I should drive them home myself, the man thought.

"But the game's starting soon," I whispered in his mind.

He checked the clock and shrugged. *Aw, who cares? They'll work it out.* I smiled. The man had potential. Soon I would return to tempt him as well.

"Justin, I thought you didn't drink," said another girl named Melanie.

"Shhh. I'm fine. Never better."

"Maybe we should call a taxi."

"I'll take you. I know the way. Let's go. See? I can stand on one leg."
They got into the car and I got in with them.

"Dude, you drive like a little kid," Marcos teased him.

I'm not a little kid, he thought.

"Prove it to him. Go faster. It'll impress her." Justin obeyed,
blinded by his desire for her. Sara whooped enthusiastically and raised
her hands in the air. He turned up the music on the stereo and stepped
harder on the accelerator, satisfied.

"Whoa, dude, now you're overdoing it," Marcos complained.

"C'mon, Justin. Slow down," Melanie added.

"What's wrong with you two? Scared of a little adrenaline?" Sara said.

"You're going too fast, for fuck's sake!" Marcos exclaimed.

All at once a moose stepped out onto the dark street and Justin
slammed on the brakes. The tires squealed across the asphalt as the car
jerked to a halt. For a second there was silence, then someone started
laughing and the others joined in.

"I thought we were done for."

"Gotta tell you, dude, you're insane."

"Guys," Melanie murmured in a tiny voice. "The train!"

"Huh?"

"The train's coming!" she cried. "We're on the tracks! We have to get
off them!" The train whistled, its lights coming closer and closer.

"Drive, Justin!" Marcos shouted. "Get this fucking car moving!"

"I can't! It won't start!" he cried.

"Let's get out of here, quick!" I smiled and jammed the locks.

"They won't open!"

"I don't want to die!" Sara whimpered. Justin grabbed the fire
extinguisher from under his seat and smashed his window. He
scrambled out of the car and stood staring at the other kids as they
tried to get out, then raised his eyes to the train. It was coming closer
and closer.

"Justin, help me!" Melanie screamed. He looked at the train again,
gauging the distance.

"You can't make it. You'll die too. Leave her there."

Justin stood there for a moment, paralyzed by my Temptation. Then
he shook his head and rushed back to get her. Anger grew inside me.
I'd lost him. He helped Melanie out and they both fell to the ground as
Marcos smashed the other window and pulled himself out as well.

"Marcos help me! I'm stuck!" Sara pleaded.

"I'm sorry," he whispered, in tears, his conscience deadened by evil.

"Marcos!" she shrieked.

The train plowed into the car, sweeping it away with Sara inside it.

"Why didn't you help her?" Justin screamed at him. "She was right next to you! You could have gotten her out!"

"There wasn't time!" the frightened boy said.

"My God . . . She's dead . . ." Melanie covered her mouth with her hands.

"Sure there was time. You didn't help her!"

"I . . . I'm sorry," Marcos whispered. "I was afraid of dying."

"Don't apologize," I whispered. *"He was the one driving."*

"You were the one driving. It's your fault! We all could have died! I'm telling the cops. I'm telling them everything."

"No you're not," Justin hissed.

"Guys, cut it out! What's wrong with you?! Sara is dead!"

Down the track, the train was slowly grinding to a halt and we could hear sirens in the distance. Marcos pointed his finger at Justin. "We're all in deep shit. We're going to stick together, got it? We need to come up with an explanation." The other two nodded.

Anya and Devina materialized beside me. "Having a good Reaping?"

"I lost him." I gestured at Justin. "He resisted my Temptation."

"It happens," Anya said.

Devina went up to Marcos. "In compensation, I see you tarnished him."

"Better than nothing," I said. The purer they were the more fun it was. That taste of the forbidden . . . I'd thought Justin was weak because they'd talked him into drinking so easily. Nevertheless, instead of succumbing to my evil temptation, he'd saved the girl.

Marcos's soul, on the other hand, was now tarnished. He could still redeem himself, but we would make sure he was tempted again and, when his time came, one of us would claim him.

A Subterranean came for the girl. I gazed at him for a long time, fighting the urge to attack him, but I had more urgent matters to think about.

"Let's go. We're done here," I told my Sisters. I was anxious to begin again.

I should stay and turn myself in, thought the man in front of me. He'd just killed his girlfriend over nothing.

"Get out of here," I whispered in his mind. I smiled, watching him run away. If he'd stayed, maybe he would have had some hope of redemption, but he'd fled. One day he would be mine.

We'd collected the souls of dozens of mortals, tarnished those of hundreds more, but I could never get enough. My thirst grew with each new conquest, my Dakor was getting stronger, and I felt more alive than I'd ever felt. Entering the minds of mortals was child's play. They were so easy to manipulate! Only a few—those with the strongest spirits—managed to resist our Temptation. All the others gave in to our lethal whispers. We listened to their thoughts and quickly discovered what tormented them most. Secrets, lies, hidden desires. Evil had a thousand disguises and we assumed them all in our efforts to corrupt the mortals. We leveraged their emotions, their fears, their weaknesses. Some wanted money and some wanted power, no matter the cost. At that point we came into play. Each granted wish was a deal with the devil. We'd amassed First-Echelon Souls, Cowards like Marcos, Egotists, Corrupt Souls, and Lechers. They were the most fun of all.

"That's enough for now," Devina said.

"No," I insisted. "I'm not done yet."

"It's time to go back to the Castle. Sophia will be anxiously awaiting our Reaping."

"One more Soul, then we can go back," I said resolutely. I wasn't ready yet.

"Agreed." Devina gave in.

We materialized in a luxurious apartment where a party was going on. The noise was deafening and colorful lights chased each other all around the room to the rhythm of the music.

"Why don't we have a little fun?" Anya suggested. Appearing in the middle of the crowd so even the mortals could see her, she winked at me, inviting us to follow suit.

I smiled and turned to Devina. "Finally an idea I like."

She, on the other hand, looked vexed. *"What are you doing, Anya? We're exposing ourselves too much."*

"Relax, Dev. You could really use it," she shot back wickedly, dancing between two young men.

But Devina was adamant. *"He'll come."*

"We can't hide her forever."

I looked at my Sisters. What were they talking about? Hide who? And from whom? Did they think the music could drown out their thoughts? Or did they think they'd blocked them off from me, like they were doing more and more often?

"Come on, Gemma!" Anya encouraged me. "Come dance! It's fun!"

I made my way through the crowd to her, dragging Devina behind me. She grumbled but then saw a man she liked and started coming on to him. We went wild in the crowd, flirting, our pheromones drawing all the males to us like bees to nectar. No one could resist our dark allure.

"Hey, Gemma, check out that guy over there." Devina pointed to a man who was dancing with his girlfriend but couldn't take his eyes off me. I probed his mind. She wasn't his girlfriend. She was a professional dancer, and this was his bachelor party. The next day he was getting married, but just then it was me he wanted. *A lecher.* As my final prey I couldn't ask for anything better than a cheater.

"The honor is yours," Devina said.

I wafted my pheromones over to him, inducing him to come closer, then danced with him, using my provocative movements to turn him wild with desire. Completely bewitched by me, he was ready and willing to cheat on his fiancée. He moved his lips toward mine but I dodged them and pushed him to his knees in front of me. He looked up at me ecstatically as I danced around him. Taking off his shirt, he reached out and put his hand on my behind, but Devina cracked her whip and trapped his wrist in it. Though he shouted from the pain, he was instantly excited when Devina joined me in my sexy dance. "Nice costumes," he told us both, trying to pull me against him.

Suddenly someone rushed him and dragged him away from me. The crowd around us pulled back as the man was brutally smashed against the wall. I sensed at once it was a Child of Eve. "By Lilith! What the— " I stopped mid-sentence when the Subterranean turned and his silvery gray eyes locked onto mine, burning into them.

"At last I've found you." His voice filled my head.

"You again," I murmured to myself. It was the young man from the forest.

"Let's get out of here!" Devina ordered, but he strode over to her and grabbed her by the neck.

"You're not going anywhere," he threatened.

"Care to bet?" Devina slipped free from his grasp and materialized beside me and Anya.

"Anya, no!" an unknown female voice shouted in our minds. I spun around and met her incredibly green eyes. By Lilith, it was a Witch!

A second later we disappeared.

"What's going on?" I demanded when we materialized at the Castle.

"I don't know what you're talking about," Devina retorted icily as Anya went to tell Sophia we'd returned.

"Maybe if you stopped blocking off your mind you'd be able to read mine. That woman was a Witch! One of us! I felt the Bond." Finally I remembered—I'd seen her in the forest too, but my hostility toward the Subterranean had distracted me and I hadn't given her another thought.

"There is no Bond. In any case, I'm not allowed to talk about it."

"Fine. That means I'll ask Sophia. At least tell me why we ran away. I don't understand—we've faced lots of Subterraneans before."

"He's different. He's not just any ordinary Subterranean. He's dangerous."

"Even better, then. Next time I want to fight him."

"No! You need to stay away from him."

"Why? Didn't you say Anya was too protective?"

"He's mine," she admitted. "I've been after him for centuries but he's never bent to my will. It's only a matter of time, though."

"He wants to kill you. I read it in his mind."

"I know. He's the most ferocious Subterranean I've ever encountered. Sexy and ruthless—that's why I want him. He's been hunting me down to kill me, and he'll try to kill you too. He has the power to creep into your mind, but you mustn't let him in. He'll try to convince you he's ready and willing to be claimed, that he worships you, and a whole bunch of other lies, but you mustn't listen to him. It's a trick. The minute you lower your defenses he'll attack and kill you. If we ever run into him again don't let him into your mind. It's his greatest power." Devina took my hands and looked me in the eye. "Do you trust me?"

I smiled. "Of course. More than anyone else in the world."

FIRST REAPING

"Welcome back," Sophìa said when we arrived. "Did you have a good Reaping?"

"See for yourself," I replied, a smug smile on my lips. I summoned my Dakor, who crawled out of my wrist and dropped to the floor, slithering over to the symbol of the Witches carved in red in the black floor. Anya and Devina's Dakor followed him.

"Come to me!" the Empress exclaimed, raising her arms in her elegant black gown. The serpents opened their jaws wide and three swarms of black butterflies flew out, merging into a single vortex like a dark tornado. Sophìa's laughter filled the hall as the myriad of Souls whirled about. "Fly, my little butterflies! This is your new realm."

The butterflies danced before the Empress. She clapped her hands and the Souls encircled her before flying up and disappearing through the opening in the ceiling. Finally she looked at me. "Excellent work. I could not be prouder. Especially of you, Naiad." I bowed to her, grateful, and looked her in the eye again. "Now tell me: did the Reaping meet your expectations?"

"It far exceeded them," I told her. My Dakor had quenched his thirst. The Souls had given him strength and I felt invincible.

"Good. Very good. Then tell me, what is it that troubles you?"

Though I'd closed off my mind, the Empress had detected my emotions. "Not what, but who. Tell me about Ginevra." Her name had come to my mind when her green eyes met mine; my soul had recognized the Bond. Sophìa cast a questioning glance at Anya and Devina. Or maybe it was one of reproach, because the two stepped back and went away, leaving me alone with her. "You told me my Sisters were dead! I'm confused, because I just ran into one of them."

Sophìa didn't reply, but instead fixed me with a guilty look. "Come," she finally said. "Let us find a quieter place to speak." She descended the steps and stood right in front of me, on the symbol. The floor trembled slightly and rose like an elevator. I looked up with surprise as the opening in the ceiling grew closer. We emerged into a well made of carbonado and the platform came to a halt. I looked around in wonder. It was the most luminous place I'd ever seen in the Castle—maybe in my entire life.

"Where are we?" I asked in astonishment.

Sophìa smiled. "Welcome to my garden." Part of the low wall surrounding us crumbled away to let us out. I took a few steps and turned back to look at it.

"It is the Well of Souls," Sophìa said as the carbonado sealed up again. "It is here that the Souls of all the Damned in the Castle converge. All my beloved butterflies." She raised her arms and let them flutter around her. Butterflies were everywhere—on the walls, on the huge glass ceiling, and most of all . . . "Come. I shall show them to you," she said, noticing my interest. Spread out in front of us was an incredible field of Devil's Stramonium. I'd never seen so much of it before. Its presence was almost frightening, as though it was alive. "You are fortunate. Few have seen my beloved crop of Devil's Stramonium." Sophìa plucked one of the blossoms and held it out to me. It was black and regal, just like her.

"The Witches' flower," I murmured. I inhaled its scent and instantly felt intoxicated. My Dakor heard the call and materialized from my skin. He too sniffed it and then gulped it down.

Laughing, Sophìa plucked a black butterfly from a flower and held it up near her eyes. "And you, were you a bad boy, my little Lecher?" It flapped its wings and fluttered away as the Empress watched it.

"This is where the Sorting of Souls is done," I said. It wasn't a question. My Sisters had told me about Sophìa's garden. I knew she often spent time there, entrusting command of the Castle to Devina, her Specter. She spoke to her Souls, cultivated Devil's Stramonium, and sorted the Damned before casting them out into Hell, where they would return to their human forms.

"Precisely," Sophìa said, confirming my thoughts. "But at times I also come here to relax. It is heavenly, is it not?" She laughed and I agreed.

Sophìa knew how to be eccentric, especially when it came to her butterflies, but I was there for another reason. I wanted an explanation. "You told me they were dead," I repeated, point-blank.

She stopped and turned her back to me. "To me they are," she replied, her voice once again serious.

"Tell me more."

"Ginevra left us."

I frowned. I would never have expected an answer like that. "How is that possible? It's madness."

"And yet it happened. She betrayed our trust and I banished her." It seemed impossible to me that a Sister could forswear the Bond like that. Sophìa was everything to us. "Not to her. When she left, my heart broke."

I snorted. "What heart? Your heart is made of ice."

"But to me, all of you are fire—the only thing that can melt my heart. You Sisters are everything to me."

"As you are to us." She was right. I knew how much she cared about us all. I shouldn't have been so unkind.

Sophìa nodded. "No other interesting encounters apart from Ginevra during your Reaping?" she suddenly asked, studying me closely.

What did she mean? "No . . ." I thought it over. "I don't think so."

"No other powerful emotion apart from your Bond with her?"

"Of course, as always, the seduction and Temptation and then the Reaping all went straight to my head."

"Excellent."

"What about the other Sister?" I said, switching to a subject that interested me more. "You said we lost two of them. Did the other one abandon us too?" The idea still seemed absurd.

"No. Tamaya was slain before she transformed. It was her husband who sacrificed her after he became a Subterranean. One cannot trust the Children of Eve. They are uncontrollable."

"What happened to him?"

"I dealt with him myself. Now that you have had the answers you sought, I wish to give you a gift."

"Being able to live in your kingdom is already a tremendous gift," I replied on impulse. Sophìa had been saddened by our conversation and I couldn't bear it.

"Do you mean you would refuse the gift I wish to give you?"

"I didn't mean that. I would never turn down a gift from you."

She smiled. "Very well. Come."

I followed her down a narrow hallway. The light had returned to normal—it was dimmer and gloomier than it had been in the field of Devil's Stramonium. The butterflies followed us, fluttering everywhere. Lining the walls were huge glass display cases, full of mounted butterflies. Only then did I notice that beneath each of them was a small, engraved carbonado plaque. I stopped to study them and Sophìa came back to join me, a smile on her lips. "It is my private collection . . . A little whim of mine. Do you like it?" There were butterflies big and small. All of them were black. I read a few of the names: *Caligula. Maximilien Robespierre. Joseph Stalin. Nero. Heinrich Himmler.* "These are—"

"My pride and joy. They are the foulest of the Damned that humanity has ever encountered, the most ferocious, most heartless mortals who ever existed on Earth. My masterpieces, if you prefer. They are those with whom I established a fruitful alliance. Some were even excellent lovers. They spread panic, terror, and death. They made people lose their faith. Under their rule, my kingdom flourished. Until, that is, their time came and they returned to me. Adding a new piece to my collection is always a momentous occasion. When it happens, I preside over an Opalion as queen in honor of my victory."

"Wow," I murmured. I'd participated in various Games in the Circle, but none of them had ever been held in Sophìa's honor. Maybe that was why I'd never seen her Champion in action. The thought of him stirred something inside me—the desire to watch him do battle.

"You have met Zakharìa," Sophìa said, sensing my interest.

I'd lost control of my thoughts. "I'm sorry, my lady."

"Do not be sorry. You know the rules of the Sisterhood: upon request, a Subterranean claimed by a Sister may be loaned to another who desires him."

"But . . . I thought it didn't count for Champions, much less yours. Devina said—"

"Indeed, that is true, but I could make an exception for you if you wish."

I stared at her, surprised. Was the Empress granting me her Champion? I couldn't imagine a greater honor. "Thank you, my lady, but for the moment I'd like to focus on Souls. Reaping is my vocation. I can't stop thinking about it. When can I go again?"

Sophìa burst into a laugh that brimmed with pride. "Soon, my black butterfly." She stopped beside a small altar and picked something up. "It is tradition for each Witch to receive the sacred token after her first Reaping. And you have proven yourself worthy to wear it." She opened her palm.

My eyes widened. In her hand was the ancient medallion I'd seen my Sisters wear: the Dreide.

EVAN

33

THE ILLUSION OF HAVING YOU NEAR

"All this time waiting for a sign from Gemma and when I finally find her I let her slip through my fingers!"

"Calm down, Evan," said Simon. "You'll have another chance."

"I shouldn't have blown this one!" I snapped.

"Don't shout or you'll wake Liam. He was crying all night long."

"You're right. Sorry."

Simon had stayed with him while Ginevra and I went looking for Gemma. Tracking her down had been hard even for her, and she could rely on the Bond. Gemma's power was strong—darkness shrouded her like a mantle. We had to be patient, wait for an opening. Without Ginevra I never would have managed. My connection to Gemma had been broken because her soul had been corrupted.

"They're ready." Ginevra appeared with an arsenal of weapons. She dropped them on the table and looked at me. "We'll see if he can catch a bullet in mid-air too."

I picked up the projectile and studied it. Inside it was venom from her Dakor. "Nice work. It's ingenious."

"It was easy, once I worked out the mechanism."

When we were still together, Gemma had told me about how they'd used weapons Ginevra designed to defend themselves from Desdemona, the Angel of Death sent in by the Màsala to kill her. They were dangerous for us and therefore effective against our enemies.

Ginevra strapped a holster to her thigh. Simon and I had already put on our shoulder holsters. "There are two guns each, plus this." Ginevra pulled out a Kalashnikov. "I'll keep this, if you don't mind. I have a score to settle with that Hunter."

"Be our guest."

"Careful with that thing," she warned, alluding to the bullet in my fingers.

"What, it might explode in my hand?" I joked.

"You never know. Your nerves haven't been reliable lately, and we need you alive." Ginevra was talking about my incident with the guy Gemma had been seducing at the party. I hadn't been able to help myself. When I'd seen his hands on her I'd lost my head and had come close to killing him. I was fierce, frustrated, and willing to kill to get her back.

I slid the cartridge into one of the guns and loaded it. "With these, the bastard doesn't stand a chance."

"Guess who's back," Ginevra suddenly said.

"He's here? Where?" Simon and I turned to look at her, gripping our weapons.

She was concentrating, listening. "Not him. It's Gemma. She's on Earth."

Emotions filled my heart: joy, fear . . . *urgency*. I holstered my weapons, staring at Ginevra. "What are we waiting for, then? Take me to her," I said resolutely.

"Good luck," Simon murmured.

Ginevra took my hand and together we dematerialized. Gemma's eyes were the first thing I saw, like two magnets that drew me to them the second I appeared. She, in contrast, glared at me with hatred, annoyed by my presence. It was like being shot in the chest with a poisoned bullet. In front of her was a newly born Soul, his dead body lying next to them.

The sight of Gemma seducing another man threatened to send me out of control again. I couldn't stand it. Fighting the instinct to shoot him, I grabbed the guy by the arm and helped him cross over, showing him the way.

"How dare you?" Gemma hissed. "He was already mine."

"Don't make me regret not killing him," I shot back threateningly.

She raised her arm to strike me but I blocked her wrist. We stared at each other for a long moment. I didn't know what was worse: the fact that she didn't remember me or the hostility I saw in her eyes.

Devina attacked me from behind and I was forced to defend myself.

"Gin, don't let Gemma get away!" I shouted, struggling with the redhead. I shoved her against the wall and pinned her there. She sneered at me as her Dakor emerged to challenge me. I tightened my grip, not even afraid of the thing. "I'll take care of this Witch."

"I know some fun games you could entertain me with," she whispered, touching her lips to my neck.

"You just don't give up, do you? What's wrong with you?"

"Sooner or later I'm going to claim you."

"Or maybe somebody else will," I said to provoke her. Her eyes burned with hatred. I'd never given in to Devina, but Gemma had a power over me Devina would never have.

"It wouldn't be a good idea for you to come back to us in Hell," she hissed, regaining her confidence.

"You're right. I'd better bring her back here to me."

Devina smiled and broke loose, attacking me again. "You'll never achieve that goal!"

"Then I'll die trying," I snarled, counterattacking.

"Evan, leave her to me!" Ginevra shouted, rushing at Devina. Until then, she'd kept Gemma, who refused to strike her, at bay. I jumped in front of Gemma. I had to keep her there. I wanted a chance to talk to her—just one. She launched an attack and then another, but I blocked them all without striking her. I barely recognized her. She'd always been a fighter, but now she was a fearless warrior. The Witches had trained her well; she was giving me a run for my money with her poisoned, curved-bladed daggers. Time was running out. I had to seize my chance. I disarmed her and trapped her against the wall, pinning her wrists to it. For a long moment we looked at each other as she caught her breath.

"You know your stuff when it comes to fighting Subterraneans."

"Especially the ones who want to kill me," she hissed.

I gripped her wrists harder. "I don't want to kill you."

"You're lying—I know you are. What else could you want of me?"

"To have you by my side," I said, determined, staring into her eyes. She held my gaze and a sneer formed on her face. She moved her lips close to mine, driving me wild. How I longed to kiss her again . . . just one kiss. Her hand rested on my thigh and slowly rose, disintegrating my every last shred of willpower.

"You're aroused by me," she whispered, thrusting her hips against me as I lost my mind. The brief contact disarmed me, but then I looked into her eyes. A glimmer of violet flashed across them, returning me to my senses. In a flash, I spun Gemma around and held her face against the wall, pressing my erection against her.

"I'm always aroused by you," I whispered behind her ear. For a moment I'd let myself be bewitched, but now I was in control again.

"You'll never have me," she said, her tone confident.

"Evan, look out!" Ginevra shouted. An arrow whistled past my ear. I grabbed Gemma in my arms and held her tight, rolling across the wall with her. Absolon was back.

Gemma stared at me, confused by my gesture, and the Hunter attacked again. "Go! Run!" I shouted to her.

"We need to get out of here!" Devina materialized beside her and they vanished.

I brandished my guns and prepared to face the Hunter. He was going to pay dearly for interrupting my encounter with Gemma. I shot at him and he dodged the bullet, surprised.

Ginevra pulled out her Kalashnikov, but the Hunter appeared behind me so she couldn't open fire. Not only was he strong, he was also agile and extremely sly. I tackled him and a furious struggle ensued. Suddenly, he tore a gun away from me, but I managed to kick it out of his hand before he could shoot.

I was trying to keep him away from Ginevra. There was no way I could go back to Simon without her. I'd experienced for myself what it was like to lose the person you love. I launched another attack and Absolon defended himself by throwing me to the floor. I slid across the ground and pulled out another gun, firing a shot that hit him straight in the gut and passed through to the other side. His eyes went wide with shock. Ginevra and I held our breath, waiting for him to disintegrate. Instead he slowly raised his head and stared at me, his lips twisted into a sneer. We stood there, stunned. The bullet hadn't killed him?

The Hunter prepared to attack again and Ginevra reacted by showering him with all the ammo in her Kalashnikov. Yet he continued to rush me, disappearing and reappearing as swiftly as a ghost. He tackled me and grabbed my shirt, but Ginevra cast a spell that hurled him away. An instant later she materialized at my side and got me out of there.

"What happened?" Simon asked, looking frightened when we appeared in front of him in the kitchen.

"The Hunter," I burst out, my nerves on edge. "He attacked us."

"The bullets, Evan!" cried Ginevra, who still couldn't believe it. "Did you see what he did? I've never seen a Subterranean like this one. How can we face him now? We have nothing that can stop him!"

"Would you two explain what's going on?" Simon insisted with exasperation. "We've faced lots of Subterraneans. One more shouldn't scare us."

"He's not like the others. My venom doesn't kill him," she explained.

Simon's eyes bulged. "How is that possible?"

"I have no idea. I hit him with an entire arsenal but it didn't leave a scratch on him. No Subterranean has ever had such power."

"But he isn't any ordinary Subterranean," I reminded them. "He's a Hunter. His priority isn't helping Souls pass on—what matters to him is killing Witches. He must have developed some sort of immunity to their venom."

"I've never seen anything like it," Ginevra murmured, incredulous.

"Yeah. He's become a serious problem."

Simon locked eyes with Ginevra. "This game is getting too dangerous for you."

"You can't ask me to stay holed up at home just because it's protected," replied Ginevra, who must have read his mind. "I'd rather risk my life than be imprisoned."

"Well, I'm not willing to run that risk," he said sternly.

"Evan needs me. Gemma might—"

"*I* need you," Simon shouted. "The topic is closed. Until we kill the Hunter, you're not leaving here." The fire in his eyes kept Ginevra from protesting, though I knew it wouldn't be so easy to keep her still—not when Gemma was involved. Bringing her home was almost as important to Ginevra as it was to me.

"Gemma? Did you find her?"

I nodded wearily. "It was no use. She doesn't remember *anything*." I sighed, at a loss.

"What now?"

"I'll keep trying. I have no intention of giving up." Somewhere beneath that Witch's exterior was my Gemma, and I would find her again.

"I spoke to her while we were fighting," Ginevra said. "In her mind."

"I'm listening," I said. What had she told her? Maybe she'd unearthed some glimmer of a memory . . .

"No, I'm sorry. She sees you only as a Subterranean, an enemy."

"No need to be so direct," Simon told her reproachfully.

"That's all right," I reassured him, sitting down on the sofa. "I already know how Gemma feels when I'm near her." Great bitterness, followed by the deep desire to claim me as her slave. My mind lost itself in the memory of her fiery gaze. "What did she tell you?" I asked Ginevra, driving the image from my thoughts.

"She was confused. She doesn't understand why I'm with you two." Ginevra chuckled. "She wanted me to come to my senses."

"What did you tell her?"

"That she was the one on the wrong side. Then I realized that only you had any chance of bringing something out in her, so I handed her over to you."

"It didn't work," I said softly, resting my head on my knees. "I can't believe this is actually happening. Me, fighting against Gemma. It's a nightmare."

"What will you do if she never comes back? Have you ever thought about that?"

"That's not even a possibility." I gave Ginevra a hard stare, almost as if her question were an insult.

"You should think about it, though."

"Never." I shot to my feet, furious. Had she lost her mind?

"You don't understand. The Sisters' Bond has taken possession of her. I felt it. Gemma was reborn through Sophia's venom. I'm not sure there's any chance she'll be able to renounce evil."

"Shut up," I ordered.

"What, you don't want to hear it? Well, you have to. We've all got a lot on the line."

"You can back down whenever you want," I growled.

"That's not the problem! I care about Gemma as much as you do. I want to bring her back too, but you need to open your eyes and face facts."

"I'd rather be blind than lose hope."

"I don't want you to give up, Evan. I just want you to stay focused. You were on the verge of letting yourself be claimed today. They were on Recon and you're a Subterranean." My eyes widened at the memory of the power Gemma had had over me. "If you let her tricks work on you, it'll end up being *you* who gives in to *her* and not vice versa. Are you understanding me? *You* need to be strong. That's the only way you'll manage to bring her back. You need to see Gemma for what she is now: a Witch. What got into you back there, anyway?"

"I . . . I lost my head," I confessed. Having her so close after such a long time had disarmed me. I'd touched her—had been on the verge of kissing her. I'd longed to hold her again so badly I'd let myself be overpowered. Her lips had been so close to mine I'd believed I'd found her again.

"Instead, she had you in the palm of her hand. She was *this* close to making you hers."

"I'm already hers."

"You know what I mean. The more you gave in to her, the more your energy flowed into her. Her lips would have made you her prisoner."

"Maybe I should let her do it," I murmured, feeling defeated.

"Don't even say that," Simon reproached me. "What would become of Liam?"

I ran my hands over my head. What I'd said was ridiculous—I would never abandon my son. "You guys are right. I'll be more careful next time."

Unless I was willing to succumb, I would have to see things for what they were. I couldn't keep on deluding myself that I'd found her again just because she seemed to give in to me. It was a trick. Gemma was a Witch and I was a Subterranean. Once again we were pitted against each other, like when it had all begun—only now our roles had been reversed: I was the prey and she was the hunter. Gemma had tried to claim me. I'd felt my soul yearning to run to her, to give in to those lips, so inviting, so desirable. Overcome with frustration, I punched the sofa. Gemma's power was so strong it overwhelmed me even when she wasn't there. Ginevra was right. I couldn't let her get into my head or I would lose sight of my objective. *I had to stay focused* to avoid surrendering. I had to see Gemma for what she'd become: a Witch. There was one thing, though, that I was wrong about: in our battle, I wasn't the only prey. We were both predators. One of us would subdue the other. Either I would bring Gemma back or she would take me.

The hunt had begun.

GEMMA

A NEW DESIRE

The doors to the kitchens flew open and all the Damned bowed, frightened, as I made my entrance. I was hungry. Very hungry. Soon we would all gather together to eat, but I couldn't wait. I pointed to one of the Gluttons. "You. Bring me what you prepared. At once."

"As you command, my lady," he said ceremoniously, fear in his voice.

I sat down on a table and tasted the meat he placed before me. It felt like I hadn't eaten in centuries, but that was nothing new. There was never enough food for me. Still, that day I was particularly on edge, which made things worse. The Damned watched me enviously as I raised the food to my mouth. They were all as thin as sticks and their sunken, bloodshot eyes disgusted me.

"Don't stare at me like that, dog," I snarled at the one who'd served me. I threw a dagger at him and it lodged in his skeletal neck. He gurgled and exploded in a cloud of smoke as all the others groaned with terror. I picked up the platter of meat and smashed it against the floor. "It's too tough." The dagger returned to me like a boomerang. I caught it and jabbed it into the table. Then I pointed to another of the Damned. "You. What do you have for me?"

"Everything I have is yours, mistress." He bowed, offering me his platter.

"Nothing you say will earn you any pity from me, bootlicker." I dug my heel into his shoulder and he fell to his knees in pain. Picking up a candy apple from the platter he'd held out to me, I examined it. "But maybe this will." Its sweetness exploded in my mouth. *"Divine,"* I moaned, closing my eyes. "Gluttony is without doubt the most delicious of all sins." I hopped off the table and tossed the rest of the apple to the floor at his feet. "Here. You've earned it."

He lunged at the food and grabbed it, holding it tight. "Thank you, my lady, thank you."

He knelt down to kiss my feet but I shoved him away. "Make more for me and my Sisters!"

"As you command, mistress. Right away."

"Now get lost before I change my mind." He crawled away, not daring to stand up. "What are you all doing, idling around?! Back to the kitchens!" At my command the other Gluttons hurried back to their posts. Actually, we Witches could have made all the food we wanted magically appear, but that wouldn't have been as much fun. Because of this, Sophìa had built huge kitchens and filled them with the finest Gluttons found during the Hunt. It was more satisfying to have others wait on us. During their lives, Gluttons had committed incredible atrocities to satisfy their insatiable appetites—not only for food, but also for money, power, and so forth. In Hell, their souls were ravenous, in a state of endless hunger that couldn't be satiated. Their lives there were very short. They lacked strength, they lacked the power they'd always yearned for, and for the other Damned they were easy prey, the littlest fish. However, some of them were granted the privilege of waiting on us, and in exchange we allowed them to live longer—at least, as long as their dishes were worthy of our palates.

Hung on a wall in the kitchens was Drugo, the first chef who'd set foot in the Castle. Legend was that, hoping to amaze Sophìa, he'd prepared an elaborate dish made of butterflies. Obsessed with her butterflies, she'd been outraged and had hung him there without killing him as a warning to all the others. Over his head she'd placed a plaque, as she did with all her beloved lost Souls, bearing the inscription "The Profaner." Since then, everyone had called him that. His suffering would be eternal.

I looked out the window and saw twilight ruling in the forest. Opening my palm to summon my Dakor, I felt the venom burn in my eyes as they transformed. The serpent hissed and slithered up my arm. It was comforting to feel him against my skin. Maybe he could banish the uncertainty that had left me so on edge: why had the Subterranean saved me from that arrow? I'd smelled the aroma of our venom on its tip. It wouldn't have had any effect on me unless the archer had used pure fire . . . and yet the young man had shielded me with his body, even though for him the arrow would have been fatal. Why? It made no sense. It must have been a trick to make me lower my defenses. Devina had warned me about him. Everything she'd told me had been right: he was dangerous—more dangerous than the other Subterraneans—because his mind worked differently. What Devina had hidden from me, though, was that his soul had such a delicious, satisfying scent. Now I understood why she wanted to make him hers. She'd tried for centuries without succeeding. It had taken very little for me to get close to achieving that goal, on the other hand. He wanted me. I'd sensed it. I'd sensed the emotions struggling inside him, utterly different from those of the other Subterraneans we'd claimed. They all reacted either with total hostility or a complete willingness to surrender, but in him there was more. He was full of desire, but his willpower was incredibly strong. He wanted to have me, yet maintain control. His was an absurd thought . . . but it excited me.

I smiled. Growing inside me was the sweetest whim, the most exciting challenge. I would bring down his defenses. I would claim him.

MILLICENT AND PRISCA

Voices touched my mind. It was Anya and Devina, and they were arguing. Again. Was it starting to become a habit? And why did I have the impression they were hiding something from me? After Devina had burned Anya's book in my chambers, I'd found a tiny fragment of paper. The words in Sanskrit were cut off and I couldn't decipher them, but the graceful handwriting belonged to neither of them.

I drew my daggers and spun them around in my hands. The gesture relaxed me. Closing my mind so my Sisters wouldn't notice my presence, I listened to their thoughts more carefully. I'd gotten good at it.

"Don't you dare, or I'll tell Sophìa," Devina threatened. She sounded confident. *"I thought you knew me better. Do you really think Sophìa would accept it? It's against her rules. Since when have you been willing to break them?"* she asked mockingly.

"Right—that's usually more your department," Anya mocked back.

"That doesn't matter any more. In that life she's dead. She came here to us and here she'll stay."

"You think I don't realize that? I just want her to find herself."

"She already has. She's a Witch."

"She could be both."

"Nonsense."

"Do I seem like nonsense to you? It wouldn't change anything for us if she knew!"

"It would change for me."

"Or maybe you mean for him? You're deluding yourself."

"Not any more than you are. No little fairy tale could undo the Empress's venom. Do you think Sophìa is a fool? She took precautions."

"What does that mean? What do you know?"

"Good!" said another voice, interrupting Anya. It was Camelia. "You're here. I'm dying of hunger. When are the others coming?"

"Gemma's already here," Devina said.

I jumped. How had she sensed my presence? I sheathed the daggers behind my back and stood up straight, entering the Hall of Sisterhood. "These Gluttons are a bunch of crybabies. They're starting to get on my nerves," I said in a steady voice. "They'd better bring me something good to eat or I'll make heads fly." I glanced at Devina and then at Anya.

Devina was pleased with me—it was clear from the way she looked at me. Anya, on the other hand, always seemed disturbed. Why? Because she was jealous of how close I was with Devina, that was why. However, neither of their opinions interested me. I was who I wanted to be, and soon I would become even more.

"Welcome, my black butterflies." Sophìa appeared in the room in an elegant black gown that left her thighs bare. The long sleeves covered her hands, showing only her sharp black fingernails. The Empress always wore magnificent gowns. At times they were sumptuous and strange, at others sober and refined. They were all made by her black butterflies, who modeled their creations directly on her body. They often changed their arrangement from one moment to the next, based on her mood, and they all gave her an irresistibly sexy look. Sophìa was the devil, but to anyone who saw her she was a goddess—the most enchanting, most dangerous creature in the entire universe. When she sat down, the strange hat on her head changed shape. As always, it was composed of butterflies. "Take your places and tell me of your victories and your failures."

"A failure is merely a victory not yet enjoyed," we replied as one.

"Excellent." Sophìa smiled, looking at us with satisfaction.

The Hall of Sisterhood was one of the most luminous rooms in the Castle. It wasn't particularly large, but in compensation it was high-ceilinged, and black butterflies fluttered far overhead, their wings producing a sound that delighted our Empress. A large chandelier hung over the table around which we sat, a perfect ring of black carbonado at which we all had the same importance, including Sophìa. Whoever sat at the Ring of Sisterhood was equal to all the others. "Tell me, Sisters, tell me everything," the Empress insisted.

Having dinner together gave us the chance to share our experiences, to tell Sophìa everything we'd done. That night Nerea and Safria began with anecdotes about the Reaping—some amusing, others gruesome.

Our maidservants served the dishes the Gluttons had prepared and went to stand behind us, one for each Witch. The ring began to turn, allowing us all to taste each of the dishes the Mizhyas continued to serve. Their tasks also included keeping our cups constantly full of Cider, but this time one of them—Millicent—spilled some on Devina's shoe. My Sister cursed, furious, and Millicent dropped to her knees to clean it as the others held their breath.

"I'm sorry! I'm sorry! Forgive me, my lady," Millicent pleaded in fright.

Devina studied her shoe and smiled at her Mizhya. "Don't worry. It happens," she said. The maidservant looked at her, stunned, and relaxed slightly. Devina did away with servants for far less. Millicent would be wise not to get her hopes up. "Now fill my cup," Devina told her, holding out her black goblet.

"As you command, my lady. At once." The maidservant obeyed, Devina's amber eyes on her all the while.

"Go on, take it," the Witch ordered her with an affable smile. Millicent stared at her, confused, but obeyed. "Now *drink it*," she snapped, her smile curling into a sneer.

Millicent stiffened. "But . . . it's poison. If I do, I'll die."

"I said *drink it!*"

Millicent looked at us Sisters one after the other, hoping someone would offer her a pardon, but no one spoke in her favor. She cast a desperate glance at Prisca, one of Anya's maids, and raised the goblet to her lips, hands trembling.

"No!" cried Prisca. She ran across the room and tore the cup out of Millicent's hands. "I'll pay for her mistake." Before Millicent could stop her, the other Mizhya gulped down the poison.

"No! What have you done?" Millicent cried, bursting into tears. Prisca gurgled, burning up from the inside out, and fell to her knees as Millicent embraced her. Seconds later she exploded in a cloud of dust.

"What a touching scene," Devina scoffed, making some of us laugh. Millicent and Prisca were lovers—we all knew that. "Still, I've never understood martyrs. Dying for someone else?" She snorted. "That's nonsense, dost thou not agree?"

"No!" Millicent dared to contradict her. "She was my great love," she whimpered, still on the floor.

"No one deserves love more than we do," Devina said. Her whip cracked through the air and wrapped around the Mizhya's neck. "It's a pity her sacrifice was pointless. I'm not one to make compromises—she should have known that." She yanked on the whip and Millicent fell at her feet. Devina shoved her heel against her neck, preparing to finish her off, but Anya rose to her feet.

"Stop!" she ordered. We all turned to look at her. "Millicent has my pardon."

"Stop getting in the way all the time. You're spoiling my fun," Devina groaned. She pressed harder, all the maidservants in the room watching breathlessly.

"You killed Prisca. She was my Mizhya, and a good one. You owe me another."

"But I didn't kill her. She did it on her own."

Everyone laughed at Devina's joke. Everyone except the Empress. "Obey your Sister," she said sternly. "If she wishes to take the servant as her own, it is her right."

Devina fumed, but lifted her foot, freeing her. Head bowed, Millicent struggled to her feet, went to Anya, and kissed her hands. A tear slid silently down her cheek and Anya wiped it away. "In your place now," she told her tenderly.

Millicent nodded and went to stand behind her. Another Mizhya came into the room and took her place behind Devina, looking frightened because she knew what she was up against; Devina was the most capricious of the Sisters, and her Mizhyas either never did enough for her or didn't battle-train hard enough.

"Very well, my fearless butterflies," the Empress said, bringing our attention back to her. "Who has another interesting story for me?" Meanwhile, the swarm of Souls descended from the ceiling and began to flutter over the table, creating amazing formations. Art in movement. Sophìa adored it.

"I have an interesting story," I began. The Empress smiled at me. "Devina and I went on Recon today."

"How did it go?"

"Excellently, I would say." I looked at Devina, who smiled at me, her amber eyes aimed straight at mine.

"The chrysalis has blossomed," Devina said, nodding. "She's getting better and better."

"We claimed various Subterraneans and brought home eleven prisoners."

"A praiseworthy achievement. I am very proud."

"Still, I'm not satisfied." I opened my mind to let Sophìa read my thoughts, but also told her aloud, "There's a Subterranean I would like to claim more than any other." I glanced at Devina, who now looked furious. But I didn't care. I had decided: he had to be mine. "He's stubborn and disrespectful. There's not the slightest trace of fear in him—only strength, determination, and desire. I want him to be mine."

"Very well, then. You have found your Champion."

"No!" Devina protested, quickly rising to her feet. "I'm going to be the one to claim him."

"You are free to try," Sophìa said to calm her, "but so is Naiad." I shot Devina a challenging look. Only one of us would manage to win him—and it was going to be me.

"I told you how long I've been after him. How can you do this *to me?*" Devina said bitterly.

"Following your own instincts above all else is the first thing you taught me," I answered, resolute. *Your instinct is the most powerful weapon, the most reliable shield. Always follow it and you'll find your way.* Giving in to my whims was more important than heeding hers. And now, *he* was my whim.

Devina pretended to calm down and addressed the Empress with greater deference. "My lady, this is madness. May I remind you how dangerous he is?"

"Don't pretend you care about her," Anya spoke up. "You just want Evan for yourself." *Evan.* So that was what the Subterranean was called. I had to remember the name.

"Devina, your concerns are unfounded. There is no chance that this Subterranean could endanger our Naiad or the Sisterhood more than any of the others. She is special. She is a powerful Witch and within her flows my own venom. She will be with me forever. No one can change that," the Empress stated matter-of-factly.

Devina and Sophìa looked at each other for a long moment. Why was Devina so worried about that Subterranean? It wasn't only jealousy—there was something else, I knew it. Was he really as dangerous as she'd always claimed? She herself had trained me so well that I could face him. Why, then, was she so concerned? Sophìa didn't seem to have any doubts—quite the opposite. Anya, who had defended me, now looked sad again—disappointed, maybe.

"Then it is decided," the Empress proclaimed. "The Subterranean will be less dangerous under our control. If Gemma succeeds in claiming him, he may become her Champion."

Devina cracked her whip. Frightened, the swarm of butterflies dissipated and flocked to Sophia. We all watched as Devina stormed out of the room.

Our challenge had begun.

EVAN

ABSOLON

I watched Simon make his way through the wreckage of the plane crash. Neither of us could wait to finish the mission and get back to Ginevra and Liam. Since our discovery that the Hunter was immune to her venom Simon had been out of his mind, knowing how reckless Ginevra became when it came to Gemma. This time, though, he hadn't given her any choice: until we found a solution she would stay at home, where she would be safe. We had no idea how to rid ourselves of Absolon. Maybe we could lure him into the magic simulation scenarios, like we'd done with the other Subterraneans who'd been after Gemma.

Simon disappeared, accompanying a Soul into the other world. I walked among the mutilated bodies in search of other Souls to ferry over. In the wreckage I noticed a young man with his back turned toward me, crouching beside his body. I approached him and noticed he was weeping. Another frightened Soul. "Can you save me?" he suddenly asked me, his head bowed.

I rested a hand on his shoulder, but nothing happened. He looked up and I saw his black eyes.

A bitter sigh escaped me. "I can't. I'm sorry." His Soul was irremediably tarnished. It was too late to help him. I felt a dark energy surround me a second before the Witch materialized in front of him.

"Who are you?" the man asked, terrified by her ominous presence. Or maybe it was her golden serpent eyes that scared him.

"You offend me. Don't you remember me any more? We've spent so much time together."

The young man didn't recognize her face, but he must have given in to her dark whispers, offering his soul to her. He tried to run, but the Witch paralyzed him with her magic and dragged him across the ground as he screamed. She swept him over to his corpse, which sucked him back up. Moments later, out of its mouth crawled a big black butterfly—one of the largest I'd ever seen. Her Dakor lunged out and gobbled it up.

"What a delight," the Witch murmured. I narrowed my eyes and she smiled at me seductively. "Bathsheeva." She materialized in front of me, her expression menacing.

"Go back to the Castle, princess of darkness. There's nothing more for you here," I told her.

"You never know what I might find in the wreckage," she replied, turning her eyes to the soul of a woman. If she wasn't completely compromised, one of us still had a chance to save her. I wasn't about to let the Witch take her. When Bathsheeva sensed my intentions, her expression hardened. "Step aside, Child of Eve. This time there's no truce to rein in my instincts." Her serpent hissed close to my face, but Simon materialized beside me, ready to hurl the fireball in his hand. The Witch glanced at it and turned to look at me. "Your reinforcements have arrived."

"You have your allies and I have mine," I told her. She withdrew her serpent and, with one last challenging look, vanished.

"Evan, look out!" Simon cried.

An arrow whizzed right by my head and lodged in the plane's fuselage where the Witch had been a moment before. I slowly turned and looked the archer straight in the eye. "Absolon."

Simon kept his fireball burning and remained at my side expectantly. "What a shame," he said. "You barely missed her."

The Hunter narrowed his eyes at us in a tacit challenge, nocked another arrow, and pointed his bow at us.

"Why are you still here? You miss the good old days of being a Soldier?" I asked mockingly. He pulled back on the bowstring but I materialized in front of him and grabbed the arrow before it could leave the bow. "Or did you want to train with us for a while?"

Throwing me a malevolent look, he tried to punch me. Simon jumped over the debris of the plane and hurled him away. My brother and I exchanged a complicit glance and split up to catch him off guard. While Simon diverted his attention, I climbed onto the roof of the plane to lie in wait for him. Immune or not, sooner or later I would find a way to make Absolon pay for what he'd done to Gemma. The second he went after my brother I caught him off guard and slammed him to the ground, but my victory was fleeting. He was too strong and would soon manage to overpower me. We struggled amid the wreckage and Simon rushed in to help me. He opened his fiery palm and clamped it onto Absolon's shoulder, burning through his leather tunic. The Hunter gnashed his teeth from the pain and with a single blow hurled Simon away, returning his focus to me. "Ye have thick skins, ye two."

"We're fighting for a good cause."

He smiled. "As am I." A dark, sharp blade slid out from his ring. He moved to stab me with it but Anya appeared behind him and dragged him away. The Hunter looked at us and tried to break free from Anya's grip, but she shoved him against the plane. Her Dakor opened its fangs.

"Anya, no!" Simon shouted with alarm. "He's immune! Your venom can't kill him!"

She whipped out a long dagger and pinned his hand to the plane with it. Absolon shrieked in anguish. Anya pulled off his ring and pointed it at his throat. "Well, maybe this can." Absolon stared at her, his eyes aflame, and tried to dematerialize, but it was no use. His skin began to shrivel, as if the Witch were desiccating him from the inside.

"Going somewhere?" Anya challenged him.

I approached them, stopping abruptly at the sight of the ring. "What the fuck?!" I muttered. Simon and I stared at each other in shock. It was the Devil's Claw.

The Hunter hadn't come for the Witch. He was there to kill us.

HIDDEN TRUTHS

"Where did you get this?" Simon shouted, pointing the ring at the Hunter's throat. The Claw glittered, dark and sharp as a razor—a messenger of death for those of my race. Its poison could banish a Child of Eve to Oblivion.

Absolon sneered in reply. He was sitting on the ground, leaning against the wreckage, his body immobilized by Anya's power. "Answer me! How did you get your hands on this?!" Simon shoved him to the ground with his foot. I'd never seen him so furious before.

"The same way he got the poison for his arrows," Anya replied, thinking out loud. "Sophìa recruited him."

"His arrow was for me, not Gemma," I murmured, remembering the last time we'd met, when I'd protected her from the Hunter's attack. "We were his targets, Simon."

"That's crazy. Not only is he a Subterranean like us, he's also a Witch Hunter."

"Only the devil in person could have given him the Claw. That's the only explanation," Anya insisted.

"Why would he want to kill us?" Simon replied, still incredulous.

"To keep me away from Gemma. How did I not see that?" I said. "Anya's right. Sophìa is behind all this. She always has been. *She* ordered Gemma's death." We'd been wrong—it hadn't been a last-ditch attempt by the Màsala.

Anya's jaw dropped in horror. "Tell us everything you know," I snarled, turning to Absolon.

"Why do ye not ask the Witch? I can feel her trying to enter my mind." I looked at Anya, but she shook her head.

Absolon laughed. He was obscuring his thoughts. "When ye spend centuries locked up like a cur ye learn to master true solitude."

Enraged, I hoisted him up and slammed him against the side of the plane. *"Tell us what you know!"*

Paralyzed by Anya's spell, he had no choice. "Why should I help ye? What have I to gain?"

Without taking my eyes off his, I summoned the ring to my hand and pointed it at him. "Is your life enough?" The Hunter tilted his head back, distancing himself from the lethal blade.

"Was it Sophìa who ordered Gemma's death?"

Absolon stared at me for a long moment before giving in. "Aye."

A sob escaped Anya. "I'm sorry, Evan. I had no idea."

"It's not your fault, it's mine. I should have been more careful. Devina must have overheard me while I was telling my brother about the plan to purify Gemma, and she ratted me out. Is that right?" I asked the Hunter, pushing him to confess.

"'Tis," he confirmed, "yet 'twas not that made her do it. Lilith had already recruited me. She personally trained me for months. Said the risk of losing the new Witch was too high. Your plan but added more urgency to hers."

My eyes went wide. "Sophìa saw how strong our bond was—that was why she didn't want to run any risks. If she hadn't intervened, Gemma might actually have been able to resist evil."

Absolon nodded. "She feared the transformation alone might fail to steal her away from ye. I saw it when she tore off her fingernail and gave it to the red . . . A demon, that one, she is."

"Wait a minute. You were with them? You mean Devina knew everything? She knew you were going to kill Gemma? *She knew* you were still alive? How is it possible Sophìa spared you after what you did to Tamaya?" Anya hissed, tears in her eyes.

"The red interceded. Once I had reduced Tamaya to ashes, 'twas *she* who saved me from the devil's wrath. She would call on me in my cell, though I cursed her every visit. I would rather have rotted alone than lie with her. At times it made me regret not being dead."

Anya looked shocked. "She's never cared about anyone, not even the Sisterhood."

"Or maybe she thought he might come in handy one day," Simon remarked.

"Aye," the Hunter confirmed, looking proud about having killed Gemma before our eyes.

I lunged at him, but Anya stopped me. We needed him alive. "What was her plan? What did you hear?" she asked, still shaken.

"She sent me out to slay the half-Witch so ye would resuscitate her with Lilith's venom. That way the lass would be hers forever."

"There was no war," I murmured.

Absolon smiled. "All an act. Lilith knew ye would never let her die. She tore a nail off her finger. Howling with pain, she was. She's mad. All of ye are mad."

"Then you know what you're risking if you don't cooperate," Simon replied.

"Tell me what she said," I growled as the anger inside me grew.

"'He himself will beg me to transform her.'" I punched the fuselage, overcome with rage, and left a dent in it.

"Evan, calm down. We were playing with the devil. What did you expect?" Simon asked. "It was obvious she didn't want to let her get away."

"What happened after that?"

"Use your imagination." The Hunter stared at me, sneering.

It was Simon who deduced the answer: "After using the Claw to bring Gemma back to life, Sophìa must have given him a new mission. So she gave him the Claw to get rid of us. She knew we would never give up. Did I guess correctly?"

Absolon looked at me. "Why are ye chasing after her so relentlessly? She's one of them now."

"She's my wife," I roared, furious.

He snorted. "Ye fight so fervently for her when your 'wife' does naught but betray ye with other men."

"Are we still talking about me or are we talking about you now?" I said to provoke him. Once he became a Subterranean, Absolon had slain his wife Tamaya before she could transform into a Witch, publicly humiliating her for betraying him.

He looked at me and smiled. "I wager she's already doing it." I grabbed him by the throat and squeezed.

"Evan, we're wasting time," my brother reminded me.

I stared at Absolon for a long moment, trying to calm my nerves. "I'm going to bring her back."

I let go of him and he slid down and crumpled to the ground, his body as dry as stone. "Did ye not hear what I said? Evil has darkened her soul. 'Tis an irreversible curse. There's no hope for her. A Daughter of Lilith, she is," he concluded with a triumphant laugh.

My good humor had run out. I planted my foot on his shoulder and kicked, smashing his head against the plane. "She's coming back to me." Fists clenched, I turned to Anya. "We have to let her know it was Sophìa who plotted her death."

"She'll never believe you," she replied bleakly. "Besides, she wouldn't care. Sophìa's power over her is very strong. Gemma was forged by her venom. She was reborn from her. The Hunter is right: Gemma's soul is an extension of the Empress's. There's no way to bring her back. I'm sorry."

"Gemma's soul belongs only to me," I hissed.

Anya hung her head, unable to reply. She wanted to believe me but couldn't. "What should we do with him?" she asked after a moment.

"Let's lock him up in the dungeon," Simon replied. "He'll be safe there."

"Now that we've captured him, nothing will keep me from seeing Gemma again."

"You're forgetting Devina," Anya said. "Gemma trusts her too much. The situation is spiraling out of control."

"What about you? Will you help me talk to her again?" Sometimes not even Ginevra could hear Gemma. We needed all the help we could get.

"I already am. *I* was the one who made sure she materialized at the party. From now on I'll let you know whenever she returns to Earth. I'm sorry, that's the best I can do."

"It's already a lot." I took the ring and studied it. The Claw was as sharp as a panther's and as black as carbonado. I cast one last look at the Hunter. "We'll keep this." I pressed the little button in the metal and the blade retracted. I tossed it to Simon. "Later on we'll figure out what to do with you." I raised my foot and kicked him in the face again. He fell to the ground, his eyes wide open, as Anya used her powers on him until she'd petrified even his face.

The Hunter had fallen into his own trap.

GEMMA

MIND AND SOUL

I was reclining on red cushions in the Hall of Perversions while my Mizhyas massaged my body with hot stones. My mind, however, was elsewhere, trapped in the eyes of ice of that Subterranean. *Evan.* Their color was the same as the other Children of Eve, yet a different sparkle animated them.

You have found your Champion. Sophia's words continued to whirl in my head. I had witnessed dozens of Opalions and some had even been held in my honor after I'd won the Hunt, though I still hadn't found a worthy Champion. But now I wouldn't give up until I'd claimed Evan, w;hether he liked it or not. I would make him my prisoner and lock him up in the dungeons, if need be. Sooner or later I would bend him to my will. The fact that I was challenging Devina for him would make everything more exciting.

My maidservants stopped and I opened my eyes to find out why. Devina had shooed them away and was standing next to me, together with two bare-chested Subterraneans wearing only the standard leather pants of claimed Executioners. All at once her black outfit changed, transforming into a long skirt in white and gold. A delicate necklace dangled to her bare abdomen and her breasts were covered only by a thin strip of fabric the same color as her skirt.

"Did you come to make me change my mind or to remind me how dangerous Evan is?"

"Nothing of the sort. I thought our challenge should be celebrated with a little party just for us." She gestured to the two Subterraneans, who began to massage my body. I closed my eyes, moaning with pleasure. Their hands were warm and strong—nothing like the maidservants' small, cold ones.

"What do you say we have a little fun? You did well today on Recon. You deserve it." Devina lay beside me and the two men admired her. One of them had blond hair tied up in a ponytail, the other short dark hair and a scar along his cheekbone. Devina spread her legs, inviting the blond Executioner to come forward, and he began to massage her hips. I took a closer look and for the first time noticed that the two were part of our most recent catch. I had claimed one of them myself, and he would obey my every order. He would do anything to give me pleasure . . . and ask for nothing in return. They'd become our love slaves, like all the other claimed Executioners. Once they succumbed we entered their minds and their souls, and all they wanted to do was please us. Only Champions had special privileges.

I pushed my hair to one side and allowed him to caress my back. His movements were slow, his hands rough and exciting. Devina ran her sharp fingernail down her chest, making a rivulet of blood seep out. He sank his head between her breasts to lick it and she closed her eyes, aroused.

"Thanks for the peace offering," I told Devina, though he wouldn't have been my first choice. We had also taken eleven prisoners, and I definitely would have preferred one of them to a claimed Subterranean. It would have been more exciting to bend him to my will.

No, said a little voice inside me. Only one of them could quench my thirst. Up until then, I'd never paid much attention to the Subterraneans. Though Devina had offered me the most intrepid of her warriors as a gift, I always ended up tiring of them and killing them before they got too close. None of them could excite me. The truth was that the Children of Eve left me bored. I preferred action, going into battle, fighting . . . stealing mortals' souls. That was what I found exciting. To Devina, sex was an obsession. She always said lust was the sweetest of sins. I, instead, was always focused on the Bond, on the Reaping, on the Hunt. *On Sophìa.* One of my greatest wishes was to please her. The biggest challenge of all was to become her Specter. Nothing mattered more to me, and one day I would reach my goal. However, now that I had chosen my Champion I was beginning to understand Devina's lustful desires. I wanted to see him kneeling in front of me, feel his mouth between my legs as his eyes gazed at me, full of desire.

The Executioner with the scar kissed my shoulder and I closed my eyes, aroused by the pictures in my mind. When I spread my legs, his hands slid up to massage my thighs. He took my foot and I watched him unlace my boot, but when he raised his eyes to mine, the spell broke. I rested my heel on his chest and shoved him away, anger growing inside me. That Subterranean was attractive, but he wasn't *him*.

"What a waste of time," I grumbled, standing up.

"Where are you going?" Devina exclaimed, sounding annoyed.

"You take him. I'm going to look for something that really amuses me."

Just then, Anya appeared. "Sophìa wishes to speak to you in private," she told Devina.

"I'll go later. Can't you see I'm busy?" she answered, intoxicated by the attentions of the Subterraneans, who were now both focused on her. "In fact, why don't you join me? These two are new. Let's teach them a little about our customs. They're fast learners."

"The Empress doesn't like to be kept waiting, and she said she wanted to see you at once," Anya insisted sternly. The looks she was giving Devina were more irritated than usual.

"A little R and R would do you good, Sister," Devina goaded her. "Are you jealous because I didn't offer them to you first?"

"You just want her to be like you," Anya said accusingly.

Devina shot her a piercing look. "She already is like me." Her lips spread into a sneer.

"Stop talking about me like I'm not here," I put in. "I'm no one's trophy. I'm not like anyone. I'm just myself. Accept it, both of you."

"She's the one who needs to accept it, given that she keeps bringing you her Soldiers," Anya said.

"They're a gift. She should appreciate it," Devina retorted.

"You just want her to lose her purity and betray him. Don't think I don't realize that."

Devina laughed. "Are you listening to yourself? She's a Witch, Anya."

"That doesn't mean she can't be herself too."

"What you're talking about no longer exists. It's a dead body in a forest. It's the past. We're her future. All this is in her nature."

"And he's in her soul," Anya said.

My eyes went to them. What were they talking about?

"Her soul belongs only to Sophìa now. She was reborn from her venom," Devina replied, sneering. "Nothing can change how things are."

"Why is it so important that it was Sophìa who transformed me?" I asked them. "All that matters to me is my life here with you. My past existence, before I was bitten, is of no importance to me now."

Devina smiled. "Forgive her, Gemma. Anya likes to brood over insignificant problems. She should learn to relax," she said, returning to the attentions of the two Subterraneans.

"Do as you like." Anya turned her back on her.

I followed her out of the room. "Anya, can I talk to you?"

She looked at me for a long moment and nodded. "First let's find someplace quieter." She took me by the hand and the entrance to the Hall of Perversions disappeared. We materialized in an abandoned wing of the Castle. I had been there only once before, during my first days there.

The large double doors opened with a creak and closed behind us, sealing us inside. We all called it the Chamber of Enchantments, not because it had powers but because it was where we stored all the magical objects created over the centuries to satisfy mortals' whims. For Witches, making deals with them was an irresistible pastime. They would grant mortals wishes . . . in exchange for their souls. Over the centuries, they had created all sorts of magical contraptions to amuse themselves, many of which were collected in that room. It was a giant circular grotto with a large oval table in black stone in its center, illuminated by a skylight in the ceiling. Energy vibrated on all its walls, which were full of niches carved to order to accommodate the various devices. There were objects that slowed time or sped it up and others that commanded the forces of the sky and earth: staffs that brought rain, stones that invoked the benefits of the sun and moon or controlled the wind, amulets that tricked the light, making whoever wore them invisible, not to mention enchanted weapons capable of annihilating armies of soldiers: swords, war hammers, spears and shields . . .

"Look, this is one of Devina's favorites: a Mirror of Shame." I looked at it, curious. "It not only shows one's reflection but delves into the heart of the person looking into it and lays bare their sins. Some mortals have used it to accuse their adversaries, others to save their own lives . . . or to get out of trouble."

"Extortion is a delicious form of wickedness," I replied, instantly grasping her allusion.

"This, on the other hand, is its twin: my favorite."

"What does it do?"

"It's the Mirror of Courage. It shows people the part of themselves they're keeping hidden. The one they'd really like to be. Some Souls lose themselves to the desire to be what they see reflected in it. Certain mortals might stray because of their longing for what they've seen. The weakest ones even go insane."

"I prefer the first mirror. It's more fun," I said as we made our way through the room. "What's that one up there?" I asked Anya, drawn to an object that sparkled high above. I jumped onto the wall and climbed almost all the way to the top, where I grabbed it and leapt down, landing in front of my Sister.

"That's a Soul Sphere."

I studied the sphere. It was sparkly, created with a myriad of carbonado prisms. "What does it do, predict the future?"

Anya laughed. "No one can predict the future—it's the result of millions of decisions. Choices are the future."

"Not even Sophìa can?" I asked. I couldn't believe there was a limit to the Empress's powers.

"I can't answer that, but I wouldn't be surprised if she could. She's the queen of the underworld, after all."

"So what is the sphere's power?" I asked.

"It's the key to Nirvana, a transcendent world suspended between our worlds."

"Does it really exist?"

"Only in the mind of he who finds it. But that's not all." Anya took the sphere from my hands and held it in front of her face, turning it slowly. "This sphere can connect the mind of whoever possesses it to that of anyone she desires, creating a path where the two Souls unite. It transcends their bodies, leaving their spirits free to follow their desires. To find peace. Soul and mind in a world all their own."

"Isn't Nirvana a state without passion or desires?"

"Not *without*, but above. It's the achievement of desires. It's an otherwise unreachable state of inner peace. It's pure ecstasy."

"If one of us infused that kind of power in this sphere to satisfy the desires of a few mortals, does that mean we have it inside ourselves too?"

"No. Sophìa made this sphere. It's one of the few objects she personally forged for men. We Sisters are strong, but she has powers beyond whatever you could possibly imagine. None of us has ever been able to connect to someone's soul like that."

"Do you think I could keep it?"

"No, I'm sorry. Sophìa's very jealous of her toys. You can ask her permission to use it, if you like. She'd probably let you."

"It doesn't matter. I was just curious."

"Did you want to talk to me about Ginevra?" she asked point-blank.

"Huh?" I replied, my eyes still captivated by the energy the sphere was emanating.

"You said you wanted to talk to me."

There was so much I had to ask her. Anya was a trusted Sister. She might have been the wisest among us, but she also had a very strong spirit: she was one of the few who could stand up to Devina. Plus, Sophìa completely trusted her and her decisions. I couldn't choose a better confidant.

"I saw her," I explained, a knot in my stomach. "I ran into Ginevra and felt both happiness and sadness."

"I know," Anya said, her face full of sorrow.

"So basically, she's our Sister. How can she refuse to stay here with us? What happened to her? Why did Sophìa banish her?"

"For the Empress it was the hardest decision, but it was either that or death. At first she'd sentenced her to die."

"You were the one who changed her mind, I'll bet." Anya smiled, returning to that memory. "I don't understand. I read the suffering in her mind. She felt the Bond uniting us too, so why is she acting this way? *This* is her realm! Her place is here, with us. Maybe if I talked to Sophìa I could convince her to let her come back."

"Even if you convinced Sophìa, Ginevra would never want to. She chose to leave us . . . so she could live with a Subterranean."

"What?! You mean she betrayed us to be with an enemy? Did she lose her mind?"

"Sophìa was deeply disappointed by her behavior. For her, the Bond is the most important thing there is."

"I understand. It is for me too."

"However, there's a bond that's even stronger, if you have the good fortune to experience it."

"What are you talking about? That's absurd."

"Love. God gave Sophìa the Bond with her Sisters, but because she hadn't returned His feelings for her, He couldn't allow her to feel toward others an emotion that surpassed the power of true love."

"You've experienced it," I murmured, reading the story Anya had hidden away in her mind.

"That's not important any more." Though she turned away to escape my eyes, I caught her wiping a tear from her cheek.

"You're right," I said, trying to reassure her. "The past doesn't matter."

"That's not always true," she told me. "Sometimes the past can help us understand who we really are."

"It's true for me. I know who I am. I know what I want and how to get it. I don't care about the past. Only together with all of you does my life have meaning. I'll never understand how Ginevra could have made that decision." Anya looked down sadly. "You and Devina have been arguing a lot lately. Sometimes I have the impression it's because of me. Tell me why."

"Nothing I could tell you would change anything. You were created by Sophìa. Her venom runs through your veins. You belong to her. Besides, I'm forbidden to even think about certain things. Only you can probe inside yourself."

"Why would you want to change anything?"

"Because you're becoming more like Devina by the day."

"What's wrong with that?" I hissed with frustration. Why was Anya always so jealous of Devina? I cared for them both, but it was very clear to me who I wanted to be. "You're a good Sister, but when Devina's around you behave differently. What's the problem between you two?"

"We often want different things."

"Different things for me too?"

"Especially for you," she admitted, making me furious.

"Well, don't worry yourselves about it. I can manage all on my own!"

"I know," Anya replied with conviction. "You're very strong. You always have been. I just want to make sure you're always in charge of your own decisions."

Our eyes met and I suddenly felt like a willful child. Anya, instead, was mature, and her affection for me was sincere.

"Forgive me," I told her. "Sometimes I get carried away."

"That's all right. You still have a lot to learn."

"How do you manage to resist the power? Evil never takes control of you—you're the one to control it."

"I'm the second Witch that awakened for Sophìa. I've had a long time to learn to control myself."

"But Devina transformed before you did. She's the first Witch, but there's so much darkness in her. She doesn't have your wisdom. Why not?"

"Because I listen to my heart."

"The first thing Devina taught me was to listen only to my instinct."

"You're a Witch, Gemma. Your instinct will always lead you toward evil, toward what you are."

"What's wrong with that?"

"Nothing," she assured me, "but sometimes you need to listen to both to be sure you're making the right decision. Don't let the darkness blind you, Gemma."

"I'll try," I promised. She hugged me. I closed my eyes, overwhelmed by my love for her.

"I see you've received your Dreide," she said with a smile.

I stroked the medallion I wore around my neck, a small black serpent in the center of it. "Yours is nice, with those shades of green."

"It's the medallion that creates its colors for us."

"I know." When I had held mine in my hand for the first time, the serpent had stirred, coloring itself black. "I haven't discovered all its powers yet."

"Oh, they're limitless. You'll use some more than others."

"Tell me about some of them," I asked, curious.

"As you saw today on Reconnaissance, the Dreide stores the purest essence of the Subterraneans we claim. The moment they succumb to us, their souls are trapped within it and as of then they belong to us. But the Dreide is also their only key to get out of Hell. A real paradox, don't you think?"

"What do you mean?"

"The Dreide controls the door to the underworld—the only way in, the only way out—on Mount Nhubii, the Devil's Plane. The Damned can't cross through the passageway between the two worlds. The Souls who try remain trapped there forever. However, Subterraneans can, once the medallion has opened the portal for them."

"Why should they do that? I don't understand."

"Not alone, obviously, but with one of us. Some Sisters have fun taking their Champions to Earth from time to time."

"But why?"

Anya smiled. "For us they're trophies. Or maybe it's simply to spite the Màsala. Don't bother thinking about it."

"Speaking of our Champions . . ."

"I heard what you said at the Ring of Sisterhood." Anya turned, hiding her face. "Are you sure *he's* the one you want to claim?"

"Do you think I'm not strong enough, like Devina does?"

"No, just the opposite. And she knows it."

"All she does is tell me I should stay away from him, that's he's dangerous."

"Because she's afraid. The challenge you proposed is more dangerous for her than it is for you."

"What do you mean?"

"She knows she might lose."

"So why do you think I shouldn't claim him?" I asked, having read her mind.

"Are you still convinced your past doesn't matter to you at all?"

"What does my past have to do with it?"

"He was part of it."

I gaped at her in shock. "What does that mean?"

"Dig deep within you, Gemma. Maybe there's still hope."

I locked eyes with Anya's, offended. "This is how I am now, whether you like it or not. I have no connection to the past. All that matters is the future, and there's one thing I can see clearly: he's going to be my slave."

EVAN

THE LIGHT OF THE SOUL

Gemma leapt up to the window of the cathedral and turned to look at me, her eyes snapping with malice. *Until next time,* she mouthed. She blew me a kiss and hurled herself against the glass, which shattered in a shower of colorful prisms. The crowd screamed in panic and swarmed outside as I continued to stare at the spot where she'd disappeared.

We were in Rome . . . and she'd escaped me yet again. I growled in frustration. I'd followed her to Thailand, Singapore, through Africa, to the farthest reaches of Earth. Each time I came closer and closer. She and her Sisters destroyed sacred sites to diminish faith among believers, spread terror, and stained mortal Souls with their poisonous whispers. Then I would show up and our game would burst into flames. She battled to kill. I tried not to harm her.

Gemma had changed since I'd protected her from the Hunter's arrow. At first I'd deluded myself that she remembered me, but then I'd realized her true intentions. Ours had become a sensual hunt in which neither of us had any intention of giving up. I wanted Gemma back by my side on Earth. She wanted me with her in Hell. She'd decided she liked my tenacity and wanted to claim me. She was both bolder and more elusive, and this made everything more difficult. It seemed like each time we met she was sexier and more dangerous, and I was more in danger of losing my mind. Every time we encountered each other I managed to pin her down, but she was the one leading the game. She would brush her lips against mine to absorb my energy, and for a moment I would lose myself in her, because that closeness was everything I wanted. Many times I was on the verge of giving in to her beguiling power, overcome by desire for her, by the overwhelming attraction she exerted on me, but then I would think of Liam, think of my Jamie, and everything I would lose if I gave up. That was when I would rebel. At times I was brutal, but I had no choice.

Our encounters were increasingly fleeting—a matter of seconds or, at most, minutes, during which each battled to gain control over the other. I wanted to make her remember. She made me forget myself.

Anya told me there was no hope. Their Empress had even given Gemma her blessing to claim me. She no longer feared I might steal her away because she was certain the old Gemma had been obliterated. I, however, refused to give up. As long as I lived, I would fight for us. All it took was for her to set foot on Earth and I rushed to her. I would follow her to the ends of the Earth.

I materialized in the garden where Simon, Anya, and Ginevra were sitting on the lawn, playing with Irony and little Liam. It was already April and spring had sprung all around us. Liam loved all the colors.

"News?" Simon asked. I shook my head, frustrated.

"Evan, maybe you should—"

"No!" I growled at Anya. "Don't even say it."

"You've been trying for nine months," Simon agreed.

"And I'm going to keep on trying. I'm never giving up."

"This whole time, nothing has changed. Maybe Anya's right," Simon urged. "Maybe Sophìa's venom irremediably obliterated her. She would never let Gemma return to Earth if she risked losing her to you."

"She doesn't care about the past. She doesn't want to remember," Anya admitted to me with sorrow. "Nothing can bring her back unless she's the one who wants it to happen."

"What if we let her see Liam?" Simon proposed.

"Out of the question. It's too dangerous," I answered.

"You're right. She might decide on a whim she wants him for herself."

I clenched my fists, making up my mind. "Simon's right. It's been too long. We need to do something, try another approach."

"No!" Ginevra protested, reading the plan in my mind.

I ignored her, staring hard at my brother. "Simon, you need to use your power on Gemma."

Ginevra stood up. "We've already tried that. You don't know what happened the first time. It's too dangerous!"

"I would risk my life to do it, but my power only works on mortal Souls," Simon replied. "It doesn't work with Witches because their souls are corrupt. We've already talked about this."

"That's true," Anya said. "Centuries ago they tried to use it on Devina to make her forget she'd seen Simon and Ginevra together, but it was useless . . . and dangerous."

"We need to at least try!" I shouted in exasperation.

Liam babbled something and we all turned to look at him. He smiled and took a few steps toward me. I sighed and tears stung my eyes. Only he could calm me. "Come here," I said softly. He laughed in contentment. I knelt down and opened my arms to him, smiling at his awkward attempt to reach me. He toddled over to me and then clapped for himself, making us all smile.

"He's modest! Just like his Aunt Ginevra," Simon remarked, earning himself a glare from her.

"We'll bring your mommy home," I whispered to Liam. I rubbed my nose against his and he tried to bite it. "I hope you didn't get her appetite too." I lay down and held Liam above me to make him fly like an airplane. He loved that game. Time had flown by in the blink of an eye and Liam was already nine months old. He was a good-natured little boy and incredibly curious. But most importantly, he was human. There was no trace of supernatural power or energy in him.

"Here." Ginevra handed me a baby bottle full of milk. "It's feeding time." I leaned back against a tree and cradled him in my arms. He looked at me as he gulped down the warm liquid and his eyelids slowly grew heavy. I spent all my free time with him. I played with him, took him with me while I worked out. Watching me do handstand pushups gave him fits of giggles, especially when I pretended to fall and hurt myself. Often I would read him the old copy of *White Fang* I'd found in Gemma's storage boxes in the attic. It was the first book she'd ever read, and I hoped that by reading it to Liam, he could in some way feel more connected to his mother.

Some time ago he'd started to babble "dada," filling my heart with emotions I hadn't thought I would ever experience. I played the violin for him, fed him, and a few times even took him for a ride on my bike in the driveway. Then there were Ginevra and Simon, on whom I knew I could count. When I was carrying out orders or chasing after Gemma, one of them stayed there to protect him. The house was well defended, but you could never be too sure, which was why we never took him outside the walls of our fortress.

As far as Gemma's parents knew, we'd moved to London be with my relatives. I sent them photos of Liam and once in a while Ginevra would talk on the phone with them, simulating Gemma's voice. It would have been different if Drake had still been around to go visit them. But then I thought it might be harder for me to be face to face with her ghost, knowing I'd lost her.

I looked at Liam and Gemma's voice filled my head: *I wanted us to be a family.* "We will be," I murmured, stroking Liam's sweet face as he slept. "It doesn't matter how long it takes." I was going to keep my promise. I got up and went into the house, opening the sliding windows in the kitchen before putting Liam into the playpen we'd set up in the living room and going back out to my brother and sister.

"I was serious before," I told Simon, looking at him resolutely. "I want you to use your power on Gemma. Only you can probe deep inside her and reach her memories."

"Not if they've been wiped out."

"You've got to try!" I shouted, pleading. "She's still there. Somewhere in her heart she'll hear you. She can't have vanished forever. No magic can take her away from me. Part of her still loves me, I know it. I just have to help her remember."

Now that Gemma had transformed, I could no longer take her to Heaven to have her drink Ambrosia, but if she managed to remember, nothing would separate us ever again. Now that she was immortal we could live together for all eternity, like Simon and Ginevra.

"All right." Simon gave in. "We'll give it a shot as soon as Gemma returns to Earth."

"She's already here," Anya told us.

Simon and Ginevra looked at each other for a long moment. She still didn't agree with letting him do it, but she wasn't going to stand in his way. Simon looked at me and nodded. I held my hand out to Anya and she guided me to Gemma. A moment later she was in front of me, at her feet a young mother who was smothering her baby.

My eyes went wide in shock. "Don't do it," I begged her.

Gemma peered at me and smiled. "I'm not doing anything," she replied, dark sensuality in her voice. The baby boy cried, squirming beneath the pillow his mother was pressing over his face. He was younger than Liam. Simon had also frozen at the sight, but we could do nothing—it was the woman who had to decide not to follow evil. Now she began to weep and shout: "Enough! Stop crying! Stop it! Stop it!"

But Gemma was there to strengthen the woman's resolve, instilling her venom in her: *"He'll never stop,"* she whispered, staring at me. *"He'll ruin everything. George can't stand him. He knows. He knows it isn't his baby. He'll leave you."*

A man materialized at the back of the room. It was a Subterranean. He'd come for the baby. "Simon, do something!" I ordered.

Despite his horror, Simon reacted instantly. Though the woman couldn't see him, he cupped her face in his hands. Beneath her skin, her veins moved like little snakes as Simon evoked memories of her and her baby in her mind. She stopped, her eyes going wide, and for a second I almost had the impression she looked Simon right in the eye. Finally realizing what she was doing, she let out a scream, flinging the pillow away. She took the little boy in her arms, trying to revive him, and called 911. "I'm sorry. I don't know what got into me . . ." she said. "I heard a voice . . ." She wept, but now they were tears of desperation.

The Subterranean in the back of the room disappeared and I heaved a sigh of relief. The child was no longer in danger, nor was the young woman's soul. Gemma looked at me with hatred in her eyes. She seemed to be deciding whether to attack or leave. Before she could escape us I rushed up behind her and pinned her hands behind her back. "Simon!" I shouted.

Gemma tilted her head toward me and smiled. "If you wanted to have a threesome, you could've told me so right from the start." Simon materialized in front of her and grabbed her face, pressing his thumbs against her temples.

"Do it! Now!" I ordered. Gemma fell to her knees and I let her go as Simon held her tight. Her face became a black spider web as Simon's power flowed through her veins. Suddenly her Dakor hissed somewhere inside her and Gemma's eyes transformed.

"What's going on? You're hurting her!" I shouted.

"She's fighting me!" Simon growled. "I can't, I'm sorry."

"Keep going! Dig deeper!" Blood trickled from my brother's ear, but he didn't stop. "Simon!" I shouted, a second before a dark force hurled him away from Gemma. I ran to him and helped him to his feet.

"I'm sorry," he murmured. "I dug deep but found nothing."

Gemma stood up and shot me an icy glare. She pulled out her curved daggers and spun them around in her hands, ready to fling them, but I was faster; I materialized in front of her and held her wrists against the wall. I couldn't accept that even the last trace of hope had vanished.

Weakened by Simon's spell, Gemma dropped the knives and looked at me, still short of breath. Maybe it was my only chance to talk to her before she could escape. "Gemma, they're tricking you."

She wormed her hands free, her gaze hard. "How dare you? They're my Sisters. They're all I have."

"That's not true. You have me," I said. "You have Liam. Do you remember him?" I asked desperately, hoping Simon's power had had some effect on her.

Gemma seemed to think about it, her brow knit, but then her ice-cold eyes returned to mine. "I don't know any Liam. And I don't know you either."

"Your Sisters did this to you."

"They made me strong and invincible."

"They tore you away from us," I contradicted her.

"I *chose* to join them. There's no other way to enter the Bond."

"That's not true. They had to kill you to have you with them."

"Sophia saved me!"

"I begged her to!" I shouted in desperation, squeezing her wrists against the wall.

Gemma stared at me, confusion in her eyes. "What do you want from me?" she asked, studying me carefully.

I loosened my grip on her wrists and opened my hand in hers. Palm to palm. "I want you," I whispered, stroking her thumb with mine. "Just you." My gesture drew her gaze to our joined hands, to the tattoos that completed each other, the symbol for infinity that formed only when we were together. She studied it for a moment, surprised, and her big black eyes fixed on mine, digging inside me, leaving a deep furrow. I clasped her hands tighter, not wanting to let her go, but she vanished, her gaze still on mine, leaving me on the verge of tears, brimming with rage, vain hopes, and frustration. I hung my head and rested it against the wall, balling my fists against the stone as the emotions mushroomed inside me to the point of devastation, then struck the wall, which shattered from the impact. The anger was too great for me to contain. Each time Gemma ran away from me it was like losing her all over again.

"Hey." Simon rested his hands on my shoulders. "I'm sorry." Once again, Simon had risked his life to help me, but despite his best efforts he'd failed.

I rested a hand on his. "Thanks for trying." What was left to me now, if even this hope had been taken from me? Was it possible my Gemma truly didn't exist any more? No. No. No! I would never accept it. I would never allow it.

For such a long time, Gemma had been my light. Now she was lost in the darkness, unable to return. But somewhere inside her, her soul still shone. I didn't care what Simon thought. It was a lie, another attempt by evil to take her from me. She still existed. I would find her and bring her home. By my side. It was the only place for her.

GEMMA

THE EYE OF DESTINY

I went up to one of the tallest windows in the Castle and crouched down, breathing in the cool air. It almost seemed like I could see the entire kingdom from up there. The thick expanse of trees, the twisted trunks in the Marsh of Stillness, the waterfalls with their comforting rumble . . . the huge volcano that watched over us like a surly giant.

I felt like queen of the world . . . yet something disturbed me, though I couldn't put my finger on what. I stood up and spread my arms, contemplating the void beneath me, then closed my eyes and leaned forward, entrusting myself to the darkness. "*Argas*," I whispered in his mind.

I felt his heartbeat. When I opened my eyes, he was beneath me. He spread his mighty wings and I landed on his rock-hard back. I smiled and he whinnied, carrying me up to where the scent of freedom could banish the doubt that tormented me.

Argas and I were deeply connected. I spent all the time I could with him and together we explored Hell, following the rivers upstream or flying over mountains and waterfalls. It felt like he'd always been a part of me, not only since I'd bonded with my Sisters. With him I felt invincible and complete.

We quickly left the Castle behind us, soaring over hidden dwellings and underground villages. I could sense the fear of the Damned who sought shelter there. It was useless: no one could hide from me. But that day they didn't interest me.

A group of Souls fled at the sight of Argas descending. While he was still galloping, I leapt off his back and walked to the river's edge, observing my reflection in the swiftly flowing water. All I could see was a blurred outline. Maybe that really was what I was. Maybe it was all an illusion.

They had to kill you to have you with them. The Subterranean's voice filled my head like a ghost determined to haunt me. What did he want from me? Why did he hunt me down so insistently? Devina had wanted him for centuries, but he had chosen me. *Just me.* Why?

Sophia saved me!

I begged her to!

His frustrated shout exploded in my head. Nothing seemed to matter to him except convincing me of his sincerity, but it was absurd. A trick. I shook my head, banishing my doubts. Devina had warned me. She knew him well. She'd told me he would try to get into my head. I had to be careful.

Lost in the image of his gaze, both proud and desperate, I bent down and picked up a clod of earth. A flower blossomed at my command. It was black, like my tormented soul. I shouldn't listen to his lies. I knew where my place was—nothing else mattered. I stroked the stem and the Stramonium lengthened, obeying my order. At my touch, the flower spread into a lush fan. I stroked its velvety petals, but my eyes were drawn to the tattoo on my hand.

Another image filled my head: my palm against the Subterranean's, the lines on our juxtaposed thumbs forming a single design.

Stay together. Fight together.

A shiver crept up my back. I had always imagined it was a promise connected to my Sisters. Why did he have the same tattoo? And why had he been so intent on making me notice? Was it another of his tricks?

They tore you away from us. What did he mean by that? For months he'd been trying to subdue me, and now I was letting him penetrate my barriers? Why was I allowing him to plant doubts in my mind? I couldn't let him fool me. Witches had only one enemy— Subterraneans—and he was one of them. My Dakor stirred inside me, plucking the cords of my reason. Drawn by the scent of the flower, he crept out onto my palm and did a slow dance around it, then opened his fangs and gulped it down, staring at me intently. Our eyes were identical at that moment. I felt them burn, reminding me where my place was. He and I were two entities but a single being. I belonged to this place. What importance could the past possibly have?

An arrow hissed through the air and a small creature squealed. I was instantly on my feet, waiting for the hunter who'd shot it to emerge from the forest in search of her prey. Her thoughts were near. Maybe I would take home some fine plunder, a fierce new maidservant who could take my mind off my dark doubts. When she appeared in the bushes, my eyes locked onto hers.

"Gemma," she murmured, caught between surprise and happiness. I frowned, confused. How did this Soul know my name? Something moved in the trees, distracting me from her.

"Don't get mad if you didn't catch one bigger than mine. You can try again next time!" a man said cheerfully, approaching her.

"Drake, look," the woman said softly.

He saw me and froze. It was a Subterranean. His grey eyes pierced me as I studied them carefully. I probed his mind, losing myself in his memories—a confused tunnel of images in which I too was there, smiling with the other Subterranean, Evan. The power of his emotions was so astonishing I couldn't move a muscle.

"Let's get out of here, quick," the man urged her, and they disappeared into the forest together, leaving me with a new doubt to paralyze me: who were those two? And most importantly, how did they know me? What possible reason could a Soul and a Subterranean banished to Hell have for knowing me, a Witch? On Earth, Subterraneans might be untruthful, showing me lies in order to confuse me and prevail over Souls. But what reason would that Drake have to do so here? Besides, our encounter had been accidental, unexpected for both of us. It made no sense.

I looked once again at the tattoo on my hand. *Stay together.* Who was I, really? Would learning about my past help me find out?

There was something I was missing. I couldn't go on lying to myself and ignoring the need stirring inside me. I craved answers. Things needed to be clarified and there was only one person I trusted, more than anyone else in the world.

I leapt onto my Saurus's back, suddenly burning with the desire to unlock the doors of my mind. And Sophia had the key.

It was easy to find her. The Bond united us like parts of the same body. She was the heart and her heartbeat gave us energy. When I appeared in the large arched entrance, she welcomed me with a big smile. She had known I would come.

"My respects, Empress," I said, bowing to her.

Sophìa raised my chin. "Please, do not bow to me, my pet." She took my hand and kissed it, looking me in the eye intensely as I lost myself in her dark allure.

"You know why I'm here."

"For some time I have known this moment would arrive," she said. "Tell me, do you have any doubts about where your rightful place is?" she asked, though she already knew the answer.

"No. Nothing could make me doubt that my place is here at your side."

She smiled, pleased, and led me into the room that she called the Eye of Destiny. The ceiling sparkled, dotted with thousands of stars that reproduced the galaxies. In the center of the room ruled a giant black globe where millions of tiny lights twinkled, some blinking on, others blinking off. They were the pride and the torment of Sophìa, who spent hours studying them, the souls of the Subterraneans we claimed and those who rebelled against us, unleashing her fury.

"Knowing one's past is a whim that every Sister longs to satisfy sooner or later, though all that matters to us is our life here at the Castle."

"It is, my lady. I can't stand it that the others know things I don't, but the past won't change what I am."

"That is certain." Sophìa smiled, confident. "The transformation cancels all memories. For some the effect lasts longer than for others. No one can make them return, yet with time they often resurface on their own. Nevertheless, that does not change what we are."

"Do all my Sisters remember who they were before the Bond?" I asked.

"All of them except Devina, because I transformed her myself and my venom is the most powerful weapon. Devina was the first of the Sisters."

"You mean after all these centuries she's never remembered anything?"

"Nothing has ever mattered to her except her place beside me."

"I understand. Nothing means more to me either," I confessed. "I was just curious."

Sophìa studied me carefully. "Devina has her moments, but she is a loyal and trusted Sister. It is for this reason that for centuries she has been my Specter."

I nodded, agreeing with her description of Devina. The Empress turned the globe slowly, reflecting on what she'd told me. Her mind was closed to me, a dark, unfathomable well. The globe stopped and her eyes locked onto mine with a mischievous smile. "I know you would like to take her place. The time has come for you to be honored with that privilege."

My eyes went wide and my heart pounded. "I've never wanted anything else," I declared, deeply proud at her words. The Bond among all the Sisters was strong, but I knew I loved Sophìa more than anyone else, and she too had always shown a special affection to me. All I had ever wanted was to please her and become her Specter—her second-in-command—and at last I had succeeded. I would be in charge of the Castle when Sophìa willed it, and everyone would take orders from me. The idea of all that power was already going to my head and I couldn't wait to put myself to the test. "How will Devina take the news?"

"Devina must accept it. Moreover, she has always suspected you would replace her," she conceded. She approached me and kissed me on the lips. "I have never hidden my preference for you, and now that you are finally ready, it is your right to be by my side."

"I swear I won't disappoint you."

"I am certain of it. Now, come. I have a special task to entrust to you. It will satisfy your curiosity."

I smiled at her. "I am yours, my lady."

"Not even I can give back to you what has been lost forever, such as your memories. However, I can give to you a gift you will deem precious. Nothing can satisfy your thirst to know your past more than the person who lived it with you. Someone who shared everything with the old Gemma. Today you may claim his soul and he will not resist you because he already loves you." Sophìa turned the black globe and with her elegant black fingernail touched a tiny village on Earth nestled among the Adirondack mountains. "His time has come. He is already yours. You need only to go and take him."

Send me to him. A white speck lit up on the globe, revealing the young man to me. I smiled. Peter was his name. And his soul would be mine.

EVAN

POINT OF NO RETURN

"Are you *sure* you didn't find anything?" I asked Simon. We'd just returned from our encounter with Gemma.

"I'm sorry, not a trace. Gemma is—"

"Don't say it!" I shouted in exasperation. "Don't *think* it."

He tried to bring me to my senses. "Evan! You need to calm down, please."

Tears started to my eyes. I grabbed my hair and pressed my lips together to prevent the words from escaping. I'd been so convinced Simon's power could change things! I couldn't accept that it wasn't so. I couldn't accept that he'd searched inside her and hadn't found a single trace, a single memory that might bring her back. I couldn't accept that all hope was lost. "I thought I saw something in her eyes."

"That's what you say every time, Evan. With every desperate attempt you make, you think you've found her again, but it's only a lie you tell yourself and it's putting you more and more at risk. She's going to end up capturing you unless you can control yourself."

"I . . . can't," I said. A tear slid down my face. "I want her back, Simon. Every time I think I've lost her, I can't breathe."

Simon was right: I was gradually losing control. I could feel I would soon go mad with rage, frustration—and nostalgia. Most of all nostalgia. I missed Gemma terribly. Every day was worse than the one before, because she was farther away, more elusive. "I have to see her again. Now."

"It won't help anything!" Simon shouted.

"What are you saying, that I should give up? That one day I should look Liam in the eye and tell him his mother's gone because I gave up on her?" How could I? "I'm sorry, I can't do that."

"What can you possibly do that we haven't already tried? Seeing her again won't have any effect on her, but you'll keep getting worse."

"The worst thing of all is being away from her." Despite the fact that Gemma had changed, seeing her lit up my heart. I couldn't stay away—my desire for her was too painful. How could Simon ask me to give up all hope? "I need her. I'm going to go look for her. I'll even summon her if I need to."

"You don't," Ginevra said, entering the room with Liam in her arms. "She's back. And she's very close." I looked at her questioningly. "She's at Peter's. You'll have to hurry, because she wants his soul."

"You mean she remembers him?" I asked, full of hope.

"No. Sophia sent her to him on a whim. I can hear Gemma's thoughts. She's seducing him and he isn't stopping her. It won't take her long to claim him. He loves her—he's not going to put up a fight."

I clenched my fists, shaking off the thought of Gemma and Peter together. "Just what I needed: an excuse to get rid of the kid once and for all."

"Don't talk nonsense, Evan," Simon admonished me. Given how things were turning out, he knew there was a risk I might actually do it.

"Now go," Ginevra urged us. I went over to her and kissed Liam on the forehead. "Good luck, Evan." My eyes met hers and I nodded before vanishing.

When Simon and I materialized in Peter's smithy Gemma instantly sensed our presence, though she didn't move. All she did was raise her malicious gaze to us over his shoulder. I had to summon all my self-control to keep from rushing over and killing him when I saw his hands on her. Gemma smiled, grasping my thoughts as I tried to calm down. "Good. The game is more exciting."

"Don't," I ordered her. Waking from her spell, Peter turned to look at us.

"What are you doing here? Go away."

"Stay out of this, kid," Simon warned, knowing my nerves were on the brink of snapping.

"You're the ones who should stay out of it. She wants *me* now."

"She's not who you think she is any more," I told him. "She's dangerous."

Gemma smiled and slid her hand down Peter's chest. "What do you imagine I might do to him? Kill him? I can give him everything he desires." Peter looked at her, captivated by her bewitching power yet confused by her behavior.

"Your offer has a steep price tag," I shot back coldly.

"What price isn't worth paying to satisfy our desires?"

"The soul," I replied, intransigent. "Gemma, listen to me. You can't take his. You don't realize it now, but you would regret it forever."

"What the fuck is going on? Is this some kind of joke? Gemma, would you tell me what's happening? And why are you dressed like that?" Peter exclaimed, now completely free of her spell.

She caressed his face, wafting her pheromones over him. The guy was tough for a mortal. Gemma's power dazed him but couldn't pull him in completely. "Peter," she whispered, "you and I are connected, you know we are. Who do you trust more: me or them?" He gazed at her, at the mercy of the passion she'd aroused in him. "Show me," Gemma whispered against his lips. "Kiss me."

Black rage rose inside me, compelling me to act. I couldn't stand around watching. I rushed at Gemma and she pushed Peter away in order to defend herself from my attack. Simon joined the fray, but she was fast, agile, and managed to hold her ground against us both. I tried to grab her, but she eluded my every attempt. She whipped out her daggers as I grabbed a long iron pole from a table and bent it to my will. "Step aside, Simon. This is between her and me." The pole glinted, turning into a sharp sword.

Gemma was more and more excited by the game. She honestly had no idea what I'd just prevented her from doing. If she'd taken Peter's soul, she would never have forgiven herself. Just like I would never forgive myself if I let her go.

"You're the one who never gives up," she said, lunging at me with her dagger.

I blocked her blow with the sword. "Never, when it comes to you." We moved swiftly around the smithy among the equipment and sharp metal objects.

"It's a shame there's still something you haven't realized about me." She did a backflip and I followed her, launching another attack.

"I know everything about you," I said.

"Then you know I don't like to lose." She stretched a hand out toward Peter and it took me a moment to understand.

"Peter, no!" I shouted. A pointed pole flew from behind him and ran him through.

Peter looked at us, his expression desperate, his hands gripping the bloody pole that protruded from his abdomen. "Gemma . . ." he murmured, dropping to his knees. Simon rushed to heal him, but Peter's mouth filled with blood and he crumpled to the ground, his eyes still wide.

"He's dead," Simon announced, unable to help him.

"What a great loss," Gemma said, a grin on her lips. With a scream of rage I attacked her again. The Gemma in front of me had nothing to do with my Jamie. She was ruthless, and the only voice she heard was the voice of evil. Maybe it was time for me to listen to it too. I'd tried in every way possible to bring her back, to rekindle her memories of us, but nothing had worked. Maybe it was time to try more extreme measures.

Gemma eyed me with a little grin as she dodged my blows, which for the first time were brutal. "Reaper Angel versus Reaper Witch. Round one."

"Evan, what are you doing?!" Simon shouted. He'd never seen me really attack Gemma, but maybe there wasn't any other option.

We were on a perfect battlefield. I didn't want to seriously injure her but I had to at least try to shake her up. The more I attacked, the more amused she seemed. She began to use magic. Every tool in the room became a weapon. Around us rose a cloud of dust, trapping us inside a little hurricane. Gemma hurled me to the far end of the room, but I sprang back to attack her. A wall of nails flew toward me. The metal melted before it could hit me, so the coast was clear to rush her and knock her to the ground once more.

"I knew I had chosen my Champion wisely," she told me in my mind, satisfied. She'd used my power.

"That isn't surprising—you've always chosen me. It's with the family that you made the wrong choice." The remark enraged her, but she immediately looked away, distracted by something.

"Evan!" Simon cried. Peter's soul had left his body. He was looking at his hands, confused by the new sensations running through him. Slowly he raised his head and his eyes pierced us, as gray as molten silver.

"What's happening to me?" Peter fell to his knees and howled in pain as black ink seared his arm like a brand. Simon and I stared at each other, astonished. *He was a Subterranean.*

Gemma freed herself from my grip and reappeared beside Peter. "I'll be back for you," she whispered in his ear, her eyes locked on mine. Then she disappeared, a victorious smile on her lips.

HEART OF ICE

"All this is insane! Tell me I'm dreaming," Peter burst out, in shock. "What the hell is this thing on my arm? Am I a ghost? And why does Gemma look like she came straight out of an episode of *Xena: Warrior Princess?*"

"Calm down. We'll explain everything," Simon replied.

"Wait a minute. If I'm dead, how is it you two can see me?" Peter took another look at his old body that lay on the floor in a pool of blood.

"Look." Simon showed him the mark on his own arm. "We've got one too. You've been chosen. You aren't a mortal Soul. You're one of us, a Subterranean."

"So you guys are dead too," he said. "I always knew there was something strange about you."

"That's not the point."

"Is the blond a 'Subterranean' too, whatever that is?" he asked cockily.

"She's a Witch."

"Oh, well, that explains everything."

"Gemma wasn't here for his mortal soul—she wanted to claim him as a slave," I reasoned aloud.

"Souls? *Slaves?* What the hell is a Subterranean? Either this is a nightmare or I've ended up in one of my comic books."

"Get him out of here before I kill him a second time," I said.

"Hey, you can't talk to me like that."

"You'll understand everything once you've eaten," Simon explained. "Let's go. I'll show you the way."

"Hold on! What's going to happen to me and my life?"

I crossed the room with long strides and shoved my face into his. "That's your life, right there," I growled, pointing at his corpse. "Forget about it, because it's already gone."

Showing unexpected courage, he didn't back down. In fact, he glared at me bitterly. "My mother can't bury another body. I'm all she's got left."

"What does that mean?"

"I don't want to *die*."

"It's too late. In case you haven't noticed, you're already dead."

"Okay, I get it—I'm dead, but why does anyone have to know that? Nobody knows you guys are. If I'm not a common Soul, if I am what you say I am, why should I disappear?"

"You're a Soldier now. You'll be given orders and they'll be the only thing that matters to you."

"I'm a *what*?" he asked in shock. Not even the sight of his bloody body had upset him so much. "I want to be normal. I didn't ask for this."

"None of us did. And you're not normal. You were chosen to serve Fate. Orders come first," Simon insisted.

I sighed in exasperation. "We're just wasting time."

"Peter, trust us. When you eat of the Tree you'll understand everything. You'll know what your place is and you'll be a lot stronger than you've ever been."

"What would happen if I didn't eat?"

"You'd get weaker and weaker until you disappeared. Evil would seize its chance to claim you and you wouldn't be able to fight it."

Peter was stressed out, but not as much as I was. I'd had enough of the guy. I didn't have Simon's patience, much less in this situation. "Do you have any idea how lucky you are? By this time you would have already been in Hell if we hadn't been here to save you. Like it or not, death exists, and we're its Soldiers."

Peter reflected a moment and nodded. "Okay, but we'll do things my way. I'm not going to leave my mom all on her own." His words impacted me, clearing a path back to the memory of my own mother. "I can be both things. You even go to school. I just need to learn your rules."

"All right. Do what you want."

Just then, the door opened and a woman entered the room. "Mom," he murmured, aghast. She couldn't see us but she immediately spotted

Peter's bloody corpse. Her scream echoed through the room and she fainted. Simon rushed to her, catching her before she fell.

"It looks like I don't have a choice any more," Peter said, tears in his eyes. He leaned over his mother and stroked her cheek, looking at her as though for the last time.

"Yes you do," I told him. "Simon can erase this memory from her mind."

"Can you really do that?" Peter asked, his voice full of hope.

Simon nodded. His power hadn't been able to bring Gemma back, but it could save the connection between Peter and his mother.

Peter turned to look at me, gratitude filling his face. "I guess I owe you my thanks."

"It's not the first favor I've done for you today," I retorted. It was true. If Simon hadn't been around, I'm pretty sure I would have killed him when I saw him with Gemma.

Simon leaned over Peter's mother and rested his fingers on her temples. The woman's face filled with thin back veins that quivered beneath her skin as he extracted her memory.

"What . . . what's he doing to her?" Peter asked in alarm.

"Don't worry, she'll recover. When she wakes up she won't remember any of this."

Peter nodded gratefully. "We need to get rid of my body. Nobody can find out I'm dead."

"We could bury it somewhere in the woods, make it unrecognizable," I reassured him.

"I've got a better idea." Peter shoved open a heavy iron door. "We'll burn it in the incinerator."

I went back to the house alone. I'd left Simon with the task of showing Peter the way between the two worlds. He wouldn't be able to accompany him all the way to the Tree of Knowledge so he could eat of its fruit, but he would explain how it was done and Peter's instinct would take care of the rest. Simon would wait for him to return and then bring him here to us, at least for the time being. More than anyone else, I understood his need not to abandon his mother, especially after I'd personally taken his father from him. But it wouldn't be easy for Peter to pretend to still be human and take on his new duties as a Soldier at the same time. No matter how hard he tried to cling to his old life, it no longer belonged to him, and sooner or later he would realize it.

The house was unusually quiet. Liam must have been sleeping. I checked his playpen in the living room but he wasn't there. Disappearing and materializing in the boy's room, I found it empty as well. *"Ginevra, where are you?"* I called in my mind. The only reply was silence. Normally she would have materialized beside me instantly. It was strange to think she'd gone out and taken the baby with her. I concentrated on Liam's soul to reach him, wherever he was. I couldn't find him. The world came crashing down around me and the room began to spin. No. It couldn't actually have happened.

"Evan . . ." My ears detected a faint murmur. It was Ginevra, in the pool area downstairs. I materialized beside her in the blink of an eye. She was on the floor, wounded and semiconscious. All around us was an imaginary forest full of life, but in my heart there was only silence.

"Ginevra! Ginevra, wake up! What happened?" I tried to bring her to, but my power didn't work on her.

"Liam . . ." she murmured in anguish.

I jerked away from her, my eyes full of tears. "No . . ." I whispered, "It can't be true. Tell me it's not true. I beg you . . ."

I turned around and saw him. Everything inside me turned to ice. "NO!" I screamed. A flock of birds took wing, frightened.

Liam's little body was floating face down in the simulated lake, his arms limp at his sides, swaying in the current that tried to push him to shore. I leapt into the water and carried him out, resting him on the rock and turning him over to look him in the face. He was so tiny, so defenseless! His heart had stopped beating. "Liam!" I cried, attempting to use my healing powers on him. It didn't work. His soul was gone; someone had already helped him cross over. How could it have happened? "No!" I screamed in desperation. I clasped him to my chest, weeping in pain. "Liam, no . . ." I repeated, holding him tight. I kissed him on the forehead and pushed the hair from his face. It was thick, like his mother's.

I had lost them both. I couldn't believe he was gone, that I would never watch him grow up . . . that I hadn't been there to protect him.

The hiss of an arrow touched my ear. I spun around and caught it, my eyes burning into those of the Hunter. Absolon. He'd broken free. I clenched my fist so hard it crushed his arrow. The shaft was metal, but within a split second I'd pulverized it in my fury. "You have no idea what you've got coming to you," I threatened.

He glanced at the baby as I rested his body gently on the ground, never taking my eyes off Absolon. Standing up to face him, I balled my hands into fists. A strong wind blew through the trees, making the forest shudder. Wild rage blinded me and pain crushed my chest with its bands of steel.

In a flash, Absolon nocked another arrow and pointed his bow straight at me. I disappeared only to reappear right in front of him, my chest touching his arrowhead. "You're going to sorely miss the Hell you came from," I promised.

He lowered his weapon and attacked me, but I was faster. No man, Subterranean, or celestial creature could have escaped my wrath. Absolon tried to defend himself but I struck him mercilessly again and again, slamming him against the rock wall, shattering stones and uprooting the trees. I wanted to tear him limb from limb before sending him back to Hell. How dare he take my child from me?

Absolon tried to escape by leaping to the top of the waterfall, but I beat him to it. As soon as he landed, I hurled him to the cold stone at the edge of the cliff and wrapped one hand around his throat. With the other I took one of his arrows and pointed it at his jugular as he tried to distance himself from me by craning his neck into the empty space below him. I knew the poison wouldn't kill him, and in any case I didn't want him dead. Not yet. First he would have to experience for himself the suffering he'd inflicted on me, that he'd inflicted on my little Liam. I wanted him to taste at least some of the Hell that had emerged inside me.

Tears returned to fill my eyes. "How could you take it out on him?" I snarled, desperate. "How dare you take him from me?!" I screamed. Blood trickled from the spot where I was pressing the arrowhead.

"'Tis only ye I'm after," he replied, undaunted.

"Then you shouldn't have taken it out on him, because all you've gained is your own death," I shouted in fury, my demoniacal eyes brimming with pain, rage, and loathing for the bastard who had stolen everything from me—first Gemma and now Liam. A shriek rose from my chest and echoed through the forest as I slit his throat with his own arrow.

He gurgled, but a burst of lightning streaked the sky above us, which suddenly darkened. "Stop!" a voice shouted.

I was so lost in my fury I didn't recognize it. I had to turn toward her to realize it was Ginevra. "He has to die," I hissed, "but first he has to endure Gemma's suffering . . . and Liam's. And mine."

"He wasn't the one who killed Liam," she revealed gravely.

I released my grip on the Hunter and dried my tears. He gurgled, pulling the arrow from his neck. I stood up and leaned over the waterfall. Ginevra had my full attention. "Who was it, then?" I snarled, seething. Whoever it was, I would find them and tear them to shreds.

"It was one of the Màsala."

43

A PAINFUL GOODBYE

I sank to my knees and embraced Liam for the last time, the excruciating fact of his absence bringing fresh tears to my eyes. "Why did they do this to me?" I sobbed, kissing his tiny cheeks. I had failed. I should have brought Gemma back so we could be a family but I had failed miserably, and now she would never see our child again. I couldn't bear it, it was too painful. Too devastating. "Liam . . ." I murmured. "He had nothing to do with this, any of this." My tears dampened his face.

Ginevra rested her hand on my shoulder. "He's in Heaven now. He'll be fine. At least he won't grow up in the middle of this war."

"I'll never see him again. I've lost him forever," I said, my voice dull.

"I'm sorry," Ginevra said. "I tried to stop him but I couldn't." She stroked Liam's forehead and her armor crumbled. She burst into tears. "I fought back, used all my magic, but it was useless. He took him away. Liam called out for you before vanishing. Then I passed out."

I squeezed my eyes shut, overcome by pain. "It's not your fault," I reassured her. "Thank you for protecting him and loving him," I murmured. Together we shed bitter tears, little Liam's body lying motionless on our laps.

"No!" Simon shouted when he appeared beside us. Ginevra and I looked at him. Peter was at his side but Ginevra didn't even notice. Nothing mattered more than our loss.

"It was the Màsala. They took him," Ginevra told him. But it wasn't the time for explanations. Simon knelt over the child and kissed his forehead, hugging Ginevra. He ran his hand over her cheek and healed her wound.

"I'm sorry I wasn't here for him," Peter said, but Ginevra shook her head to silence him.

I stood up and gathered pieces of wood. Ginevra watched me bind them together as she cradled Liam. Absolon was tied to a tree, unconscious. Ginevra had paralyzed him again with her magic. I built a little boat, making sure the structure was sturdy. Liam loved boats. Simon had carved him a wooden toy boat, and Liam loved to watch it float in the pond at the back of the gardens. I gently rested him inside it and a tear slid down my cheek as I prepared to say goodbye.

"Wait." Ginevra touched the wood and a bed of flowers appeared around his little body. She leaned down and something sprang from the ground. A white orchid. She knew how much they meant to me. It was my mother's favorite flower, and she'd always kept one on her piano. I would sit beside it and stare at it as she composed new melodies just for me. Ginevra plucked the orchid and offered it to me. I kissed the flower and rested it on Liam's body. My mother would protect him. A new shudder of grief left me sobbing as a white flame emanated from my palm.

Seeing that I couldn't bring myself to move, Simon set the boat adrift. When it had moved onto the lake, I cast my fireball onto it and the wood burst into flames, shrouding Liam in the heat of the fire. My fire . . . my last embrace.

Goodbye, my little warrior.

SEDUCTION AND TEMPTATION

I was sunk into the sofa, cradling Liam's toy boat in my hands. I would cherish it forever as the most precious of treasures. "How are you?" Ginevra asked, sitting down beside me. We'd watched the funeral pyre all night long, until Liam's little body had turned to ash. Only then did the others manage to pull me away. Ginevra had deactivated the forest simulation scenario and my dream of fatherhood had vanished along with that illusion. I'd spent hours in the darkness on that sofa, contemplating my suffering. Irony stayed beside me the whole time, as though he understood what had happened. We'd lost Gemma and now Liam as well.

"Tell me again," I begged her, my voice empty. The fire of my pain was beginning to give way to ice. "Tell me everything you know."

"His name is Adhémar. He's one of the twelve."

"Sounds like you know them well."

"Only because I was Sophìa's Specter and, like her, I had privileges. It's never a pleasant experience meeting members of the Brotherhood. The mere presence of the Màsala leaves you petrified. Few have seen them, since they're superior beings and never show themselves to anyone—they always wear a red hood to hide their appearance—but I have. It's like they have no face. Their eyes look like glass. They're blind, because they see through Souls. Their voice is as dark as the depths of the abyss, their power immense."

I understood what Ginevra must have felt. I'd met with one of the Màsala when I wanted to back out of my orders to execute Gemma. I'd summoned them, imagining they would pay no attention, but one of them had actually shown himself to me. The entire forest had reacted to his presence and time had frozen. His eyes were hollow, empty. Meeting his gaze was like staring into a hole that looked out onto the universe. It made me dizzy. Back then I hadn't known how important she was to them—important enough to show themselves to me to make sure I killed her. What they couldn't have foreseen was that she would fall in love with me.

"We don't know why they took Liam's life. I doubt his time had come, but at this point even they are breaking the rules. Maybe they were afraid Gemma would take him with her and use him in the name of evil."

"To do what? Liam didn't have any powers. He was human," I said. "He was only a baby."

"Maybe they weren't sure of that."

"So just to be on the safe side they took his soul?!" I shouted, furious.

"They saved it," Simon reminded me, a firm believer in his Subterranean values.

Right. Why was it so painful, then? Once again, the desire to keep someone with me had taken precedence over my principles as a Soldier. It was just like when I'd spared Gemma. Saving her back then would have prevented her from transforming and serving evil. By killing her I would have spared her Hell. Still, I would have done it a thousand times if it meant being able to be with her. It was self-centered, but there was nothing I could do about it. Liam wouldn't have had to die so soon either. I balled my hands into fists. I'd lost my son forever, but Gemma was still out there and I had no intention of letting her go.

"I know what I have to do," I declared. Ginevra looked at me, shaken. She already understood. "There's nothing keeping me here any longer. I'm going to Hell and I'm going to bring her back."

"Are you out of your mind?" she said. "It's madness and you know it."

"Evan, you're devastated over losing Liam. Please, think carefully," Simon cautioned me.

"I already have."

"You can keep trying from right here, you know."

"For how long? What has it gotten me so far? Weeks, *months* of frustrating expectation, to spend how long with her? Five minutes? No. That's not enough. I need her. I have to see her, *touch her*, convince her to unearth her past with me. I can't do it unless I have enough time."

"Not even Simon's power worked. You may never succeed."

"Then I'll stay with her in Hell."

"You've already been there. They locked you up and tortured you. You can't have forgotten. You still have the scars."

"The scar I have in my heart right now is more painful," I growled in frustration.

"Are you even willing to accept that it might be Gemma who inflicts all that pain on you this time? Will you be able to bear such suffering?" Simon warned.

"I won't go as a prisoner." I looked him straight in the eye. "I'll let her claim me."

"That won't help anything. It'll only be surrendering," Ginevra murmured.

"My mind's made up, so save your breath."

"I don't want to stop you, but you need a better plan than that."

"Sorry, I don't have one. I've tried fighting to bring her back, but that didn't work. I have to go. I owe it to Liam. It's not going to end like this—I'm not giving up on us." I ran my hands through my hair. A silence fell among us. Simon and Ginevra realized that nothing could change my mind. "It doesn't matter where. My place is with her." *Stay together. Fight together,* I thought, gripping my thumb in my fist. The promise wasn't just tattooed on our hands—the words were also branded deep in her heart. I knew they were. They still burned, and I would reawaken their power, no matter what it cost.

Simon rested his hand on my shoulder. "You're right. You have to go."

I raised my eyes to him and even Ginevra nodded in resignation. "Just don't ask me to say goodbye to you."

I smiled at her. "I won't." I got up from the sofa, hugged her, and fist-bumped Simon.

My thoughts returned to the cenote where the mouth to Hell was located—a timeless place whose dangers lurked beneath its dark waters. Back then I'd been escaping from a nightmare. Now I was about to enter it willingly.

"That's not a plan. It's a suicide mission," Peter said, his tone critical.

"Why are you still here?" I said, annoyed. I'd forgotten he was even there. Peter had eaten of the Tree, thereby gaining the knowledge of our worlds. Still, everything was new to him and what had just happened had floored him, leaving him wordless this whole time.

"Hey, why are you always so pissed off at me?" he shot back, frowning at me as he approached. I stepped up to look him square in the eye, ready to take him on.

"Calm down, you two," said Simon. "Fighting won't help anyone."

"You guys are crazy," Peter scoffed.

I snorted. "What, you would abandon Gemma to evil? Didn't you used to claim you were her best friend?"

"That's exactly why I think it's crazy for you to go there alone. I want to help you. There must be a better solution."

"What would you know? You haven't spent the last few months looking for a way to bring her back while your family was being torn apart."

"Evan, you can't blame him for thinking it's risky. He's right," Simon put in.

"I don't need him, and I don't need to stand here explaining it to him either."

"Actually, you do," Ginevra contradicted me. "You need him." I looked at her, dubious.

"How are you going to get yourself captured, Evan?" Simon asked. "We can't wait for Gemma to return to Earth—that could take weeks."

"Maybe not," Ginevra said. "She killed Peter to claim him, and she won't give up so easily. She'll come back looking for him soon enough."

I thought it over. All things considered, Ginevra was right.

"I have to act as bait?" Peter protested.

"Whoa, you're a genius—I never would have guessed it!" I said sarcastically.

"Guys, don't fight," Ginevra yelled. "We have far more important things to discuss."

"You said you wanted to help," Simon reminded Peter, who nodded.

"Do you feel up to facing Gemma?" Ginevra asked him. "Think carefully—Witches will entrance you with their beauty and subjugate your mind unless you defend your thoughts. Seduction and temptation are their most powerful weapons. Think you're strong enough to resist Gemma's power?"

"I can do it," he said, determined. "I'm not afraid and I'm not backing down."

"I still can't believe you're a Subterranean," I muttered. It was strange seeing him there in our living room, talking to him about things like Hell, Witches, and being claimed.

"It explains why he's always been drawn to us . . . especially to Gemma," Simon replied. "He grew up at her side because the Màsala *knew*, and they put him near her."

"It also explains why he had something against me right from the start," Ginevra said, throwing him a provocative look.

"Plus his fear of snakes," I added, taking full advantage of this opportunity to point out his weaknesses. I couldn't bring myself to see him as an ally or dispel my urge to kill him, especially now that he had so much power over Gemma.

"He's always been fairly resistant to our power," Simon pointed out, "but we never imagined he had the Subterranean gene in him."

"Only Sophìa can track down the descendants of the Children of Eve. She poured some of her power into a large globe so all her Sisters would be able to identify their enemies. It's also the tool she uses to bend the forces of nature to her will. Sophìa is obsessed with Earth and likes toying with mortals. All she has to do is choose a spot on the globe and toss a little water into the air to cause a storm, flood, or tsunami, spreading panic, death, and destruction. It's been the most complicated of her magic spells. Right after creating it, she burst into thousands of fragments—butterflies as black as her soul. She managed to reconstitute herself, but only partially," Ginevra told us, evidently reliving the memory. "I was with her at the time. Her beautiful face was like a puzzle with pieces missing. She lost consciousness for a long time, though I was the only one who knew it. I was her Specter and took her place until she returned."

"What does a Specter do?" Peter asked.

"She takes over command of Hell and all its creatures," she replied, her tone solemn. "The Sisters are connected by a bond of equality, but even they must bow to the Specter's orders. Whoever has been appointed Specter holds vast power, and not everyone is capable of handling it. That's why Sophìa's Specter is ruthless and unscrupulous."

"Who took your place?"

"Devina. No one deserves the scepter of evil more than she does. I think she's still the Empress's second-in-command."

"Do you think she'll try to subjugate Evan again once he's back at the Castle?" Simon asked.

"If Gemma claims him, she would have to leave him alone—though knowing Devina, that can't be ruled out. What's certain is that she will try to stop you, Evan, since she knows your true intentions. Gemma trusts her—it won't be easy to compete with that."

"Devina has no power over me and never has. I'll fight her like I've always done."

Ginevra nodded.

"What do we do now?" Peter asked.

"We wait. She'll come looking for you when the time's come," Ginevra said. She gave Simon a telling look. He went over to Peter, placed his hand on his neck and looked him straight in the eye. The veins on Peter's face squirmed as a dark memory ran through them, flowing toward Simon.

"Go home," Simon ordered. Peter nodded and disappeared.

"Why did you do that?" I asked hesitantly.

"I only canceled his memory of this conversation. It's better that he not know our plan, or Gemma will discover right away that he's only acting as bait. He hasn't learned to block off his mind yet."

"It's more dangerous for him. Will he be able to resist Gemma's power?"

"He's a Subterranean," Simon replied. "He knows where his place is."

"But he loves her, and that hasn't changed. He won't hurt her even though he knows she's a Witch—but she might hurt him."

"That's why we need to act fast."

"I agree with you," Ginevra said, nodding. "I doubt he'll be able to resist Gemma's seduction. We need to get to them before it's too late or we'll have another problem. We need to be prepared."

"How long do you think it'll be before she comes back for him?" Simon asked her.

Ginevra smiled. "There's one thing all Witches have in common."

"What's that?"

"We hate to wait."

"She's already here," I murmured, frowning. Inside our house, Peter had been hidden by our protective barriers, but once he'd left she'd tracked him down.

"This is it." Ginevra came up to me, in her eyes a trace of bitterness. This might be goodbye. None of us knew if I would return. I would let Gemma claim me, and there was only one way she could do it: with a bite from her serpent. The first time Witch venom had killed me, death had torn me away from her. Now it was my only hope of winning her back. The burn was still vivid in my mind, like fire in my veins. But I wasn't afraid any more.

Ginevra locked eyes with me. "Are you ready to die for Gemma?"

"I have been since I first met her," I replied confidently.

Simon gave me a bear hug. "Good luck, brother."

I pulled back to look at him, my eyes turning gray as I transformed. "I'm afraid I'm going to need it this time." He and Ginevra silently watched me as I disappeared, guiding my steps toward death. Toward Gemma.

GEMMA

KISS OF DARKNESS

Around me danced a swarm of black butterflies, fawning over me. They felt the power I emanated and fed off it. Sophìa had left, leaving me in her garden right in the middle of the Reaping. Only she could sort through the Souls, but I was her Specter now so I had certain privileges. No one else had permission to witness the Sorting. For some, Sophìa's garden was a forbidden utopia. I closed my eyes and spread my arms, allowing the Souls to alight on me, venerating me and clinging to my body like they did with the Empress.

One of them came to rest on my hand and I eyed it carefully. It had bold, powerful wings. My Dakor sensed its power and materialized. The other butterflies all rose into the air at once, like an explosion, but the one on my hand didn't move. It must be an interesting Soul. My serpent hissed, creeping toward it, but I called him back, calming his impulses. I wanted it for myself. I knew it was forbidden, but I felt an overwhelming curiosity to know who it was, so I released my pheromones, immediately drawing the swarm back. The butterfly sensed my energy and bit me, wanting to feed off it. A second later a man took form before my eyes. He had well-developed muscles, a shaven head, dirty skin, and a scar along his cheekbone. He looked like a barbarian warrior and had such a virile air it seemed impossible he was the Soul of a mere mortal and not a Subterranean. The man bowed to me, resting one knee on the ground. "At your command, my queen," he said, subjugating himself to my power.

He was a First-Echelon murderer—I had felt it the minute he bit me. That was how Sophìa sorted Souls: with the Butterfly's Kiss. Sophìa plumbed their depths, knew their souls' darkest hue, and sorted them, based on the crimes they had committed, assigning them to an Echelon—the punishment they would have to undergo. First Echelon, Second, Third—she classified them into hundreds of subcategories.

The butterflies would dance through the air, obeying her orders as they avidly awaited their turn. The large windows in the ceiling would open like a blossoming flower from whose heart they would be spit out into Hell, their new realm.

A Soul like the warrior before me would be in great demand during the Hunt for the Opalion, but before they were recruited, Souls had to endure the great trial of Hell: surviving so as to prove themselves worthy. If they remained sane, they proved their strength. Only the toughest endured. Rarely during the Games did the Damned survive the Subterraneans, let alone our Champions. This one, however, had a fearless air and a powerful body. Maybe I should keep him for myself . . . The temptation was strong, but I knew Sophìa wouldn't approve. I would definitely go out looking for him later, though. *If you're strong enough to resist, one day I'll find you and you'll return to me.*

"What are you doing here?" Devina's voice sounded behind me. My Dakor lunged and bit the warrior, who vaporized in a cloud of dust.

"What a shame," I sighed, shrugging.

"You're not allowed to awaken the Empress's Souls. It's not your task."

"I was only contemplating them. Is that forbidden too?"

Devina's mind was in turmoil. She knew Sophìa had passed the scepter of command to me, and it had to have incensed her. However, her thoughts were distant and unfathomable. Why did she continue to keep me out? I already knew she was furious with me—what else did she have to hide?

"I heard Sophìa has given you a great gift."

"Yes, soon there will be an Opalion in my honor and everyone will learn that I am the new Specter."

"My congratulations. But I wasn't talking about that." Devina studied me, her expression sly. "I mean the boy, Peter. You didn't manage to claim him, it seems."

"Not yet," I corrected her. "He's already mine. It's only a matter of time."

"I hope so, or it would be a real disappointment for the Empress." I glared at her. "What about the other one, Evan? You haven't claimed him yet either? Didn't you want him to be your Champion?"

I thought of the Subterranean and his impertinence. There was something about him that irritated and attracted me in equal measure. Devina had tried to subjugate him for centuries and failed. Perhaps I should leave the tedious task to her, since he'd done nothing but make doubt creep into my mind. I was Specter now; I'd obtained what I most desired. "You can keep him," I said. She smiled at me enthusiastically, forgetting our conflict. She was my Sister, and after all, I had to make it up to her for taking command away from her.

On the other hand, Peter seemed like a fine prize to claim. I hadn't sensed him again after he'd disappeared. Those two killjoys must have shown him the way to eat of the Tree. Now he had Knowledge, and he must also have acquired his Subterranean powers, but that wouldn't keep me from subjugating him.

As if he'd sensed my need for him, I detected his soul again. "Well, I suppose you have unfinished business to take care of," Devina remarked, having read my mind.

"Would you see to Sophìa's Reaping?" I asked.

"Of course." Devina smiled at me. "After all, I always have."

I went up to her and kissed her on the lips. "Thank you. You're the best of the Sisters. Well, I'm off. A gift was given to me. The time has come to claim it."

I followed the young man's call and materialized next to him. He was turned away from me, but when he sensed my presence he spun around. "Turn around again—I was admiring you," I told him mischievously. He had firm buttocks and a well-trained body.

"Gemma . . ." he murmured, shaken. His breathing suddenly went ragged. Though he no longer needed air, he was still attached to his human habits. Novices were so sweet. He leaned back against the workbench, gripping the edge of it in a useless attempt to maintain control.

"Were you expecting me?" I asked, my voice charismatic.

Seeing me approach, he didn't budge and allowed me to move in between his legs. "You have to go. I don't want to fight you."

I pushed the curly locks from his forehead as he stared at my lips, at the mercy of his emotions. "I don't want to fight either. There's a bond between us. Can't you feel it too?" I whispered. "I won't hurt you. All I want is a kiss." I moved my lips closer and he stood there, paralyzed. I hadn't yet unleashed my powers of seduction, but he already seemed utterly at my mercy. I smiled. Taking him would be child's play. But maybe I could amuse myself with him a little more first. "You can touch me, if you want," I whispered to him, guiding his hands onto my sides.

He ran his nose down my neck, his hands trembling. I could read his desire for me in his thoughts. He wanted me—he always had. And now he could have me. Still, part of him resisted me; the Subterranean in him was rebelling against the Witch.

"Maybe Devina is right," I said softly. He listened to me carefully. "What Sophia gave me is a great gift."

If I took him it would satisfy that part of me that wanted to reconnect to the past. Claiming him would be enough to quench my thirst. Peter was a fascinating Subterranean. He had always loved the old Gemma and he would learn to love the new one too. Soon there would be an Opalion in my honor and I needed a Champion. I stroked his bulging biceps. He was strong and would be trustworthy and loyal. I moved my mouth to his ear and emanated my seductive power. My Dakor emerged, hissing with impatience, but Peter didn't even notice.

I bit my lip, causing a drop of blood to seep out. "At last I've found my Champion," I whispered. I moved my lips close to his and he was on the verge of touching them.

"Stop!" A voice thundered in the room, interrupting our tête-à-tête. I whirled around and my eyes locked onto Evan's, which were as sharp as ice. "I'll be your Champion," he told me in a determined voice.

In a split second I was in front of him. "You're lying." I studied his face and he made no objection, allowing me to explore his mind and comb through his thoughts.

"I have nothing left to lose," he said, his voice low and resolute.

Behind us, Peter stepped forward in protest, but I stilled him with my powers. My Dakor drew near Evan's face and he didn't move, his dauntless gaze locked on mine. There wasn't a trace of fear in his eyes. "A tempting offer," I admitted. Devina had chased that Subterranean for centuries and now he was offering himself to me—not as a prisoner but as my Champion.

"Don't miss your chance, then," he provoked me, his gaze proud and sharp.

"Normally we're the ones who hunt Subterraneans, but you're different from all the rest. You're stubborn. Why are you willing to die of your own volition?"

He looked down and took my hand. "Sometimes you have to die to be reborn."

I studied our joined palms and shook my head, banishing my doubts. "Fine. Then you'll die for me." I touched my finger to my lip, dabbed it in the blood, and raised it to his mouth. He accepted it, caressing it with his tongue, and an image exploded in my mind.

I never want to be separated from you again. Promise you won't leave me. Samvicaranam. Samyodhanam. *Stay together. Fight together.*

My heart belongs to you forever.

I jerked my hand back in shock as a shudder gripped me. I had been the one to say those last words. I looked him in the eye. What had happened? What had I seen? It was the two of us locked in a desperate embrace, as though it were my own memory.

No. It couldn't be—he was deceiving me, and I wasn't about to fall into his trap. I grabbed his chin and touched his lips with mine, absorbing his essence with my kiss of darkness.

"Evan, no!" Ginevra screamed, appearing in the room, but it was too late. My Dakor attacked, sinking his fangs into the neck of the Subterranean who stared at me, wracked with the first tremors. Through his mind I sensed the pain he was experiencing—but there was no fear.

He vanished, destination Hell. I clasped the Dreide I wore around my neck and studied it as it filled with a soft light.

I smiled. His soul was mine.

SWEET POISON

I materialized in one of the rooms we reserved for rebels—or, as we called them, Torture Caverns. Usually only Subterraneans who refused to bend to our will ended up in them. Those we claimed were set free in exchange for having surrendered their souls to us. Different accommodations, though, had been prepared for Evan. He would pay for that last little trick he'd attempted to play on me. Ginevra had read my mind just before I took him and had tried to stop him.

Evan appeared, his back to me. He looked around and instantly understood where he was. Spinning around, he stared at me boldly. "What's going on? Why am I here?" he asked, furious.

Smiling, I grabbed his shirt and tore it off him. "You won't be needing this." As I studied his body he didn't take his eyes off me. Two Drusas approached to discourage any attempt at rebellion.

"Seize him," I ordered, turning my back on him.

He struggled and broke free from my Sisters, grabbing me roughly by the wrist. "Gemma, wait!"

Two panthers landed beside him, growling threateningly. "Halt!" I ordered them. I tilted my head toward the Subterranean without turning around. "Let go," I hissed, my voice so icy he released his grip. "Lock him up. But first give him a shower."

"As you command," my Sisters replied, bowing to me.

"As you command?" Evan asked with surprise. "What does that mean?"

I smiled and turned toward him. "That I'm in charge here." The Subterranean's eyes went wide, his mind grappling with what I'd just said. My Sisters forced him to his knees and bound his hands behind his back with poisoned chains.

I turned my back on him and leapt up to one of the high windows. Giving him one last look, I found his gray eyes trained on me. I grunted with annoyance. Who did he think he was? He was a Subterranean like all the others. And now I had claimed him. If he thought he could make demands, I would put him in his place. Slipping out the window, I drew my knives and jammed them into the wall above me. Pulling myself up, I began to climb the Castle wall.

The air was cool in the gloom of the kingdom. I liked being high up—higher and higher. What I needed, after all those strange emotions, was my Saurus. When I reached the roof, I went into the stable to wake him and he welcomed me with an enthusiastic whinny while all the others bowed before me. I stroked Argas and he unfurled his mighty wings. Pulling myself onto his back, I spurred him to a gallop, his hooves echoing through the silent twilight.

"Away, Argas," I whispered in his mind. *"Carry me far away."* He took wing, sensing my need. I wanted to feel free, but I hadn't been able to for a while now. My mind was imprisoned by the past, by my doubts, by those eyes of ice. I lowered my eyelids and tilted my head back, letting the wind lash my face. I hoped it would wash away the thoughts tormenting me, but it was no use. The image I'd seen returned to fill my mind.

Promise you won't leave me.
My heart belongs to you forever.

What was that flashback? Could it actually be a memory?

Argas flew over the volcano and I ordered him to descend into it. I quieted the rage of the eruption, which diminished to a sputter on the surface. Nature bent to my every wish because I was its queen. My Saurus landed on a rocky outcrop and let me dismount. The scorching heat reddened my cheeks. The air was incandescent, but not even those temperatures could scathe my invincible body. Quite the opposite—a strong dose of boiling poison was what I needed. Maybe it would clear my mind. I unfastened my corset and took off my weapons, along with all my clothes, then sank down into the liquid, feeling its energy envelop me. The poison was just like me: lethally dangerous. Below the surface I felt the heartbeat of my Dakor, intoxicated by all that power. I slowly emerged, my eyes burning and glinting with purple tones, the eyes of my Dakor, who exulted inside me. I *was* a creature of Hell. I was Hell.

I swam inside the volcano, thinking of Evan. The flashback had occurred the moment his tongue had touched my thumb. The contact had triggered some sort of energy between us—or maybe it was something else.

What was it that had changed in me lately? My encounter with those two Souls by the river must have destabilized me. Through their minds I'd also seen images of Evan and me together. What could it mean? It had been a mistake to let them go. I had to find them and kill them. She would be easy prey since she was just another one of the Damned, but as for the other—Drake—he was a Subterranean and couldn't die. Still, I would find a way to silence him. Our dungeons always had room for rebels. That was where I would have Evan locked up. It had been a great victory. I couldn't wait to show Sophia my trophy. I smiled. Devina wouldn't believe her eyes.

I should have ordered that Evan be brought to the spa, where the Champions entertained their Amìshas. Instead I had decided to grant him access only to the showers where the rebels were sent, despite the fact that he'd given himself to me and my Dreide now contained his deepest essence. Why couldn't I treat him like the others? Why did I still feel the need to fight him? I closed my eyes. He had clouded my mind, forcing me to remain vigilant. Yet now that I'd claimed him I could no longer hide my desire for him, my desire to carefully watch him subjugate himself to me.

I opened my eyes. The landscape around me had changed. I was no longer in the volcano. I looked around, confused. Hearing water crashing down furiously against rocks, I advanced and peeked around the wall. Evan was turned away from me, completely naked, his hands resting against the wall, muscles tensed, head bowed as the water ran down his golden skin in a sensual caress. My heart was pounding. How had I ended up there? And why was I experiencing those strange sensations? I felt vulnerable.

I approached him, obeying my desperate need to touch him, the burning desire to feel his hands on me . . . like sweet poison. He turned, the hair hanging over his forehead dripping wet, his gray eyes locked onto mine. He swallowed, at the mercy of his emotions, and gazed at my naked body. His thoughts lost themselves, drifting. I wafted my seductive power to him as I advanced beneath the stream of water. He seemed dazzled by me, but in a different way from the others. There was a glimmer of awareness in his eyes.

He ran his thumb over my wet lips and contemplated them for a moment, letting me read the desire in his mind. Then he kissed me—a sweet, sensual kiss that soon turned into a desperate need. Evan rounded on me and trapped me against the wall, our naked bodies touching as I surrendered to his kiss.

A whinny from Argas filled my mind, bringing me back. I looked around, disoriented. *I was still in the volcano.* What the hell had happened? Had I imagined it all? It hadn't been another flashback. It had been a vision of the present. It seemed so real I couldn't believe it had happened only in my mind. Still dripping wet, I went to Argas. Had all that poison made me hallucinate?

Dressed again, I leapt onto my Saurus's back, still shaken by the vision. Maybe I'd been wrong to claim the Subterranean who'd hunted me down so stubbornly. Maybe I really should have left him to Devina. But I couldn't resist. Challenges excited me, and he was different. He triggered sensations in me that made me fight yet also attracted me. Was that why my mind had so avidly sought him out?

I flew to the Castle and hurried to his cell, slamming the door behind me. He was sitting on the floor, his back against the wall and his chained hands resting on his knee. He raised his head and his gray eyes shone through the half-light, instantly finding mine. "Welcome back," he said sardonically.

I probed his thoughts. He was still unsettled by my role as commander and the reception he'd been given. Still, he wasn't giving up. I'd never met a more stubborn Subterranean. Nevertheless, sooner or later I would bend him to my will.

"Is this how you treat your Champion?" he asked with arrogant defiance.

I approached him and planted the heel of my boot between his legs. "You'll have to earn that title first." He slowly rose to his feet, brushing his body against mine, and looked into my eyes. The sparkle illuminating his own was maddening. Neither rebellious nor subdued, I could see he didn't want to bend. He wanted to bend me, but I would never let him. "Your mind is different from the others. It's not trustworthy enough. What most distinguishes a Champion is his loyalty to his Amisha."

"You can trust me," he replied, "but I bet that's not your real problem. Maybe you're afraid you won't be able to trust yourself."

"Nonsense!" I replied irritably, looking away. "Don't think you're the only one to aspire to the position." I walked over to the Subterranean standing guard, staring at us through the bars of the cell. Upon my command, one of the bars disintegrated and he made his way toward me through the thousands of metal shards, utterly at the mercy of my power. "I've claimed many of you since I've been here. Any of them could become my Champion." I touched the Subterranean's muscular chest, staring steadily at Evan in a tacit challenge.

He looked furious, his thoughts a black cloud that threatened to unleash its power. His gray eyes were tempestuous. Smiling, I pulled the guard to me and brushed his ear with my lips. He reacted and grabbed me by the hips, yearning for my kiss, but a howl of rage filled the cell as Evan lunged at him and hurled him to the floor. He pinned me against the wall, his hands still bound and his gray eyes locked on mine. The Subterranean got up to face him, prepared to protect me, but I raised my hand and stopped him. He bowed before me as my gaze remained steadily on Evan's. I was more curious than ever about him. Perhaps the key to discovering the secret behind him was to go along with it. "At ease, Soldier. What makes you think you're so special?"

"Your body," he replied impertinently. "You're attracted to me."

"I'm attracted to all Subterraneans."

"No one attracts you more than I do—admit it," he dared me.

I locked my eyes on his, standing up to his insolence. "You have no effect on me," I lied, enunciating each word.

"You didn't seem so indifferent back there in the showers." I jumped in shock. What was he saying? It hadn't only been a vision in my mind? "You look surprised."

"Did you do that?"

"No, not at all. It was you who came to see me. I was in the shower. I was thinking of you and all of a sudden you were there. You let me kiss you," he added, pleased. "Then you disappeared and I found myself with my hands against the wall again, as though it had never happened. But I know it's not true."

"How do you know that?"

"Because you've done it before."

I turned my back on him, nervous. "You're lying."

"No I'm not, and you know it. Read my mind if you don't believe me."

"I don't trust your mind."

"Don't you trust your own? You experienced that moment in the shower with me too. It was our desire that broke through the confines separating us."

Nirvana. It liberates spirits from their bodies, leaving them free to follow their desires. Soul and mind in a world all their own.

"That's impossible," I murmured. "Only Sophìa has such great power." It was the same power she had imprisoned in the sphere. That Subterranean was capable of awakening it in me.

Evan walked up behind me and his mouth brushed my ear. "Our minds are bonded together."

I rubbed my cheek against his, overcome by the energy that quivered between us, but then shook my head. "There is no bond!" I snarled, furious.

He took my hand and held it up before our faces. "So how do you explain this?"

I stared at our two tattoos. He didn't take his eyes off me. There was no doubt they had the same calligraphy. But why? It made no sense. How could my life before Sophìa be connected to a Subterranean's?

"Give me a chance," he whispered.

"Why should I believe you?"

"Because I'm your husband."

"That's absurd."

"No it isn't. I bet your Sisters didn't bother to tell you that."

"Even if they had, I would never have believed such blasphemy. You're a Child of Eve."

The Subterranean ran his chained hands over my head and drew me to him tenderly, trapping me in his arms. "You haven't always been here. Before, you were with me," he whispered against my lips. *"Mamåtmå mari, yati tvayå saha."*

I frowned. *My spirit will die with you and rise again with you.* The words meant nothing to me but they seemed important to him. There was something I was missing. His lips teased mine hungrily. Maybe he was trying to cloud my mind. Devina had told me he was dangerous. And yet . . .

I rested my hands on his chest and pushed him against the wall, taking control. I instantly felt his erection against me and touched it through his pants as he bit my lip. As swiftly as a ghost, he grabbed my bottom and drew me to him, inverting our positions. His mouth moved avidly down my neck, his body pressed against mine, his hands inflaming me as they gripped me firmly by the buttocks.

My Dakor awoke, inebriated by Evan's presence, and his hiss snapped me out of my daze. I grabbed my dagger and shoved its blade against his throat, stopping him instantly. His eyes bored into mine, full of challenge. Part of me was irresistibly attracted to him. He'd given himself to me, surrendered his soul to me so I could claim it, yet I couldn't subjugate him. That rebellious spark still lingered in his eyes of ice. "We're the ones who hunt you down," I hissed furiously. "We're the ones who toy with you. Not vice versa."

"This isn't a game," he insisted.

"It is for me." I broke through his chains and strode past him, still clutching my dagger, but before I could walk out the door a shadow in the corner caught my attention. Nothing was there, but the second I looked at it an image burst into my head.

Gromghus. Is that your name?

Who we are isn't important in here.

"Gemma, what's happening?"

I emerged from the vision and turned to look at Evan, who seemed worried. "Gromghus," I murmured to myself, to remember it. I felt the name was important, though I didn't know why. What had just happened? I'd seen a strange creature hiding its face under a long hood, and I'd been speaking to it.

"What did you say?" Evan asked, now looking shocked. Might he know the answer?

"Who is Gromghus? Stop putting images in my head!" I snapped.

"They aren't images. They're memories," he exclaimed in surprise, his eyes lighting up. "Simon's power is working!"

"What power? What have you done to me?!" I felt a fire building inside me, ready to explode. A wave of energy burst from me and struck Evan full in the chest, sending him crashing against the wall.

I stared at him as he hit the ground on his hands and knees. This Subterranean was poisoning me. Why did I keep seeking him out? I gripped my dagger. The whole thing had to end. It wasn't important any more whether they were lies or whether this Child of Eve really had been part of my past. Hell was my world now, and I was its queen. I went to him and leaned over him. He raised his head slightly, his dark hair falling over his forehead. "I'll send my maidservants to prepare you," I told him icily. "You'll soon have an excellent opportunity to demonstrate your loyalty. If you wish to become my Champion, you'll have to prove you're worthy."

My Dakor lunged and sank his fangs into Evan's flesh. He raised his eyes to look at me one last time, then collapsed onto his side. I stood up and walked to the door as he struggled to resist the poison and stay conscious. "Now rest, Soldier," I told him before closing the door. "The Games are about to begin."

EVAN

UNFORGIVABLE INSULT

A murmur brought me back to the light. "He's so cute!" What had happened? Had Gemma really recalled an old memory? Or had it just been a dream?

"Shh! Do you want to get yourself killed?"

"Freia's right. The mistress claimed him. You're not allowed to say such things."

"Well, if she claimed him, why is she treating him like a prisoner?"

"Be quiet! He's coming to!"

I struggled to emerge from the darkness. When I finally managed, the three young women smiled at me. "Welcome back," one of them said. The others laughed, putting away some herbs which they must have used to wake me—they were still smoldering and my nostrils were full of the sweet, spicy odor.

"Who are you? What do you want from me?"

"I'm Emayn," the liveliest of them said. "Her name's Meryall, and she's—"

"We're Mizhyas," the last one said, cutting her off. "We need to prepare you for the Opalion."

I'd heard her name as I was waking up: Freia. "Why? This isn't the first time I've taken part in the Games," I told them. When I'd been a prisoner before I'd participated in them many times, in what they called the Circle, but I'd never needed any preparation. They'd simply thrown me into the arena and I'd battled to defend myself for as long as my strength held out.

"This time it's different. You were chosen by our mistress, so you'll be battling as her Champion. She's Sophia's Specter now, and today everyone will bow before her when they hear the news."

A pang of bitterness ran through me. It meant the devil in person had recognized the evil inside her. I sighed, thinking of the serpent's bite. I'd suffered the torture it inflicted on me and its poison had hurt even more than Devina's. "Where is she now?"

"That's none of your concern. She'll come to you when it's time."

I shook my head, trying to remember what was true and what I'd dreamed after losing consciousness. If Gemma was beginning to remember, maybe there really was hope. "Where are we?"

"In the gymnasia around the Circle. All the other Champions are preparing as we speak." I looked around. It was a well-lit room full of weapons and equipment. "Don't even think about it," Meryall warned me, thinking I wanted to make a break for it. "The panthers are already outside."

"I have no intention of escaping," I reassured her.

"Good, you're better off that way," Emayn continued. "I don't know why my mistress is keeping you prisoner after choosing you, but this is a big opportunity for you and you'd be wise to seize it. You're lucky. Our mistresses' Champions are the only ones who enjoy certain *privileges*, if you know what I mean." The maidservant winked as she spread salve on my arms. "On the other hand, if you rebel, you're done for."

"Thanks for the warning," I said, giving her a smile.

"Don't mention it. Here, eat these." Emayn offered me a bowl full of seeds. I looked at them dubiously. "They might not taste like Ambrosia, but you can't be fussy here. They'll give you strength."

I swallowed them as the other woman, Meryall, smiled sheepishly. "Our mistress's vital essence—that'll definitely boost your strength."

"Gemma's blood," I murmured, remembering all the times I had refused Devina's.

"You have to drink it if you want to fight as her Champion. She'll transmit her energy to you. If you win, she'll personally train with you. It's a great honor."

"How long has the Opalion existed?"

"As long as Hell itself," Emayn answered. "For fun, Sophìa also took it to Earth, though in a primitive version, without levels or enchanted scenarios—just battles and death. The mortals called the Games *Munera*, lethal battles among armed gladiators or even against animals, in which case they called them *Venationes*. The most famous of them were held at the Coliseum in Rome. I was there back then. I was a

Mizhya to the Empress, along with Freia. You can't imagine the atrocities mortals are capable of under the influence of a Witch."

"That's enough talking," Freia said. "Leave him be." The whole time she'd been silent, busy with a mortar and pestle, engrossed in crushing black flowers to extract their poison, which she spread onto various weapons. Just touching them would have burned her flesh, and if she cut herself it would be the end of her.

"Don't worry," I reassured her. "It's not a problem."

"For you, maybe, but we know our place and we mustn't forget." Freia cast a glance at the other two maidservants who looked down before backing away.

"They'll come for you when it's time. Meanwhile, I advise you to warm up your muscles." She nodded at all the equipment. "In case we don't see each other again, good luck." The Mizhyas bowed and left the room, closing the massive wooden door behind them.

I sat on the cot and looked around. The room was huge, with weapons and equipment of all kinds. There was still a trace of venom in my body. My muscles were burning and I knew what to expect in the Opalion. It was best I took the Mizhya's advice and warmed up before the battles. I would have to fight bloodthirsty Souls captured during the Hunt, then a ferocious beast, and finally I would come up against one of their Champions. Whoever won would bring glory to his Amisha and obtain her as a reward. The Witches claimed Subterraneans for their amusement, often sharing them with each other. The Champions, on the other hand, were the only ones to whom they gave themselves completely. And the only way to achieve that was to win the Opalion. But the Witches were lusty creatures, so the Opalion just happened to be held frequently. They were also capricious and competitive, which was why they held a Hunt before being able to satisfy their needs. One of them had to win it to become the Witch of Honor at the Opalion, which meant she became the "prize" and could lie with her Champion. Watching Subterraneans engage in mortal combat aroused them.

If the competitor made it through the first two trials, a Sister challenged the Witch of Honor with her own Champion. Sophia was the one to choose the challenger. If the rival Champion won, the Witch of Honor lost her title, passing it to her Sister, who could then lie with her own Champion and obtain glory and the envy of the others. At the end of the match, true victory didn't belong to the Champion but to the Witch who'd outdone her Sisters.

The Witch of Honor could send in whomever she wished, and Devina had always chosen me—a prisoner—though I refused to drink her blood to fight as her Champion. I fought for myself. I'd beaten all my adversaries except the challenging Champion—not because I hadn't been capable, but because I preferred to be defeated rather than give Devina the satisfaction of seeing me win for her.

This time it was different. The Opalion was being held in Gemma's honor. She would be the prize and this time it meant only one thing to me: I had to win.

I jumped off the cot and tested my hand muscles, opening and closing them. There were metal bars suspended from the ceiling, positioned at different heights. I went over to one of them and jumped up to grab it before slowly pulling myself up. I could feel my back muscles tighten with every pull, but the more I warmed them up the more my strength returned as my blood rid itself of the last remainders of the poison. I hoisted myself up and stood on top of the bar. In front of me wound a path all through the room, rising and falling at different heights. With a leap, I grabbed the next bar and used my abdominals to swing myself over to the next. I continued upwards, climbing and spinning through the air. Grabbing hold of a bar with my legs, I dangled my upper body to work my abdominals in a long series of pull-ups.

"By Lilith, what a show."

I vaulted to the ground and grabbed a gladius from the wall, pointing it at Devina's throat. She didn't move, staring at me steadily with interest. "At ease, Spartan. The Games haven't begun yet. You'll have time to vent all your ardor."

"What do you want? Why are you here?" I snarled, still aiming the blade at her throat.

"What silly questions. I'm here to enjoy the show, like everyone else." She moved away from the weapon and circled me, moving her lips to my ear. "However, I was hoping to watch it from closer up." She stroked my chest as I stood still, muscles tensed.

"Gemma claimed me. You should know that," I reminded her, clenching my jaw.

"That doesn't mean she can't share you with me. We Sisters are very generous among ourselves. It's part of our blood bond. I myself have shared my Soldiers with her many times," she whispered in an attempt to provoke me.

I spun around and pushed her against the wall, pressing my forearm against her throat. Her serpent emerged to threaten me but I didn't move a muscle, continuing to look her in the eye. "Don't you dare say that again."

Devina smiled. "You're so sexy when you get rebellious."

"What's going on?" I turned toward Gemma, who'd just entered the room. The sight of her left me transfixed. She wore a tremendously sexy black gown worthy of a queen of darkness.

"I just stopped by to wish the new competitor good luck, but he turned out to be rather *hostile*," Devina told her with a malicious air. I pressed my arm harder against her throat.

"Let go of my Sister at once," Gemma commanded me. I glared at Devina and she flashed me a smile. "Step away, I told you. Immediately." I gave the Witch one last shove before loosening my grip and lowering my weapon. Gemma nodded at the gladius and it flew to her hand. "You don't need this yet. Devina, leave us, please."

"Wait," her Sister said. "I thought maybe you'd allow me to share the prisoner with you this time."

"He isn't a prisoner. He's my Champion."

"Not yet," her Sister reminded her. "He hasn't yet drunk your blood. He hasn't battled and won for you. He's not your Champion yet. You're his *Amisha*, that's true—you claimed him—but he may be asked for by your Sisters as long as he's a Soldier like all the others. And this is my last chance, is it not?"

"I have no intention of going along with it," I warned Gemma. "She's a witch."

"We all are," Gemma replied icily, "and you may not disobey me."

"After all, you owe me," Devina insisted.

Gemma reflected. "You're right, dear Sister. It would be selfish of me not to share with you the Subterranean you hunted for centuries and I ultimately claimed."

"Gemma, what are you saying?" I protested in shock.

She raised her chin and looked me straight in the eye. "So be it," she declared.

Smiling, Devina grabbed me roughly and flung me to the other side of the room. Seconds later I found myself on a large round bed hidden behind broad curtains. The red silk sheets contrasted with the black carbonado background. It was adorned with plush cushions and draperies that hung from the ceiling. I stared at the two Witches as they approached.

"Do not disobey my command or I will not think your loyalty worthy," Gemma warned.

Devina dropped her long black cloak to the floor. She pulled out her faithful whip and rested her knee on the bed. I was petrified. I'd always rejected Devina and now Gemma was surrendering me to her. I looked her in the eye, hoping to find a trace of regret. "Is this really what you want?"

Gemma climbed onto the bed and moved toward Devina. "It's what we all want." She touched her Sister's lips with her own. "It is my gift to you, Sister," she whispered.

Devina smiled at her and came toward me, crawling sensually over my body. I never would have thought that one day she would make me her own, but she'd been very good at manipulating Gemma's trust, and now I was forced to give in to her dirty tricks.

The Witch brought her lips to mine and I indulged her, staring at Gemma, who didn't take her eyes off us. I rested my hands on Devina's hips and she brushed her whip across my chest. "I knew sooner or later this moment would come," she murmured against my mouth. Pointing her fingernail at my bicep, she traced the scar she'd left on me the last time I'd been in Hell. "I'm a very nasty Witch. Punish me."

I grabbed her wrists brusquely and inverted our positions, trapping her on the bed. If they wanted to play, I would do it my way. Devina squeezed my buttocks and pulled me against her, moaning with pleasure. She undid my pants and sank her nails into my sides, scratching my skin.

"Enough!" Gemma snapped, stopping her.

"What's the matter? Why don't you come and have fun with us?" Devina said, irritated.

My gaze locked onto Gemma's. "I've changed my mind," she said, still staring at me.

"You can't!" her Sister said, cracking her whip in the air. "You owe me."

"Evan, move aside," she insisted, enunciating each word. Hearing my name on her lips again hit me straight in the heart. I rolled over, freeing Devina from my grip. The Witch looked furious. "Now get out," Gemma ordered.

"You can't give me a gift and then take it back like this," her Sister retorted, her pride wounded.

"Yes I can. I'm the Specter now and you will obey me."

Devina got up from the bed and approached her Sister, defiance in her eyes. *"Nïak suh hamet."* I didn't speak the Witches' tongue, but her tone was definitely full of resentment.

"I'm telling you for the last time: get out of this room."

Devina bowed to her contemptuously. *"Kaahmì."* That one word I knew well. I'd heard it often during my imprisonment. *As you command.* Without moving, Gemma held her gaze until she walked away. Before leaving the room, Devina turned to cast me one last glance and her lips mouthed the words *Goodbye, Soldier.* Then she leapt forward and turned into a panther, ready for the Opalion.

"Why did you do that?" I asked Gemma. She turned her back on me but I grabbed her wrist and made her look at me. "Why did you stop Devina?" I insisted.

Gemma looked away. "It was bad timing. The Games are about to start."

"You had another flashback," I murmured. "You remembered something else, didn't you?" I let go of her wrist.

"I've already told you I care nothing about the past." She moved away but I followed her and took her by the arm, forcing her to face me.

"But I care."

Gemma broke free from my grip and slammed me against the wall, furious. But I knew what was hiding behind her anger: fear. She was starting to remember snippets of us and couldn't explain what was happening to her.

I wasn't about to give up. I grabbed her and trapped her against the wall. "What did you see?" I insisted, holding her tight.

"It's your fault. What have you done to me?!" she snarled. "You've polluted my mind. Rid me of your poison!"

"I'm your poison, and you're mine. There's no antidote for us. There's nothing we can do," I whispered against her lips and kissed her passionately. She struggled but I could feel her resistance waver and held her hands against the wall. She was aroused and I risked losing my head right there. Outside, an entire arena was waiting to watch me do battle. In there, I could have died of love just for her.

"You're a Subterranean. It's normal for you to be in love with me," she said, reading my mind.

I cupped her cheek in my hand and stroked her lip with my thumb. She couldn't hold back and brushed her tongue against it. "And you're a Witch, so why do I set fire to your venom?"

"I feel nothing for you."

I kissed her neck and her breath came faster. "Liar."

She grabbed my arms and a second later I was on the bed, Gemma straddling me. "All I want," she purred, her voice sensual, "is for you to be my Champion."

"I'm ready to become your Champion."

"Receive my blood inside you," she whispered, looking me in the eye. She bit her lip and leaned over me. I could hear her heart beating quickly, our breathing becoming one. *Taste me,* she whispered. I licked the blood from her lips, losing my mind, then closed my eyes, pervaded by a powerful feeling of ecstasy. She smiled and sank her nails into my shoulders as I kissed her again, hungry for her vital essence, a venom so powerful it broke through all my defenses.

"Easy, Champion, or you'll pass out."

"You have no idea how long I've waited for this moment. How long I've waited to touch you again, to feel your lips on mine . . ."

"Fight for me. If you win the Games, you'll have what you want for an entire night."

"I'm not willing to wait," I said, determined. I slipped her daggers off from behind her back and tossed them onto the floor. She allowed me to take off her crossbow while looking me in the eye, probing inside me to discover my intentions. I pulled her against me and rolled over, pinning her to the bed. I nibbled her neck, her shoulder, descending toward her breast.

"Stop," she whispered, at the mercy of her emotions.

"No."

"I command you."

"Your voice lies. It's your body I'm listening to. Your lips." I kissed her and she let herself be drawn in. "Your eyes." I stroked her lashes with my thumb, gazing at her intently. I leaned over her ear and touched it with my mouth. *Your breath.* My hand slid over her breast and she looked at me, helpless. "Your pulse. Listen to how your heart is racing."

"You have no effect on me," she replied defiantly, rebelling against the sensations she was experiencing, but I knew her well—I knew everything about her.

"You keep lying." I lowered myself onto her and brushed my nose against her cheek, sliding my hand up her thigh. "Make love with me," I whispered against her lips.

"No. It's forbidden."

"If you remembered, you would know I've never cared about the rules. Your blood flows within me. I am your Champion."

"You have to win for me before you can have me."

"I'm going to win for you. I'll kill them all just so I can touch you again." I kissed her on the neck and she closed her eyes, excited by my promise. Clasping her buttocks, I held her tight against me so she could feel how much I desired her. "But first tell me why." She looked me in the eye, weighing the answer to the question she'd already read in my mind. "Why did you stop Devina? It was a serious insult, but you did it anyway. *Say it.*"

"Because you're mine," she hissed, staring at me intensely, leaving me on the edge of insanity.

"You're wrong." I spread her legs roughly and pulled her even closer. My fingers clutched her undergarment and tore it off. "It's you who are mine." I entered her and kept her tightly pressed against me as she cried out. I rested my cheek on her chest, on the brink of exploding from the emotions rushing through me. Gemma clung to the cushions, her muscles clenched to hold me close. Her nails scratched my back as I moved inside her. All my frustration faded, swept away by the passion only she could nourish. I held her hands over her head and kissed her with desperation.

Unwilling to be tamed, she was on top of me in a flash. For a moment I was afraid she was going to make me stop, but then she gazed into my eyes and removed her bodice, freeing her supple breasts. My hands slowly moved up her sides to stroke her nipples and she moaned, moving slowly on top of me. I was breathless. I'd spent months chasing her, longing for her. And now she wanted me. I was inside her and didn't want to let her go ever again. I propped myself up to be closer to her and caressed her back through her long hair.

"You're a madman," she murmured, her arousal growing. "I should kill you for this affront."

"You won't," I assured her. "You'll come to visit me every night, against all the rules." I ran my thumb over her lip and she took it into her mouth. "Because you're like me: we aren't made for rules."

"Why are you doing this to me?" she gasped, crying out with pleasure. "You've taken my body. Let my mind be free."

"I am in you as you are in me," I told her in Sanskrit. "In my heart. In your soul. I'm not giving up until you remember." I began kissing her again passionately and she scratched my chest, her poisoned nails leaving marks. I groaned, caught between pain and pleasure. "Were you with others before me?" I asked, the blood boiling in my veins at the thought.

"No one," she replied, a helpless victim of the power that ruled us both.

"Devina's Soldiers?" I insisted. "Tell me and I'll kill every last one of them."

"You're my Champion. No one else."

"Jamie," I moaned.

She squeezed her legs around my waist and arched her back, reaching the climax of her pleasure. I rested a hand on her nape and ran my lips down her neck. "I missed you so much," I whispered, brushing my cheek against her skin as our intertwined bodies trembled from having found each other again. "It's amazing to hear your voice again. Keep talking to me. I've waited an eternity. I thought I would die without you."

She was silent, letting my words wander inside her. For a moment I deluded myself that I'd finally found her. Her fingers stroked the tattoo on my thumb, so similar to hers, then rose up my arm and traced the deep scar that ran from my bicep to my shoulder. When she lowered her eyes to the one on my chest, her brow furrowed. "You've already been our prisoner," she said softly, guessing it for the first time.

"I'm not your prisoner," I stated, drawing her against me to kiss her. But she moved away and stood up, her back to me. I admired her naked body, her long hair flowing down her back, her toned muscles and golden skin. She was a goddess. "I'm here only for you, to remind you of what we had . . . to take you back."

A maidservant burst into the room. "Everything is ready, my lady." It was Meryall. She went to Gemma and helped her dress, stealing glances at my naked body.

"Inform the Empress that she may announce me." Her command called the young woman to attention and she immediately looked down, embarrassed. "Today a new Champion battles in the Opalion."

"Yes, my lady." The maidservant bowed and left the room.

"Forget the past, Soldier," Gemma said, sheathing her weapons behind her back.

"No!" I got up from the bed and approached her from behind, taking her by the arms.

"We're here in the present and you will battle as my Champion. My blood flows inside you. What more could you possibly want?" she said without turning around.

"Your body isn't enough. I want your mind. Your heart belongs to me and sooner or later you'll realize that for yourself," I promised. I wasn't willing to give up now that I was so close.

Gemma moved away, stopping at the door. "My heart belongs to Sophìa. You will never have it. And you'd better fight well or you won't have anything else either. Go and kill them all, my Gladiator. Be my Champion or die for me. Good luck. *Gahl sum keht.*" She looked me in the eye one last time and left the room, leaving me alone.

I knew those words in Kahatmunì, the Witches' tongue. They meant "Forge your glory." I couldn't believe that after making such passionate love to me her coldness had returned so quickly. If her expression had been a blade, it would have pierced my heart.

I laced up my brown leather pants and sat on the bed, disheartened. In those moments when I'd been inside her, I'd deluded myself that everything had returned to what it was before, that she was mine again. I rested my elbows on my knees and covered my face with my hands, frustrated. I couldn't give up. Not now, of all times. I would win the Opalion for her—with her blood in my body nothing could stop me. During battle she would ignite it, making it burn in my veins, giving me supernatural strength. I would slaughter them all just to be with Gemma again, because the thought of not being able to have her again was killing me.

"Evan."

My head shot up as a hooded figure stepped before me. I recognized the voice instantly, there was no doubt about it. "Ginevra. What are you doing here?" I gasped, approaching her.

She pushed her hood back, revealing her face. "You're in danger, Evan."

I looked around, on my guard, and tried to touch her but found myself grabbing only air. She was an illusion. "What's going on? Why are you here?"

"There's no time for questions. Listen carefully. Simon's power is working. It took root inside Gemma and continues to unearth her memories. Sophìa knows it and you've become a threat to her. She's afraid of losing Gemma because of you. That's why she called for an Opalion in Gemma's honor and is letting you fight for her—she wants to get rid of you. Anya warned us just in time."

"I'm going to fight," I growled fiercely. Nothing was going to keep me away from Gemma.

"No. We won't let you. Sophìa gave the order to kill you, Evan. You're going to die in the arena today."

"Does Gemma know?" That possibility alone was enough to kill me.

"No, of course not. She chose you as her Champion—she would never accept it. But if you die in battle she won't be able to object."

I clenched my fists. If Sophìa felt I was such a threat, that meant I had an actual shot at getting Gemma back. "I can't give up now, of all times. She's starting to remember!" I insisted.

"That's not enough for her to cast off evil. She needs to remember everything before she can find herself. I've been through it."

"I need more time."

"You don't have any! And neither do I. We need to act fast, before they discover I'm here."

"Here where?" I asked, voicing a terrible suspicion.

"In Hell, Evan. I'm already here, with Simon, Drake, and Stella."

I knit my brows in shock. "Are you out of your mind? What does Simon have to say about this? I can't believe he approved something so insane."

"It was his idea and I backed him up."

"You were both banished. Sophìa put a death sentence on you."

"We're prepared to fight—for you and for our lives."

"It's too risky. You have to get out of here!"

"It's too late. We're not going to let them kill you. We're going to attack the Castle."

"No! I can do this. Don't risk your lives for me. I can't allow it!"

"It's already been decided. We've gathered an army under my command, and there's an entire militia of rebels inside the Castle who will help us. We're getting you out of here."

"I'm not going anywhere without Gemma."

"You won't be any good to her if you're dead!"

"I don't want to put you in danger. It was my decision to come here. I'm going to see it through. I'm fighting."

"You can't. They'll kill you!"

"I'll die if I have to. I'm not leaving here without Gemma."

"We'll take Gemma with us," Ginevra said.

"How?"

"We'll take her, I promise you. Trust me, Evan. Trust all of us. There's only one way to save your life: by forcing Sophia to let you go."

"How can anyone force the devil to do something?"

"By declaring war." Ginevra stared at me, in her eyes pure determination.

"You know what a war would mean, don't you? Your Sisters would be in danger. Are you willing to run that risk despite the Bond?"

"My bond is with you now. My Sisters gave me destruction and death—the death of those I loved, of those I didn't know, the death of my soul. You gave me back myself. You're my family now. Besides, don't think it's so easy to face them in battle. They know how to defend themselves from your angel fire, though for them it's as lethal as the death of their serpents."

I nodded. It must have pained her greatly to say it. "Kill a Witch's Dakor and the Witch dies with it."

"I hope it won't come to that," she murmured, distraught. I could see that the idea of joining forces against her Sisters caused one part of her tremendous pain—but the other part had chosen Gemma and me. She looked at me. "What about you? Are you ready to battle the Witches?"

"I've been training with one of them for centuries," I replied with a laugh, feeling not a shadow of fear. "What's the plan?"

"We're attack—"

The doors swung open all at once and I spun around. Ginevra vanished an instant before four Soldiers burst into the room to escort me out. The horn blew, announcing the beginning of the Games. The Subterraneans gathered my weapons and walked me to the threshold. For a moment there was silence, then the doors were opened. I strode out and everyone in the stands cheered when they saw me.

The courtyard had been transformed into an amphitheater. I made my way to the center of it and looked around. All of Hell seemed to have flocked to the event. The stands were packed with the Damned—brave Souls who were risking death just to experience the thrill of witnessing the Games. The Opalion was the only occasion for which

Sophìa opened the Castle gates, and for this one she must have spread the word far and wide throughout the kingdom. I scanned the crowds, searching for my friends among the hooded faces. Ginevra hadn't had time to explain their plan, but her promise was enough for me: *We'll take Gemma with us.* Until then, there was only one thing for me to do.

Fight.

The Witches were already in position—nine black panthers in a circle, staring at me. Devina's amber eyes flashed at me. I would have recognized them in whatever form she took. Even now they had a defiant gleam and suddenly I remembered what she had said as she took her leave: *Goodbye, Soldier.* So she'd known about Sophìa's plan—she must have.

"Silence!" thundered a commanding voice. The entire arena fell silent. I turned and saw her. Sophìa was standing on a dais reserved for the Witches. Beside her was Gemma. They both wore bizarre steampunk outfits with dark yet sexy tones and, on their faces, black markings that looked like tattoos.

Sophìa and the Witch of Honor were the only ones who would preside over the Games in their human form until they were joined by the Sister who would offer up her Champion for the duel. The others had the task of guarding the edge of the Circle in their animal form, prepared to tear to shreds any of the Damned or Subterraneans who dared set foot outside of it.

"My dear lost Souls," the Empress began. "I am pleased you have come in such great numbers, as today is an important day—not only for the Sisterhood but for all of you. What better occasion than an Opalion to give you such happy news? It is with immense pride that I announce to you that the kingdom has a new commander: our Sister Naiad." Gemma rose to her feet and the crowd cheered for her. "Honor her as you have done with those who came before her over the centuries. Obey her commands and be willing to die for her."

The snarl of a panther filled the arena—Devina opposing the affront—but the other panthers instantly drowned her out, rejoicing for Gemma and her new appointment.

"This Opalion is for Naiad and it will determine the valor of her new Champion. He will undergo grueling trials and challenges. If he is valiant enough a worthy opponent will be chosen to face him in a duel. Only one will be declared the victor, rendering honor and glory unto his Amisha. May the show begin! Good luck, Champion. Forge your glory."

Sophia sat down and I prepared to fight.

THE OPALION

I stood at attention, muscles rippling, as I awaited the first challenge. A swarm of black butterflies flew in my direction. I watched them as they circled me and immediately flew away. Each transformed into a threatening-looking Soul. In a flash I was surrounded. The spectators held their breath until the first one came forward. He was a tall, dangerous-looking man wearing seventeenth-century clothing. He'd been the first to make a move, but that didn't make him any braver than the rest—it just made him my first victim. I smiled, my eyes trained on him in an ominous invitation. The man leapt toward me and attacked with a dagger he whipped out at the last second. I dodged it though he dealt me a glancing blow. I grabbed the Soul by the arm and head-butted him. Black liquid gushed from his forehead and he fell to the ground, dazed. He tried to get to his feet, reaching for the dagger he'd dropped, but I crushed his hand beneath my foot. Tearing away from him a piece of sharpened wood he'd kept hidden behind his back, I swiftly slashed his throat.

The crowd remained silent for a moment, stunned by how quickly I'd killed him, and then burst into enthusiastic cheers and shouts. The decapitated body fell to the ground and exploded in a cloud of smoke. I raised my eyes to the other Damned, daring them to make their move. One of them let out a cry of fear and fled toward the edge of the Circle, but a panther chased him and tore him to pieces. Seconds later all that was left of him was ash.

Two of the Damned advanced together. They must have been brothers, because they resembled each other greatly. They too were armed. With my foot I flicked my first opponent's dagger into the air and caught it. I flipped the weapon in my hand, waiting for the brothers' move. They looked bloodthirsty, and with good reason: their survival was at stake. But I had an even stronger motivation: I was fighting for Gemma.

One of them gave a war cry and launched his attack, but I wasn't about to be intimidated. I waited until he was close and grabbed him, using his own momentum to flip him and send him crashing into his brother. They got up and attacked together. I blocked a punch from the smaller one and used his arm for leverage as I jumped up and delivered a double kick to the larger one, who ended sprawled on the ground. But my grip was too brutal; the smaller one's arm snapped and he fell to his knees, screaming in pain. I seized my chance and drove the dagger into his throat.

"Sorry," I told his brother. "Didn't want to make him suffer."

He glared at me with hatred and launched another attack. Just then the smaller one turned to dust and I snatched up the dagger as the second Soul rushed at me, sinking the sharp blade into his neck. He gurgled, black blood gushed from his mouth, and he too was reduced to ashes.

Overjoyed, the spectators went wild, but I was just warming up. I raised my eyes to the Panthior, the platform of honor, and Gemma gave me a pleased look. *"I'm going to win for you,"* I told her in my mind, and she smiled at me, her Witch eyes glittering craftily.

At her side, Sophìa stared at me with fire in her eyes. At the tournaments she acted as Stage Director, transforming the playing field and increasing the difficulty of the trials. When she made her move, I wouldn't be unprepared. She flung out her hand in a challenging gesture and heavy bars sprang from the ground and bent around me, sealing me inside a small cage together with my new adversaries: the most ferocious Souls selected during the Hunt. Against some other Subterranean they might have had a chance, but not against me. I was the most ruthless of them all. In that arena, I was the lion.

Some of them climbed onto the ceiling of the cage and crawled over my head while others crept up behind me. I studied their movements. All my opponents were armed and I was surrounded. My only defense was to attack. I charged at one of them, dropped to my knees, and slid across the ground. Wresting the sword away from him, I struck a brutal blow, chopping two adversaries in half. Black blood spurted from their bodies. As I was getting up I threw a right hook at another one and took his sword. I spun around and two heads tumbled to the ground. With Gemma's blood in my body I felt invincible. A Soul swooped down onto me from the ceiling of the cage but I shot backwards and slammed him against the bars. The blow left him dazed and he let go, but two more dropped down and held my arms as a third came and bludgeoned me in the face. Blood filled my mouth. I slowly turned my head until my eyes met his. The ferociousness on my face was enough to leave him unsteady on his feet. I spat out the blood and freed myself with a backflip as the third Soul fled—but he wasn't going to escape me. I chased him down and slit his throat.

Only two were left. I looked from one to the other. It was clear from their faces that they were wondering which of them would be next, but I was tired of playing. Spinning both swords in my hands, I threw them at the same time, pinning both Souls to the bars. Like two filthy, impaled vampires they disintegrated, returning to ashes.

The crowd cheered for my victory. I'd exterminated them all. I looked around, still trapped behind the bars of the cage, and a black butterfly fluttered up to me. I watched it as it landed on the ground nearby. Before it could transform I picked up a dagger and stabbed it. The creature wriggled and flapped its wings. I raised my eyes to Sophìa and twisted the blade in my prey. The last of the Damned.

MORTAL CHALLENGE

The bars withdrew, signaling the end of the first challenge. The spectators were delirious and couldn't wait to see me face my next trial: a battle against a beast. After a momentary pause, flames rose up all around me and the ground began to shake. I picked up a javelin, squeezing my fingers around its grip.

A blood-chilling grunt announced its arrival behind me. I spun around and saw it. Instinctively, I tried to back up but the flames blocked me. The crowd had fallen silent, holding their breath. The beast was huge. It looked like a giant buffalo with leathery skin and massive horns on its head. Even worse, it was staring at me as though it hadn't eaten in months and I was its next meal. "Sit, boy, sit . . ." I said in a low voice. Enraged, the beast grunted and charged. I hurled the javelin, but it parried the blow with a head butt and continued its advance.

I dodged it in the nick of time and ended up sprawled on the ground. "Oh, sorry, are you a she? Didn't mean to offend you!" Maybe it wasn't the best time to crack a joke, but a fire was burning inside me that was hotter than the flames surrounding us. Gemma's poison was instilling confidence and strength in me.

When the creature charged again I ran toward the fire and at the last second did a backflip out of its path while the beast continued through the wall of flames. Seconds later it returned, moving slowly toward me through the incandescent tongues of fire that hadn't harmed it in the least.

As though offended by the affront, the circle of fire broke up and dozens of flames began to dance across the battlefield like whips that lashed to and fro, making my every movement perilous. However, the fire was a problem only for me. The animal didn't fear it and was ready to attack once more. I looked at Sophia and she smirked. Was this how she planned to kill me? I would never give her the satisfaction of dying right before Gemma's eyes. I focused on the beast and prepared myself for its next charge, which came soon. When it was close enough I grabbed hold of its horns and tried to leap onto its back, but the animal shook its head fiercely, making the endeavor impossible. In the end it won out and flung me away.

I rolled away from the flames and crumpled to the ground, surprised by a shooting pain. Touching my side, I stared at my fingers. They were bloody. The beast had gored me. I gritted my teeth, the dirt making the gash burn.

The ferocious creature snorted, stamped its hooves, and launched another attack, forcing me to spring to my feet before it could crush me. I staggered to where the dagger lay on the ground and picked it up. At the first opportunity I drove it into the beast's chest. "Now we're even."

The animal reared up, letting out a strange wail of pain. I seized my chance and climbed onto its back. It tried to throw me to the ground again but this time my grip was firm. I drew my dagger and plunged it into its skull. The beast's eyes went wide and it froze, then crashed to the ground like a huge boulder, sending up a massive cloud of dust that covered everything. I pulled myself to my feet and waited for it to settle, my hand firm on the bloody dagger and my eyes locked on Sophia's. I was ready for the next challenge.

Gemma rose, gazing into my eyes with pride. The panthers roared in their circle. In the stands, the spectators were ecstatic—not because I had bravely triumphed in the first two trials, but because the most difficult one awaited me: the duel against another Champion.

All around the arena, the massive doors to the gymnasia opened and a band of Subterraneans emerged. They were all barefoot and bare-chested, clad in brown leather pants like mine, muscles tensed and prepared to do battle. Each panther came onto the field and positioned herself beside her Champion, all anxious for the Empress to choose my challenger. She rose and stood beside Gemma, offering me a contemptuous smile. For a second everything fell silent in expectation of her verdict.

"You have battled valiantly," she admitted, her gaze as sharp as a blade. "I must choose your opponent carefully. Naiad is my Specter now, and our new commander's Champion must prove that his valor goes beyond that of all others. Only a Soldier worthy of her may be by her side. That is why you are to fight Zakharìa, *my* Champion." A gasp escaped the crowd and Sophìa smiled.

Another door opened—the largest one—admitting the last of the Subterraneans to the arena. The panthers roared angrily while all the spectators' eyes turned to him. He was a tall, powerful man with dark skin and gray eyes as sharp as ice that challenged me. He strode to the center of the arena and knelt before his queen. I glanced at Gemma: her expression was concerned but she didn't protest the choice.

This was what Ginevra had been trying to warn me about: Sophìa's Champion wasn't just dangerous—his blood was lethal. Since time immemorial he'd been nurtured on his Amìsha's vital essence and, like her, he could send a Subterranean to his eternal death in Oblivion. That was why the Empress had decided to send him out: to kill me.

"What is it? You look concerned. Do you wish to ask me to withdraw you, perhaps?" the devil provoked me, her tone mocking.

I trained my eyes on her fearlessly. "I'm ready to fight." Gemma nodded, her eyes gleaming with pride.

"Your courage is admirable, I must admit. It will be a true pity for Naiad to have to give you up."

My eyes locked with Gemma's for a long moment, and

then a group of guards marched onto the field and escorted

me out of the arena.

TO THE DEATH

Ginevra's last words filled my mind. That was what she'd been about to tell me: I would be up against Sophia's Champion. The Empress had planned this from the start. I'd gone through the first two trials wondering how she intended to get rid of me, and now I knew—by pitting me against Zakharìa in the most difficult challenge of all: the duel.

Soldiers escorted me back to the gymnasium, where Gemma's Mizhyas awaited me to dress my wounds. I scanned the crowd in search of my friends, but there was no sign of them. I tried to concentrate on the battle ahead. I couldn't lose focus. A million reasons could have prevented Ginevra from reaching the Castle with her army. It was almost insane to think they might come to our rescue. I could count only on myself. The doors closed behind me and the three maidservants greeted me and had me sit down. They examined the gash in my side and prepared an ointment, then stanched the bleeding on my cheeks and shoulders and oiled my muscles. I let them do it, my mind fixed on Zakharìa's gaze and its promise of death. I clenched my fists. I couldn't let him kill me with Gemma watching. I had to fight and defend myself. It was my only chance of being with her again. I had to become her Champion. I tried to free my mind, but her blood was a powerful poison that obscured every other thought except those connected to her.

I raised my head when the doors opened and Gemma entered the room. "Leave us," she ordered without taking her eyes off me. The Mizhyas made a little bow and left. I strode to her and pressed my lips against hers. She kissed me back, taken by surprise. I closed my eyes and rested my forehead against hers, forgetting everything around me—the bloodthirsty arena, the duel I was about to face. I could do it all if I had her.

"You fought bravely," Gemma said in a low, sensual voice. "I knew you would be a fine Champion." She turned her back to me and walked away, her skirt's long train leaving her sides bare. "However, you're quite presumptuous in your ideas about your prize. You must first win the tournament for me if you wish to be rewarded."

I went up behind her and was about to grasp her shoulders to turn her around, but stopped with my hands suspended in midair, limiting myself to touching her arms. She didn't move. "You can't ask me to stay away from you," I whispered into her hair, closing my eyes.

She turned and stroked the cut on my face. "Win for me," she said, probing my soul.

Everything was about to be decided out there in that arena. Our fate would change forever if I lost. All we'd fought for was at stake. Gemma didn't know my opponent was planning to kill me. I might die, but I was prepared to do so for her.

"*Kaahmì*," I replied. *As you wish.*

An irresistible smile appeared on her lips. I stroked them with my thumb and she moved them close to mine, igniting my desire. Drawing her against me tenderly, I demanded another kiss. My tongue touched hers and I no longer knew who I was. Gemma bit her lip and I sucked it, hungry for more of her vital essence. All I needed was one drop . . . She gave it to me, making my head spin and my body turn to flames, burning with desire.

Gemma rested her hands on my chest and her fingers traced the scars for a moment. Then she pulled her lips from mine, leaving me breathless. She looked at me and her voice enveloped me: "I wanted to give you another taste. Do not disappoint me."

She turned her back on me and walked out, leaving me in a daze. I tried to control my breathing as the blood burned inside me, igniting all my senses, but there wasn't time. The doors opened again and guards burst into the room. To my surprise I recognized one of them. It was Faustian. What was he doing there?

As he passed he bumped my shoulder and slipped something into my hand. I closed my fist, looked away and straightened up. The doors reopened and the spectators cheered in anticipation. Keeping my arm at my side, I opened my palm a crack to see what Faustian had given me. My eyes bulged. It was Absolon's ring—the Devil's Claw. I stared at Zakharìa at the opposite end of the arena and smiled. Now it was a fair fight.

The Empress rose to announce the beginning of the challenge but I didn't take my eyes off him. "Fight, my Gladiators, and may the more valiant of you win. Forge your glory!"

The guards escorted us to the center of the Circle and I found myself face to face with my adversary. I'd never seen the Empress's Champion take part in the Games; it was certainly a rare occurrence. The panthers were already in their positions, tensely prowling back and forth, patrolling their assigned areas. I glanced at Anya and touched the ring I'd hidden in my pocket. She nodded slightly. The duel was the final challenge, and only one of us would come out of it victorious.

I looked Zakharìa straight in the eye as the crowd held its breath. "It honors me to know that Sophìa had to inconvenience her Champion in order to defeat me." He stared at me in silence. We were both on guard, a gladius gripped in our fists, as the first round required. "What a shame," I continued. "I was hoping we could get acquainted before I hacked you to bits."

My opponent gritted his teeth and charged, knocking me on the shoulder so hard I fell right next to the edge of the Circle. The stands exulted while, with a ferocious roar, a panther bared its poisoned fangs and raised its paw toward me. If it wounded me I would lose consciousness and Sophìa would win the tournament. I would, however, remain alive. Only the Empress's venom could send a Subterranean to oblivion, and Zakharìa's body was full of it.

I stood up and faced him again. "I get it, you don't care for introductions," I said with a challenging smile. "Shyness is a terrible thing, you know? Your mistress should let you get out more often."

The mention of Sophìa made him react. He charged again, but this time I was more prepared and dodged his attack. I leapt onto him from behind, toppling him backwards, and dragged him toward the Witches. The crowd gave a start of surprise.

I turned to stare at Sophìa on her platform. She had a victorious expression on her face, but I was going to wipe it off. All the spectators and even the Witches thought the Opalion's final battle was being waged. She and I knew the truth: there was much more at stake. The real prize was Gemma, and Sophìa and I were the ones fighting for it.

Zakharìa got to his feet and I shifted my attention back to him. Every shred of humor in me had vanished. I had to defeat him before he defeated me. This time I was the first to attack. He took the blow and counterattacked. He was the most skilled opponent I'd ever fought, but

I knew how to defend myself. The second I shoved him to the ground the horn signaled the end of the first round.

I continued to hold him down until the Soldiers pulled me off him. They handed us two long metal-tipped staffs as the ground shook beneath our feet. The pavement crumbled and a gaping chasm opened up all around us. We found ourselves on a pillar of earth with smaller ones nearby. Around those, empty space. The horn blew once more, marking the start of the second round of the duel.

All my senses alert, I searched my opponent for a weak spot and launched my attack. I was good with a staff—I'd trained long and hard using them with my brothers—but my opponent was the Empress's worthy Champion and skilled at expert maneuvers. I leapt onto a nearby column and he followed suit, jumping onto the one beside it. Our staffs collided, their pointed tips threatening first me, then him. My muscles strained from the effort, but Gemma's blood was an inexhaustible source of energy. A mere glance at her set it on fire, making me fight with new vigor.

He dodged my lunge and began to run, jumping from one pillar to the next. I chased him until he reached the edge, one step away from the panthers. Turning just in time to see me leap onto his column with my weapon pointed at him, he parried my blow but lost his balance and fell. I pounced on him and we rolled across the ground until he managed to overpower me, pinning me down and pressing the shaft of his staff against my throat. I tried to shove him away but he was too strong. Zakharìa pushed me forward and I found myself with my head dangling over the void. The crowd cheered for the Empress's Champion. I looked him in the eyes, which for the first time sparkled with the anticipation of victory. I couldn't accept it. Driven by desperation, I struck him with all my might and swiftly broke loose. He spun around but then froze, disconcerted—another sharp point was now pressed against his throat: the Devil's Claw. Just then the horn blew, decreeing the end of the round. I hadn't defeated him, but at least now he too knew it was a fair fight.

I turned to Sophìa with a defiant glare as the abyss sealed up. She'd risen in alarm. Still, there was nothing she could do to stop me. I picked up the sword that had appeared on the ground, my eyes locked onto Zakharìa's. "You are shrewd," he said, speaking for the first time. "Now I see why the Empress feels you are a threat."

"You'd better focus on your own problems, because I intend to give you lots of them," I shot back, attempting a lunge. He parried, giving rise to the most ferocious of duels.

A layer of water formed beneath our feet, soon turning to muck. There was no rule limiting the number of rounds—they could be infinite, as could the scenarios Sophìa conjured up for the duels. They would continue until one of the two contenders was defeated. However, now that I'd revealed my secret weapon to Zakharìa, he and I knew this round would be the last one. It was either him or me.

Our swords sang with each increasingly brutal blow. "You're good with a sword, I'll give you that," I told him as he warded off my attack by thrusting his sword against mine. The force was so great it sent me staggering back into the mud, dangerously close to the edge. A panther snarled, prepared to pounce. Seizing his chance, Zakharìa disarmed me and kicked me hard, sending me to my knees.

The spectators burst out in a deafening roar. They too realized the end was near. I raised my eyes and through my mud-splattered hair watched the Damned going into raptures. "What, no one's rooting for me?" I joked before turning back to look at my opponent.

He ran his sharp blade across his chest, making a long incision, and then pointed it—now edged with his poisoned blood—at my throat. A hush fell over the crowd as I stared him straight in the eye. I looked at Gemma, who had risen from her seat to witness my execution.

In the silence, a single voice rose. "*I'm* rooting for you."

Drake. I whipped my head up as a panther pounced on Zakharìa, tearing him off of me. In seconds, Ginevra's army swarmed into the arena, attacking everyone and everything. I raised my eyes to Sophìa, whose expression was one of utter shock, and this time I was the one to smile at her.

The Games were over. The war had begun.

THE WHISPER OF DEATH

The panthers rushed to attack, ripping a group of the rebel Damned to shreds. In seconds the arena had turned into a battlefield on which chaos had exploded. Drake ran toward me but darted to the side at the last second to knock down one of the Witches' Soldiers. He reached me as a new group surrounded us.

"You took your sweet time," I joked, leaning my back against his.

"You know Ginevra. It takes her ages to get ready," he said. Together we attacked. "I have to admit"—he did a backflip, landed behind an enemy, and slashed his throat—"you put on a good show."

"I was practically phoning it in." I parried a lunge and rammed the Claw into my adversary's throat, then spun around and did the same with a Subterranean who was closing in on Drake. Both the Soul and the Subterranean exploded in a cloud of ash. Drake and I gave each other a bear hug. "I missed you, bro," I said.

"Sorry you had to come all the way back here to hang out with me again." He grinned. "Anyway, I missed your ugly mug too."

"We'd better save the sweet nothings for when we're out of here." I ducked to avoid the arm of a Soul someone had lobbed at me.

"For once, I agree with you."

Around us, the war raged. Ginevra had gathered an incredible army: the Damned, zombies, and various types of ferocious beasts defended our cause, battling the Witches' army, which was composed of subjugated Subterraneans and a multitude of battle-trained Amazons. In the fray I recognized many prisoners I'd seen before in the Castle, including Faustian, who had joined our side. The rebels confronting the Witches were in the thousands, but our adversaries seemed infinite. The Witches summoned Hell-spawned creatures that swarmed in from all corners of the underworld. They conjured up statues of animals, which they then brought to life.

Ginevra battled like a lioness, Simon and Peter at her side, while Drake had joined Stella. She was so skilled and so fierce in battling the Mizhyas that she seemed like one of them. I scanned the battle for Gemma and spotted her not far away, keeping the Souls of the Damned at bay. As I struggled through the crowd to reach her, my sword turned even against my allies to defend her. I would allow no one to harm her. "Gemma, we need to get out of here. My friends will help us escape."

"You will all die for this affront to the Empress!"

"We're taking you away from here whether you like it or not!" I shouted over the din. She pulled out her crossbow and aimed it at my face. "Please, come with me," I pleaded. "Your place is with me."

"My place is here. With Sophìa."

"Sophìa betrayed you, can't you see that? She didn't hesitate a second to order the death of the Champion *you* chose."

A mighty boom drowned out the frenzy of the battle. We stopped, alert, and a large blue-eyed gorilla barreled toward us, raging. Gemma leapt out of the way and I dodged it a second before it could crush me. I watched her rush to her Saurus that had swooped down to her rescue. She grabbed hold of it with a single hand and leapt onto its back. Argas took wing. I struck down every creature in my path in my attempt to follow Gemma. She came to a halt above her Sisters, who were battling in the form of panthers, slid off Argas, and joined forces with them. One by one, the Witches morphed back into their human forms. All at once, the sky darkened and a barrier surrounded them, advancing with them and destroying everyone it touched. All the Damned retreated, but Ginevra stood her ground and faced them.

"Step aside," Gemma ordered her.

"Come away with us and no one will get hurt," Ginevra promised.

"You've lost your mind!"

"You're the one who's not thinking straight! You're blinded by love for Sophìa. She ordered the death of your Champion. We're here to save him *and* you."

"I don't need to be saved."

"I'm your Sister."

"No you aren't. Not any more. They're my Sisters. Did you really think you could defeat us with a bunch of rebels? Consider them dead meat."

"Don't count on it—they all have my blood in their bodies."

"Then this means war."

A lightning bolt streaked the sky and Ginevra's entire army returned to the fray. I found Simon and Drake and joined them in battle. The Witches weren't ordinary adversaries; their powers were immense. The air itself was imbued with black magic and it took all our strength to withstand it. Each Subterranean summoned the elements to help: air, earth, water, and fire—the fire that the Witches so feared and that now threatened them in their own territory, within their Castle walls. Their serpents hissed, sinking their fangs into Damned Souls and rebel Subterraneans alike. They fell like leaves in the wind. Peter was on his knees, Devina's whip coiled around his neck. I hadn't yet learned what his special power was but it must have been strong, because he freed himself from the whip and pinned the Witch against the wall.

Absolon was also there, longbow in hand. He quickly killed off the Empress's guards and headed straight for the Witches. Somewhere in the distance the massive volcano erupted, making the ground quake. I used my power over the earth to summon the poison that impregnated the soil. It rose up, forming a giant arch. Simon set it on fire and hurled it against the Witches, who defended themselves by creating a vacuum around them so the fire would have no oxygen to feed on. But the spell weakened their protective shield, opening a gap that we took advantage of to launch a new attack. Against their Soldiers we used the poisoned weapons Ginevra had prepared. Our lances and arrows burned with angel fire.

A Witch hurled a lightning bolt straight at me, but at the last second Argas pushed me out of its path. Gemma looked in our direction, surprised by her Saurus's action. Anya also came running. She'd stayed close to Gemma since the revolt had begun. Though she hadn't openly joined our side, she had to have been the one who gave Faustian the Devil's Claw. Anya was there not to stand in our way but to protect Gemma, and I hoped she would help persuade her to come with us.

A Subterranean nocked two flaming arrows. I realized too late whom he was aiming at. "Gemmaaa!!!" Horror filled my eyes. I tried to stop them, but one of them flew toward her, the fire piercing the twilight. Anya looked at me in shock and pushed Gemma out of the way, taking the arrow in the chest. A tear slid down her cheek before a wave of flames engulfed her. Her body instantly exploded into thousands of black butterflies.

"Anyaaa!!!" Gemma screamed, kneeling where her Sister had been a second before. In despair, Ginevra slew the Subterranean who'd killed

Anya. Sophìa's shriek echoed throughout the realm. For an instant the battle halted as the sky transformed, filling suddenly with a tempest of lightning bolts that hurled their fury down on us. Gemma's eyes transformed, becoming inhuman, as she flung herself at her adversaries.

All at once something stopped her and she crumpled to her knees. For a second I feared someone had hit her, but then she raised her head and her eyes met mine. It was like finding each other again after centuries. She clenched her fists against the ground, her eyes fixed intensely on me, as a burst of emotion struck me full in the chest. "Evan," she murmured.

She remembered. Tears filled my eyes. *"Jamie."*

My Jamie—I had found her! I ran toward her, killing anyone who got in my way, but a swarm of black butterflies descended upon us like the darkest of prophecies, lifted some of the Damned from the ground, and tore them apart in midair before lashing out at me and hurling me away.

"Sophìa, no!" Gemma screamed, her voice cracking with desperation.

The Empress materialized in front of me, in her eyes all the world's evil. *"You* are the cause of this!" she thundered. "Now *die,* Soldier!" She hurled her serpent straight at me and I realized that this was the end. Now that I had finally found my Jamie, I was about to die.

Gemma's agonized shriek shook the sky. "Noooo!!!" As Sophìa's Dakor opened its fangs, there was a deafening boom, like a wave of energy holding back time. Gemma's voice filled my mind. *"He must live."*

"It will be forever and there will be no return."

I cringed, my blood running cold. It was the Màsala.

"It doesn't matter. As long as he's alive, my soul will be at peace."

The strange power subsided. I glimpsed another blurred form darting past me and realized to my horror it was Gemma's serpent. I turned toward her, desperate, but it was too late. A tear slid from Gemma's eye an instant before Sophìa's Dakor sank its fangs into her serpent, ripping off its head.

Gemma's eyes, still fixed on mine, grew wide as the pain her Dakor had felt flooded through her. Ever so slightly, her lips moved: *"Atyantam."* Her body exploded into a swarm of black butterflies.

My mind reeled from the shock and tears flooded my eyes. I clenched my teeth and let out a shriek of pain that pierced the sky. Dazed, I watched the battle raging all around me. Ginevra was on the ground, sobbing and clutching the earth where a moment earlier Gemma had been. Sophìa sank to her knees, paralyzed.

No! No! No! It couldn't end like this. I couldn't finally find her only to lose her again. Why had she done it? She'd sacrificed herself for me, dying in my place. I sobbed. The pain was unbearable; it wracked my chest. I turned toward the battle and realized I'd undertaken a journey with no return. Without Gemma, nothing had meaning any more. I began to run, tearing a sword out of the hands of one of the Damned, lopping off heads and venting my rage on anyone who stepped into my path. Argas's cry of anguish rose up in the night as he circled in the air above us. I ran to him and he swooped down so I could leap onto his back and continue my massacre, hurling fireballs at the accursed Witches as the Saurus charged ahead in a futile attempt—like my own—to escape the pain. Subterraneans, Witches, the Damned—I didn't care who I struck down. I didn't care about anything any more. I had lost everything. No one deserved to live more than Gemma. They all had to die.

Brandishing my sword, I was rushing at a group of Soldiers when a voice filled my head. *"Evan, stop."* A shiver crept through me and I froze. It was Gemma. I turned around and her big dark eyes locked onto mine. "Enough," she said softly.

I slid off Argas's back and rushed to her, wiping away the tears that blurred my view of her. I crumpled to my knees at her feet and wept. She cradled my head and I held her tight. She too knelt and I stroked her hair with the desperation of a man condemned to death. I rested my forehead against hers, our eyes exchanging forbidden promises.

"How . . ." It was Gemma's soul I was embracing. She wasn't there to stay.

"You're free. Your soul no longer belongs to me." Gemma touched her neck. The Dreide with which she'd claimed me was gone.

"I don't want to be free of you. My soul will belong to you forever."

"Evan . . ." she murmured, taking my hand. I squeezed my eyes shut as more tears flooded them, shaking my head because I knew what she was about to tell me—what was about to happen.

"No. Don't say it. Please don't say it," I begged her.

"I'm here to say goodbye to you."

I held her tight against me, clenching my fists. I couldn't accept it. I couldn't let her go. "Stay with me," I whispered, on the verge of madness. "Stay with me, I'm begging you. I can't lose you now that I've found you again."

"I can't stay. I prayed for forgiveness and it was granted to me." She stared at me, her eyes mirroring my desperation. "I couldn't leave without thanking you for fighting for me up to the very end."

I shook my head. "Without you, nothing I did means anything any more."

"It means something to me, Evan. You freed me."

"It wasn't supposed to end this way. We were supposed to be together forever."

"This was how it had to end all along, but meanwhile you gave me the world. Death has whispered its last song to me."

"I didn't save you."

"Yes you did. My soul will be at peace now."

A hooded figure appeared behind Gemma. It was one of the Màsala. Her great sacrifice had delivered her from the darkness, but crossing over into the light would take her away from me forever. I held her tight, refusing to let her leave me. "No. I won't let you go." A tear slid down my cheek. Never had I been so desperate. "This shouldn't have happened." I shook my head. "It shouldn't have happened."

"We fought to prevent it but fate was against us, Evan. I'll never regret having tried. I've lived moments with you I'll never forget."

"There won't be any more. There won't be any more moments for us together!" I whispered. "You know the curse I'm under. If you pass over, I'll lose you forever. Why did you do it? Why did you stop fighting?"

"I only stopped fighting for myself. Now it's time for me to protect you. If you had died today, I never would have forgiven myself. There won't be any more wars to fight, Evan."

"This is the end—the end of everything."

Gemma took my hand in hers and raised it, gazing at our joined palms, our vows interlacing for the last time. "There will never be a true end for us."

Our palms pressed closer, caressed each other, explored each other for the last time. I looked at her fingers, stroking them, trying to memorize her touch. I would never experience it again. The Màsala behind her approached. Gemma's gaze plumbed mine in a final farewell as a tear slid silently from my eyes. Then she disappeared.

I sank to my knees. I had lost her forever.

"Enough!" A commanding voice resounded through the night, and the battle all around me ceased. I was still on the ground, dazed and heartbroken. Slowly I raised my head, but only because it had been Ginevra's voice.

I started when I saw she was at Sophia's side. "The war will come to an end. Now!" she ordered. Everyone looked around, suddenly freed from her dark spell. I stared at her, bewildered, and she detected my thoughts. "It's over, Evan," she whispered, looking devastated. "We lost, but at least you can save yourselves."

"There's nothing left in me to save."

"Yes there is. I led this revolt. I'll be the one to pay the price . . . in exchange for your lives."

"No!" Simon stepped forward, emerging from the crowd.

Ginevra turned to look at him and a tear slid down her cheek. "Earth isn't a good place for those like us. I'm sorry. I have no choice."

"But I do," Simon replied, and she nodded. If Ginevra had decided to remain in Hell to put an end to the war, Simon would stay there with her. A band of panthers surrounded me and a Witch bound my wrists behind my back. I stood and let them lead me away, casting a final glance at Simon and Ginevra.

The air shimmered in front of me as the portal opened. I saw Drake staring at me from his position at the head of our army. He was covered with blood and ash, and his powerful body was shielding Stella's protectively. We looked at each other one last time. Driven forward by the Witch and the panthers, I crossed through the portal and all the chaos disappeared. The Witch didn't speak; the panthers made not a sound. They too were mourning. I allowed them to lead me to the center of the Dànava, my eyes lost in the void as the mechanism was activated and a whirlwind of butterflies came to life around me, dragging me out of Hell.

But a worse Hell dwelled in my soul that had been darkened forever. I had lost Gemma. I had lost everything.

Thunder. Inside me and out.
Bolts of lightning. They crash down onto the confines of my
reason.
Light. Darkness. Shadows.

Vain hope.

A FINAL PROMISE

I stared at Gemma's casket as they covered it with dirt. It was empty, like my heart and everything else that remained of me. Even the sky wept, bathing the black umbrellas of the community that had come together to say a final farewell to my wife and our child. I let its tears fall on me. I didn't deserve its consolation.

Breaking the news to Gemma's parents had been the hardest thing I'd ever done. Their grief was like salt in my bleeding wound. Her father had collapsed to the floor in tears. Her mother had hit me over and over, refusing to believe it. At the end she had clung to me as we wept bitter tears together, tears that burned like the deadliest of poisons.

I gripped the violin tighter, squeezing my eyes shut as I moved the bow across the strings, playing a final lullaby for Gemma and Liam. I would never see them again. The notes cut into me, exposing my pain as Gemma's eyes returned to fill my mind. Every time those eyes looked at me, my heart broke in two to let her in. She was inside me and no condemnation could ever move her from there. But death had breathed its last whisper into her ear. There would be no happy ending for us—for any of us.

Ginevra had sacrificed her freedom in exchange for my life and Simon's. He too had made up his mind, refusing to leave her. And so he'd stayed with her in Hell.

Someone rested a hand on my shoulder. It was Peter. When I looked up, I saw that the crowd had dispersed and we were alone. "I'm sorry," he said.

"They let you go," I remarked.

"Simon intervened for me. He stayed in the Castle with Ginevra."

"He'll get by. He's strong."

"I know. Ginevra imposed some conditions."

"You fought well. Thank you for protecting Gemma."

"I didn't do it for you." He looked down. "You know, when I got back from Hell I went to eat of the Tree," he admitted. He was talking about Eden, but not even he dared say the name aloud, almost as though it had become a forbidden place. "It's strange, knowing she's there and I can't see her." I closed my eyes. I hadn't found the courage to do the same. "I stayed a while, listening. I tried to imagine her there next to me. Maybe she really was there and I didn't know it. It's frustrating. But you—you haven't eaten of the Tree since you got back from the war, have you?"

I didn't reply. Peter was right, but I couldn't go back there. I'd once told Gemma there was no world where we could be together. Inside me I'd always hoped it wasn't true, but it was. We were separated, in two different worlds, lost Souls who would never meet again.

It had happened. What I'd feared from the very start had happened: Gemma had crossed over. I'd lost her. Like a dream that fades with the morning light, it was the end. The end of everything. The end of *me*.

"I know I can't replace your friends, just like no one could ever replace the one I lost," Peter continued, "but I want you to know you can count on me, for anything." I nodded my thanks. "I have to go now." Peter turned and walked away, leaving me alone with Gemma.

I stared at the engraving on her headstone. Leaning over, I stroked the stone. The words transformed beneath my fingertips and my final promise to her appeared.

Atyantam

I turned down the car stereo as I stopped at the light. Pink Floyd was playing *Wish You Were Here*. I looked out the window. Outside, standing on the sidewalk, Gemma gazed at me. She smiled . . . and then vanished. I gripped the steering wheel. Her soul lived on inside me.

ETERNAL PEACE

I went to the lakeshore to watch the water ripple as the wind caressed it like a lover. Filling my lungs with air, I closed my eyes and smiled. Gemma's image was still vivid in my mind, a salve for my soul tormented by her absence. I sought her inside me whenever the pain filled my chest as I waited for it all to be over. I'd been waiting for such a long time, but now the end was near—I could feel it. Soon I too would find peace.

I looked at the lake house and imagined Gemma standing in the doorway, waiting for me with Liam in her arms. It was a lie, I knew it—a lie to lessen my pain. I couldn't be honest with myself.

After Gemma's funeral I'd gathered her things from the family manor, set fire to the house, and watched it burn until nothing was left. Drake, Simon, Ginevra, Liam . . . Gemma. One by one they'd vanished like ghosts, leaving the huge house empty. When all that remained was ash, I'd returned to the house on the lake, seeking refuge in the memory of us, and waited for Death to finally claim me as well. Without having eaten of the Tree, I'd lost first my powers, then my strength. I struggled against gripping hunger and my blood burned with the desperate need for Ambrosia.

A few days before, Devina had returned to me, proposing I stay with her, speaking to me for the first time in a serious tone. I even noted a glimmer of sadness in her eye. She'd promised me peace, but for me, peace had one name only, and that name had been eliminated from that world. I no longer wanted to be there.

I'd been left all alone because of the decisions I'd made. That April morning when Gemma had missed her appointment with Death, I'd destroyed the lives of everyone I cared about: Drake, Simon, and Ginevra had ended up in Hell; Gemma and the baby were in Heaven, far from me. I was trapped, exiled from everything I loved. I should have gone to Hell to receive the punishment I deserved, but I wasn't brave enough. Not because of the torture—I could have withstood the Witches' torture for all eternity if there had been hope—but I couldn't live another day knowing I'd lost Gemma and Liam forever. My heart had disintegrated and the crumbs were too small to piece back together. And so I had decided I would dissolve. A few more hours and everything would end in Oblivion. I would have peace—a peace I didn't deserve, but without which I could no longer continue.

Ginevra had snuck back for a visit and begged me to eat of the Tree, but my mind was made up. I wasn't even carrying out my orders any more. What was the point? Even worse, the idea of helping a Soul cross over was unbearable, knowing that everyone could see her except me.

Since the dawn of time, the sun had risen and set every day and time had moved inexorably forward as millions of Souls passed through life, one after the other. Gemma was one of them. Her time was up. And though I'd tried everything to keep her with me, nature—the nature she'd loved so dearly—had taken her, to restore balance. In the order of the universe, she was but one of countless Souls. To me, she was the whole universe.

I raised my hand to my neck and took off my dog tag, to which I had linked Gemma's necklace, and looked at them one last time, reading the engravings.

Gevan
Atyantam

I tied the two chains into a knot that would never be undone, eternal witness to our love, and cast them over the water. At the peak of their arc they sparkled, kissed by the light of the sun as it gave them its blessing. They hit the surface of the lake and sank, settling on the lakebed where no one would separate them ever again. Together. Like Gemma and I could no longer be. A solitary tear slid down my face.

I lowered my hand and examined it in the morning light. It was almost transparent. I smiled. I was beginning to fade, and there was no better place for it to happen than the lake house, our special hideaway. It was there that we'd made love the first time, there that our child had been born. It was there that I wanted it all to end. I would finish in Oblivion, but a shadow of me would wander the woods for eternity, reliving the magic of our times together. The first time she'd promised herself to me as I held her against that tree. I stroked its bark, where she once had stood, as though I could touch her again . . . just one last time before vanishing forever.

Her laughter still filled the air. Her gaze burned inside me each time I closed my eyes.

Are you here to protect me? Is that your mission?

A reckless Angel.

My heart belongs to you forever.

Inside, I was happy because no one could deprive us of our memories. They were a priceless gift. They were my expiation.

Keep playing for me, Evan.

Wherever I went, I would take them with me. And even if the two of us were apart, those memories would be eternal.

Out of the blue, someone grabbed my leg. I spun around and my eyes went wide with surprise. It was a Subterranean, on the verge of vanishing. "H . . . eeelll . . . help . . . me . . ."

Thoughts crowded my mind. He needed to eat of the Tree. I could help him cross over—but I couldn't go back there because in my condition the lure of the fruit would be too powerful to resist. I had to decide fast. The young man fixed his eyes on me, pleading for my help. Suddenly I thought of Liam, of the man he might have become, and of whoever one day might have had the power to decide whether to spare him or end his life.

I reached out and rested a hand on his shoulder. The world around us transformed and disappeared. *"Go. Follow your need,"* I told him in my mind.

"Thank you." I could hear his voice, but he'd already vanished.

I was back in Eden. Alone. I looked at the row of pillars surrounding me where I'd once been with Gemma. They called it the Celestial City, but inside me everything was dark. Knowing she was there and I couldn't see her drove me mad. Maybe she was talking to me and I couldn't hear her voice. I closed my eyes, praying for her to speak louder so I could hear. The scent of the fruit filled my nostrils and I clenched my fists. I had to be strong, one last time. I had to leave before the temptation became too difficult to ignore. Soon I would disappear—it wouldn't be long.

I prepared myself to return to Earth, but a sudden stinging sensation spread over my left arm, a pain I'd never felt before. Had Death come to take me? Would I disappear right there, with Gemma so close to me, hidden from my eyes by my curse? It was a good place to die.

The stinging grew stronger. I turned my hand over and my eyes widened in bewilderment. I wasn't vanishing. It was the mark of the Children of Eve that was burning. Its claws withdrew like a snare unraveling, freeing me from its punishment. In shock, I examined it, trying to understand what was happening to me.

A voice broke my eternal silence: "Finally." I stood stock-still. Was madness claiming me just before I vanished? It couldn't be. Slowly I turned around.

She was there. "It took you long enough." Gemma smiled at me and my eyes filled with tears.

"Daddy!"

My eyes shot toward the second voice and Liam ran up to me. I swept him up in my arms and lifted him into the air, my heart bursting with joy. "Liam!" I exclaimed, hugging him tight.

Gemma watched us, a smile on her lips and her expression radiant. I put our son down and gazed at her for a long, eternal moment before smothering her in my arms. Then I broke down and wept all the tears left in me.

"We've been waiting for you for so long."

I closed my eyes at the sound of her voice. "It's really you . . ." I murmured. I cupped her face in my hands and kissed her as desperation returned to torment me, telling me it wasn't true, it must be a dream or a mirage my mind had sought refuge in to cope with the pain. I held Gemma even tighter, touching her face, her skin, to make sure she was real. "I'm afraid that if I let you go you'll disappear again," I confessed, squeezing my eyes shut.

"I'm here," she reassured me. "I'm not going anywhere."

"But . . . how is this possible?" The mark of the Children of Eve had disappeared and I could see the other Souls around us.

"You had your expiation, Evan. Your curse is lifted."

"Did you do it?"

"It's not every day that a Witch renounces evil and chooses to die in the name of love. I kept my promise: I searched inside myself and there I found you."

I held her tight. "What's going to happen now?"

"Our souls will be immortal."

"You were here and I . . . I'm sorry I kept you waiting."

"I would have waited for you for eternity."

"Jamie." I rested my forehead against hers and smiled, my eyes full of tears.

She took my hand, biting her lip. "There's someone else who's been waiting for you too."

I looked at her questioningly as a woman in a white dress appeared. My eyes went wide. "Mother!"

"Hello, Evan." My mother smiled and walked up to me. It seemed impossible that at last I could hug her again. I held her close and invited Gemma to join us as well. Liam grabbed hold of my leg and we all laughed. I had reunited with my family.

I was in Heaven. And this time it would be forever.

EPILOGUE

High atop our vast treehouse, I rested my hand on a small branch to help it grow as I watched Gemma playing with Liam at the edge of Red Lagoon where the Moon Maidens sang, warming us with their breath.

The house was almost ready. I'd fashioned a corner of Heaven just for us and soon it would become our hideaway. To build it I hadn't needed to chop down trees—just the opposite: I'd made their branches grow and intertwine over our heads, leaving ample spaces to watch the light displays in the sky. Inside, everything was made of woven branches, including a large bed I would cover with soft petals, a reading corner for Gemma and, most importantly, a large bookcase where she could keep the books I'd brought for her.

I leapt down and ran over to them at the water's edge. "Well? What do you think?" I asked Gemma, stealing a kiss.

"It's lovely." Flowers blossomed on the windowsill, filling it with colors. I lay on my stomach beside her and the water drenched me up to my waist. Gemma looked at me, a little smile on her lips. "Did you really have to take off your shirt to fix up our hideaway?"

I smiled. "Actually, no. That was for you. I was hoping to arouse sinful thoughts," I shot back, one eyebrow raised. "Did it work?"

She bit her lip and sought my mouth. "What do you think?"

"Daddy! Look what I can do!"

We both turned toward Liam, who disappeared under the water and attempted a handstand but failed. Gemma and I laughed, but the instant he emerged, bursting with enthusiasm, we grew serious again.

"That was really good, sweetheart. Keep trying," Gemma told him.

For a moment we watched him in silence. Liam was a bright, exuberant child. Not a day went by that he didn't learn new things or discover new places. He'd grown a year older in Eden—the same amount of time that had elapsed since his death, as though it had never happened. He wasn't a Soul like the others and none of us could understand why. Sometimes I imagined it was because his soul had been taken by one of the Màsala, but then I would convince myself it made no sense.

Days had passed since we'd found each other. We both missed Simon, Drake, and Ginevra, but our family was finally together for the first time, and that was what counted most. My brothers and sister had all made their own decisions and our paths had parted, but nothing—neither death nor destiny—could destroy certain bonds, and one day we would all find a way to be back together again.

On that now-distant April morning, my decision to save Gemma from the semi that was supposed to run her over had changed our fates and led us to that final agonizing battle. In Hell things had come to a head and it had seemed there was no longer any hope for us, but Gemma's ultimate sacrifice, made in the name of love, had put an end to it all. It had been rewarded with redemption: Gemma's and my own.

My fear had never been that Gemma would die, but the fact that once she passed on I would never see her again, since death would separate us due to my curse. As it turned out, the solution to the problem wasn't Gemma's immortality but my expiation.

She'd told me what actually happened during those terrible moments when I'd lost her. Just before she fell to her knees on the battlefield, her mind had flooded with memories: her shrieks of pain filling the forest, the wailing of newborn Liam. My voice calming her. The joy that filled her heart as Liam looked at her. She remembered that I'd been there to squeeze her hand.

When Sophìa hurled her deadly serpent at me, Gemma had sent a desperate cry for help to the Màsala. Time had stopped as they surrounded her. She asked that I be saved. The Màsala replied that it had all begun with her and that only she could put an end to it all. She could save me by choosing to renounce evil, sacrificing her life for mine. No Witch had ever done so before. Sophìa's poison had spawned her and in the same way only her venom could break the bond and free her from evil. Sophìa had been both her punishment and her atonement. When time began to advance again, Gemma hadn't hesitated to pit her serpent against the Empress's.

Kill a Dakor and his Witch dies with him. Her sacrifice had saved us both. At that moment, not even she knew that by asking to save me she would also be redeeming my soul.

"Liam, look who's come to visit you," Gemma called to him.

He emerged from the lagoon, cheeks bulging, and spat out a mouthful of water. "Grandma!"

"Welcome back, Danielle," Gemma told her. My mother came to see us often. Liam adored her and she'd stayed with him when I wasn't there.

"Hello, Mother."

She smiled at me and leaned over to kiss me on the head. "Liam, what do you say? Shall we go for a walk, you and I? I saw some red butterflies down in the valley."

Liam's eyes went wide with excitement and he ran to Gemma. "Can I go, Mommy?"

"Of course, sweetheart."

"Let's go! Let's go, Grandma!" he exclaimed, tugging on her arm.

My mother laughed at his enthusiasm. "I'll bring him back later." She and Gemma exchanged a strange look and my mother winked at her before disappearing with Liam.

"What's going on?" I asked suspiciously.

Gemma brushed it off. "What? I don't know what you're talking about."

"Oh, you don't?" I straddled her and tried to tickle a confession out of her.

She managed to break free and pin me beneath her instead. "Your mother is happy to see us together, that's all."

"Oh, now I get it," I whispered, moving closer to her mouth. "Keeping my shirt off worked. You wanted to be alone with me," I said to provoke her. "I'm warning you, our hideaway isn't ready yet. They might see us."

She ran her hands down my bare chest and her eyes sent me a sensual challenge. "Just because we're in Heaven doesn't mean we shouldn't break the rules any more."

I raised an eyebrow and pulled her against me. "Little witch," I murmured, craving her lips. She obliged me and our kiss grew hot and passionate. I rolled over on the sand and trapped her beneath my body. Her eyes pierced me whenever they rested on mine. Gemma wasn't a Witch any more, but I was still prey to her spell. My soul was hers.

"Kiss me, Evan," she whispered, and I obeyed. The hot water of the lagoon bathed our intertwined bodies as we made love, hidden in our little corner of Heaven, contemplating our eternal love.

The fire inside us eased into a sweet warmth as we held each other close, listening to the sound of the Moon Maidens. "I told you, Jamie,"

I whispered, watching the shimmering particles drift through the air, "in the shade of that maple tree, when we pledged our love for the first time, I told you."

"What?"

"That we would find a world where we could be together. This is going to be our world." Gemma rubbed her head against my chest and began to hum a little tune. "What's that?" I asked, curious. Suddenly I remembered Eden was full of trees with trunks that looked like overlapping reeds and produced incredible music. I often stopped there to compose melodies using my power to control the air, and soon I would show them to Gemma.

"It's been in my head for a while—a song that's always made me think of us: *Uncover* by Zara Larsson."

"I'll show you an incredible place here in Heaven where everything is music."

"Is there really one? And can I listen to whatever I want?"

"Everything. Every form of art is a window to Heaven. We can go there now, if you like."

"No, let's stay here a little longer—just us."

I rested my chin on her head. "Sing it, then."

Gemma sighed and tenderly took my hand. *"Nobody sees, nobody knows. We are a secret, can't be exposed. That's how it is, that's how it goes. Far from the others, close to each other . . ."*

"You're right. It's perfect. Please, don't stop."

We were hidden in a dream that was all mine and Gemma's—a dream that would never end. No one could see us in that new world of ours. Gemma and I were a secret that couldn't be exposed. Far from everyone else, close to each other.

A butterfly with transparent wings alit on her hand and she contemplated it, fascinated. I closed my eyes and she began to sing softly again. I never wanted to stop listening to her voice. Being there with her was so wonderful it all seemed like a dream and I was afraid it might end at any moment.

But a whisper filled my mind, and I knew I had to go. Those were the hardest moments—when I received a mission and the fear of not finding Gemma upon my return came back to torment me. "Evan, can Souls return to Earth?" she asked me out of the blue. "Before you showed up here, I tried to."

"Souls can't cross over." Gemma grew sad. "Not on their own . . . but you have me. I can ferry Souls, remember? If you want, we can go back now and then."

Her face lit up. "Do you think Ginevra and Simon could also return once in a while?"

I laughed at her enthusiasm. "It was supposed to be a surprise, but at this point I guess I have to spill the beans. Ginevra and I have already talked about it. She misses you and wants to see you again. We'll be meeting secretly in our hideaway one day each month so we can be together again."

"When?"

"Soon. *And* . . . Drake will be there too. He's eager to meet Liam." I smiled. Earth, which had divided us, would now be our meeting place.

Gemma's eyes filled with tears. "How is that possible? What about Stella?"

"The Souls of the Damned aren't like Subterraneans. Simon and Drake can cross through the portal, thanks to Ginevra, but for Stella it would be too risky."

Gemma nodded. "Now you need to go," she said, sensing that I'd gotten a mission, though I hadn't said anything.

I stood up. "I'll be back soon. I promise."

She pressed her knees to her chest. "Don't worry, I'll be here waiting for you."

Smiling at her, I vanished. Though I was now free from the curse of the Subterraneans, orders had continued to appear in my head, and despite not being obligated to any more, I'd decided to continue my mission. No Soldier ever really stopped being a Soldier. I'd been to Hell, I'd seen the evil that corroded the world, I'd seen mortal Souls lose themselves to the darkness, but I could help them find the light again. I could save them. I'd been given a gift—being able to find the person I loved when everything seemed lost forever. They all had the right to that same chance, and I helped them achieve it by helping them cross over.

I found myself on a desolate road, the same one where a few days earlier I'd come for a young man who'd been speeding on his motorcycle. The car I was waiting for came around the bend. Inside it was an elderly couple. I wouldn't take their lives—their time hadn't yet come. I was only there to make sure their fate took the right direction.

I had to make them turn back in order to avoid the accident that later would claim the lives of others.

I carried out my mission and got the couple to make a U-turn. A car behind them stopped to give them room for the maneuver. I was about to leave when something made me freeze. Behind the wheel of the car was a young woman . . . *and she was looking at me.*

I frowned and stared into her eyes until she passed me by. She pulled over up ahead and looked behind her. Had she really seen me, then? I materialized beside her and studied her from close up. No, she couldn't see me. Her gaze was lost in the void, her expression focused, as though her mind were quickly processing information. She grabbed a tissue from the glove box, rifled through her purse, pulled out a pen, and began to jot something down. Soon she pulled out another tissue and another still.

One glimpse of the snippets she was writing made me start.

. . . incredible gray eyes. What if only I could see him? And what if he had come for me?

I studied the young woman again, but no, she couldn't see me, nor did she seem aware of my presence. Shaking my head, I laughed at myself. It must have been a coincidence. I turned around and focused on Gemma.

She welcomed me upside down, hanging from a branch by her knees, her head dangling in front of mine. "That was quick," she said.

I looked at her and grinned. "Get down from there, you little squirrel."

Gemma let herself fall, challenging me to catch her. "Well? Where were you this time?" she asked. Now that Death wasn't hunting her any more, Gemma had stopped fearing the darker side of me and always wanted me to tell her every detail.

"In a little town in Sicily."

"Sicily? Fascinating," she said enthusiastically.

"Yeah."

"What is it? You look shaken."

"Something weird happened," I admitted. She was all ears. "I was there to make sure an elderly couple made the right decision, but then a woman drove by and she . . . *saw me.*"

"What do you mean, she saw you?" Gemma asked, puzzled.

"I had the impression she looked me straight in the eye. She even pulled her car over to look back."

"Do you think it's happening again?"

"No, I don't think so. It wasn't like when it was you seeing me. It was different. It was like she saw me in her mind's eye . . . Like she'd only imagined me. I don't know how to describe it."

"And then what happened?"

"She took out a pen and started writing."

Gemma's eyes lit up. "What if she's a writer? Maybe her imagination pushed her mind beyond the confines of the mortal world!"

I sprawled out on the grass and chuckled. "You've got to stop reading those paranormal novels."

"Lots of writers don't know they *are* writers until they find the right story. Maybe you inspired her and she might become one," she continued, ignoring me. "Let's tell her our story, Evan! Let's whisper it in her mind. You know how much I love books. We could have one all our own."

I looked at Gemma dubiously. "Are you serious?" She didn't need to answer; her eyes spoke for her—*sparkled* for her. I smiled. "All right, let's do it. That way the whole world will know our story and will know true love exists."

Gemma smiled back at me and took my hand. "And that death isn't the end."

The room was illuminated by light from the window. Outside, birds chirped in the blossoming lemon trees. The young woman was there, her back to us, leaning over a blank sheet of paper.

"That's her," I told Gemma.

"I'm so excited!"

"Why are you whispering? She can't hear us," I teased her. It was true, but why, then, had the woman's pen stopped? She seemed to be listening.

"Look, she's writing about you. You were right. She saw you."

I moved closer and read what the woman was writing.

His eyes. They'd enchanted me like a dark spell, carrying me away to their fortress dungeon. As clear as crystal, as ardent as fire, they stirred up a whirlwind of uncontrollable emotion inside me. I watched them narrow, sharp as ice, as he stared at me in astonishment, but there was no trace of coldness in his gaze. It was warm, comforting. Like a mystical connection, it drew me to him and wouldn't let go.

I jumped. It really was bizarre. "You sure you want to do this?"

Gemma nodded, a light in her eyes. She peeked at the page and frowned. "She set their first encounter in an alley."

I laughed. "Gasp! We'd better roll up our sleeves, then!"

Gemma shot me a dirty look like she did whenever I teased her. She leaned in close to the young woman's ear and began to whisper to her heart. The woman's hand stopped on the page. She thought for a moment, then crossed out the word "alley" and above it wrote "woods."

Gemma continued with great joy and the woman followed her lead, racing her pen across the page to avoid missing a word. She seemed excited about our story. At times she laughed, at others a tear slid down her cheek. Whenever Gemma stopped she would appear to grow nervous, look at the page, gnaw on her pen, and await another whisper. Meanwhile, I looked through the woman's books and read a few of them. From time to time I would fill in for Gemma so the story could have my point of view as well.

"All right, that's enough for today," I told Gemma, who looked at me sadly. "It's already dark out. She's been writing nonstop for over six hours. She'll get cramps in her hand."

"Is it so late already? I was having loads of fun!" Gemma looked out the window. Night had fallen, shrouding everything, but neither she nor the woman had noticed.

"We'll come back tomorrow," I promised. "Right now there's someone else who can't wait to see you. Let's not keep them waiting." I squeezed Gemma's shoulders and we turned around, ready to leave, but Gemma stopped.

"Wait! We don't even know her name."

At my command, a breath of wind slipped in through the window, flipping over the pages of her notebook and closing it. The woman started and looked around as though she'd sensed our presence.

I squeezed Gemma's hand. It was time to go. I read the name written on the cover of the notebook and smiled before vanishing. *Until tomorrow, Elisa S. Amore.*

The air was cool, the bikes' roars filled the night, and Gemma was behind me, like in the old days. "You should ride with me instead," Ginevra told her. "It's a lot more fun to watch the others from the finish line."

"That's a lesson I taught you myself, little sister. Catch me if you can." My bike reared up and Gemma squeezed her arms around me.

"Man, have I missed you guys!" Drake exclaimed.

"We've missed you too, bro," Simon replied, jamming on the front brake to raise his rear wheel.

"I didn't mean you. I was talking about our bikes. Duh!"

Gemma shook her head. "I missed our nighttime races. You're lucky I don't have a bike of my own. I would cream you all!"

"I would never challenge a woman who's ridden a prehistoric horse," I joked.

"He's not a prehistoric horse!" Gemma laughed, thinking affectionately of Argas. "Okay, actually I guess you could call him that."

We looked at each other, our bikes lined up on the starting line. "First one across the Tri-Lakes region and back?" Simon challenged us.

"Lake Placid, Saranac Lake, and Tupper Lake. A joyride," I said.

"Prepare to eat my dust." Ginevra winked at me.

"I'm in." Drake gunned his engine, making the bike beneath him smolder. "Let the party begin."

The motorcycles roared, zooming off like missiles toward our new future. *"Hold on tight, Jamie."*

"I'm a Soul now. I can't die, remember?"

"I wasn't saying it for you, but for me." Gemma held me tighter and I reared up.

We were ready to race: three Subterraneans, a Witch, and a redeemed Soul, separated by different worlds but united by the same emotion. Because bonds—be they of love or friendship—know no bounds.

Nobody sees, nobody knows.
We are a secret, can't be exposed.
That's how it is. That's how it goes.
Far from the others, close to each other.

Atyantam.

A few years later

"*Liam! Where have you run off to?*"

"*Here I am!*" *he answered his mother.*

Playing with the butterflies was Liam's favorite pastime. He would study them when they alit on his fingers, watch them flutter about, and spend hours lying in the fields letting them cover him.

"*Liam!*"

"*Coming!*"

Reluctantly, the boy let his red butterfly go, promising he would be back. He turned to leave, obeying his mother. From the rock where it rested, the butterfly watched him walk away. Something had happened after the boy touched it. The creature moved its big red wings as it transformed. At last it spread them and rose into the air, displaying to the world what it had become.

A magnificent black butterfly.

ACKNOWLEDGEMENTS

Here we are at the end of this long—and, for me, unforgettable—journey. Gemma and Evan's love story has made me experience incredible emotions and touched my heart. As always, I hope you felt some of those emotions too. I'm grateful for the affection that all my readers and bloggers have lavished on these two star-crossed lovers, and it is most of all to you that I owe heartfelt THANKS for reading my story. Thank you for all the messages and emails, all the support and word-of-mouth publicity . . . Thank you for loving Evan and Gemma, for rejoicing and suffering along with them. Thank you for believing deep down in their true love. It means the world to me!

This journey wouldn't have been possible without the support of my husband Giuseppe. Thank you, my love, for your trust in me and your understanding during my intense writing sessions. And thanks most of all to my greatest treasure, my son Gabriel Santo. You're myreason for everything. I hope you learn from my experience to always pursue your dreams and fight with everything you have to achieve them, because no goal is ever too far away if you don't stop chasing after it.

I owe a debt of gratitude to my family for their support and unconditional love, and for all the chores they took over for me so I could work on my writing! Thank you,Mamma and Papa. I love you with all my heart!

Much-deserved thanks to the fantastic team at Editrice Nord publishers for the trust and enthusiasm they showed for Evan and Gemma's story right from the start. My dream was my passion, but thanks to you it also became my profession, and I couldn't be happier. In particular, I'm grateful to Cristina Prasso, who chose each title with great care and enthusiasm. It takes a great person to run a great publishing house, and I'm honored to have been chosen. Thanks most of all to my Italian editor Giorgia Di Tolle for being among the first people to experience Evan and Gemma's adventure at my side.

My final, heartfelt respects to the late Luigi Bernabò, who believed in me right from the start. I'll never forget his words when, after reading the first Italian draft of The Caress of Fate,he told me the text needed more work,but that my story had struck him because it had a voice. Thank you, Luigi, wherever you are.

I'm grateful to my American translator Leah Janeczko and my editor Annie Crawford, because thanks to them, Evan and Gemma's story crossed the border and won over thousands of American readers in a very short time. Okay, I admit it might have been partly because of Evan too!

Once again, my gratitude to Professor Saverio Sani for his translations into Sanskrit and Devanagari. And my appreciation to all the readers who got tattoos! If you got one too, or are thinking of doing so, please send me a picture!

An infinite THANK YOU to Alex McFaddin and Rhiannon Patterson, whose indispensable help allowed me to enrich the Touched saga with actual details about Lake Placid and its school, Lake Placid High. Thanks to the artists I mentioned in the books; I wanted Evan and Gemma to hear their songs because they gave me inspiration for many scenes. All my gratitude goes to Lana Del Rey, James Blunt, Hans Zimmer, Amy Lee,and Zara Larsson. Also, many thanks to the administrators of the saga's official page. You're FANTASTIC and your help is priceless to me!

I couldn't write these acknowledgements without thanking my pug Bam Bam—who inspired the character Irony—for keeping me company during my countless hours of writing, from the first to the last book—even though he slept the whole time!

I must admit I procrastinated in writing these acknowledgements— maybe because I didn't feel ready to write the last page of this great love story. But deep down, Gevan will live on in my mind and I hope in yours too. If you'd like to share your thoughts about them with me, write to me. You can find me on my Facebook page! I always read all the messages I receive, and I try to reply to most of them. And don't forget to stop by the saga's official site at www.touchedsaga.com, where you'll find quizzes, polls, and lots of exclusive content created just for you. Again, my thanks to all the bloggers who welcomed Evan and Gemma into their reading circles, and to all those who will welcome them in the future. Your support is truly precious!

And so here we are at the end. When I first imagined Evan and Gemma's love story and pulled over to the side of that road to jot down my ideas, I wasn't sure how it would end, but now I know there couldn't be a more fitting ending for them, because love—the true love we hold inside, the love we truly believe in, for which we're willing to fight against everyone and everything—that love always prevails.

Until the next adventure!

Oh! One more thing: I'm working on a new project, a spin-off series that I'm sure you'll love.

Sign Up Now and I'll personally email you as soon as it is ready. Go to:
http://eepurl.com/bR8EuT

Affectionately,
Elisa

THE AUTHOR

Elisa S. Amore is the author of the paranormal romance saga *Touched*. She wrote the first book while working at her parents' diner, dreaming up the story between one order and the next. She lives in Italy with her husband, her son, and a pug that sleeps all day. She's wild about pizza and traveling, which is a source of constant inspiration for her. She dreamed up some of the novels' love scenes while strolling along the canals in Venice and visiting the home of Romeo's Juliet in romantic Verona. Her all-time favorite writer is Shakespeare, but she also loves Nicholas Sparks. She prefers to do her writing at night, when the rest of the world is asleep and she knows the stars above are keeping her company. She's now a full-time writer of romance and young adult fiction. In her free time she likes to read, swim, walk in the woods, and daydream. She collects books and animated movies, all jealously guarded under lock and key. Her family has nicknamed her "the bookworm." After its release, the first book of her saga quickly made its way up the charts, winning over thousands of readers. *Touched: The Caress of Fate* is her debut novel and the first in the four-book series originally published in Italy by one of the country's leading publishing houses. The book trailer was shown in Italian movie theaters during the premiere of the film *Twilight: Breaking Dawn—Part 2*.

Sign up for the TOUCHED saga newsletter at:
http://eepurl.com/bR8EuT

Find Elisa Amore online at www.touchedsaga.com
On Facebook.com/TheTouchedSaga
On Twitter.com/TouchedSaga
On Instagram/eli.amore
Add the book to your shelf on Goodreads!

Join the Official Group on FB to meet other fans addicted to the series:
facebook.com/groups/251788695179500

If you have any questions or comments, please write us at
touchedsaga@gmail.com

For Foreign and Film/TV rights queries, please send an email to
elisa.amore@touchedsaga.com

***

If you enjoyed this book, consider supporting the author by leaving a review wherever you purchased it. Thank you.

17998354R00254

Printed in Poland
by Amazon Fulfillment
Poland Sp. z o.o., Wrocław